Swallowing hard, palms feeling a little damp, she moved toward the bed. She'd already thought about the different scenarios for waking Elliott, and had discarded the idea of actually touching him. Which was good, because he seemed to be wearing nothing but the sheets that were twisted around his hips. The thought of touching his warm, smooth skin made her belly tighten . . . and not in an altogether unpleasant way.

Instead she bent toward him to whisper his name, but she'd hardly drawn in a breath when he moved suddenly. She squeaked in surprise and shock as his hand lashed out and strong fingers closed around her wrist, giving her a little tug so that she bumped her thigh against the mattress.

"What are you doing here?" he asked in that smooth voice. Too smooth for him to have been sleeping.

Romances by Joss Ware

BEYOND THE NIGHT

Forthcoming

EMBRACE THE NIGHT ETERNAL
ABANDON THE NIGHT

JOSS WARE

Beyond the Night

AVON

An Imprint of HarperCollinsPublishers

This is a work of fiction. Names, characters, places, and incidents are products of the author's imagination or are used fictitiously and are not to be construed as real. Any resemblance to actual events, locales, organizations, or persons, living or dead, is entirely coincidental.

AVON BOOKS
An Imprint of HarperCollins*Publishers*
10 East 53rd Street
New York, New York 10022-5299

Copyright © 2010 by Joss Ware
Excerpt from *Embrace the Night Eternal* copyright © 2010 by Joss Ware
Excerpt from *Abandon the Night* copyright © 2010 by Joss Ware
ISBN 978-0-06-173401-4
www.avonromance.com

First Avon Books paperback printing: January 2010

Avon Trademark Reg. U.S. Pat. Off. and in Other Countries, Marca Registrada, Hecho en U.S.A.
HarperCollins® is a registered trademark of HarperCollins Publishers.

Printed in the U.S.A.

10 9 8 7 6 5 4 3 2 1

With love to Emma

ACKNOWLEDGMENTS

I have so many people to thank for their support and feedback regarding this book.

First and foremost, a big thanks to Erika Tsang and everyone at Avon for their enthusiasm for my vision of a post-apocalyptic world and the heroes—and heroines—who inhabit it. It's been a delight working with all of you!

Also to Marcy Posner, as always, for her savvy support and encouragement of my work.

A big hug to Tim Gleason for all of his computer expertise—Lou and Theo wouldn't be the computer geniuses they are if it weren't for you. (And, yes, any mistakes are mine, not yours.)

To Dennis Galloway and Scott Turner in particular for their feedback and brainstorming on post-apocalyptic worlds during those Thursday-night sessions, and for letting me bounce ideas off them out of the blue.

And a happy fist bump to Zach Winchell for giving me a fun escape plan one afternoon from his hammock.

Thanks to Tammy Kearly and Holli Bertram, who've read so many iterations of Elliott's story that their eyes are probably permanently crossed, yet who continue to give thoughtful and welcome feedback. And especially to Tammy, who said early on, "Why don't *you* write a post-apocalyptic story?"

Also to Jana DeLeon for always keeping me on the straight and narrow, and to my mentor, Robyn Carr, for her unfailing support and advice. Thank you too to Kathryn Smith and Jeaniene Frost for their support and enthusiasm, as well as to Jackie Kessler and Trish Milburn.

Hugs to my mom and Gary March, D.O., for their medical knowledge and suggestions.

And, finally, much love and many big, squishy hugs to my husband and children—thank you for understanding when the deadlines loom, and for all those plot discussions around the dinner table. I couldn't do it without you!

Sometimes a man must awake to find . . . really . . . he has no one.

Jeff Buckley

Beyond the Night

PROLOGUE

Night closed upon them.

All of the young people realized it at the same moment, as the sun dipped suddenly behind the jagged horizon, permitting only a thread of gray to illuminate their stark faces. Laughter and conversation evaporated, leaving them silent and uneasy.

Their vehicle sat where they'd left it, a few miles away. The stupid thing had clunked to a halt two hours ago, and wouldn't start again. With the optimism of youth, fueled by the frenetic energy of the verboten crystal dust, they'd decided to continue to the meeting place on foot, unaware of how quickly the sun would slip beneath the horizon. Anything had seemed possible at the time they set out from their broken-down van.

But now. . . .

The buildings—mossy, moldering ruins, which during day might offer shelter—now loomed over them, close and eerie with their pitched angles and jutting beams broken by the sprout of a tree or hanging vine. Large trees grew in the middle of what had once been streets, and the glint of eyes low to the ground accompanied the scamper of animal feet.

Even without the influence of the crystal dust, the place

would have been sinister and alarming . . . but the gritty, mind-altering dust made it more so.

The smashed and rusted-out vehicles with missing windows and upholstered with fuzzy green moss lined the street, appearing larger and more fearsome than the inanimate lumps they really were. None of these abandoned cars, sitting next to broken and bent signs and parking meters, had been started for decades and wouldn't be of any help to them.

What had once been ten- or twenty-story buildings had tumbled into angry mountains of brick and beam, ragged glass and metal, folded in on each other in an unnatural terrain, softened by a thick layer of lichen and moss. What had once been smooth, landscaped walkways and wide thoroughfares jutted and cracked beneath their feet, making each step in the dark unsettling.

They'd never seen this world as it once had been: tall, glittery buildings, lit so brightly that night held no more secrets than day, filled with throngs of people, cars, noise; smooth and hard and spare.

"How much farther, Geoff?" asked one of the girls. The effects of the dust ebbed as real fear began to sink in. What had they done?

Since they were children, they'd been warned: how, in the blink of an eye, the sun could sink, and take its frugal warmth and light.

And release the fearsome things.

"It can't be much farther," he said brightly, neglecting to admit that he'd left the map in the van. But he remembered the way well enough. "And Nurmikko will be there, waiting for us, and then he'll take us on to Hemp's Point." To safety, freedom . . . and more dust.

That was what they'd come for.

Then another of the teens, Linda, choked on a shriek when

she saw the orange glint. It blinked before its other eye came into view from around a ragged, viny brick wall. Two orange eyes were joined by two more . . . and more and more. They came from the shadows, filtering from somewhere below ground where they lived in darkness, spilling onto the streets from all directions, released by the setting sun.

Moving slowly, steadily, they came. Much taller than a man, with massive legs and bulky arms. Grayish skin, tight and bone white under the sliver of moon, orange eyes, black holes where a nose might have grown. Gaping mouths and powerful, clawed hands moved in a horrible parody of the humans they'd once been. The *ganga*.

The teenagers huddled together, too paralyzed to save themselves. The last vestiges of their optimistic, frenetic mood disintegrated, leaving them cold and dark and frightened. They bumped up against a large vehicle, whose roof had been crushed into a vee, and sprouted grasses from beneath its hood.

One of the creatures growled *ruuuth . . . ruuuth.*

Geoff gathered his shattered wits and dipped to the ragged ground below, scooping blindly for a stone or some other object to throw. He rose, a hefty rock in his hand, and flung it at the nearest creature, at the same time shoving at the group of his friends. "Go!" he shouted, his head pounding.

The stone thudded into the chest of one of the creatures, but it seemed to have no effect.

The creatures were close enough now that their rank scent filled the air. The young people gaped at the huge hands that reached for them, bumping into each other, stumbling and tripping in their efforts to elude the dangerous grasp.

Benji screamed, staggering away even as she stared back with bulging eyes, holding her hand out in front of her as if to ward off the creature. Marcus picked up a rock and pitched it at one of the monsters, striking its shoulder, but it only growled more loudly, lunging at its attacker.

The creatures continued to swarm, Zac fell and was grabbed by two skeletal hands the size of dinner plates. As Geoff watched in horror, his friend was mauled by the teeth and hands in a horrible parody of old slasher movies. Only, this wasn't a parody. The sharp smell of blood, the dull scent of exposed human entrails tinged the night air, and Geoff's belly lurched.

Benji, too, fell prey to the nearest of the creatures, but instead of tearing into her with claws and teeth, he—it— flung the blonde over his shoulder as if she were a rag doll. She screamed, pounding on cold gray flesh that was barely covered by tattered clothing, terror choking her cries as he plodded away like a Frankensteinian monster of old. Horrified, Geoff snagged another stone from the rubble and lobbed it even as more of the creatures lunged toward him.

Then a shout reached their ears, accompanied by the sudden pounding of hooves as a wild mustang galloped toward them. The woman riding bareback clung to the horse's mane, her long hair streaming behind her as she stampeded into the cluster of monsters, sending them scattering heavily.

"Run!" she screamed, and even in the dark Geoff recognized her. She wheeled her horse around and started back into the group of orange-eyed creatures as they pressed closer.

One of them grabbed at her, and she must have kicked her horse, for he reared up and clocked the monster in the face with a solid hoof. But the undead creatures surged closer around her, inexorable and strong. "Run, dammit!" she ordered again, when the stunned youth still hadn't moved.

Suddenly, a man's voice shouted. "This way! Now!"

Geoff looked into the darkness and pointed, began to stumble toward the disembodied voice—which had come from a completely different direction as the horsewoman. The others followed as quickly as they could.

Benji struggled against her abductor, screaming. But there was nothing they could do for her as she was toted in the opposite direction, and nothing they could do to help the horsewoman as the monsters closed in around her.

Then, from the direction of the voice, something flew out of the night. Something that glowed and made a streak of light in the air. It landed on the ground between the slowest of the humans and the surge of creatures, exploding with such force that the lagging man was pitched forward. The horse reared again, screaming crazily, but the woman remained seated as flames burst around them.

The explosion sent several of the creatures crashing to the ground like a rampage of boulders. Their clothing and skin scorched and burned, flames dancing eerily in the darkness. The mustang leapt from the burning circle as another streak of light arced through the air, landing with a crash and an explosion at the second wave of the attackers, destroying even more of them.

The screams of the kidnapped girl rang through the night, growing more distant as a third missile pitched and crashed. By that time, the cluster of humans had moved out of sight of the creatures, leaving them growling in the darkness.

Ruuuth . . . ruuuth.

CHAPTER 1

"Damn, she went after them," Elliott Drake said as he leapt over an old sofa to join two of his four companions. The others had gone on foot after the abducting *ganga* and the woman.

"Where the hell did she come from?" asked his friend Quent, still peering through an ivy-curtained window that had lost its glass long ago.

"I don't know, but, my God, she rode like a fucking rodeo queen." Elliott looked off in the direction she'd galloped, crouching low over the mustang's neck, her hair streaming out behind. The rider had already disappeared into the darkness, a nameless, faceless heroine. But not without giving him a peek of moonlit skin where her shirt rode up from her jeans.

The rest of the zombie-like *gangas* had also scuttled off into the night, leaving their six would-be victims shaking and clinging to each other until Elliott rounded them up and brought them inside. Unable to see any other sign of movement, Elliott at last turned from the second-floor window of the shadowy, bedraggled buildings, and headed across the room to where the surviving teens had huddled. None of them had appeared injured, although they'd certainly had the shit scared out of them.

Despite wanting to lecture these kids about what the hell they were doing out after nightfall, with no protection—and not a wit to spare among them—Elliott merely gave them his physician's smile, one meant to soothe and calm. Poor kids. Whatever mistakes they'd made by venturing out at night, they'd learned their lesson: one of their companions had been mutilated beyond recognition, and the other had been carted off.

And if Elliott and his companions—along with the surprise Annie Oakley—hadn't intervened, it would have been much worse.

He'd seen the remnants of *ganga* attacks, and they weren't pretty.

"Is anyone hurt?" he asked the teens, keeping his voice soothing and easy. Their eyes were wide with shock, but he quickly noted that all six were standing upright, there wasn't any blood, and no one seemed to be protecting or holding any injury. Definitely a good sign.

They seemed to cluster together even more tightly at his approach, so he halted and raised his hands in an open gesture. "Are you all right?" Elliott asked, looking at the girl who seemed to be slightly more composed than her sniffling, gasping companion. As he'd done countless times in the ER—God, a *lifetime* ago—he made certain that his voice was calm and low, but also commanding enough to penetrate her shock.

She looked at him with big dark eyes, hiccupped, and nodded. For an instant, she reminded him of his favorite niece Josie, with her pretty, round-cheeked face, innocent and tear-streaked. Grief swarmed Elliott for a moment, making the back of his throat ache. They were all gone now. Everything was gone.

His family, his job, his hopes, his dreams.

Oh, and the rest of the damned world too. He had nothing left but this band of motley guys he called friends.

He swallowed and pushed away the wave of disbelief that occasionally rose to hamper him. "Are any of you injured?" he asked again, looking at her, then meeting the eyes of the others, one by one. They shook their heads, and he noticed with satisfaction that some of the shock seemed to be easing from their faces. "Are you cold? Hungry? Thirsty?"

Of course they were hungry. They were teens. There might be no more YouTube, cell phones, rock concerts or malls, but some things didn't change.

Elliott produced dried venison and apples from his pack and some bottles of water. The offerings of food seemed to ease their fear and suspicion.

The tallest of the group, and the first one who'd had the brains to pick up a rock and throw it at the *gangas*, finally spoke. "So who are you? Where did you guys come from?"

Who are you? Good fucking question.

Where did you come from? An even better one.

Elliott had been wondering that himself for the last six months—ever since he and his friends had emerged from a cave in Sedona to find the world completely and utterly changed . . . and fifty years older than it had been when they went in.

It was still impossible to comprehend.

He rubbed his forehead, brushing the fringe of hair out of his eyes. It was the exact same length it had been fifty years and six months ago when he, Quent, and Wyatt had gone on what was supposed to be a weekend caving trip, led by a local guide nicknamed Fence and his partner.

Elliott had met Quent and Wyatt on a volunteer humanitarian mission to Haiti in 2004, shortly after finishing his medical residency. Both Wyatt, a paramedic firefighter who had also been part of the National Guard in Colorado, and Quent, a bored and rich playboy who'd loved to go against his parents' wishes, had been assigned to Elliott's team.

Despite their different backgrounds, they'd become fast friends, bonding as men often do when faced with life-altering circumstances. Their work to help the people of the poverty-stricken, devastated island nation after Hurricane Jeanne had been that sort of life-changing experience. Because of the horrors they'd seen, and the people they'd helped in Haiti, their bond was strong, and they remained close friends over the years that followed.

The trip to Sedona, Arizona, was only one of many such adventures on which the three had embarked since. Quent, as the heir to Brummell Industries with unlimited funds as well as an Indiana Jones-like fascination for antiquities and treasure, usually arranged the trips based on one of his outlandish theories about the location of a lost artifact. Elliott and Wyatt were more than delighted to accompany him because the trips were always exciting, exotic . . . and dangerous.

The visit to Sedona should have been their least-exciting and briefest adventure . . . but it had turned out to be impossibly long.

Fifty years long, in fact.

"I'm Elliott Drake," he said to the teens at last. "That's my friend Wyatt over there, with the dark hair. And Quent's the blond one with the bandanna. Our other two friends went after the *ganga* that took your friend."

That was the easy part. But there was no way he could explain what they were doing here; that, while they were exploring a cave, all hell had broken loose. Earth shaking and splitting, rocks and boulders tumbling, odd smells and sounds, sharp and sizzling shocks of energy . . . and then everything had gone dark.

And they'd awakened a half-century later, Elliott, Quent, Wyatt, and the two guides who'd taken them deep into the caves. Unscathed and unchanged.

Well, not completely unchanged.

They—along with their guides, Fence and Lenny, and Simon, a man they'd found in the caves—spent the last six months in a combination of disbelief, anger and grief, trying to understand what had happened. "What's your name?" Elliott asked, looking at the boy who'd spoken.

"Geoff."

"Do you know where they might have taken her, Geoff? The *ganga*?" It was probably a futile question, for none of the few people they'd met in the six months since they'd emerged from the caves knew much about the *gangas* . . . except to avoid them when they came out at night.

Geoff shrugged and looked miserable, rubbing his arm. "I don't know. Will they find her?"

"They'll try their best." Elliott looked over at Quent, who'd walked over to look through a different window. Cracked, covered with mildew spots and encrusted with dirt, the glass was nearly opaque. But he had scratched away some of the grime and peered out onto what had been an avenue or thoroughfare below.

"You see anything?" Elliott asked, suddenly feeling a wave of the exhaustion that never seemed to leave him anymore. That was what happened when you hardly slept for six months . . . and when you did, you woke sweaty and out of breath from the nightmares.

"Nothing. It's quiet out there." Quent shifted his stance at the window so that he could peer straight down. "Nothing moving but a few rats."

In another lifetime, another world, Quent had been known as Quentin Brummell Fielding III, complete with not only a silver spoon, but the whole fucking place setting. Now he was simply Quent.

Though there was nothing simple about him.

Or any of them, anymore.

"They should be back by now, unless they ran into trouble. She was riding like hell, and the *gangas* couldn't have gone far. They're pretty fast but not too agile," Elliott said. Damn. His fingers closed tightly, and he itched to go after them himself.

Where had she come from? Did she know these kids? What was she doing, traveling about at night when the *gangas* were out?

He wanted to meet her, the bold woman who'd torn through the overgrown town and trampled the *gangas*, then flashed a tantalizing bit of skin above her jeans as she barreled off in pursuit. That sexy little swell of a curve just above the ass.

Christ, El, get a grip. It was a flash of skin. It's not as if you haven't ever seen a slew of bare asses in hospital gowns.

Needing a distraction, Elliott looked around the room to consider the sleeping arrangements. He and the others hadn't planned to stay here tonight, but now it looked as if they'd be shacking up with the kids in an old office building in this . . . whatever it had been. Some town in the middle of some county in what probably had been northern Arizona, but who the hell knew what it was anymore. An overgrown, jungle-like wasteland.

"What's your name?" Elliott asked the girl who reminded him of Josie.

"Linda," she replied, smiling bashfully.

"Pretty name." Though he felt light-headed and weary, Elliott smiled back, keeping his expression gentle. "How far are you from home? Do you all live in the same place?"

"Yeah. Our parents are going to be all nuclear by now." Her large eyes swam with tears. "We sneaked out and didn't tell them, and now we're so far from home." A little wail caught at the end of her sentence.

Elliott patted her arm, giving it a little squeeze. "We'll get you back home, safe and sound," he promised. "You'll just have to tell us how to get there."

He hadn't seen any sign of recent human civilization in their last day of travel, coming from the south, so the kids were either really far from home—or they lived in a settlement large enough to produce at least seven teens of the same age.

"Are you from Envy?" Elliott asked, as he did anyone they met.

Linda nodded.

Excitement spiked through him. "And you can get us there?"

She nodded again.

Elliott smiled, and the fog of exhaustion eased. *At last.* They'd found Envy.

After they'd emerged from the cave, Elliott and his friends had traveled on foot, horrified at the change in landscape. They scavenged for food and shelter for more than a week before they actually met any people. When they learned that fifty years had elapsed—an inconceivable concept—they were fairly numbed, paralyzed for a time.

How could one comprehend that the entire world had been destroyed? Most of the human race and its infrastructure—gone? Civilization annihilated?

It was beyond comprehension.

At last, trying to find answers to what had happened fifty years earlier—and how—Elliott and his companions had been unable to find anyone who'd actually lived through the destruction, and who could answer their desperate questions. Over and over, during their months of travel in a slow, concentric circle from Sedona, the band of men had occasionally encountered small settlements of people. Finally, about three weeks ago, they met someone who suggested that they go to Envy, the largest known settlement of people. Almost a city, in fact, where some of the survivors might still live.

Once they learned the city was north, they had at least had a direction in which to travel. And now they were closer than they'd ever been.

Wyatt interrupted from his position by the window. "Dred, they're back," he said, using Elliott's nickname.

Below, he heard the faint squeak of the rope ladder and the sniffling, snuffling sound of sobs. He immediately discarded the thought that it could be the woman. She wouldn't cry. Not someone who came blazing in like fucking John Wayne.

His guess was confirmed as the young blond teenager emerged, sniffling and sobbing as she rose from the top of the ladder. When she saw her friends, she gave a wail and stumbled over to them without hesitation.

"Dred!" Fence, their original guide from the caves, called for him as he appeared from behind the girl. The muscular black guy was carrying the bareback-riding woman in his arms as if she were nothing more than a kitten. Limp and unmoving, bruised and bleeding, at first she looked as though she'd been beaten to a pulp.

But *gangas* didn't punch or strike. They tore and devoured.

"Put her here," Elliott told Fence. His nickname had come naturally when he started med school and his friends had started calling him Dr. E.D. in texts and emails. Even though he joked that "Dred" made him sound like one of the X-Men, he didn't mind the moniker . . . though it did give people pause during first introductions.

"What happened?" he asked Fence, looking down at her. Putting all thoughts of that up-riding shirt from his mind.

"Looks like she fell off her horse fighting the mother-fucker. Horse was gone, and she was lying near a mess of *ganga* roadkill. Or would it be horsekill. Hoofkill?"

As he felt her warm throat for a pulse, Elliott couldn't help a smile. There was little to joke about nowadays, but that didn't stop Fence from finding a bit of levity whenever he could.

"Blondie—her name is Benji, for chrissakes—was run-ning away. We found her not too far from this one. I guess she was coming back for help, 'cause she couldn't lift her," Fence replied, gesturing to the unconscious woman. "Didn't get too far before we found her, and Benji brought us back to where she was, on the ground by a pile of *ganga* crap," Fence continued, a note of relish in his voice at the descrip-tion. "The job was already done, and we didn't even have to use any more bottle bombs."

Which was a good thing, since they couldn't just walk into a CVS and buy more alcohol.

"Benji seems all right," said Elliott as he considered the rider's pulse; it was steady and strong in her narrow wrist.

Her skin felt warm, but not overly so. And in a moment, he'd know exactly what was wrong with her, thanks to what-ever the hell had happened to him during the fifty years he'd been suspended in time.

Then he noticed a leather pack strapped under her shirt. He gently pulled it away, its heavy contents clunking me-tallically, and set it aside. The removal of the pack's wide band exposed some very perky curves covered by the thin white shirt. A fit female patient, likely in her late twenties, observed Elliott the Physician. With a smoking-hot body, noticed Elliott the Man, who was usually tucked away when Elliott the Physician was on duty, but who hadn't had sex for fifty years. Or at least, for six months.

"Girl's scared pissless," Fence remarked. He grinned, his smile clear and white in his dark face. "But if you want to check her out, feel free. She'd probably love a handsome doctor like you taking care of her."

"She's a bit young," said Elliott. Not the case with the woman in front of him. From what he'd seen, she wasn't too young at all. In fact, she was just about right.

"Yeah, for a guy who's eighty years old," Wyatt, who'd just walked up, added dryly.

"But I'm a young eighty, and still two years younger than you," Elliott returned with a smile. "Now let me see what I can find."

Taking a deep breath, he closed his eyes to concentrate, for this was still new to him. Then, scanning his hands just above the woman's body like a human MRI, he waited for the images to appear in his mind. Like full-color X rays.

He still found it unfuckingbelievable, this amazing ability he'd somehow acquired while hibernating, or being cryogenically frozen, or time traveling—or whatever it was, for fifty years. Too damn bad he hadn't had this gift . . . before. Think of the lives he could have saved.

Before.

His concentration broke for a moment, and the internal images turned to gray mush.

Lips curling tightly inward, he pushed away the thoughts and felt the strange hum that skipped through him. He focused on the internal buzz, scanning the images that reappeared in his mind.

No head injury. No internal bleeding . . . just a fractured ulna, and the fifth rib. Some kind of meat for her last meal, and some vegetation. She was at the middle of her menstrual cycle.

His eyes flew open in chagrin.

Christ. Like he needed that damn information.

Then he realized the teens were all staring at him.

"Do you know her?" he asked, suddenly uncomfortable, though he didn't know why he should be. For all they knew, he could have been praying over her. They couldn't have any comprehension of what he was doing—he barely did himself.

No one responded to his question, though he saw a few furtive glances between them. Great. They looked more awkward and nervous than they had after the *ganga* attack.

Drawn back to his patient, he looked down. "What the hell was she doing out here by herself?" Elliott muttered. Bruises and lacerations all over her face, Elliott the Physician noted. Thick hair of an indiscriminately dark color, snarled and ratted from that wild ride. And fine, long legs that had to be strong as hell if they held on bareback like that. Elliott the Man's mouth went ridiculously dry at the thought of her riding bareback.

Okay. Get a grip, Elliott.

Yeah, it'd been fifty years and seven months since he'd had his hands on a woman's body. But it wasn't like he hadn't slept through most of it.

Be a fucking professional. She's your patient.

With that pep talk mentally ringing in his ears, he reached over to her left arm, the one with the fractured ulna, bared by the short sleeve of her shirt.

Fully registering the warmth of her skin, he gently examined the bone beneath, concentrating, keeping it impersonal.

She stiffened with discomfort beneath his light fingers, and he felt and saw the disjointed ulna. He'd have to splint it up, and that was going to make it difficult for her to ride again. Damn shame, when she was so good at it.

He stopped his thoughts right there before they could go down some wayward path with creative images of *his patient* riding bareback.

Good. Very good. Raging hormones under control.

Closing his eyes, Elliott focused and saw the fracture again in his mind, a slender, jagged break, the bone slightly misaligned . . . and he felt a surprise sizzle of energy flit through him.

Elliott resisted the urge to open his eyes, focusing instead on the hot rise of power flowing through him. This was new, this flush of energy. Was it because he was concentrating more carefully?

Of course, the whole fact that he could scan someone and read their insides was new, but this was something he'd never experienced before. His brows tightened together, he ignored the soft rustling of the watching teens and their hushed whispers, and steadily focused on his mental images.

Suddenly, a sharp pain sliced through his own arm. He gasped in shock and his eyes flew open, but he didn't release her. His arm ached like a bitch. His left arm. It didn't just ache, it was beginning to fucking hurt. Like someone had stabbed him.

He looked back down at the woman, who hadn't moved. If anything, her face seemed to have relaxed. Elliott focused again on her broken arm, looking for the image in his mind, still feeling the pounding of pain in his limb.

He understood that he was somehow transferring her pain to his own body. Wow. He was even more talented than he thought.

Maybe she'd rest easier. He could bear the pain for a bit, give her some relief.

And then he focused on the image in his mind and realized that he couldn't see the break any longer. Her ulna was now a pristine, white bone.

What the fuck?

Had he healed her?

Elliott stared down at his hands around her arm, realizing that the pain still blasted through his own limb. He'd healed her and taken the pain into his own body?

Unbelievable. Absolutely amazing.

What the hell would have happened if she was having a heart attack? Or if she had cancer? Could he absorb the rest of her pain by concentrating over other areas of her body?

This was miraculous. Learning that he had acquired the ability to read the internal state of a person's body had been an accident in itself. And now this? Excitement and disbelief washed over him. Not only could he actually diagnose an injury or illness, but now it appeared he could also heal them.

The implications were staggering.

"She's a Runner," said Linda suddenly, breaking into Elliott's wild thoughts.

He turned to look at her, his mind swirling with the impossibility and the implications of what had just happened, and at the same time, focusing on the girl, who suddenly looked terrified.

A *Runner.* Clearly spoken as a proper noun. He hadn't heard that term from anyone else in this world before. People had mentioned bounty hunters. And whispered about the Strangers. But he'd never heard mention of Runners.

Of course there were a shitload of things he didn't know about what this world had become.

Six months after waking up in this post-apocalyptic hell, and Elliott had stopped trying to figure it out. He'd almost stopped wondering why he and Quent had awakened with extraordinary capabilities—like his being a human MRI machine and Quent being able to touch something and "read" its memories—and Fence and Wyatt and Simon, who'd also been caught in the cave during the catastrophic events, hadn't.

If they ever found someone who'd lived during that time, maybe, God willing, they'd have some answers.

Or maybe they'd just have to get through the rest of this damned life never knowing. Why. How.

And why the fuck *him*?

Linda shook her head mutely, as if she'd been elbowed. Or kicked. Big tears had gathered in her eyes, and Elliott felt the wave of antipathy from the other teens. Clearly, there was something else going on here.

Silence.

His arm still screaming with pain, Elliott looked over the group of them. He sat back on his haunches, which were in much better shape than they had been six months ago. Nonstop physical activity, and walking hundreds of miles—not to mention fighting *gangas* and living in survivalist mode—had turned him from the fit jogger he'd been into a lean, muscular candidate for the Special Forces. Not that they even existed anymore. He didn't think.

Another one of the kids spoke up. "It's nothing. Just heard the word 'Runner' before."

"But she wasn't running," Elliott reminded them, very, very gently. He reached over to touch the back of Linda's hand, meeting her gaze steadily, paring through the shock that still lingered in her eyes. "Who is she? How do you know her?"

But the girl just shook her head and looked down, biting her lip.

What the *hell* was the big secret?

Hiding his frustration, Elliott looked back down at his patient, noticing the perfect almond shape of her eyelids and the short, very faint crinkles at their corners. Not wrinkles—he knew better than to even think that word near a woman, but . . . laugh lines, maybe, or the evidence of time spent in the sun. A beautiful woman, even beneath the cuts and grime. Beautiful and gutsy.

What had she been doing out there alone?

At last one of the teens, the kid who seemed to be the leader, asked, "Is she going to live?"

They did know who she was. So it must be Elliott that they didn't—or wouldn't—trust.

He nodded, realizing that the pain in his arm had dissipated. That was pretty fucking amazing. A little bit of pain, and he could heal someone's broken bone. Cool. "Yes, she's going to be fine. But we need you to show us how to get back to Envy so I can take care of her."

The leader, who'd nudged Linda into silence, looked at him with blatant suspicion. "I don't know if we can trust you." He closed his mouth mutinously.

"At least tell me her name," Elliott said.

Just then, he felt the change. He looked down right as her eyes began to open. She shifted slightly, her movement accompanied by a small groan. She looked up at him, and even in the dimness, he could see that her eyes were cloudy and dazed.

"It's . . . Jade," she said on the gust of a soft breath. "Name's Jade." Her lips, split and cracked with blood, moved in either a grimace or a smile.

Elliott saw her gaze shift unsteadily from his face to

beyond, scanning over the hovering teens, snag for a moment, and then back to him.

"Who're you?" she asked, her lips stretching again, and some of the murkiness leaving her gaze. Their eyes met and he felt a whoosh of . . . something. Hot, heavy, and strong.

Hoo-boy.

"Are you . . . an angel? Raphael maybe?" Her voice sounded deep and husky, not unusual for someone awakening from an injury.

Elliott smiled back, wondering how much of his expression she could see in the low light. "Sorry to disappoint you, but I'm just a doctor." That's right. *Her* doctor.

"Mmm," she replied as her gaze shifted to land on one of the kids behind him. Her voice was still rickety and deep, and her breathing unsteady from that aching fifth rib, but she continued, "Not an angel . . . damn."

Her eyes fluttered closed, but the little temptation of a smile remained. Blood oozed from a cut that she touched with the tip of her tongue as if to relieve a twinge of pain. And then she shifted again, her lids opening wider, clarity bursting into them. "A doctor? There aren't anymore doctors."

The sultry pleasure—real or imagined—was gone from her voice, and the note that replaced it was decidedly displeased. He could see her try to focus on him, even felt her gather herself up as if to resist.

"Who are you?" she asked, her voice stronger now. "Take off your shirt."

What the *hell*? He frowned, wondering if she was hallucinating—but she was looking at him with lucidity in her eyes. Not invitation, but blazing suspicion. Her heart rate had increased, and so had her breathing.

"Ow!" someone cried out.

Elliott turned to see Linda, holding her arm as if she were

in pain. The other kid standing next to her looked surprised, so it was clear that he hadn't just slammed his elbow into Linda's arm.

"What is it?" Elliott asked, recognizing more than minor discomfort in the kid's face.

"I dunno. It's my arm," she said, her voice rising into a sob at the end. "It started to ache a little. Now all of a sudden, it *really* hurts!"

Frowning, Elliott reached to touch her, gently palpating the girl's arm. Her left ulna.

An odd sort of frisson sizzled along his spine and Elliott closed his eyes to concentrate on the mental scan, his belly feeling heavy.

No fucking way.

But he saw it there, in the full-color image in his mind: the fractured ulna.

The one that Elliott had somehow transferred from Jade to Linda, simply by touching her.

CHAPTER 2

"Everything all right?" Quent asked Elliott as he came over to join his friends.

Elliott nodded, but his head was still spinning over what had just happened. What *had* just happened?

He'd touched the girl's arm and tried to absorb the pain again and heal the fracture, but whatever had worked a few moments ago on Jade was apparently out of order. Dumfounded and unsettled, he'd wrapped the injury in a makeshift splint and left the group of teens. Now he found himself flexing his slender fingers, examining his hand for any sign of . . . something.

Was it him? Or was it that he'd touched Jade? Or was it some other cosmic fuck-up that had given him a miracle—and now had turned it into a weapon?

"Dred?"

He looked at Quent and Wyatt, who were watching him closely. He nodded again. He'd tell them . . . later. He wasn't quite ready to talk about it because he didn't fucking *understand* it. "They're from Envy," he said.

"The kids?" Quent asked, adjusting his bandanna. "That's bloody lucky."

"I hope to hell they know their way home," Wyatt said grimly.

"They say they do," Elliott replied. "And not only will they show us the way, but they confirmed what we've suspected: that the *gangas* only take blondes—men or women. Better keep that kerchief on, Quent, or we might have to save your ass too," he added, only half joking.

"They've seen them before?" Wyatt asked. "And they didn't learn anything—like to stay inside at night?" His mouth tightened as he glared over at the young people.

"Give 'em a break, Earp. They're kids. Practically kids," Elliott replied, thinking of his nieces, and the sorts of messes he'd helped them out of—without their mother, his sister, knowing. Fairly harmless ones, like helping Trudi replace her brand-new iPod that had been a hard-won birthday gift and had ended up smashed under a tire, or picking Josie up from a football game when her date had turned out to be a drunken dickhead. Sure, their escapades had resulted in lectures from their Uncle E, but they'd preferred that to being grounded or losing their cell phones. Or facing their loving, but strict, mother.

Now he'd never see his nieces, grown up and matured, hopefully married to non-dickheads. Hell, the stark fact was they never even had the *chance* to finish growing up. God damn it all.

Elliott shoved the thought away as he'd learned to do. There was nothing he could do about it, so he'd best focus on the problem at hand. He told Wyatt, "The kids' van broke down. It's sitting up the street—and I use that term loosely— a couple miles away. I told them we'd take a look at it."

"A vehicle?" Quent raised his brows.

They hadn't seen a running vehicle since coming out of the cave. And it was no wonder, for even if there was a cache of gasoline, or some other way to fuel a car that wasn't overgrown and rusted out, the buckling, cracked, potholed roads would be hell on the wheels. Literally. It'd be worse than driving cross-country.

"Believe it or not, they had a working van, but it's at least a five-hour drive on these roads. Figure they couldn't go more than five to ten miles an hour, if they were lucky—so we're talking a day of foot travel if we can't get the damn thing working again. But if we can, then we don't have to stay here tonight. We can drive through the *gangas* if we have to."

"What's the plan?" Simon asked as he approached. He was a quiet, brooding guy none of them knew much about. Elliott and the others had found him in the same Sedona cave only a few yards away from where they'd awakened when they'd reanimated, or whatever the hell they'd done. He, too, had been in the cave for fifty years, alone—and that was all he'd told them. Elliott and the others had not pressed him for more details—for it no longer mattered how he'd come to be there anymore than their story did.

Elliott explained to Simon about the van, and the fact that the kids were from Envy.

"These kids are lucky we even stopped here tonight," he added, nodding at Simon. Normally, they'd travel till the sun went down, all the while listening—and sniffing the air—for the *gangas*, but Simon had sliced his leg on a rusted piece of metal and Elliott had insisted that it must be washed out with alcohol and bandaged.

Although Simon had resisted Elliott's doctoring efforts, he'd taken the alcohol and administered it himself. No one argued over such simple first aid, for they'd already lost one of their companions due to an infection.

Lenny, the man who'd been Fence's co-guide, had cut himself severely on a piece of aluminum three months after they emerged from the caves. When he finally told him about it a day later, Elliott had treated the infected cut, and by the next day, it looked as if it would heal nicely. But then a few days later when they'd stopped in the small settlement of Vineland so that Elliott could help an old man with a septic infection, Lenny's own infection blossomed again. Within a day, he was dead.

Since then, everyone immediately reported even the slightest injury to Elliott. And they always made sure they carried a bottle or two of wine or liquor, scavenged from some demolished party store or restaurant.

Elliott had seen his share of unlikely items that had survived the earthquakes, fires, and other events that had crumbled buildings and cleaved the ground while he and his buddies were hibernating. He considered it one of the universe's little gifts when they came across an unbroken bottle of Scotch or jar of pickles, or, better yet, an unmildewed, unopened package of boxer briefs. Constant hiking, climbing, and dodging *gangas* was hell on skivvies.

Especially when, as Fence teased, one had as big a package as he did.

Elliott snorted to himself, allowing a smile. If he had to be stuck in a brand-new, fucked-up world, at least he was with guys he'd come to know and trust—Fence and Simon included.

Wyatt stood. "Let's take a peek at that van, or we're not going anywhere tonight. Quent and I'll go check it out. No sense in everyone trekking over there if we can't get it working, notifying the *gangas* that we're out there," Wyatt said. "They're dumb, but they can scent human flesh better than a bloodhound.

Elliott hid a wry smile. "Take a few bottle bombs with you." What Wyatt really meant was that he wanted to work on the van away from the kids, who'd scored pretty damn low on his tolerance meter for pulling a stunt like this. And yet Wyatt was infinitely more patient with his own children. He had a smart, hot wife, two children, a dog, and a little green bungalow—the family unit that Elliott had always yearned to have. Wyatt had just happened to find it first.

Had found it . . . and lost it, decades ago. Without even knowing.

The brief flash of humor disintegrated, and Elliott felt the weariness and grief descend again. What the hell kind of life could he expect here, in this world? Certainly not like anything he'd ever envisioned for himself. No exciting, rewarding hospital career. No little house with a white picket fence and his own smart, hot wife waiting for him—or getting home from work herself just as he pulled in the driveway from a grueling, but satisfying, day at the ER. Or there'd be days that would have sucked, and she'd be there to listen to him talk about it over dinner. Maybe a glass of wine or two after the kids were in bed, then a roaring fire in the fireplace and a bit of nookie in front of it.

Oh, he'd had it all planned out.

But those plans had gone up in smoke the day the world died.

And now he had yet another unimaginable problem: how had he healed Jade, and then transferred her injury to someone else? If he touched another person, would he break their ulna too?

Had he done the same thing to anyone else without realizing it?

Who had he actually touched, skin to skin, besides Jade and Linda? Lenny. And the old man in Vineland.

Elliott froze, his mouth going dry. *Lenny.* He'd been

taking care of the old man, trying to make him comfortable
. . . and then he'd turned to check Lenny's healing infection.

Good God. Had he killed Lenny?

Jade moved so that her right hand touched the bracelets
around her left wrist. They were still there. All three of
them, woven to fit snugly, and each with twelve stones—
representing the months of her captivity. Three years.

She lined them up, inching them so they were stone to
stone instead of catty-wonker. It was a sort of therapy, a
meditation. A way to organize and steady her thoughts when
they became dark.

A reminder of how far she'd come from the days when
she'd made them.

When she first became conscious and realized she was in
the company of a group of men she didn't know, Jade had
panicked. Full-force, heart-stopping, gut-clenching panic.

There, she admitted it. But at least she'd done so privately,
without even opening her eyes. No one would ever know.
She'd adjusted her bracelets, calmed, and pushed the panic
away.

So when she finally did open her eyes, still weary with
pain, Jade found herself looking up—right up—into a man's
face. She was prepared for the worst, tense beneath her skin,
face carefully blank. But it wasn't Preston. And it wasn't
Raul Marck.

Nevertheless, she twitched deep inside, wanting nothing
more than to leap up and get out . . . but that would show her
fear. So she smiled. Even told him her name. Sort of.

Jade couldn't see much detail of his face, shadowed as it
was by the dim light and the way he bent toward her. She dis-
cerned little but dark hair and heavy brows, and the glimpse

of a very nice chin when he turned to the side. Solid, square, but without a cleft that would have made it effeminate. He'd be wixy handsome in full light, she was sure.

Laced with lingering pain, Jade thought back over the murky blend of memory and dream, trying to determine if he'd said or done anything that threatened her. She hoped the part where she babbled something about him being an angel then demanded that he take off his shirt had been a dream. She really hoped.

At first, she had thought she'd died and gone to heaven. And what a bummer that would be, after all she'd endured to keep herself alive. To have only had three years of freedom after a decade of hell.

But the pain soon disabused her of that notion. There wasn't supposed to be pain in heaven, and despite the agony, she didn't think the discomfort was bad enough that she'd gone the other way.

Of course, she might very well end up there some day, but not yet.

But the angel . . . the man who'd bent over her, feeling the injured parts of her body with skilled, capable hands, didn't frighten her, despite his fearful sounding name.

This man called Dread. What kind of person had a name like Dread?

Not an angel, but a doctor. Or so he said. An impossibility, of course, for the closest she or anyone else had come to experiencing a real doctor were those in the old DVDs they watched when they could find them unscratched and intact.

But even if his medical knowledge had come from tattered, moldering books, she couldn't deny the fact that the pain had almost disappeared.

Jade had no idea how much time had elapsed since she'd first awakened to see Dread bending over her. Night, tinged

pale by a shaft of moonbeam, still colored the window openings black, so it couldn't have been long. Her arm, which had
been screaming in agony with every breath, no longer hurt,
and seemed to be movable. She lifted it slightly, just to see
if she could. No pain.

No pain anywhere. Huh.

She rolled her head to look over at the men clustered
in the corner, around a low light, speaking quietly. She
counted three. Hadn't there been five earlier? Where were
the other two?

From their shadowy figures, she could see they were muscular, solid men, and even from a distance, she sensed. . . .
There was something different about them—something big
and forceful and dynamic.

Jade swallowed, her stomach swishing with nausea. Could
she have fallen into a band of Strangers? She didn't see the
telltale glow of crystals seeping from beneath their clothing.
Either it wasn't dark enough, or their clothes were too heavy.
Or they weren't Strangers.

Possibly bounty hunters, but . . . no. She didn't sense
the same desperation and mercilessness as men like Raul
Marck. At the thought, his craggy face popped into her
mind, greedy and desperate. No. She was safe now.

She hoped.

But Jade had never seen these men in Envy—and as dazed
as she might be, she knew if she'd seen this band of men, she
wouldn't have forgotten them. So who were they?

And more importantly, did they know who she was?

Dread had given no sign of recognition, and she was
grateful for the low light that would make her hair simply
look dark instead of mahogany, and her eyes an unremark-
able color instead of brilliant green. Plus, though dazed and

in pain, she'd remembered to give her name as Jade. As far as Preston and his bulldog Raul Marck knew, Diana Kapiza had been dead for more than three years.

Despite the fact that they seemed to mean her no harm, she wasn't about to trust them. And the less they knew about her, the less likely word would get back to Preston about a green-eyed woman whose dark red hair had grown out again.

But now she needed to get out of here. She'd have to take Geoff and Linda and the others with her, too, she supposed—though that would certainly slow her down. What the hell had they been doing out, away from Envy? She couldn't wait to corner Geoff, who had to be the instigator, and find out what stupid stunt the kid thought he was pulling.

But most importantly, she had to get back to Envy, to find out if Theo had returned.

She'd expected to meet up with him just east of here, and he hadn't shown up by dusk, so she started off in this direction, thinking she might find him. Instead, she discovered the rusted-out van she recognized from Envy, and knew right away that Geoff had devised something foolish.

By the time she caught a mustang and figured out what direction the kids had gone, the *gangas* had attacked and the only way to help was to try and flatten the creatures.

Jade hadn't expected to get her ass dumped and be saved by a group of—whoever they were. Now her plans were all nuked up, especially since she was pretty sure that, unless she'd been unconscious longer than she thought, it was Friday night. Which meant that tomorrow was Saturday and she was due to perform in Envy and if she didn't show, she'd have some explaining to do. A situation that would raise questions better left unasked. No one knew she'd left the city.

Crap. She really had to figure out a way out of here.

She noted that the teens had settled down in a different corner to sleep—at least, she surmised that was what those shifting lumps were in the corner. Surreptitiously, she felt around for her pack. It was no longer hanging over her shoulder, and another wave of worry caused her to bite down on her lip until she felt the tenderness of a cut.

She had to find that, too, then, if she hadn't already lost it when she was thrown from the mustang. What if Dread or his friends had looked inside? Would they realize what the contents were? Most people wouldn't. But if they did. . . .

Jade gritted her teeth. One step at a time. Find the pack. Find a way out. Get the kids. Keep them safe.

It could be dangerous to leave the building, but she couldn't hear the *gangas* anymore. She could lead the kids out and hide somewhere nearby for the rest of the night. As long as they were above ground and there were no stairs leading up, the *gangas* couldn't get to them. She could start the journey back to Envy as soon as the sun started to rise.

She strained to listen as the trio of men seemed to dissolve from their cluster. Though she couldn't hear what they were saying, it appeared that they, too, were going to get some rest. At least two of them were. They left one man on guard—Dread, who looked about to settle himself near an eastern window.

Now would be a good time to escape.

She closed her eyes quickly when she saw Dread turn and move in her direction. She forced her breathing into a slow, regular rhythm, and relaxed.

"Jade?" he said, and she felt him crouch next to her. "Are you awake?"

And so what if his voice sounded so rich and gentle she wanted to look up at him? She wasn't about to open her eyes just because he spoke to her. Even though what she really wanted to do was *get up* and away. Far away from here, from him, from them.

So Jade feigned sleep, opening her eyes just a bare slit that he wouldn't be able to see in the dim light. He knelt next to her, giving a better view of his face thanks to the low trail of moonlight filtering through the ivy-covered windows and small light in the corner. She still didn't see any sign of a glow beneath his shirt.

Maybe he wasn't a Stranger. And surely if he was a bounty hunter, he'd have said something about a reward or whatever by now.

Bracing herself to remain still and relaxed when he touched her, she was surprised when, moments later, he rose quietly without doing so. Through slits in her eyes, she saw his broad shoulders and easy movements in the dim light as he went over to check on the teens. Low murmurs reached her ears, including a soft, sleepy chuckle from one of the kids, and then silence.

Safe in the darkness, she watched through fully open eyes as Dread extinguished the small light and settled on the floor near the low window. He leaned to the side, against the wall, arms folded over his middle, and turned to stare out into the darkness.

Weariness slumped his shoulders, outlined by the faint gray at the window. The moon shone full and round, but the darkest part of night had passed. It would be only a matter of hours before the sun began to color the sky, and Jade knew she needed to go soon if she wanted the cover of shadows. She could move quickly and silently—it was the teens she was worried about.

She'd sneak out of the building alone, first, and find a safe place for them to hide, then maybe she could make some sort of distraction that would draw the men out. She could then double back somehow and get Geoff and the others to sneak out. . . . It could work. But first she had to get out herself and look around.

Just as she was about to rise from her makeshift pallet on the floor, she heard voices and a soft rhythmic squeak from below. Dread rose from his relaxed stance, and moments later, a head appeared from the dark opening in the floor. The other two men had returned.

She'd lost her chance.

June 8 (?)
Two days After.

I don't even know for sure what day it is to date this journal entry, but I have to write something down. Figure I better leave something in case I die too.

Unbelievable. The smoke and dust. The fires. The aftershocks. Horrible storms with lightning, hail, tornadoes, wind, for hours and hours and hours. Days maybe. Is this the Big One we've been warned about? Why is the weather going haywire too?

It's been too dark to know how many days have really passed, but I think it's been two. Two days since all hell broke loose, so that makes it June 8.

I don't know whether to stay in and maybe get squashed by a building or go outside and get swept or washed away, so have been staying inside. Figure if the building didn't go during the quakes, it won't go now.

Hope so.

The only sound is the wind and the roar of fires. And the occasional crash of a building.

Can't find Theo, but sense that he's still alive. What a miracle that would be.

Can't find anyone else alive.

Cell phone won't work. Been trying laptop, but no Internet. Battery is almost dead.

No sound of rescue teams. No airplanes, helicopters. Nothing.

Where is everyone?

—from the journal of Lou Waxnicki

CHAPTER 3

Elliott turned from his contemplation of the moon—and the nauseating possibility that he could be a walking time bomb of illness and injury—when he heard the rope ladder begin to creak softly. Quent and Wyatt had returned.

Once they'd figured out that *gangas* couldn't climb any way but by stairs—either they were too dumb, or not co-ordinated enough—Elliott and Fence had woven a durable, lengthy rope ladder. They'd fashioned grappling-type hooks on one end for stability, and thus were able to take it with them and use it as needed. When camping for the night, they'd either destroy an already rotting staircase to keep the *gangas* away, or toss the ladder up onto a higher place that had no other access.

"You on guard duty again?" said Quent, walking toward him. "Instead of sleeping?"

Elliott shook his head. It wasn't as if any of them were sleeping that well, thanks to an unshakable case of PTSD, but he found that the moment he tried to close his eyes he was assaulted by images and memories both real and imagined about the Change. "You know me. Always willing to help."

"Right. When's the last time you slept?"

"About fifty years ago. So did you find the van?"

"It's deader than a fucking cell phone," Wyatt said. "No chance to get it working again. Kids patched it together from a bunch of parts, and they rusted right through the damn floor. I can't believe it made it five hours on this terrain." He walked away, clearly disgusted with the situation.

Quent crouched next to Elliott. "The bloody van wouldn't work, and then a band of *gangas* showed up. Just before we tossed in a bottle bomb, some Robin Hood shot a few of these arrows and scrambled a bunch of zombie brains. I pulled this out of the back of a *ganga* skull." He showed him the slender rod he was carrying. "It's an arrow. Or crossbow bolt. Look at this. Bloody clever design."

Quent demonstrated how the shaft worked. It had slits near the sharp head, and when the tip met resistance—such as slamming into the skull of a *ganga*—a weight inside the hollow shaft released and slammed forward, shooting out five lethal petal-like points like a starburst around the tip.

"A little more innovative than our Molotov cocktails. But not nearly as efficient," Elliott said, taking the bolt—but without touching Quent's fingers. Last thing he wanted was to break his friend's arm too.

He turned the bolt over in his hands, tilting it from side to side. The dull slide of the weight shifted back and forth, and the spikes fell in and out around the tip. *Pretty fucking cool.* "So not only does it penetrate the skull, but it makes mashed potatoes out of the brain."

That was the only way to stop a *ganga*: destroy its brain. Smash it. Burn it. Explode it.

"Got three of them, the last one right as I threw our only bottle bomb. Three shots, three victims. Boom, boom, boom." Quent peered over Elliott's shoulder into the night. "A Robin Hood like that would be handy in our little band of Merry Men."

"You didn't see anyone?"

"Not a hint."

"You couldn't tell anything about him by touching the arrow?" Elliott asked, knowing that Quent was still learning the extent of his ability to read inanimate objects.

"A little. Not much." Quent shoved his hands in his pockets. "Hey, I'll watch for a bit if you want to rest. Dawn'll be here soon."

Elliott shook his head. Tension rode along his neck, aching his shoulders. "I'm fine. Go on."

Moments later, Elliott found himself staring out the window again. He leaned against the wall, tipping his head up and back, folding his arms over his middle. The only sounds were the distant rustling of a breeze through the leaves, and the quiet scrabbling of some rodent or other nocturnal creature on the hunt. The moon cast a swath of pearlescent light over the choppy, shadowy ground beyond.

Funny. It was the same moon he'd stared at back in Chicago, fifty years ago. The same moon under which he'd strolled hand in hand with Mona, listening to the fringes of the blues fest, thinking about whether she was the one he wanted to spend the rest of his life with. The very same moon had shone down on him when he'd walked out, sweaty and pumped, from a fierce basketball game. The same one glowed while the sky lightened with dawn as he drove home from an afternoon shift after saving the life of a hemorrhaging woman.

Hard to believe it was the same one when everything else was so different.

A different sound caught his ear and he stilled, listening. He didn't turn because . . . well, because he knew it was coming from the corner where Jade was sleeping.

Or, rather, pretending to sleep.

Always keen, his ears seemed even sharper now, and he could tell she'd risen from her place on the floor. If she was in pain or needed him, she would have called out. Or said something.

But . . . then he heard the soft metal clunk. She'd found her pack and picked it up. Preparing to leave? Or simply needing something from the bag?

He waited until she was well away from her pallet before he turned his head. "Jade? Is everything all right?"

"Oh," she said, her voice still low and husky. "I didn't mean to wake you. I was just . . . I needed to. . . ." Her voice trailed off in embarrassment.

"I wasn't sleeping." Elliott pulled to his feet. "Sorry we don't offer indoor plumbing here," he said, moving toward her, willing to pretend he didn't know what she was up to. And, good God, the white T-shirt she wore was like a magnet for the moonlight, showing off the curves of her torso. As if he needed a reminder.

Her face remained shadowy and she seemed to be moving smoothly, without pain. Had he really healed her completely, then?

"I'm afraid you'll have to go down and outside. I'll come with you," he said.

Holding the pack she'd slung over her shoulder, she shifted on her feet and looked up at him. "Well, isn't that awkward. You don't need to come—I'll be fine. There aren't any *gangas* around—we'd hear them if there were."

"Or smell them."

She gave a soft laugh and nodded. Elliott gestured toward the opening in the floor where the rope ladder hung. "Awkward or not, I'm going with you."

"If you want," she said as if it was her idea, when she clearly preferred to be left alone. Then she turned and started down the ladder.

Elliott followed and remained a prudent distance away, standing in what had been a street a half-century ago, as she disappeared into the shadows. Scanning the area for the orange eyes of *gangas* or the yellow ones of wolves, he waited, resisting the urge to follow her.

As nearly everywhere he'd been, decrepit, overgrown buildings loomed over and around him, barely recognizable as the establishments they'd once been. A diner, with its sign peeling away. A gift shop. A pharmacy. In the morning, he'd check to see if there was anything salvageable for his bag of medical supplies.

Far as he could tell, this had been the downtown of a quaint little Main Street USA town. Probably one that had already been on the verge of extinction fifty years ago, with its Mom-and-Pop shops threatened by big box stores and lifestyle malls on the outskirts of town. But big box or little, all of them had been reduced to jungles of bush and vine. Not for the first time, Elliott wondered what town this had been, once upon a time. And who had died here, and who had lived, when It all happened.

Then he realized that Jade had been gone for quite a while, and he sharpened his attention, turning toward the shadows.

A few steps toward the darkness, listening carefully, he wondered if she had indeed melted into the darkness, never to return.

Just like the mysterious Robin Hood Quent had told him about.

Would it matter if she had? Other than the fact that she

was a woman alone in the night, with *gangas* and wolves and other dangers, would he care?

Obviously, she had already been alone earlier, when she blazed in Annie Oakley-style . . . hadn't she? Or was Jade secretly returning to her own band of companions, now that she was healed?

"Jade," he called, stepping closer to a shadowy alley, now overgrown with bushes and trees. "Are you all right?"

His heart was suddenly pounding. He was worried about her being alone in the night . . . but he also didn't want her to be gone. To just *poof* . . . and disappear.

A soft rustle drew his attention, and then she reappeared. He felt a leap of relief . . . and delight . . . as she emerged from behind a tree. "I didn't mean to be gone so long."

"I thought you might have taken the opportunity to run away," he said, looking down at her, trying to catch her eyes in the dim light. He felt oddly off center, unusually tentative.

"Run away?" Jade stilled and returned his gaze, easing back a bit. "Would you have tried to stop me if I had?" The bruises and scrapes on her face looked like dark splotchy shadows, but her eyes gleamed up at him, steady and sharp. Tension fairly quivered from her.

"Only because I'd be worried for your safety. Not because . . . not because you wouldn't be free to go."

"Really. So if I said I wanted to leave right now, you'd stand aside and let me?" Her hands settled on her hips in that way women had when they challenged their menfolk, but her voice was mild. Ready to pick a fight, but not quite there yet.

"I'd think it was pretty foolish, but I have no reason to keep you here. I saw your performance tonight, riding in to save those kids. It was brave and beautiful . . . and reckless."

She seemed to relax a little, her shoulders easing and her hands dropping from her hips. "Reckless?" she laughed, and the sound lingered, low and dusky, in his ears.

"But nevertheless effective." His smile faded. "So are you going to leave?"

She shrugged. "I might. If I want to." But she made no move to go.

"You seem to be feeling all right. Are you in any pain?" he asked, realizing that if they were talking, she'd be less likely to melt into the shadows again.

"For flying through the air and landing on my ass, I'm feeling surprisingly well," she replied. "Maybe you are a real doctor."

"I told you I was." He wished suddenly that he could see her face better, but the close buildings and trees cast shadows that kept them nearly in the dark. "But as I recall, the last time we were having a conversation about my credentials, you demanded I take my shirt off. I confess, I wasn't sure whether I should have been flattered . . . or worried."

"Oh." She looked up at him, and, wonder of wonders, stepped into a patch of moonlight. Her upturned face, scraped and half shadowed by her thick hair, was nevertheless arresting in its simple beauty. He saw the smooth rise of a scraped cheekbone and the soft angles of a perfect nose. "I had really hoped I'd dreamt that."

"We could pretend it was a dream and never mention it again," Elliott said, his mouth twitching in a smile.

"That would be good. Can we do that?"

"Done."

"So . . . is your name really Dread?"

"It's Elliott. Elliott Drake. My friends started calling me Dred when I . . . when I became a doctor. Dr. E. Drake was shortened to Dred."

"Oh," she said, as if considering this information. "So who *are* you?"

That damn question again . . . but for some reason, he didn't feel that same blast of frustration he'd had earlier. Not that the explanation was any easier now. . . . "You had a fractured ulna—a broken arm," he said instead. "How does it feel now?"

She reached automatically for her left arm, closing her fingers over the bands she wore around her wrist. "It's not broken anymore. It feels normal."

"I told you. I'm a doctor." He smiled, but it felt rickety. He was a doctor . . . and now, thanks to some oddity, he was also a healer that taketh the pain away . . . and giveth it back. Wham-bam-thank-you-ma'am.

And then she tripped or slipped or something, reaching toward him, but he reared away before her fingers could brush his arm. "*Don't!*"

Jade caught herself and sort of stepped back, looking up at him with wide eyes. "I'm sorry. I just . . . tripped."

"No," Elliott said, feeling foolish. "I'm sorry. I . . . didn't mean to startle you." *Christ.* How much should he tell her? "You just surprised me. I didn't . . . uh." He sounded like a fucking idiot. "I think I might have something . . . contagious. I don't want you to get sick. Again." He tried to sound blasé, but from the way she was looking at him, he didn't think it was working.

What *would* happen if she touched him? Would her arm break again? Or nothing?

How was he ever going to find out? Because, holy hell, he really wanted to touch her. As in *touch her*, as Elliott the Man who hadn't had sex in five decades, not Elliott with the Hippocratic Oath and hospital ethics board breathing over his shoulder.

Just then, he heard it . . . the low grating, groaning. *Ruuu-uuthhhh.*

"They're back," he murmured, moving automatically toward her, but without actually touching her. "Are you coming inside?"

"You'd better come inside," she ordered as if it was her idea. As if she were going to protect him.

That clinched it. He had the hots for a control freak.

She slipped ahead of Elliott, taking obvious care not to brush against him in any way, and started up the rope ladder.

Which meant that he was right behind her and got a first-hand glimpse of the way her jeans shifted lower than the hem of her shirt as she climbed, showing that bit of skin. What was it about such an innocuous sight that made his gut tighten, and yeah, sue him, but his cock shift? If he got a hard-on every time he saw a flash of white ass in the hospital, he'd have spent the majority of his days walking around with a woody.

And it was just ridiculous that he was distracted by a little flash of skin when there were fucking *gangas* coming after them.

At the top, filled with disgust for himself, Elliott pulled the ladder up after them, coiling it in a circle on the floor.

The sounds of the *gangas* drew closer, and Jade moved to the mildewed window to look down. As much as he felt compelled to be near her, Elliott resisted and walked over toward the cluster of teens as the groaning of the night creatures became louder.

All six of them seemed to be sleeping soundly.

Six?

He paused and counted again. Aw, hell. One of them was missing. He looked closer. It was one of the guys. Geoff.

Maybe he'd just stepped aside somewhere to take a piss. Out a window, he hoped.

Turning to look around the darkened room, Elliott hissed, "Jade."

She turned from the window, fully outlined by the moon, and for a moment, Elliott's words dried up in his mouth. Her face glowed like porcelain, and for the first time, he could see the hint of a red nimbus in her thick, dark hair.

Just then, a loud shriek pierced the air.

The *gangas* had found their prey.

From a vantage point high above, Zoë Kapoor heard the shriek of fear rise beyond the groaning of the *gangas*.

Stupid kid. Now she was going to have to waste another of her arrows.

Glaring down into the darkness, she fit one of the precious bolts into position on her bow and eased closer to the edge of her perch. Looking down at the cluster of five *gangas* that had begun to converge on the single teenaged boy, she tried to determine the best angle to take one of them out.

Just then, a group of men burst from the safety of the brick building and Zoë slipped back into the shadow of a moss-covered dormer. She lowered her bow, relieved to save another arrow—at least for now.

And hot damn . . . one of the five men charging out was wearing a bandanna. He was definitely the guy she'd been following—the one who'd been by the rusted-out van she'd been investigating earlier.

Not only had he and his grumpy-ass friend interrupted her, sending her slipping into the shadows, but he'd stolen her arrows—yanked them right from the steaming mass of *ganga* brains. In fact, he was carrying two of them in his hands, using them to stab at the creatures, trying to distract them from the kid.

Gripping her bow, Zoë eased deeper into shadow, feeling the comforting shift of bolts in the quiver slung over her shoulder, watching carefully. Five strong, agile men versus five clunky, slow *gangas*. *No fucking contest.*

Moments earlier, from her perch across the street, she'd seen the kid sneak from the building, just as she'd noted the man and woman below on another side of the building. She'd been trying to figure out if there was a way to slip in and find her arrows after following the two men back from the vehicle they'd been working on.

After she'd helped save their asses from the *gangas*. Why the bandanna'd one had taken her arrows, she didn't know, but it pissed her off.

They weren't easy to make, and she wanted them back.

What the hell did he need them for anyway? He and his friends had their loud, fancy explosives.

Then she saw the cluster of orange eyes approaching from another street. She counted at least a dozen more *gangas*. Perhaps as many as twenty, moving quickly if not awkwardly, around the building toward their comrades.

Shit. Hope those guys have more of those fancy explosives.

Just as the five men finished the last of the cluster of creatures, a second group of *gangas* surged onto the street in front of them.

Zoë heard a woman's warning shouted from somewhere as she fitted an arrow into place. The group of men shifted quickly, scattering. She watched them with interest and grudging admiration even as she let the arrow whiz through the air. *Bull's eye.*

Her quiver was feeling uncomfortably light, and Zoë swore again. But she grabbed another one and nocked it. She watched as the big black man whaled against one of the creatures with the broadside of a . . . what was that?

She peered down. One of those things they used to put money in for parking. *Crap.* The dark man was wielding a parking meter like a mace, slamming the heavy end up over his own head into *ganga* faces, splattering flesh and brains every which way.

The other four—no, three—including the one who wore the bandanna, were no slouches themselves when it came to fighting off the gray-skinned thugs. Whatever they could find, they used to beat off creatures nearly twice their size and strength. With surprising effect.

These men had speed on their side. Speed, strength and intelligence—and, in relation to the *gangas*, smaller frames. They ducked and spun so fast the *gangas* had no prayer of trying to follow them.

Zoë's eyes narrowed as she continued to watch, and saw how the one with the bandanna swung out with her arrows, one in each hand, whipping and slicing, always aiming for the head. Once he actually jammed one through a *ganga* eye, clear through to the brain. And twisted. *Score.*

But he had his back to the others, and somehow three of the creatures had begun to edge him away.

He didn't seem to realize it as he fought—or maybe he did—but the others were engaged in battle as well and couldn't see what was happening. Then one of them smashed him from behind and his bandanna went flying, exposing his blond hair to the full-on beam of the moon and stars.

Oh shit.

The three *gangas* crowded him as he staggered against

the wall, their deep croons more excited as they surged forward. Zoë didn't hesitate; she sent her arrow down into the back of one of their skulls.

But it was too late. The other two had cornered the blond man, who, despite his stumble and obvious pain from the blow, still held her damned arrows, using them to stab and bash at his attackers. They'd moved beyond the crumbled corner of a collapsed building, and were out of sight of his companions, soon to be out of sight of her.

Fuck. She was *not* going to lose her arrows.

She might as well save him too.

Zoë rarely came down to ground-level when there were *gangas* around, but this time, she didn't hesitate. Down and out of the opposite side of the building, she moved quickly and lightly, following her nose, which, like her ears, had become sharply attuned to the presence of the dead thugs.

What had been a very narrow alley had flooded decades ago and was now a shallow stream, dark with shadows from roofs that tilted in toward each other. Zoë could hear the splashes ahead and started off quickly, edging along the wall nearest her.

Grasses and reeds sprouted where water and brick met, and who knew what lived in the small canal, but she had sturdy boots (if a little too small) and determination. A rat scuttled past her, bumping her leg, and slid into the water. Zoë's lip curled in revulsion. No matter how many of those rodents she saw, lived with, crawled with . . . they still disgusted her.

It wasn't long before the narrow space ended, opening into a wider area lit by the moon. She saw the outline of the *ganga* who carried the bandanna-man, and froze against the mossy wall. Where was the second creature?

Zoë listened, sniffed, waited. But not for long, for she

couldn't let them get too far ahead of her in case the bounty hunter who sometimes rode with the *gangas* was waiting this time. Then there'd be no way she could help the blond one, or get her arrows back.

She sensed no other presence, saw no orange eyes, and, most telling of all, smelled nothing but the familiar scent of waterlogged vegetation and mildew. Picking up her speed, she hurried along, breaking out of the canal-alley and promptly stumbled into something at the edge of the water.

A *ganga*. With one of her arrows jammed into the back of his head.

Well, damn. At least he was putting them to good use.

Zoë couldn't resist a smile. She yanked the arrow from steaming *ganga* brains and, with a sharp flick, flung away any clinging remnants, then swished it quickly into the water to rinse.

Two down, one to go.

Her hesitation had caused her to lose sight of them, but when she came to another crossway, she heard the shuffling, plodding creature. He wasn't far ahead, and, although she didn't like to climb through buildings she didn't know— rotting floors, broken stairs, crushed roofs, animal lairs, and all—she slipped into a nearby doorway and sprinted along the ground floor of the structure, praying all the while that she would not go through the floor.

Making her way through slanted boards and around de-caying furnishings, she got close enough to the *ganga* for a good aim.

He was coming toward her, and the man, who must have been struggling before when he slammed the arrow into the other thug's head, wasn't moving.

Didn't bode well, though Zoë had never known of a *ganga* to attack a blond person.

She didn't waste any further time, but fit the arrow and let that baby fly through a window.

Score.

The *ganga* froze, staggered, then gave a horrible grimace of pain and crashed to the ground. Its burden hit the ground, too, his head bouncing enough to make Zoë wince.

She waited for a few breaths, but everything was quiet. So she slipped out of the building, the hair rising at the back of her neck, feeling as though she was completely exposed.

She walked quietly toward the two unmoving figures.

CHAPTER 4

Jade peered down from the window, watching the battle below. Dred—no, Elliott—and his companions had all rushed down and out to fight off the small group of *gangas*. She would have followed, but Elliott turned and said, "Stay with the rest of them."

"I'm staying here with them," she told him, so he understood it was her own decision and not that she was letting him tell her what to do. The last thing they needed was for the other kids to get spooked and rush blindly out.

Or, if the worst happened—which, by the looks of the battle below, was unlikely—and Elliott and his friends didn't return, at least Jade would be there to help the kids.

What the *hell* had Geoff been thinking anyway? First, leaving the city—and now this? She was going to murder him for messing up her plans if she finally got him back to Envy. Maybe even before.

And how had she and Elliott missed seeing or hearing him, unless he went out of the decrepit building a different way? So was he purposely sneaking out, trying not to get caught—or had it simply been a half-sleepy young man looking for a place to relieve himself?

Hah. She didn't think that for a minute, though she was certain he'd try and sell it that way. Geoff might lack some common sense, but he wasn't a complete fool. In fact, the kid was pretty smart, even if he had a misplaced sense of immortality.

The other youngsters had awakened by now, and crowded around Jade, watching the battle below. Just as the last *ganga* found himself engaged by the tall black-skinned friend of Elliott, Jade caught sight of the figures, lurching from around a shadowy corner onto the overgrown street below.

Oh God. More *gangas*. There were at least fifteen of them . . . maybe more.

Wishing she had something to throw, some weapon, Jade leaned forward, half out the window, and screamed, "Elliott! Behind you!" But her shout was lost in the sudden swarm of confrontation, and she found herself gripping the rotted edge of a wooden windowsill in fear. Suddenly, it didn't look quite as likely that they'd walk away the victors. Five men versus fifteen—no, twenty!—*gangas*?

But as she watched them scatter and turn to face the onslaught of a small *ganga* platoon, Jade relaxed her grip—just a bit—on the windowsill. No panic, no desperation . . . just capable, fierce intensity as the band of men fought back against the moaning creatures.

They possessed speed and agility, strength, and an innate skill that seemed to lead them through the confrontation. She'd never seen anything like it—the way a single man could take on three or four of the *gangas*, half again his size, stunning and beating them off, holding his own as they staggered back for more. The weakness of the *gangas* was that they were too big and awkward for more than one to get close at a time, or to coordinate their attacks, so the men were able to keep them at a distance by beating them back, one by one. And occasionally stabbing or crushing the skull to kill them.

Jade noticed that all five of them—no, four . . . she didn't see Quent, the bandanna'd one—had grace and strength, but it was Elliott who drew her attention, who had her lungs filling and catching, her heart pounding. Even from above and in jinky light, despite the fact that he was crowded in by the large creatures, she could easily identify him . . . and couldn't look away.

Her fingers began to uncurl slowly, loosening with optimism as she watched Elliott spin around with power and grace. She even forgot to shout suggestions to him, she was so caught up in the view. He held some long pole, thicker than her wrist, that he used like a baseball bat, then like a sword, then like a battering ram, shoving, slamming, whipping it at his attackers.

Just because watching him fight—all those muscles and that speed and wow, the way he whipped that pole around and sent *ganga* brains flying—made her all flushed and warm didn't mean he was a good guy. Nope.

And . . . oh, my, a desperate *ganga* had torn his shirt. As it fell away in tatters, Jade could see the fluid slide of his pecs and shoulder muscles outlined in the moonlight. And she could tell that, once and for all, he had no crystals.

A blossom of relief washed over her. He wasn't a Stranger.

Now she really wanted to get back to Envy as quickly as possible. Not only to make her gig and confirm that Theo was all right, but also to tell him and Lou about Elliott and his friends.

If there was anyone who would be able to help them in their fight against the Strangers, it might just be Elliott and his equally fascinating friends.

Quent felt something touching his face. A hand, warm and alive. Gentle. Scented with dirt and something organic that he couldn't identify. He turned his face, and the hand slid away.

He opened his eyes to find someone bending over him. Shadowed by the moonlight from above, the face left only the impression of large eyes, an outline of short, ragged hair, a high, curving cheekbone.

"You'll be fine." The voice, dusky and rough, sounded as if it wasn't often used. "Now, will you give me back my arrows?"

Quent tried to look closer at the warm, wiry figure crouched next to him, but his head hurt like a bitch and everything was all shadowy.

"Thank you," he said, knowing it was this person—male or female, but he was leaning toward female based on a sort of crackling awareness shooting through him—who'd helped stop the *ganga*. After he'd smashed one of his captors' brains, the other one had cracked him across the face with a massive, cold hand . . . and that was the last he knew until now.

"My arrows," the voice said again, then, as if realizing how rude that sounded, added, "Can you sit up?"

Quent could and did, though his head pounded like hell. He grasped the figure's arm. Smooth, muscular, but delicate. Exposed by a sleeveless shirt, skin a shade darker than his own.

He caught a profile. Definitely a woman. If a boy had such feminine features, it'd be a pity—not to mention a danger for the poor sod.

And then there were the sleek curves of her torso. The strap from what must be a quiver cut diagonally between two plum-sized breasts.

Definitely a she.

And definitely the owner of the arrow he'd been holding

earlier, the one that gave him murky images and memories, laced with impatience and anger . . . and determination. Loneliness.

"You're alone," he said, hoping he didn't sound like a bloody rapist. But he had a feeling she was the kind of woman who could take care of herself.

She sat back on her haunches, and he saw wide dark eyes in a face darkened by shadows. "I like it that way. My arrows. Please."

"You saved me," he said. "Thank you."

She eased back, and he realized she'd closed her fingers around the arrows. "That's what I do." The darkness swallowed her.

"Wait," he said, scrambling to his feet, embarrassingly unsteady. His head pounded harder now, and he felt more than a bit shaky and nauseated from the close proximity to the *gangas*.

"It'll go away," she said from the shadows in that low, husky voice. "The dizziness and weakness. And you'd best use this."

Something whuffed out of the darkness and he had the wherewithal to snatch it out of the air. His bandanna. "Where do you live? In Envy?"

Silence. Quent peered into the shadows, taking a step toward the place from where his bandanna had come flying as he tied it back into place.

"Come with us," he said. "We could use you."

"No."

He heard a soft trickle-like sound of lapping water and knew she was gone. Quent thought about following her, and even started in the direction where she'd disappeared . . . but then he remembered something. "I still have one of your arrows." He made sure his voice carried, certain she'd not gone too far. "You can have it whenever you want. Your arrow."

He waited, heard nothing but the soft splash of water, and the scamper of small rodent feet. "We're taking those kids back home. To a place called Envy."

"What the hell're you doing? Giving the *gangas* our fucking itinerary?"

Quent whirled to see Simon standing there. Despite the edge to his words, there was a glimmer of dark humor in his handsome, chiseled face. "Not that they could follow it, dumb wanks. And where the hell did you come from?"

Simon shrugged, and Quent saw that he carried a two-by-four-sized branch as a weapon. Something steaming and rank still clumped on the far corner.

"I saw you were missing. Got one, but not before he swiped at me." Simon gestured to his arm, which had a deep gash that would match the one on his leg from earlier in the day. "Fucking nails on those bastards are sharp. You okay?"

"That archer, the one who shot a couple *gangas* when Wyatt and I were checking out the van, saved me," Quent told him as his friend gestured in the proper direction for them to walk. Bloody good thing, as he'd been out cold for part of his trip and didn't know which way to go. "Wanted the arrows back." It wasn't like him to drop pronouns. *Interesting.* Quent tickled that around in his mind as they started back.

Simon, who wore his shoulder-length dark hair in a low ponytail, walked alongside him with long strides, though he still limped a bit. Quent didn't know him that well, but, he supposed, when your life changes the way his had—all of theirs had—you get to know a man pretty bloody quickly when you've got all that to deal with. And what he'd gotten to know about Simon was that, though quiet and private, and stinging at times, he was brave and fought tenaciously. He was trustworthy and intelligent.

"You give them back to him?"

"Yes."

Except the one in his hand. He was keeping that one . . . until she came back for it.

The *gangas* were gone, Geoff had fled back into the safety of the building, and Elliott and his friends had sustained little in the way of injury. Even Wyatt had resisted the urge to lecture Geoff, who claimed he'd left simply to find a place to piss, and got turned around in a dark and unfamiliar place.

As soon as he reached the top of the rope ladder, Elliott found himself looking for Jade. Sweaty, exhilarated from the adrenaline rush of battle, and pissed that one of his few shirts had been ruined, he saw her talking to Linda and another of the teen girls. She cast a quick glance toward him, but didn't break off her conversation.

That was fine with Elliott. He had some patching up to do on Simon, who'd taken a nasty hit by a set of *ganga* claws, and some serious thinking ahead.

At least he knew the answer to one question, sort of. After the battle with the *gangas*, he'd been unable to avoid Wyatt clasping his hand in a victory shake. Nothing had happened.

At least, so far.

It could mean that once he'd "transferred" the injury to someone, it couldn't or wouldn't be transferred again—hell, he hadn't even been able to heal Linda after he'd given it to her.

Or maybe it meant that the ability to transfer it had worn off after a while. Or maybe he had to be thinking or concentrating about it when he absorbed the injury and then transferred it.

The implications were enough to keep his mind on that labyrinthine trail for a while. There was also the possibility that it had been something about Jade herself that had caused him to take on her injury and transfer it to himself, and then to Linda.

He glanced over at the woman in question and happened to find her looking at him. She looked away quickly, but it was too late. He couldn't hold back a smile of delight and a rush of attraction.

Something about Jade? Most definitely.

"Look what I found."

Simon's richly satisfied voice had Elliott starting awake from the best dream he'd had in a long time. It starred him and the intriguing, bareback-riding woman who was supposed to be his patient. There'd been lots of bare ass and smooth white skin, and he wasn't playing doctor.

Shaking off the dream, trying to ignore the raging hard-on that reminded him that, yes, his parts still worked and his jeans were a bit tight, Elliott rubbed his dry eyes and realized that not only had he actually slept, but that the sun sat fully on the horizon.

Then he saw what Simon was holding. "Duct tape. Holy crap. Six rolls? Unopened, dry, unmildewed?" He grinned and took one of the precious objects. "We could build a bloody house with this stuff. Could probably even tape that damned motor back together."

Simon gave a rare laugh. "Tell me, man."

Until now, until he'd had a chance to pull back on his raging hormones, Elliott hadn't allowed himself to look toward Jade's pallet. But now that he did, he saw that she was gone.

"Where's Jade?" he asked casually, looking around the

area arrayed with stripes of sunlight. The illumination revealed dust motes that had been stirred up by the unusual
activity of human occupation, and the mildew spots on what
had been drywall but was now torn and sagging, infested
with vines, rodent holes, and insects. The teens had begun
to awaken, and it was immediately clear that Jade was no
longer in the room.

Elliott walked over to her pallet and saw that the pack
he'd taken from over her shoulder was gone. He resisted
the absurd urge to kick at the pile of blankets that probably
smelled like her and turned back to the others.

At least she'd been smart enough to wait until dawn to
leave. He was fairly certain about that because he remembered seeing the faint gray from the sun before drifting off
into a hard-won sleep.

"I dunno."

It took Elliott a moment to realize that Simon was answering his question; but he didn't need to hear it. He already knew she'd gone back to wherever she'd been, and he
doubted he'd see her again. Unless. . . .

He looked at Geoff, who looked fairly miserable. Obviously the kid knew Jade. All the more reason to get on their
way and find this mecca known as Envy.

They gathered up the teens, and, now that it was daylight
and there was actually decent illumination, Elliott could
see how miserable and tired they really were. And young.
Definitely no more than seventeen, all of them. They all had
parents that were likely worried sick about them too.

They started off, heading north, bearing slightly west,
walking along an overgrown road that led toward a nearby
fringe of looming mountains.

Once paved, the thoroughfare—probably a highway
of some sort, though any signs had long rusted over—had

become home to full-grown trees and bushes, thrusting up from cracks made by stubborn seedlings and temperature changes. Clusters of saplings and patches of grasses and low-growing bushes filled out the sides of the highway, not quite forests yet but definitely on the way to becoming them. Elliott found it amazing how quickly man's world had become destroyed and overgrown after half a century.

Mother Nature was one hell of a ball-buster.

June 10 (?)
Four days After

Ventured outside for the first time since the earth-quakes began. Horrible sight. Unbelievable destruction. Dead bodies, crushed cars, parts of buildings gone. Dust and debris everywhere, clouding the air, my lungs. Puked three times.

Amazed and sickened to find that half of the Strip is underwater. Completely gone.

Have been able to find more bottled water. Some plastic bottles. Some food, too, in a fridge. Found an-other survivor, a woman named Diane. Arm broken but otherwise okay. We scavenged together and found a safe place to stay. Have tentatively agreed it's been four days, making today June 10, 2010.

The buildings aren't falling so often anymore. Only one or two crashes per day. The storms continue. Can't see much through the rain, but the dust and debris is being cleared by it. Spent very little time outside. Just enough to call out. No one answered.

Where's help?

Found an intact cell phone and tried to call 911. No bars. Nothing.

Still sense Theo's presence. How will I ever find him?
　　　　　　　　—from the journal of Lou Waxnicki

CHAPTER 5

Jade bent over the mustang's neck, its mane sweeping rhythmically over her cheek as they galloped across the terrain. She held on to a handful of mane and looped her other arm around and beneath the horse's neck. Her pack hung comfortably over her shoulder, jolting against her hip, and though she hadn't slept much last night, she felt exhilarated as they pounded through grassy meadows and around and through what had once been small cities. *Free*.

She loved the wind in her face, the sunshine on her skin, the scent on the air, still damp after the morning dew, the warmth and movement of a living being beneath her. Those were things she'd never take for granted again. She reminded herself of it every day.

With only a little stab of regret, she'd left Elliott and the others the moment dawn began to gray the horizon. By then, the *gangas* would be seeking the protective darkness of large buildings or wading deep into the ocean.

If nothing unexpected happened, she'd get back to Envy in just enough time to clean up before her gig. She prayed Theo had made it to Envy by now too. There seemed to have been a lot of *gangas* out and about last night. A trickle of worry nagged her, but she tried to put it out of her mind because there was nothing she could do about it until she found out whether he was safe or not.

Jade wondered if Elliott was angry that she'd left. Not that it mattered. Just because he'd somehow healed her didn't mean that he had any control over her. And since she'd seen him with his shirt torn off, she knew for certain he wasn't a Stranger.

That was the only reason she'd been looking at him so closely when he climbed up the rope ladder last night. Just to make *sure* he didn't have any crystals. But he'd caught her watching for him, and he probably thought she was ogling his bare chest. Which she hadn't been. Except to look for crystals. Even though it had been a very wixy chest.

Jade gave her head a little shake to dislodge the image of that very wixy chest, and felt the pleasant reminder of her long hair flip and flow behind her. It had taken her three years to grow it out again and although it could be a liability in some ways, she refused to cut it. The heavy length, despite the tangles and impracticality, was another reminder that she was free and in control of her own life. And her own body.

There were nights when dark dreams brought back those days in the sunny, spare white room, the constant rush of running water, the large white upholstered bed. Even now, when she approached a river or waterfall, the sound gave her pause for a moment, sending a little trickle of unease over her shoulders. Foolish, she knew. Foolish and weak.

But for the most part, she was free of the dreams, the catch of the memories. Her past could have deadened her, induced her to stay locked safely away, but she refused to cower. She enjoyed life—the life she'd fought so hard to preserve—too much to be restricted.

By the time Jade saw the walls of Envy, the sun was leaning well toward the western horizon. Instead of going to the main gateway, on the southern side, she dismounted about two miles away, near an overgrown structure that might once have been a small house. An oak thrust from its decrepit roof, and none of the windows retained their glass panes. Buckled concrete led up to an entrance large enough for one of the big vehicles the Strangers liked to drive. Jade gave her mount a hug, a pat, and an apple from her knapsack, then slapped him on the rump, setting him free to return to his herd.

Mustangs were plentiful in the meadows, tame and easy to catch if one knew how, so she had no need to pen him—or any of them. Jade had a particular affinity for the horses, and she went to where they gathered and whistled when she needed a ride. Most of the time, one would respond to her call—and the apples they'd come to expect.

Having set her mount free, Jade walked toward Envy. She took care to be as unobtrusive as possible, keeping trees, buildings, and any other object as a shield between herself and anyone who might be watching from the city walls. The three main gates were large and obvious and drew the attention of any approaching traveler. And no one but Jade, Lou, and Theo knew about the hidden entrance positioned on the southwest side beneath an old sign with a girl called Wendy on it.

That was because the Waxnicki brothers had built the hidden entrance long ago, when the walls were first being erected to keep out the *gangas*.

If only they'd kept out the Strangers too. Not that Strangers were plentiful in Envy, or even often ventured into the city walls. At least, as far as they knew.

Jade easily slipped between the heavy bushes that grew along the protective walls, which had been made from old train cars, semi-truck trailers, and a variety of stacked debris. They'd also used big house-sized signs called billboards and even some bricks and metal sheeting taken from the destroyed buildings. The walls, which in places were little more than a mountain range of junk, rose more than twenty feet high. In fact, they could be used to keep Envyites in as well as *gangas* out.

Uncomfortable with that very possibility of being penned in was the reason Lou and Theo had created their own passageway, using a large culvert. They'd secretly positioned the metal pipe—which was large enough for a man to walk through—beneath collapsed billboards and tumbling walls. Then, they had obstructed both ends of it with more debris, causing it to blend into the piles of rubble that had been formed by the cleanup after the Change.

Only someone like Jade, who knew which objects to move and how, could find and utilize the passage.

Now, she emerged from the inside of the culvert and found herself in an old boxcar. Feeling her way in the dark, she moved through the car and through a trapdoor in the floor, easing herself onto the ground three feet below. She crouched, hurrying out from under the boxcar, slid from behind a warped sheet of metal, and found herself on what had once been a street.

The sun had dropped farther, and with the height of the wall, Jade was well hidden on the overgrown street. She slipped quickly and silently along the dim alley between the building and the barricade of debris. All was quiet but for the soft rustle of some animal scuttling through the dark, and the far-distant sounds of voices and activity.

But . . . she heard something else. Something that didn't belong.

The back of Jade's shoulders prickled. She slowed and

slid into the shadows, feeling the rough, age-pitted wall beneath her hands. Voices. Low and careful.

Unusual for this area of the city, where few people had the need or desire to venture. There was nothing here but piles of rubble, and a few half-walls from destroyed buildings. Whatever might have been of value had been scavenged long ago.

The voices were deep, indicating they were men. They spoke quickly and quietly, their feet kicking up old sticks and dislodging stones, taking little care to hide their presence. Or perhaps they simply didn't expect anyone to be here.

Jade knew she had to make a decision—whether to hide, or to go boldly forward and bluff her way through a possible meeting. It could be a perfectly innocent situation . . . but something felt wrong. She'd never encountered anyone else in this area, and she realized suddenly why it felt wrong. They carried no light. No illumination. But anyone else, without a nefarious purpose, would want to safely light their way.

Of course, she wasn't carrying a light either . . . so what did that say about her?

Jade pushed against the wall, feeling her way for an opening or indentation in which she could hide. The voices were coming closer and she'd hardly moved.

Her heart picked up speed and she moved as quickly as she dared, taking care to lift her feet carefully and deliberately, placing her steps smoothly so as not to rustle or scuff. At last . . . the wall angled beneath her fingers and she edged sharply into unknown darkness. The brick or concrete seeped chill into her back and palms, and leaves from its overgrowth brushed her face and caught at her hair.

Something moved . . . slithered . . . over her foot and she barely contained a surprised—and horrified—gasp, muffling it with a hard, horse-scented palm over her mouth. *Oh*

God! Mice, rats, possums . . . she could handle any of the four-footed creatures and some of the eight-legged ones. Just not the ones that slid on their bellies.

Then . . . no more slithering. A faint rustle from where the snake glided off, hopefully far away, and Jade realized that the men were approaching. So much for the hope that they might not come in this direction.

Peering around the edge of her hiding place, Jade saw the two figures. They were outlined in the gathering shadows, black against the blue-gray of falling night. And beneath one of their shirts, faint but unmistakable, she saw a faint glow. Very subtle, hardly noticeable if you weren't looking for it and if the fabric wasn't too heavy.

A Stranger.

Here in Envy, lurking in the darkness.

Jade's heart ramrodded in her throat and a trickle of nervous perspiration rolled down her spine. But her shock increased as they drew closer.

For, even in the low light, she recognized one of them—the one without the crystal glow of immortality. Rob Nurmikko, one of the plastic workers. He melted down a variety of objects left over from before the Change—milk cartons, parts of cars, toys, whatever he could find—and created furniture and other goods from them. Jade had one of his heart-shaped chairs in her room.

He was working with a Stranger?

Jade held her breath as they drew nearer.

"It's not my fault they never showed last night," Rob was saying. "I can't exactly drag—"

"I'll be happy to give your excuses to Preston," interrupted the Stranger coolly. "You know how well that'll go over."

"No, wait. *Wait.* I'll get 'em. How much time?" Rob's voice was strained and thready.

"The shipment's going on Friday," replied his companion flatly. "Everything's got to be ready by then, or he'll have your fucking head. If you screw up this shipment, he'll send the Marcks after you."

"I'll have the cargo by then." The plastics maker's voice didn't sound very convincing.

"Either that, or you'd best disappear. Because if you don't manage it this time—and he's expecting prime goods—then you'll be *ganga* lunch." The other man laughed as they passed by Jade's hiding place and she closed her eyes, praying that they wouldn't look into the darkness.

"I need more grit," Jade heard Rob whine as the two men faded into distance and darkness, but she could discern nothing else after that, for the ominous conversation still rang in her mind.

Preston. Just hearing his name was enough to make her knees tremble and the bottom drop out of her stomach . . . but to know that someone here, in Envy, had a connection to him . . . was preparing a cargo for him . . . threatened to give her nightmares. She'd hoped, maybe in the deepest part of her heart, that something had happened to Preston in the last three years . . . but what, after all, could happen to an immortal man?

Not much, as long as he had his crystal.

But the other thing that settled in her mind, besides the fear that she would be discovered as Diana Kapiza, was Rob's plea for more grit.

Crystal grit. Also known as pixie or crystal dust.

A hallucinogen she'd become horribly, frighteningly familiar with during her captivity. What had Rob gotten himself mixed up in?

* * *

The daylong trek took Elliott and his friends north through the mountains, and by the time they made it through the pass, the western horizon had bisected the sun. Darkness would soon come, and with it, the night creatures, and according to the kids, they still had about an hour's worth of travel.

Fence and Wyatt each carried a bottle bomb, ready to be lit. Quent had his arrows, and Simon and Elliott each had one of the group's precious firearms, loaded with even more precious bullets.

Bullets for the wolves, bottle bombs for the *gangas*.

During the day, Elliott saw several old and rusted-out vehicles along the side of the overgrown road, but he'd stopped wondering where the rest of them had gone. Just as he no longer expected to find bodies, or even skeletons, lurking in the buildings into which they'd ventured. If there had been any, they'd disappeared long ago, perhaps taken off by wolves or wild dogs . . . or perhaps not.

Perhaps something else had happened to them.

"Is that a lake over there?" Fence asked, pointing toward the setting sun. They were standing on a high point just beyond the mountain pass.

Elliott turned and saw nothing but gray-blue ridges of low mountains; but, then, he wasn't Fence.

"I don't see nothing," said one of the boys. "But Envy's right by the ocean." He pointed. "See that bit of light? That's Envy."

Elliott saw the patch of lights. From the size of the cluster, it looked like a fairly large settlement. And if they wanted to get there before dark, they'd better hurry.

"The ocean," Fence murmured. Elliott, who walked just behind him, could almost hear the wheels turning. "But that's not right. It can't be." He looked at the boy who'd answered him. "How do you know it's an ocean?"

"Salt water," Geoff said. His voice held a cocky edge that Elliott could relate to from his own youth.

Apparently even the apocalypse hadn't changed teenaged attitude.

"The Great Salt Lake maybe?" Fence murmured, mostly to himself. He'd paused walking and Elliott saw that he'd closed his eyes. "That might make more sense. But no . . . we're too far west."

"It's an ocean," Geoff said. "Not a lake. Seashells." The *duh* remained unspoken, but hung there nevertheless.

"We're not that far west," Fence replied.

Before they could continue, a strange trumpeting sound filled the air. Elliott turned toward the noise. No way.

"Bloody hell, that sounded like an elephant," said Quent.

"Yeah. There's a big herd of 'em," said Marcus, one of the other boys. "They live here." As if a herd of elephants were as common as deer.

"No fucking way," Simon replied.

"Where the hell are we, Fence?" asked Elliott.

They reached the bottom of the incline and one of the girls stopped and pointed to the southwest. "See?"

And there, silhouetted by the orange ball of sun were the very definite outlines of four elephants, looking like something out of *The Lion King*. They trumpeted again, and in what became clear was a warning, they began to stampede into the darkness, trumpeting and thundering and stirring up dirt.

Fortunately, they were running away from their path . . . but the distant roar that overrode the sound of elephantine steps had Elliott stopping cold. No way.

"Tiger?"

"That or a lion," said Wyatt. "And I'm not thinking mountain, though I wouldn't want to meet an angry one of those either. Christ. Elephants, *gangas*, tigers. Where the hell are we?"

No one mentioned Kansas. That joke had become old six fucking months ago.

The lights were closer now, for they'd kept up their pace despite the fascinating zoological sights.

Was that the . . . Statue of Liberty?

It was crooked as all hell. And bent.

But, unfuckingbelievable, it looked like the damned Statue of Liberty.

The small cluster of lights around and below it glittered like gems of red, blue, yellow, green, and white. This was definitely the largest—or at least, the most well-lit—settlement they'd seen in their year of wandering.

"Holy shit," Fence said. "The Statue of Liberty? No fucking way, man. I'm not that confused."

At that moment, Elliott saw the shape of a massive golden lion, looming like an off-kilter shadow in the darkness, beyond the lights. And a collection of huge toy-castle turrets, silhouetted against the orange sun.

Then suddenly Simon started laughing. A little crazily.

"It's Vegas, you ass-wipes. We're in fucking Las Vegas."

CHAPTER 6

New Vegas, N.V, or Envy—whatever the hell you wanted to call it—wasn't exactly Sin City.

It was half of Sin City.

Less than half.

Elliott blinked again and resisted the urge to rub his eyes.

According to Geoff, the same devastation that had annihilated pretty much all of California also destroyed most of Las Vegas.

Which explained the ocean.

The ocean that now sat about where Caesar's and Harrah's used to be.

Holy fucking shit.

Simon pointed out landmarks he was obviously familiar with. "The Statue of Liberty—she used to be at New York–New York. The MGM lion there, and that castle was part of Excalibur." His voice was dulled by the same surprise and shock that Elliott felt.

Lady Liberty looked more like the leaning Tower of Pisa, precariously tilted to one side, but still gamely clutching her torch. And the massive golden lion from MGM, along with the castle towers of Excalibur looked a little like Toyland, unaccountably rising above jagged walls, buckled roofs, and piles of rubble that had once been luxury resorts.

"Well," said Fence with a forced chuckle, "you know, what happens in Vegas, stays in Vegas."

No one bothered to respond.

Seeing Vegas as it now was seemed to put a lid on any possibility that the world they'd been living in for months was just a bad dream, or an anomaly limited to a relatively small geographic area. The sight of the beleaguered city, its desperation clear through the multicolored lights illuminating jagged rooftops, caved-in buildings, and, above all, an eerie stillness that the Strip had never seen, also served to quiet the five of them.

If they'd harbored any hope that things might not be as bad as it had appeared, that optimism was now gone.

As the last vestige of sunlight faded, they reached what could only be described as the city limits. A wall had been constructed around the settlement, reminding Elliott of the kind of guarded village in epic sci-fi or fantasy movies. The barrier had been made of a variety of objects—wheelless semi-truck trailers, bricks, cars piled atop each other, steel beams, and even ragged billboards. In some places, it looked like little more than piles of junk.

As one might expect, guards tended the entrance of the enclosure. Although they didn't have gates blocking the way, ready to be raised if those who approached were deemed worthy, it was clear that permission needed to be gained before entering.

But before anyone spoke, Geoff pushed his way forward. "It's us. Let us in."

"Geoff Pinglett? Linda Royce?" One of the men standing guard obviously recognized them, and with undisguised relief and delight. "You're back! Grady! *Grady!* They're back! They're here!"

Everything happened very quickly after that. The next

thing Elliott knew, his group was welcomed in amid shouts and exclamations of joy. Apparently, some of the teens' parents, led by a fellow named Grady, had just returned from a search trip of their own, seeking the shelter of the walls when darkness fell. The reunion was joyous and raucous, filled with embraces and cries of delight, but Elliott knew admonishments would follow in the privacy of their homes. But for now, everyone seemed happy and relieved.

"They saved us," Linda, the one who reminded Elliott of his niece Josie, was saying. She looked worshipfully up at him from the safe embrace of her mother, her broken arm tucked protectively against her chest. "From the *gangas*. And they brought us back."

"Thank God," said one of the mothers, tears glistening in her eyes, and a father reached out to clasp Elliott's hand, shaking it firmly.

"We're greatly in your debt," another parent said, as Elliott, Wyatt, Quent, Simon, and Fence were urged beyond the entrance and into the safety of a well-lit city—no questions asked. Not even their names.

Yet the gates and guards left Elliott to wonder uncomfortably whether they'd have gained entrance if it had only been the five of them and if they had not done anything to render themselves heroes.

But why would they not? The walls and gates were to keep the *gangas* and wild animals out, not people.

Unless they were also meant to keep people *in*.

Elliott shoved away the dark thought. There was no reason to think that. But he would keep his eyes and ears open, and pay attention to their surroundings. He still didn't fully understand this world—how it worked, who lived here, why it had all happened, and what the Change meant to society.

Nevertheless, Elliott tried to absorb every detail as a

group of ecstatic parents escorted them down a very different Strip than the one he'd visited once with a bunch of ski
buddies. He avoided the cracks and buckles in the sidewalk
and the avenue itself, noticing that there wasn't as much
natural growth here in this inhabited area as in other abandoned cities that had little or no population. Obviously, the
presence of man had kept Mother Nature in check.

He saw people too. More people than they'd seen in
any one place—and more than they'd seen in total—since
coming out of that cave. How many people lived in Envy?
A couple thousand? The other settlements they'd found had
consisted of forty or fifty people at most, some with only a
dozen or so. Envy was definitely the bastion of civilization.

As they walked, Geoff slipped away from his parents and
sidled up to Elliott. "Dude . . . don't mention Jade, okay?" he
said in a low voice.

Elliott read concern in the boy's eyes and didn't hesitate.
"I won't." Of course he wanted to know why, but this wasn't
the time or the place to interrogate the boy.

Hm. Well, at least Jade was known here in Envy. Which
meant that he might just see her here.

The thought lightened his step and caused him to look
around even more closely, as if he might catch a glimpse
of her.

They hadn't gone far from the main gate of the city before
they veered off their path toward the damaged Statue of Liberty, and turned down a walkway onto the Vegas version
of the Brooklyn Bridge. The copy of the New York skyline
was no longer intact, though parts of it remained erratic and
dark, looming above their path. Obvious care had been taken
to maintain what parts of the resort remained.

Beginning to feel more and more like an errant knight
seeking entrance to a medieval keep and being ushered in by

a man-at-arms, Elliott glanced at Wyatt. Their eyes met, and he read the same alertness there. Elliott had a knife in his belt, and he felt his hand straying toward the leather sheath.

But once inside, instead of being confronted by a dais sporting some sort of enthroned ruler, they found themselves in nothing more than a functioning restaurant.

The smell of food, cooked food, *real* cooked food, had their eyebrows rising and mouths watering.

"Is that steak?" murmured Quent. "I think I've died and gone to heaven."

The next thing they knew, they were seated at a table in the middle of the room and food, drink, and rambunctious gratitude for saving the teens were pressed upon them. Names and faces blurred in upon each other, interspersed with tears and reprimands from parent to wayward teen.

Elliott looked up and caught Fence's eye. The other man grinned and began to whistle the *Cheers* theme under his breath. It did feel as though everyone knew their names—or at least, everyone else's names. And the atmosphere was one of congeniality and familiarity.

Elliott thought this might be what it had been like in small towns before the Change, where the central gathering place revolved around food and comfort. And perhaps that instinct of people, to gather together to eat and gossip, to have a hub for social outlet, had been a saving force in this new world.

Perhaps later, specific names and faces and people would separate from this whirlwind, and there might be something resembling real conversation—and some of the answers they needed to have—but for now, it wasn't worth fighting. They were fed, and safe, and as comfortable as they'd been since leaving Sedona.

Maybe he'd even sleep in a real bed tonight.

Quent had indeed smelled steak—real beef, not the venison they'd had a few times—and along with that were potatoes and tomatoes, oranges, apples, and even beer. And not Budweiser or anything else in a can that might have survived the calamity, but a home brew.

And a damned good one too. Heavy and dark and nutty.

As they ate, feeling somewhat as if they were in a fish-bowl—but the food was too welcome for them to care—Elliott observed the people. These residents of Envy. He noticed that hardly any were overweight, most were younger than forty, and there were a lot more crooked teeth and over-bites than he was used to seeing. And there were so many pregnant women the restaurant looked like an OB/GYN waiting room.

There was, to his disappointment, no sign of Jade.

And there was also no one who looked older than fifty. No one who would have been here when the Change happened.

No one who could help them understand what had happened between the time they entered that cave and the time they came back out.

Elliott asked Geoff's father, who was sitting next to him drinking a beer, whether there was anyone old enough to remember the Change.

Sam Pinglett shrugged. "Not really. Not anymore. There's an old man named Lou Waxnicki, but he's a little . . . off. Guess I would be too if I'd lived through something like that." He gave an uneasy laugh. "Technically, he was around then, but I'm not sure how much of what he remembers is real and what isn't, you know. Only other person I ever talked to who was around died three years ago."

"Where would I find Waxnicki?" Elliott asked, meeting Wyatt's glance.

Sam shrugged again. "Have no idea. He keeps to himself,

comes out for a meal once a day, I guess. Usually I'm busy working, don't see him much."

"Working? What do you do?"

"Help keep the power supply running. Electricity."

Elliott nodded, trying, and failing, to imagine going "off to work" in this strange world. How did one make a living? "From the Hoover Dam?"

"Naw. That failed 'bout twenty years ago, I guess. We get most of our power from wind and water. Some solar. A bunch of different things they set up years ago, and we just keep 'em running. Say, why don't we go on over to The Pub for a drink? Sometimes we got some entertainment there too. At least the waitresses are cute." He glanced over to see if his wife had noticed. She was petting Geoff's cowlick, which appeared to be a losing battle. Sam looked back at Elliott with an abashed smile, but before he could repeat his invitation, his wife stood.

"I think it's time we went up and had a family chat," she said meaningfully. "You too, Sam." Maybe she *had* heard his comment. Or maybe it was just time to lower the boom on Geoff for his little stunt.

"Nice meeting you. And thanks again," Sam said as he stood. "Pub's down that direction if you guys want to head there anyways."

"Did I hear someone mention a pub? Getting pissed sounds like a great idea," Quent said, standing. "Since no one's got to stand guard for *gangas* tonight, and they're giving us real beds, I say we all go for it."

Sure. What the hell else were they going to do?

The five of them stood, and one of the other parents offered to show them the way to The Pub. As they followed him from the restaurant and down a wide corridor, Elliott noticed a neat sign on the wall by the door. *Tonight's Feature*: *The Bourne Supremacy*.

Huh. A bit of normalcy in this fucked-up world.

He thought about how the setting of that movie must seem so foreign, so outlandish to the people of Envy. Cars, planes, cell phones, huge cities with millions of people . . .

The reality staggered him as he recognized once again that that world—the world he knew—existed no longer.

God. How? Why?

He swallowed hard. *Get a fucking grip. You're alive.*

And you're a doctor. A fucking healer.

Think what you can do for these people.

If you don't kill them by accident.

Elliott took a deep breath. Yes. He could make a difference. Save lives. Be a miracle worker. If he could figure out how to use his power . . . and if he didn't lose his damned mind first.

Why would he be given a gift that he couldn't use? A gift that only taunted him? *Why, dammit?*

He blinked, shook his head to clear it, and realized he'd lagged behind.

"Yo, Dred, you coming? There's entertainment," said Fence. "Sounds good too."

Elliott heard it then . . . music. And a low, smoky Sarah Vaughan voice. He might have walked right past if he hadn't caught a phrase of the lyrics . . . something about a man waking to find he had no one.

That sounded just about right. He'd awakened to find he had no one. And nothing.

Talk about hitting a guy right where it hurt.

He followed the others in, glancing toward the stage automatically to see what the woman who sang like that looked like. The bottom fairly dropped out of his belly. Jade. Up there. Singing.

Not sure whether he should be elated or simply shocked, he managed to keep walking, suddenly a ridiculous, pubescent bundle of hormones.

Here she was, just as he'd hoped . . . but not exactly what he'd expected. Standing there up on a stage, dressed in a low-cut, shiny dark red shirt, accompanied by a single keyboard player. She looked long and lean and confident, her dark hair glowing mahogany from the lights, her eyes dark and smoky. Her lips full and glistening, the cuts and scrapes unnoticeable.

Christ, were his palms sweating?

"Is that Jade?" Fence muttered in his ear. "Man, she musta ridden like a mother to get here before us. And what a voice."

What a voice, indeed. She sounded like sex and promises.

Elliott moved into the club, felt Quent and Fence behind him, and selected a table off to the side. Off to the side, but where she could see him when she looked over.

For a moment, he felt as if everything were normal. He sat with two of his buddies, he ordered a beer from a server who approached, he looked up and saw a beautiful woman singing in a bedroom voice. And he hoped like hell she'd be leaving with him.

And then reality, the bastard, reared its monstrous head. The beer was placed before him, and he realized he had nothing to pay with. He had no idea *how* to pay, even.

Unpleasant shock settled over him as he reached for the wallet that had been—fifty years ago—in his back pocket. Oh, he still had it, tucked away with his other belongings, but it held nothing but worthless credit and debit cards. Maybe a crinkled bill or two—would they take that? Probably a long-expired condom, which was no doubt as brittle as the smile that he knew was on his face.

"Don't worry about it," the server said. As she told them her name was Trixie, her sloe eyes lingered on his face. "You're heroes . . . it's on the house, according to Mayor Rogan." She smiled, then walked away.

Okay. Good. But. . . .

What *did* they use for money now? Regular U.S. currency? It wasn't that much of a long shot—since they were in Las Vegas, there had to have been a supply of cash somewhere. But how would they have divvied it all up among the survivors? Did it even mean anything anymore? After all, there was no backing by the full faith and credit of the U.S. government.

Because it was clear the U.S. government no longer existed.

Elliott took a long drink from the beer mug, glad that Trixie had left even though it was obvious she'd have liked a reason to loiter, glad to have something cool and smooth going down his throat that might just give him a bit of a buzz.

The song was ending, Jade's voice, sultry and clear as she finished the ballad about a lover who should have come over, about a tear hanging in someone's soul. He watched as she reached out, stepped near the edge of the stage and gestured to a rangy-looking man sitting there, front and fucking center.

What passed between Jade and the man in that moment was little more than an exchange of glances, a brief flutter of her fingers over the shiny red blouse, a nod . . . but there was no misreading it. The familiarity, the connection. The intimacy.

Well, didn't that just suck.

And then as the last notes from the keyboard filtered away, she released the mike and stepped offstage to join the guy, who looked like a Marlboro Man wannabe.

Elliott picked up his beer and buried his face in the mug. And drank.

Getting pissed, as Quent put it, suddenly sounded just about right.

Ten days After

No help is coming.

Diane and I found forty-three others. 43. Of everyone in Las Vegas, only forty-five of us survived?

Bodies everywhere: on the streets, beneath the rubble. Everywhere.

One of the survivors—a man named Rowe—said he was with fifty others who lived through the earthquakes, but then all but himself died the next day for no apparent reason. They simply dropped like stones.

He was the only one who didn't.

Why? Some weird-ass result of severe PTSD? A gas released by the quakes? A disease?

After some (sometimes heated) discussion, all have agreed that today is June 16.

No more aftershocks. Storms have stopped. Got some generators working, siphoned gas from bus and truck tanks. Have lights and some power for a while.

No Internet. No cell.

Trying to find medical supplies for injured people. Sending parties to forage for food. Some don't come back.

Where is everyone else?

I have to find Theo. He's still alive. I can feel him.

—from the journal of Lou Waxnicki

CHAPTER 7

Jade slipped the flat plastic card into the slot, heard the familiar click of the lock, and silently eased through the door. Thank goodness for Lou's master key.

Inside, the room was dark but for a brush of moonlight that gave gray highlights to a smooth bed, a wing-shaded lamp, and a hulking armoire.

On silent feet, she hurried across what had once been a well-appointed hotel room at New York–New York Casino and Resort, and just as quietly to the adjoining door, carefully jimmying the lock . . . and into Elliott's room.

She glanced at the bed, saw the unmoving figure of a man and swallowed hard. Even from here she could see the rise of a broad, square shoulder illuminated by the faint gray seeping through the window. She looked away, toward the door that opened onto the hallway down which she'd just padded. Good plan on her part, coming in through the next room—he'd used the security lock, and she wouldn't have been able to get in through that door. Jade smiled to herself for her foresight and began to move quietly toward the bed, realizing her heart was beating loudly in her ears.

She felt more than a little odd, being in Elliott's room, but it was the best way to make sure they weren't seen together, and to get him to Lou.

If he was willing. And if she wasn't wrong about him. *Please God.*

That was the biggest risk of all, but one Lou had been determined to take. "I'll know the moment I shake his hand," he'd assured her. "Before any damage is done."

Theo wasn't back yet, and although he'd tried to hide it, Lou was worried about his brother. His elderly face had shown its creases even more deeply after Jade told him about the conversation she'd heard near the Wendy passageway.

Friday. Something was going to happen Friday. Whatever it was, if it had to do with the Strangers, if it had to be done in secrecy, something was wrong. Just the fact that a Stranger was here, secretly, set her hair on end.

Jade had seen what the Strangers did. She dreamt about it, and when she was alone, often woke up sweating and trembling. That was precisely why she did what she did, and why she risked herself on the Running missions. Because they had to be stopped from killing more children, from torturing more women. From using mortals for their experiments that left them mutilated and ill.

And no one believed her about all the things she'd seen. No one but the Waxnicki brothers.

Jade hesitated. Should they really be wasting their time with Elliott and his friends—people they didn't know— instead of doing something about Rob and his cargo?

But what could she do, aside of questioning Rob? Subtly, of course. Which, by the way, she'd intended to do, but hadn't been able to find him.

As it was, Jade had barely made it back in time to clean up for her gig tonight—thank God for Flo, who'd helped her get put together. The woman was magic—fixing her hair and face to make her look as good as if she was one of those old actresses. Angelina Jolie or Scarlett Johansen, Jade wasn't, but at least Flo had helped hide the remnants of Jade's cuts and scrapes.

And then of course Vaughn Rogan had shown up, sat right in the front so she couldn't ignore him. She couldn't exactly blow off the mayor of Envy, especially considering their history.

But here she was now, in Elliott's room, after extricating herself from Vaughn and actually snatching a few hours of sleep. It was the wee small hours of the morning, as one of the songs she sang went, and most everyone was sleeping.

She wasn't stupid. She had a knife. She slid her fingers surreptitiously toward the pocket of her loose tunic. She could have it out and in her hand in an instant.

Swallowing hard, palms feeling a little damp, she moved toward the bed. She'd already thought about the different scenarios for waking Elliott, and had discarded the idea of actually touching him. Which was good, because he seemed to be wearing nothing but the sheets that were twisted around his hips. The thought of touching his warm, smooth skin made her belly tighten . . . and not in an altogether unpleasant way.

Instead she bent toward him to whisper his name, but she'd hardly drawn in a breath when he moved suddenly. She squeaked in surprise and shock as his hand lashed out and strong fingers closed around her wrist, giving her a little tug so that she bumped her thigh against the mattress.

"What are you doing here?" he asked in that smooth voice. Too smooth for him to have been sleeping.

"You're awake," she said needlessly, trying to settle her racing heart.

The bed was right there, flush up against her thigh, and she could see the darkness of his skin contrasted against the white sheets . . . shoulders, torso, and the muscular arm attached to the hand that held her wrist, the black hair brushing his forehead and temples.

"Of course I am. I don't sleep." He kept hold of her and she saw the faint shine of his eyes in the dim light. "Are you here to join me? I definitely wouldn't want to sleep through that." His voice became even smoother, promising, and he gave a gentle little tug on her wrist, as if to coax her down next to him.

"No." The word came out flat and sharp, and more panicked than it should have, considering the fact that she was the one who'd sneaked into his bedroom. Reminding herself of that should have steadied her, feeling her fingers settle over the knife handle should have given her comfort, but her heart was racing and her mouth had dried, and a little of that old fear began to crawl up her spine.

She tried to tug out of his grip and Elliott must have sensed her apprehension, for he freed her immediately. Jade stepped back from the bed, releasing the knife in her pocket. Her jinky nerves calmed as she mentally chided herself for going a little panicky. Well, more than a little. Truth was, if he hadn't released her, she might have gotten a bit nuclear. Used the wicked blade on his smooth, tanned skin.

But what else was he to think, for crying out loud, when she shows up in his room in the dead of night? And besides, if he'd wanted to . . . do anything to her, he'd had ample opportunity last night. And he hadn't touched her but to heal her. Miraculously healed her.

"Then let me guess. You're here to take something. Or to try and kill me. Although I suppose if you wanted to do that, you'd have done it before you ran off this morning."

As he spoke, he sat up and swung his bare feet off the

bed, settling them on the floor. It was probably a good thing that he kept the sheets in his lap, for she swore she saw a flash of bare hip as he did so.

She would not think about the fact that he was most likely naked under those sheets. Definitely not. *Quit gawking and answer the question, Jade.*

"No," she said, and her voice was stronger now that she'd put distance between them. "Don't be ridiculous. I just didn't want anyone to see me—us—talking, so I sneaked in here."

"So you came in here to *talk*. In the middle of the night. When I'm in bed."

Put that way, it did sound kind of suggestive. Didn't that sort of thing happen in those old James Bond movies all the time? And then 007 and the woman ended up going at it? And sometimes she even tried to kill him.

Or vice versa.

Jade took another step back.

Elliott reached over and turned on the bedside table's lamp, which counted among the original furnishings in this hotel room. He and each of his companions were given their own rooms in what had once been a high-rise casino resort. The rooms were clean and furnished, if not dated, with running water and power.

Jade focused on answering his question instead of noticing the details of his newly illuminated torso. "I wanted to ask if you'd come to meet a friend of mine. He'd like to talk to you. And I didn't want anyone to see us together." His chest was sleek and angular, dusted with a light patch of hair between two firm, square pectorals. A muscular arm held the bunch of sheets in his lap. She felt warm all of a sudden.

"Why? Is your cowboy boyfriend the jealous type?"

Cowboy boyfriend? Jade frowned. "It's complicated. I want Lou to explain it to you."

She could practically see him come to attention. "Lou? Waxnicki?"

"How did you know that?" A burst of worry flashed over her. She and Lou were careful not to appear close in public; in fact, she tried to avoid being seen with him as much as possible. But had someone begun to notice? Rob Nurmikko?

"A lucky guess. As it happens, I'd be happy to meet your friend Lou." Grabbing the sheets, he warned, "I'm going to stand up to get dressed."

She spun on her feet and heard his low chuckle as she did so. But she wasn't about to completely turn her back on him, and angled herself so she could see a bit of him in the mirror. Purely just to make sure he didn't sneak up behind her. The flash of a pale flank confirmed her suspicion that he slept in the nude, and Jade felt a combination of wariness and warmth sweep over her. Then she heard the soft swish of his clothing being pulled on and relaxed a bit more.

"So you left this morning just to head back here to Envy. What was the big hurry?" he asked, and she heard a soft zipping sound. Jeans.

"I had something to do. I didn't want to be late."

"Were you not supposed to be gone? Was it a secret that you had left?"

Judging him dressed by now, she turned. He was fully clothed and she felt even more at ease. "I just didn't want to be late."

"For your gig."

She hid her surprise that he knew about that. But come

to think of it·. . . Trixie had been blathering about the new
arrivals when Jade went back behind the bar to get a drink.
"Right," she said.

"So how are you feeling?" he asked, tucking the shirt into
his jeans. "After riding—I assume you rode—all day? That
was quite a fall you took. Are you in any pain?"

"No. I'm feeling perfectly fine. Surprisingly fine, in fact."

"Good," he said, stepping closer to her, a smile pulling at
his mouth. "That means I can give you a clean bill of health
. . . and I'm no longer your doctor."

"What does that have to do with anything?" she asked,
her voice suddenly unsteady.

"Because doctors don't do this to their patients." He
reached for her, easily but purposely, as if aware that she
was skittish—but nevertheless determined to touch her.

Jade should have panicked . . . but though her heart
skipped and her lungs filled, she didn't move. She couldn't.

She didn't want to.

Holding her gaze with his own, the gentle smile lifting
one side of his lips, Elliott drew her closer. The next thing
she knew, his mouth descended, his arms enveloped her and
crossed loosely over her back, fingers brushing the ends of
her hair.

She closed her eyes and took his kiss, lifting to him for a
long, sleek swirl of lips and tongue. His mouth moved over
hers, his tongue swiping deep and hot as though he needed
to taste every bit of her. His body was strong and solid, warm
and comforting as he gathered her closer. Desire shivered
deep in her belly, flushing and curling down into her core.

When had she ever felt like this before?

His hands cupped the back of her skull, holding her there,
kissing her as though he had all the time in the world. Long,
slow, thorough . . . gentle, and yet edged with need. Some-

how, her hands found their way, curling onto the tops of his shoulders, solid and square beneath the cotton shirt and she tasted him, feeling a long-submerged pleasure rush through her. She forgot to breathe, caught in the flush of awareness of this man, this mysterious stranger who made her feel weak and warm.

"Jade," he said against her mouth, urgent, breaking the kiss as he gasped for breath. His chest moved against hers as if he'd run miles, his arms banded more tightly around her, and for a moment she forgot where she was, who she was with . . . and panicked.

She must have stiffened, must have done something to signal the sudden bolt of ice down her spine, for he pulled back and released her so suddenly that she staggered back a step.

"That," he said, his voice not quite as smooth as before, "is not supposed to happen between a doctor and his patient." His eyes glittered dark, fastening on her for a moment before he turned away. "Which is why I'm very glad you're not my patient anymore."

Fingers shaky, knees weak, Jade watched silently as he retrieved his boots and sat on the edge of the bed to draw them on. Her heart still raced crazily and her lips felt full and puffy, but it wasn't a bad thing. She wouldn't let it be. He'd thrown her off her game for a moment by kissing her, but she was back to business. "Lou's waiting for us."

"My friends will want to be there," Elliott said, the laces whipping through his fingers as he tied the boots.

"Of course. I was going to get them too," she said, her attention drawn from his slender, capable fingers by the question. "The only reason I came to you first was because your room was the easiest to get to."

"Is that so?" His eyes gleamed sharp and black, boring

into her for a moment as he yanked the second lace into a knot.

Jade swallowed, her heart pounding, and she was reminded suddenly how powerful this man was. How he'd beaten back *gangas* and pummeled them so thoroughly last night, then returned with hardly a mark on him. Yet, beneath the dark glitter there, she read anguish in his eyes, anguish and emptiness. And grief. Deep-seeded, heavy grief.

What had happened to him?

"Let's go," she said, turning away from that inscrutable gaze. "I don't want Lou to worry."

"Worry? Sending you unescorted into a man's room in the middle of the night? He *should* worry," Elliott muttered. But he started for the door, leaving her to follow in his wake.

"He didn't send me," she retorted, pushing past him so that she led the way down the hall. "I decided to come myself."

"And it was only convenience that had you breaking into my room first?"

"I didn't break in," she began, but he frowned so darkly she clamped her lips shut and strode on ahead of him.

He let her get all the way to the end of the hall before calling quietly after her. "Jade. My friends are down this way."

She spun and stalked back to the corridor that branched off. Just great. One kiss from this guy and she was all discombobulated.

For the first time, she hoped she was wrong about him and that he would soon be on his way. Somewhere else. Far away.

CHAPTER 8

Lou Waxnicki's face showed every bit of his eighty-odd years, though his gray eyes were still bright and sharp. The original color of his hair, which was worn in a ponytail that stretched longer than Simon's, was indistinguishable, for now it was silver. Not white, not the dirty pale yellow of aged locks, but pure silver—and the same wiry hair grew in the form of a neatly trimmed goatee. That, combined with the faded *WarGames* T-shirt and a pair of trendy wire-rimmed glasses that sat on the bridge of his nose—at least, they'd been trendy fifty years ago—made him look like a nerdy hippie with a hint of Asian heritage around the eyes and cheekbones.

He certainly didn't look like a guy who was a little "off" as Sam Pinglett had indicated last night. In fact, as he found the man's eyes searching his gaze, Elliott had a feeling this guy's brain never rested.

He caught himself just before he reached for Mr. Waxnicki's hand. Instead, Elliott merely nodded and said, "I'd shake your hand, but I think I've got something contagious. I don't want to give it to you." A little something he'd just recently picked up, so to speak, since leaving his room with Jade and stopping off to collect Simon.

The elderly man looked at him keenly, withdrawing his hand. "You're a doctor. A healer."

Elliott nodded. "Yes, I am. I have to take care not to pass on illnesses that I might have been exposed to."

What a load of crap, Waxnicki's eyes said, but they also glinted with curiosity. He turned away. "I trust the rest of you don't have the same problem?"

Glancing curiously at Elliott, Wyatt nevertheless extended his hand. As their palms touched, Elliott saw Waxnicki's eyes widen just a bit. The older man gave Wyatt a knowing look, a little nod, and a bit of a smile tipped his lips. "Sit down, please," the older man said after he'd shaken the hands of the others.

Elliott chose a seat where he could eye Jade without appearing obvious, then he instantly regretted the blatant move. Especially when Fence gave him a knowing grin. *Christ.* Was he in fucking high school again? No . . . that was more like a middle school move.

He and his hormones still hadn't fully recovered from that long, lush kiss in his room. Nope, even a quick glance at Jade had him thinking about the taste of her, the feel of her fingers closing over his shoulders, even the innocuous lemon scent that wafted from her hair. Her wide, sensual mouth had the sexiest little curl at the edges when she smiled, and he well knew exactly how soft it was.

Probably had been a stupid thing to do, but even though he'd seen her apprehension, he figured he'd better take the opportunity to touch her when he was certain he wouldn't be passing on some illness or injury. Extenuating circumstances and all.

And the feel of her soft mouth, which turned up at the corner when she smiled—as she did now, at Lou Waxnicki—had been worth the chance.

Problem was, he wanted more. A lot more. And he still didn't know what was up with the Marlboro Man. Nor was he going to be able to touch Jade—or anyone—again for a while.

A painful twinge in his chest and over the top of his shoulder confirmed that train of thought, and Elliott resisted the urge to touch it. He'd expected this to happen after healing Simon's *ganga* scratches this morning.

When he and Jade had gone to waken the others, Elliott decided it was time for an experiment he'd been considering during the night, when he was trying, in vain, to sleep. Which was why he'd sprung fully awake the moment he heard the door from the adjoining room scuff quietly open.

So, a short time ago, he'd checked Simon's gashes, which had begun to heal very well, thanks to some natural salve Elliott had given him to spread over them.

Until today, Elliott had been afraid to touch Simon himself, until he learned more of how his weird ability worked. But this morning, the scratches were no longer puffy or oozing blood, and had started to form the shiny covering as a precursor to scabs. "I'm going to heal you," he told Simon after Jade had left the room to knock on Wyatt's door. "At least, I'm going to try."

He placed his hands over the thick gashes that curved from the top of Simon's right shoulder down over the top of his chest and closed his eyes, concentrating on the spark of energy . . . that same spark he'd felt when he healed Jade's broken ulna . . . and let it flow through him.

The scratches had healed under his very hands, under Simon's very eyes, as a low throb of pain settled over Elliott's own chest and upper arm. And when he pulled his fingers away, Simon's tanned skin was as pristine and smooth as— albeit darker than—a baby's. Even a few blemishes from earlier injuries had been healed.

"What the fuck. . . ." Simon had breathed. It had been more of an exclamation than a question, and Elliott hadn't bothered to answer.

But he'd taken care not to touch anyone since then, and he noticed that the dull pain he'd absorbed when he'd healed Simon had begun to twinge more sharply as time went on. Gathering at the top of his shoulder, the discomfort radiated down over his chest and centered right where Simon's gouges had been the deepest.

Pulling his attention from the nagging pain, Elliott glanced up as the others took their seats. Jade was looking at him with curiosity . . . and something else that he hoped was interest.

Elliott smiled back, trying to keep his cool when his pulse was suddenly trammeling through him at warp speed. Yeah. It had been fifty years since he'd had sex, and his body was definitely reminding him of that lapse. Right now. Because of a single kiss. Well, a kiss, and that particular slanted look.

Hoo-boy. He was completely screwed.

Or, at least, he'd like to be. Long and slow and easy. His mouth dried and he felt his smile falter.

"We've been looking for Envy for months," Wyatt was saying, and Elliott realized that everyone had settled in a group of chairs. They were in a small room near the restaurant where they'd eaten last night. It might have been one of the administrative offices or even a small gift shop when the hotel was in operation. Now, with its array of sofas and low coffee tables, it appeared to be a sort of communal gathering place. But since it was closing in on four in the morning, no one seemed to be around.

And Lou had closed the door, affording them a little bit of privacy.

Why had Jade been so insistent that they speak to Lou—

and in secret? It must have something to do with her being a Runner—whatever that was.

"And now that you've found Envy," Mr. Waxnicki said in reply to Wyatt, but he looked at all of them in turn, "do you find your curiosity assuaged, then?"

Considering the fact that their curiosity—hell, it was fucking desperation—burned like a never-ending flame, it was a ridiculous question. But then, of course, Lou Waxnicki could have no idea what had happened to them.

Nor could he be expected to believe it.

"Our curiosity might be assuaged if we could get some details about what happened fifty years ago. From someone who was actually there," Elliott said, plunging right into the reason *he*'d wanted to speak to Waxnicki. He wanted some answers before he learned what the old man had on his mind.

"The Change, we call it. Or, simply, 'After.'"

"You were there when it happened. Was it everywhere?"

"Everywhere." Mr. Waxnicki's voice dropped, roughened. The sharpness in his eyes lessened as though he focused on something far away. Fifty years away. "So few of us remained."

"How few?" asked Elliott.

Mr. Waxnicki's gaze focused again. "Hundreds, perhaps." *Hundreds?*

"You mean here in Las Vegas—Envy."

"Yes, in Las Vegas." Mr. Waxnicki shot Elliott that keen, considering look he'd given Wyatt earlier, then continued. "The survivors came here after, drawn by the lights. The only lights in a dark, changed world."

"But what happened? Nuclear war? Global warming? Crazy weather?" Elliott pressed, even as the thoughts echoed in his mind.

Hundreds of survivors . . . instead of thousands? Millions? Mr. Waxnicki had to mean here in Vegas. Not . . . not the whole world. How could they know anyway, as isolated as they must be?

Then he remembered the ocean—apparently the Pacific Ocean—now sitting where Harrah's used to be, and he felt like vomiting all over again. He hadn't felt this sick since his first sight of a cadaver in med school.

He'd gotten over that. Would he ever get over *this*? Could he?

Would he ever sleep again? Feel normal? Have a life?

The very possibility seemed inconceivable.

Surely if there had been more survivors, if this had been just an isolated geographic area, there would have been some rescuers or explorers to find them in the last fifty years.

"The annihilation of humanity happened in a variety of ways," Waxnicki replied. "It started with simultaneous massive, 9-point earthquakes throughout the world and from what we can tell, and what we experienced here, that in turn caused tsunamis and nearly a week of other natural disasters and devastation. Raging fires, mighty storms, aftershocks. We didn't have a chance."

"So everyone's really gone." Wyatt's voice was quiet, dead with pain.

Mr. Waxnicki nodded slowly but firmly. "Fifty years ago, there were few survivors. And of the few that survived the physical devastation, the majority of them literally collapsed, dead, in the days following. We don't know how or why some people simply died, and others, like me, didn't. There was no explanation for it. They just dropped dead."

Silence reigned for a long moment as Elliott and his friends tried to assimilate this information.

Impossible to believe. Simply impossible that most of the human race had been destroyed.

After a moment, Mr. Waxnicki spoke again. "Where are you from?" His expression had altered and now he was looking at Elliott more intently. "And you're a doctor?"

Dare he tell him the truth?

Something about the elderly man with the sharp eyes, who didn't seem the least bit senile or "off," tempted Elliott to trust him. "Chicago," he replied, holding the man's gaze . . . and his breath.

There was silence as they waited for Mr. Waxnicki's response.

"Chicago." His eyes gleamed with fascination, and Elliott fairly felt the electric energy snapping in the air. "I wonder how that can be."

But before they could respond, the old man stood with a surprising agility. "Will you all come with me? I believe we have things to discuss that might best be done privately."

Elliott glanced at Jade, whose eyes held the same note of enthusiasm as Mr. Waxnicki's. That was all he needed to agree.

He hoped he didn't come to regret the decision later.

Mr. Waxnicki led them through what had been the lobby of New York–New York and down a hallway that once might have led to the catering and housekeeping staff areas. Elliott noticed that this building, which seemed to be a central point of the settlement of Envy, was in almost normal condition as compared to the other structures they'd seen in their other travels.

Mother Nature might be a ball-buster, but man could hold her back if he put his mind to it. Obviously, that was the occasion here. He saw a few cracks that had been patched, signs of normal wear and tear in the carpet, and scuffs and dents in the walls.

He could imagine how they'd done it—scavenged to find unbroken lightbulbs and perhaps window glass from other areas of the hotel.

They followed their guide, along with Jade, deep into the building, and as they proceeded, saw that the area showed more and more disrepair. In fact, the further they went, the darker it was. Perhaps only one out of every five lightbulbs worked, showing sagging doors, animal nests, rubble, and dust. They passed no one during their walk down the hallway, but Elliott could hear the faint sounds of life in the distance. And as he walked, Elliott felt the twinge of pain radiating over the top of his shoulder with the movement of his arm.

He slipped his hand beneath the collar of his shirt and touched the area . . . and felt the ridges of *ganga* gouges. What the . . . ? Not only had he healed Simon, but he'd taken on the cuts as well?

That was different. When he'd healed Jade, he'd simply felt the pain in his arm.

And moments later, had given the actual fracture to Linda.

Elliott frowned. He'd touched Simon and healed the deep cuts—fortunately, they'd already started to scab over and begun to heal on their own—and now he not only had the pain, but he'd also accepted the actual injuries.

Elliott kept walking and, as inconspicuously as possible, simply felt around beneath his shirt. The gashes hurt like a bitch, pounding and throbbing through his body, but he knew the injury wasn't serious. With care, it would simply heal, just as it would have on Simon if Elliott hadn't interfered.

In the meantime, Elliott would have a bit of discomfort. And he just had to make sure he didn't touch anyone.

But what happened if he bumped into someone as he walked by? Or did it have to be flesh to flesh, hand to skin?

At last, Mr. Waxnicki paused at an elevator and, using a crowbar, took a moment to open it. The clunking and clinking sounds indicated that there was some sort of combination or lock to release, but when the doors rolled open, a bold light glowed up into the semi-darkness. The elderly man stepped back and gestured them to enter, directing, "Down the stairs, if you will."

Elliott followed Jade down a circular stairwell built into the elevator shaft. Definitely *not* looking at the way her hips swayed with each descending movement.

His first impression of the room below was that it was a combination of Dr. No's underground lair and the villain's hideaway in *The Incredibles*.

Yeah, he'd seen *The Incredibles*. It had been one of his nieces' favorites, and Uncle E was a sucker for his girls. His lips flattened as he had a flash of memory . . . then pushed it away.

The subterranean room was vast and brightly lit. Computers and their monitors were arranged throughout on a variety of furnishings—cabinets, desks, tables—and even a few printers hummed. Wires led up into the ceiling and walls, and lined the floor.

Other than the electronics, the room was empty except for a woman who sat at one of the counters that held five different screens. Her back was to them, as she worked industriously, her fingers flying over a keyboard as she stared intently at the center screen. She had long golden red hair with thick waves and delicate, narrow shoulders.

She turned from her work, half rising as if to move to a

different chair, and froze. Her gaze cast around the room as though startled to see the five men, Jade, and Mr. Waxnicki standing there, which was a bit surprising as they hadn't exactly been silent. Not loud, but not silent by any stretch. She must have been very intent on her work.

"Lou," she said, getting all the way to her feet, removing small earbuds. Ah, that explained it. Had she been listening to music? Or blocking out the constant whirr of the multiple computers?

She couldn't be more than thirty, and Elliott knew most men would consider her beautiful, with fair skin dusted by golden freckles and all that great hair. But he was more interested in the cinnamon-haired, green-eyed witch with the curly-edged smile and the smoking body that had, just an hour or so ago, been plastered up against his.

Elliott pulled himself back to the moment and noticed that the strawberry-blonde didn't look pleased at all.

Her voice carried a sharp warning. "What are you doing here?" Elliott recognized that the "you" actually meant the five of them, not Mr. Waxnicki or Jade.

"It's all right," Mr. Waxnicki said, "Jade and I believe they can be trusted. Everyone, this is Sage Corrigan." And he completed the brief introductions.

Elliott nearly laughed at the choked look on her face, complete with prune-like lips—pink and full, but definitely pissed *off*—as she glared at the elderly man. He could almost read her mind: *You* believe *they can be trusted?*

"They helped me and Geoff Pinglett last night," Jade said quietly. "You know Lou wouldn't take a chance unless he was certain."

"Why did you bring them down here?" she asked, persisting as if they didn't exist.

"Let's all have a seat, shall we?" said Mr. Waxnicki. "And

I believe things might become clear. Any news from Theo yet?" he asked as he opened another door. Beyond, Elliott saw a space furnished like a small flat.

Sage's face lost the pissed look and took on a hint of worry. "No."

"Theo is my brother," the old man explained. "He's a Runner."

"Lou," Sage said, her voice and lips tight.

Mr. Waxnicki waved off her warning and them into the room. "Sit, everyone. And let's have some tea, shall we?"

"I don't suppose you have anything stronger than tea," said Wyatt. Elliott could see the lines growing deeper in his face.

"It's six o'clock in the morning," Sage responded in affronted tones.

Mr. Waxnicki gave her a look meant to flatten out those pursed lips, and she seemed to take the hint and settled in a chair in the corner.

"Are you going to tell us why you've brought us here?" Wyatt asked, with a half-glance at Sage, who'd settled, glowering, in a corner. "Before someone blows a gasket?"

Mr. Waxnicki gave a little laugh that made his eyes grow narrower. "I haven't heard that phrase in a long time. 'Blow a gasket.'"

"How old are you, Mr. Waxnicki, if you don't mind my asking?" Elliott asked suddenly. He'd noticed that the old man didn't speak like an old man . . . at least, the old men he'd known. He talked . . . well, like they did. Which would make sense if, as he suspected, they had all been raised in the '80s.

"I was born in nineteen eighty-three," he said. "I'm seventy-seven years old. Perhaps you'd like to assuage my curiosity and tell me the same for you."

Tension crackled in the room for a moment, and Sage seemed to be the only one who wasn't sitting on the edge of her seat.

Elliott replied, "I was born in nineteen seventy-seven."

He could almost hear the sigh of satisfaction from Mr. Waxnicki. The man's dark eyes brightened with interest, and he looked at Jade, whose green ones widened in surprise. But to his surprise, she didn't ask how or why. He saw that the pinched, worried look had eased from Sage's face, replaced by an intelligent, thoughtful one. *Huh. Not so much of a surprise.*

Why was that?

"I suspected as much—not the particular year, but that you were . . . different," said the older man. "What happened to you?"

"We were in a cave in Sedona," Elliott said. "Quent, Wyatt, and I. Fence and his buddy Lenny were our guides. Suddenly, it felt like an earthquake, and everything began to shake and fall, and then we felt a sizzle of energy. A burning sensation, not really painful . . . and there were some flashes of light. The next thing we knew, we woke up. And everything was different. We found out fifty years had passed."

"We discovered Simon nearby—" Wyatt began.

"Did you have to waken him?" Lou asked, leaning forward eagerly. "And do you know what awakened you?"

"I put my hand on his shoulder to see if he was alive . . . after all, our last memories had been of this powerful earthquake," Elliott said. "He was breathing, he was warm. And I don't know what, if anything, woke us."

"We figured we'd just been caught in the earthquake, knocked out maybe by some gasses being released—since we weren't blocked in or hit by rocks or anything. But when we came out and saw how everything had changed. . . ." Wyatt's voice trailed off.

"Unbelievable," Mr. Waxnicki said. His eyes were shining with excitement, and he glanced at Jade. "It makes sense . . ."

"Makes sense?" Wyatt said. "How the fuck does being asleep for fifty years when everyone else around us died *make sense*?"

"You were in Sedona, an area known for its mystical properties—an area in which many sources of energy seem to collect. That must have put you into the . . . freeze . . . I guess I'd say."

"So what happened fifty years ago?" Elliott asked. "Why and how? I have a feeling there's more than what you told us upstairs."

"Yes," Mr. Waxnicki said. Despite the fact that Elliott had been born before him, he found it impossible to think of the elderly man by anything other than his title. Damn good manners, drilled into his head by his *abuela*.

"My twin brother Theo and I happened to be here in Vegas—that," he added, looking at Elliott, "was what made me realize that you're . . . different. No one would speak of this place as Las Vegas any longer. No one your age, anyway."

"Is that really the fucking Pacific Ocean out there?" Fence asked, leaning forward in his chair. His large hands and solid wrists rested on his knees, bared by the cut-off shorts he'd dragged on when Elliott woke him.

Mr. Waxnicki nodded. "Yes, it is. My brother and I were here at the time everything happened. Not for fun, but for work. Computer geeks," he said with a wry smile. "I haven't used that term in a long time either."

"For good reason," Sage put in. Her voice had turned

pleasant and lilting now that she wasn't pissed off anymore. She looked around the room. "The computers are a secret."

"We figured that," Wyatt said, not bothering to hide his sarcasm. "The secret lair in the unused corner of the hotel and all."

Sage's gaze frosted, but she didn't respond.

"Go on, Lou," Jade said. "Tell them how it all happened."

"Very simply, all hell broke loose," Mr. Waxnicki said. His voice became a bit thready, his eyes a bit unfocused, but he didn't pause. "The buildings shook and the earth erupted. This was no ordinary earthquake, nothing like anything we'd ever experienced. People died in the quake, but they also died from . . . I don't know for certain, there's no way to know now, but it seemed as if some gasses were released from the earth, or somewhere. Like I said earlier, people just died. Dropped like flies everywhere."

"But you didn't? You and your brother?"

"I didn't. A very few of us escaped injury and death. My brother . . . he. . . ." Mr. Waxnicki hesitated, glanced at Jade. "Well, things were different with him. I'll tell you more about that later."

"People died in the quake," Fence said. "But how could California and half of Nevada and who the hell knows what else just fucking drop into the ocean? I mean, there were always fears about the San Andreas Fault, but this is not just the San Andreas Fault," Fence said.

"Oh, no, no it's not," Mr. Waxnicki replied. The sharpness returned to his face, and the unfocused look eased from his eyes. "It wasn't Mother Nature who did this. And it didn't just happen here."

"But how can you know that if the place was destroyed?" Wyatt demanded. "There could be other parts of the country—there have to be. A quake wouldn't destroy all of the United States."

"My brother and I aren't just computer geeks," Mr. Waxnicki said. "We're fucking computer geniuses. We were poised to be the next Don Knuth or Linus Torvalds. In fact, we may as well be."

Elliott found it quite an anomaly to hear the elderly man use the F-word. Senior citizens in his day just didn't throw that word around. Of course they didn't generally have ponytails either and he supposed if the guy had lived through the apocalypse, he had the right to say fuck. And whatever the hell else he wanted to say.

"It was *many* months later," Lou Waxnicki stressed, and Elliott thought he might be able to think of him as Lou now that he'd shown off his dirty mouth. "Many months before we were able to do much of anything but look for food and water and see who'd survived. But once we realized this was what we had to live with and work in, Theo and I and the other few survivors began to organize ourselves.

"We'd been running electrical generators on gasoline stores that we found, and Theo and I were able to find a few computers and set them up. Eventually, maybe a year after all of this happened, we were able to hack into weather satellites, and some other ones. That," he said, looking at Wyatt, "is how we know that these catastrophic events happened worldwide. And," he added, turning his gaze at each of them in turn, "that, just a bit northeast of where Hawaii used to be, a small continent the size of Colorado had erupted in the Pacific Ocean."

A continent?

"But the most important thing we've come to believe is that the cause was man-made."

"Lou believes it wasn't an accident. It wasn't Mother Nature going haywire," Jade put in, her eyes sober. She was looking directly at Elliott.

"And it wasn't a materialization of the Mayan End of Times prophecy," Sage said in precise tones, sounding a bit like a lecturing professor. "They'd predicted great devastation or, at least, a great change in the world, and many people expected it to happen on December twenty-first, two thousand twelve. But this happened two and a half years earlier, in June of two-thousand ten."

"The bottom line is, the destruction of the earth—and humanity—was deliberate." Lou's words settled flat and heavy in the room.

Elliott was the first one to find his voice. "But . . . how? By whom?" *Maybe Sam Pinglett wasn't too far off when he said Lou Waxnicki was crazy.* "Nuclear war? Aliens?" He couldn't believe he said it with a straight face. But this world was so bizarre, he didn't think twice. Anything could happen.

"We call them Strangers." Lou shrugged, a brief glint of humor in his gray-blue eyes. "For lack of a better name . . . because that's what they are. Strangers. To us." The light moment passed as quickly as it had come, and a shadow crossed his face. "For a variety of reasons, Theo and I have come to the conclusion that the Strangers caused the Change. We believe they wanted to take over the earth, and somehow caused all the destruction as a way to destroy the human race—or most of it."

Elliott stared at him and felt the same disbelief from the others. He felt the urge to pinch the shit out of himself in hopes of waking up from this dream, and once again considered sympathizing with Sam Pinglett's impression of Lou.

But . . . no. This man was too intelligent. Too sane, too focused and clear-eyed to be a paranoid conspiracy theorist.

Wasn't he?

"So, the Strangers aren't *gangas*. So they're . . . what? Aliens? Something else?" Wyatt asked.

"They look like us, but they're different. No one's sure if they're human or not," Lou explained. "But Jade knows as much or more about the Strangers than any of us. She lived among them for three years."

"In captivity," Sage added flatly. "She was kept a prisoner."

Elliott's gaze shifted to Jade and he felt an uncomfortable twist in his belly that had nothing to do with the *ganga* gouges on his shoulder.

Three years. What had they done to her?

Jade met his gaze with clear green eyes, as if she had nothing to be ashamed or afraid of. She spoke in her low, husky voice, "The Strangers are immortal—or, at least, they can't be killed. You can tell a Stranger for sure when you see them without a shirt on."

Their eyes met and Elliott swore he saw a light rose tinge her cheeks and she looked away. His lips twitched in a little smile. No wonder she'd asked him to take his shirt off right away.

"That's why I believed we could trust you. I saw Elliott after the battle with the *gangas*, after they'd torn your shirt off." Jade looked at him sidewise. "The Strangers breed and control the *gangas*, so they'd never want or need to fight them."

"The *gangas* are their mercenary army. Strong, easily controlled, and dispensable. If not dumb as rocks," Lou put in. "Like the Orcs, from *The Lord of the Rings*."

"They're too dumb to be more than an inconvenience," Fence said.

"Unless you're really outnumbered," Wyatt added. "Then it might get hairy."

Sage lifted an eyebrow, turning a frigid stare at them. "People are killed by *gangas* all the time. Don't underestimate them."

But Elliott's thoughts had stayed on a different train of thought. "And how can you identify the shirtless Strangers? A marking on the skin? A missing navel? A third nipple?"

Christ. This sounded like . . . well, something out of a science fiction novel or a *Star Trek* episode. But he was fucking *living* a science fiction novel now . . . one that was getting more frightening by the moment.

"They have a stone embedded in their skin, right here," Jade said, pulling the neckline of her shirt away to expose her delicate clavicle. Elliott was fairly sure he was the only guy in the room whose mouth went suddenly dry as he looked at the smooth, sexy hollow.

"There's a little gem or crystal right here, in the soft part of the skin just below the collarbone," Jade was saying, oblivious to Elliott's inappropriate fascination. "Some of them have one on each side, some have just one. It's what gives them their immortality and their power."

She brushed the neckline of her shirt back into place and settled back in her chair.

Elliott drew in a steadying breath, thinking of all the information they'd obtained in the last day . . . hell, in the last thirty minutes. He found it impossible to assimilate it all: beachfront property where the Strip had been, lions and elephants roaming wild, *gangas* . . . and humanlike aliens with crystals in their skin. Aliens who were trying to control the human population, according to Lou and Theo.

Maybe Lou and his brother *were* crazy. Maybe it was that simple.

But Elliott hadn't imagined the *gangas*. Nor had he imagined his double-edged sword of a superpower.

If *gangas* and superpowers were real, it was just as likely that these crystal-ridden aliens were too.

"So are you and Theo the only ones who think the Strangers are out to get us? From everything I've seen, the human race doesn't look suppressed. It just looks as if it's trying to recover from massive annihilation." Wyatt was speaking to Lou.

The elderly man looked grim. "The truth is, most people don't think much about the Strangers, and if they do, they think of them as our friends and allies. Cohabitants of our world."

"And they're not?"

"No." His answer was definitive and hard. "Most of them don't see it, or haven't experienced their evil. They're afraid of the *gangas*, of course, but the Strangers look and act just like us. So they figure if they don't bother the Strangers, the Strangers won't bother them."

"Wrong," said Jade flatly. "Completely wrong."

"But what do they *do* that's such a threat?" Wyatt demanded. "We've been traveling around for six months and we've never run into any of them."

"That you know of," Sage added archly. "Anyone you met might have been sporting a crystal beneath their clothing."

Jade spoke quietly. "They kidnap women and enslave them, for one."

Elliott's heart lurched. *Was that what had happened to her?*

"They do experiments on humans. People disappear sometimes, taken by the Strangers. There are mass executions—

that way no one is alive to tell the tale," Jade continued. The room had fallen silent. "I witnessed one take place in a small settlement of fifty people. They locked them in a large, open building and set the *gangas* in on them. Even the children."

"But everything they do is in secret," Lou continued. "It can't be attached to the Strangers, because then they would be in danger of us fighting back. And that's what we do here, in this little room." He said, gestured at the array of electronics. "This is the headquarters of the very secret, small but growing Resistance. Against the Strangers.

"Case in point—last night, Jade overheard a conversation between a tradesman here in Envy, and a Stranger." He looked at her.

Jade's eyes fastened on Elliott once again. "That's really the reason you're here. We hope you'll help us—to join the Resistance and help us try and learn about the Strangers, and to help stop them from enslaving and killing humans."

"Why us?" asked Simon, breaking his silence.

"Because you're . . . different."

That was an understatement.

A quiet *ding* sounded, and Sage whirled her chair to face the closest computer screen. "It's an email from Theo."

"About damn time," muttered Lou.

"It's coming in under a new ID," Sage said. "That's weird."

"Maybe he's afraid someone found his old one," Jade suggested. "Is everything all right?"

The sound of computer keys clicking filled the room as Lou and Jade rose to stand behind Sage. They looked at the screen over her shoulder, and the three of them must have read the email or seen whatever it was—*they couldn't have email, could they?*—at the same time, for Elliott saw Lou's shoulders draw back and tighten and Jade's slump almost simultaneously, before turning from the computer screen.

They faced each other, and she squared her shoulders as if preparing for a fight. "I'll go get the stuff for Theo. Greenside's only a few hours from here and I'll be back by nighttime. Besides, it'll give me the chance to talk with Luke and see if he has any other news."

"Jade, you just got back. The stuff in Greenside can wait until Theo gets there."

"But what if something's wrong with Theo? We haven't heard from him in days, and now we're hearing from him under a different account. It just feels like something's wrong. Maybe he's actually in Greenside himself—maybe that's the important 'data' that he's sending us to get. Maybe he's injured. Maybe that's why he's communicating under a new ID."

"Maybe, maybe, maybe," Lou said. "He's so damn brief sometimes. I wish he'd be more specific about why he didn't make your meeting."

"You know how he is. Short and to the point. He wouldn't be sending messages if something was wrong. Anyway, you need to be here in case he checks in again." Jade's words sounded easy, but even Elliott, without knowing the situation, recognized a little bit of bullshit when he heard it.

"I'll go with you," Elliott said, leaning forward. As he moved, his shoulder screamed with pain and he nearly gasped at the shock. *What the hell?* It seemed to be getting worse.

The elderly man looked at him, and Elliott saw real fear in his eyes. "All right. You two go. Get the stuff from Luke that Theo thinks is so important, and get back here as soon as you can. I'm not liking this whole thing with Rob Nurmikko either, Jade. Something's going on. You can fill Elliott in on what we know, and let's hope the stuff Luke has is worth the trip."

Elliott looked at Jade. "When do we leave?"

"As soon as you're ready."

That was when Elliott realized that he'd just signed up for a possibly dangerous mission with a gorgeous woman . . . that he couldn't lay a finger on.

Just fucking great.

Three weeks After

Found Theo!

He was just where he should have been, in the subterranean backup room. Took two days to dig through by hand. He's not dead, but was in sort of a coma. Woke him up with difficulty, but now that he's awake, he seems fine.

Don't want to do this without him.

Our number has grown to nearly a hundred here in what used to be New York–New York. And there are another hundred in the Mandalay hotel. More people arriving every day, but in trickles.

Have taken charge of getting the power working again. Still using generators, and some power still coming in from the station. Rowe and I discussed sending a group to Hoover Dam to see if that's where it's coming from. I suspect it is if the dam wasn't destroyed. Remember from a TV show that it could run for a year without human intervention.

Maybe there are other survivors there too.

So we have some lights. Plugged in computer. No Internet. No cell phone.

The world beyond us is silent. But Theo's here.

—from the journal of Lou Waxnicki

CHAPTER 9

Elliott had learned how to compartmentalize his mind during the long, brain-sucking hours of his medical residency and four years working as an emergency physician, plus his volunteer time rebuilding the hospital in Haiti. He could block out emotions or thoughts while focusing on his current situation, saving them for later when he had the luxury to indulge.

He could put away the tragedy of a young boy who died from gunshot wounds before Elliott could even start the surgery that would save him, and focus on the next patient—a young woman, who needed her appendix out pronto—without letting it slow him down, or distract him.

The tragedy would come back to haunt him later, when he lay dry-eyeball-up, staring at the ceiling and trying to sleep. But for the time being, he could stash it away.

Which explained why, even after hearing all that Lou Waxnicki had told them that morning—which was only the tip of the iceberg of what they wanted and needed to know—Elliott was able to block the horror, the reality of it all, from his mind. At least for now. He'd get the answers to the infinite questions he had . . . but later. When he'd had time to let it settle.

Because . . . damn it. *Damn it.*

Even though he'd been traveling around for the last six months, he hadn't fully accepted that this world was no more than what it seemed. These last few months had been an adventure, a journey. A nightmarish one. He was going to go home at the end of it, back to his normal life.

Only . . . he wasn't.

Ever.

He simply couldn't imagine living here. How? Where? What would he do?

Would he ever feel at home again?

So he compartmentalized. He fought it back, afraid of what would happen if it overwhelmed him. If it took over. There'd be time to think about it later when he stared at the ceiling, or the starry sky, or the rotting timbers of the roof of a half-demolished building.

For now, he needed to pack a few things to take with him on this mission with Jade. And for some reason, that steadied him. Knowing he would be with her, even though their task was uncertain and could be dangerous.

It wasn't because of the potential of them getting together.

But maybe it was. Maybe he needed to bury himself, his body, his *brain*, in something that promised to be good. Very good.

Elliott wrenched his thoughts away and yanked up his pack. A searing pain stopped him and he couldn't contain a grimace. This was definitely getting worse.

Clamping his teeth down on a string of nasty words, he paused in front of the mirror in his room and noticed that his shirt was stained with blood streaks. An odd feeling tipped him off-balance as he peeled the cotton T-shirt—damn, that was the second one ruined in as many days—away from the sticky, oozing blood . . . and stared in horror at the deep gashes over his shoulder and arm.

Five deep gashes, wide and oozing dark red blood.

Simon's chest had looked nothing like this when Elliott healed him only a few hours ago.

A sudden wave of uncertainty flooded him.

Would it heal? Or would it get worse and worse until he either died . . . or, *good God* . . . gave it to someone else?

What the hell was going on?

Jade splashed alongside Elliott, holding a torch that cast a generous circle of light in the creepy place. This was the part she hated, slogging through this slimy, dark passage. Waterweed and algae slicked the walls, and creatures that she preferred not to identify sleeked past in the knee-deep water. The ceiling rose in a low arc above their heads. Curtains of roots that had grown through the concrete and stone were festooned with spider webs, and seemed to constantly be brushing over her face and arms. Normally when she left Envy on a mission, she used the secret Wendy entrance. But there were times when the Tunnel was the only way to go, and they were in a hurry. And didn't want to be noticed.

She hoped Vaughn wouldn't come looking for her at Flo's house.

And, oh God, she hoped Theo was okay. Sure, he'd checked in, sent that message to Lou—but it told them nothing about why he hadn't been at his meeting place with Jade. And he was using a different ID. As if he were afraid someone was monitoring their communications.

All she could think of was him lying somewhere, injured, unable to move. What if he were outside and the *gangas* found him? Or worse, what if the Strangers or bounty hunters came upon him and discovered his equipment? All those electronics . . . they'd know something was going on. But that was silly. He'd tell them if something was wrong.

Theo'd been so vague—maybe that was why. He didn't want to take any chances of the information being picked up. The problem was, their communication abilities were hit or miss, which was why Sage or Lou were nearly almost always on the computers. They couldn't communicate remotely with Theo unless he was actually plugged into the network, which only happened occasionally and for brief spurts of time due to the dangers of the transmissions being intercepted, as well as the necessary energy to run the equipment.

Jade remembered suddenly that, in his previous communication, Theo indicated that he'd managed to find a physical access point into Chatter, which was what he and Lou called the communications system used by the Strangers and their bounty hunter allies. It would be just like him to be so engrossed in trying to hack into the system that he'd lost track of time and everything else. That made the most sense, now that she thought about it. And the tension that had begun to ride up into her shoulders eased. Theo was likely just being Theo.

But, that made it doubly important to find him quickly, for if he was able to hack into the Strangers' communication system, he might be able to find out more about the cargo that was to be delivered on Friday.

Today was already Monday. They only had four days.

Jade curled her fingers deeply into her palms and organized her whirlwind thoughts. One step at a time. Get through the Tunnel, get to Greenside to get the disks from Luke, and see if Theo had been there. Maybe by the time they got back to Envy tonight, there'd be another message from him with more updates.

Suddenly, Elliott spoke, breaking their silence and bringing Jade back to the damp, creepy Tunnel. "Why do we have to sneak out of Envy? Is there a law against leaving?" His voice sounded a little . . . strained.

"No, of course there's no law," she replied, casting a speculating glance at him. Something seemed to have changed since they left Lou's presence to pack up. He seemed to be moving differently, and he'd stopped giving her the sidelong looks that made her belly feel warm and squishy.

"It's just that we prefer to keep our comings and goings as unobtrusive as possible. It's safer that way."

He didn't ask the obvious follow-up question. In fact, he hadn't asked a lot of questions she thought he might after they left Lou. Instead, he moved along in silence, holding the dangling roots and cobwebs out of her way, and seemed to be focusing on . . . something.

And, to Jade's strangely acute disappointment, it wasn't her.

The fact that he was Lou and Theo's age was just beginning to sink in. He'd been alive fifty years ago when the Change happened. That made him probably eighty years old. *And he'd been in a cave, in some sort of stasis, all this time?*

Elliott was tall enough that the ceiling nearly brushed his head in some areas where the top had caved a bit or where a large tree trunk had sent out thick roots that broke through. He wore a dark shirt that appeared to be damp with water or stained on the front of his shoulder, and rugged jeans that hung just right over his hips. His shoulders were broad, his hair thick and dark, brushed back from his forehead and temples. He had a solid, square chin and dark blue eyes the color of the ocean on a hot day. And a mouth that kissed like an angel. Or a devil.

Jade wasn't certain which one she'd prefer, but she was leaning toward the devilish side. After all, her knees had still been trembling and her palms damp during their meeting with Lou. And every time Elliott looked at her, she felt a flush of warmth.

When was the last time she'd felt that way about a man?

How about . . . never?

Not even with Daniel. With him it had always been so harsh and overwhelming, even at the beginning, when she thought that was how love was supposed to be.

"What's that?" Elliott hissed suddenly, his voice deep and eerie in the round space. He stopped abruptly, catching her off guard. His powerful arm swung out, as if to hold her back and behind him.

Jade listened, but she didn't hear anything but the constant dripping. She was about to open her mouth when he raised his hand. He took the torch from her and, edging forward, brandished it in front of him like a weapon.

Then she heard it. A soft sloshing sound. An irregular movement in the water. Too large to be another rat or even a snake. She hoped. Oh God, she hated snakes. She resisted the urge to grab on to his arm in case one erupted from the water.

"Take this, and stay back," he said, handing her the torch again. "Hold it here."

She took it and watched as he crept forward, something silvery suddenly gleaming in his hand. A knife?

Then everything happened all at once. A loud splash, a shadow rearing high up. The glint of his weapon and the slap of flesh against . . . something. Crazed, turbulent splashing. Jade tried to hold the torch level, but with the slick footing and slimy wall, she found it difficult to keep her balance in the suddenly turbulent water.

Whatever it was had no intention of being easily subdued,

and she heard Elliott grunt and more violent splashing. She lunged forward, brandishing the torch and had the impression of gleaming golden green eyes and glistening body.

Oh, God, it *was* a snake. A huge, thigh-thick snake.

Elliott gave a loud cry as he lunged. The gleaming snake twisted around, pulling him off balance, and Jade yelled, brandishing the torch at the creature, reaching to pull Elliott up.

The basilisk's tail whipped out, snapping into Elliott's shoulder and arm. She heard him cry out and saw the knife flip into the air as he lost his grip. *No!*

Jade surged toward the weapon, but it plopped into the mud at the base of the wall. Desperately, she scrabbled around in the sludge, her fingers sliding through putrid, cold muck as Elliott wrestled with the massive snake. Still clinging to her torch, she caught glimpses of his hands, grasping the trunk-thick body of the snake, pale and small against its scales. He was fairly hugging the beast, rolling and roiling about in the water and slamming against the stone wall.

Then suddenly, the creature began to thrash harder, whipping about frantically, and Elliott gave a loud gruntlike shout, as if expending some great exertion. Just then, Jade's fingers closed around the hard metal knife. She yanked it up out of the water and whirled toward the writhing snake.

But before she could strike its dull green scales, the creature whipped and twisted and then flopped down. Jade glimpsed deep, bloody gashes on its pale belly before it sank below the water.

And then all was quiet but for Elliott's heavy breathing and the ever-present trickle of water. "That," he said, staggering to his feet, "was not my idea of a good time."

He leaned against the wall, illuminated by the torch she still held. Water and the bloody insides of the snake dripped from his hair and streaked his handsome face. His cheek was red from a scrape that must have happened against the wall, or even the ground, but the expression in his eyes was one of fierceness and triumph.

He bent to splash some of the water—which was only marginally cleaner than the junk all over him—over his face. And then he took off his shirt, wadding it up to wipe his face and . . . that chest. Look at his buff chest . . . those wide, square shoulders, the right amount of dark hair, the ridges of his belly. Jade swallowed.

Jade's own heart was racing, and it wasn't just from fear. Elliott had moved so fast, and with such strength. He'd battled a massive snake with nothing but a knife. A knife that he'd lost halfway through the battle.

She frowned and looked down at the blade. There wasn't a trace of blood on it, and although it had fallen into the water, it still wouldn't be completely clean. *Would it?*

"I mean," he said, his voice steadier and his breathing evening out, "if I'm going to be playing around in the water, I'd rather it be with something that doesn't have scales." He smiled a devilish smile that made Jade's heart do an extra little bump. "Or fangs."

"That was a wixy big-ass snake," she said, trying to keep her own breathing under control. He was very close to her, and the torch made everything soft and muted. *Deep breath.*

"A *wixy* big-ass snake?" he said, his eyes crinkling at the corners. They were dark and penetrating in the flickering light.

"Yeah. I don't like snakes, so when I say thank you, I really mean it."

He gave a light laugh as their eyes caught. Then he sobered and pulled away from the wall, standing upright. "You and Indiana Jones." Then he frowned, looking back at her. "Do you even know who that is?"

"Of course I know who Indiana Jones is. Who doesn't?"

In the flickering torchlight, she could see Elliott raise his brows as if in surprise, then lowered them. "I guess if people're watching Jason Bourne, they're also watching *Raiders of the Lost Ark*. Glad to know that at least some pop culture survived." Then he frowned, looking at the shirt wadded up in his hand. "This is the third shirt I've ruined in the three days since I've met you. Considering the fact that I've only got two more, I'm not sure that's a very good track record." He cast a quick look at her, a flash of humor in his eyes. Then, holding the ruined shirt, he started sloshing through the water.

Jade allowed him to lead—in case there were any more big-ass snakes—and lifted the torch high as she watched for a sign of rippling water. "You need to take better care of your shirts, then," she said archly, giving him the same side-long look. "I don't see how you can blame me for the *gangas* and a snake attack. What happened to the third shirt?"

"I got some blood on it," he said. "So where do Envyites get clothes?"

"Some are scavenged from stores—but those are few and far between nowadays. In the older times, there were a lot more of them. But we can still find some new ones, if they're well wrapped in plastic. Or in car trunks or anything metal that wouldn't have begun to rot away or break. Once a friend of mine found a car trunk with three intact suitcases in it—a treasure trove of shoes and clothes."

"Fascinating," he replied, slowing so they could walk side by side.

"And then there are people like my friend Flo, who takes

old clothing or pieces of fabric and redesigns them. Like my jacket," she said, lifting her arm to show him the sleeve that had been built by scraps of cloth. "And then there's the wool and cotton cloth that can be used. Leather too. Even some silk. It's not that different from the way your world was, only on a much smaller scale."

Elliott nodded, clearly fascinated by the discussion. His face didn't seem quite as tight as it had before the battle with the snake. Something had changed.

Just then they came to the elbow turn around which came a dim glow of light. When they finally reached the entrance, Elliott took her arm and helped her keep balanced as she climbed up and out on the crude steps.

At the top, they found themselves in a wide cement culvert that opened from the side of a small hill. Grass and trees covered the ground, with bits of concrete showing in patches where nature hadn't quite overtaken man's footprint. Buildings long abandoned and destroyed stood in uneven rows, with jagged brick half-walls covered by vines and moss, windows broken and bushes sprouting. Trees and bushes abounded. Birds sang, and the distant whinny of a horse reached her ears. A common scene to someone like Jade, who often ventured out from Envy's protective walls.

They emerged into the sunshine, which was welcome and warm after the dank of the tunnel. It took a moment for her eyes to adjust, and when they stopped watering, she noticed that Elliott was staring about him as if he'd never seen such a sight.

"It's funny," he murmured as if to himself, smoothing the toe of his boot over a small cement area.

Jade moved closer. "What is?"

He shook his head, looking down at her with a sort of bleakness in his eyes. That anguish again. "I always thought it would be like the Thunderdome. Empty, arid, cold . . . a wasteland. But it's not. It's . . . green and overgrown. Sort of wild. Not what I would have expected."

Before she could reply, his mood changed abruptly. "So now we have to find a horse," he said, looking around again, but with a sharper gaze trained toward the horizon.

"That'll be easy," she told him. "The mustangs run wild all over the hills out here."

"And catch one."

She shrugged. "I have a way with horses."

She was right.

Elliott watched as Jade, her hair gleaming cinnamon in the sunlight, her face flushed with exertion, whistled loud and long. Once, twice, and by the third time, he heard the soft thud of hooves as a small group of mustangs trotted up from behind an old Mobil station.

"I can't believe how tame they are," Elliott said after choosing from one of the five horses that nuzzled Jade as she produced a handful of sugar lumps.

"They have no reason not to be," she said, directing her mount next to a fallen tree. She stood on the trunk and vaulted onto the mustang's back, holding its thick golden mane in her left hand.

Smooth, fluid, and whoa-baby sexy.

The good news was, he could touch her now that he'd transferred Simon's injuries to the snake. At least, until he healed someone else.

But he really didn't need to be thinking about that until they finished this trip and got back to Envy, where he could actually think about utilizing a real bed. For more than just sleeping.

Elliott mounted up. Not quite as smoothly as Jade, but much more easily now that his chest and shoulder had healed. "So we're heading to a place called Greenside?"

"It's about three hours from here," Jade said. Elliott could have sworn she'd been checking out his ass when he threw his leg over the horse's back, but he wasn't certain. And, really, they had more important things to think about.

"So is that what a Runner does? Visits different places and picks up and delivers . . . what? Information? Mail? Goods?" Elliott asked as they started off. "You're a Runner, aren't you?"

Jade looked at him, shading her eyes against the bright sun. Not for the first time, he noticed the slender bracelets she wore on her wrist, studded with colorful beads. "Where did—oh. Lou. Yes, that's sort of what a Runner does. I guess we're like couriers, and we have our regular routes. Greenside is part of Theo's area, but I've been there twice myself." She pointed east and said, "That's where we're headed. Follow this road—what's left of it—and we'll get to Greenside in a few hours if we ride hard—which we will, as soon as we get past this rocky area."

"So, a Runner. You collect and deliver computer hardware? Hard drives, disks, and so on? At least, that's what was in your pack when we found you."

"And you would recognize that stuff, wouldn't you? Most people wouldn't anymore." She shifted, leaning forward to pat her horse. "We transport it from place to place, secretly, because we don't want the Strangers to know about the network we're building. See, there's no way for any of us to communicate with any other settlement—or even among those of us who live in Envy. That's part of the Resistance. Lou and Theo are working to build a network that can be used if . . . *when* . . . we get strong enough to make a show against the Strangers."

"Sort of like a new Internet?" Elliott asked, wondering if she knew what that was. But of course she must if she'd spent any time with Lou and Theo, self-proclaimed computer geeks. No, wait. They were fucking computer geniuses.

"Sort of. Mainly for communication, although we haven't used it much yet. Theo's been setting up wireless network access points that run on solar power. He hides them on rooftops or wherever he can, and he's slowly building a network."

"So he's also been looking for a way to hack into whatever communications system the Strangers use?"

She nodded. "He and Lou insisted there must be something like that, but it was only recently that they found evidence of what they call Chatter. His last message said he thought he'd found a good point where he could break into the system, so I'm thinking he's just really wrapped up in the job and doesn't want to leave yet. Which is why he asked me to go to Greenside to get the stuff from Luke."

"Well, I'm glad you're not going alone." He looked at her, and at that moment Elliott felt something he hadn't for a long time. Something . . . solid, something good, tugged deep in his belly.

"I always go alone, Elliott," she replied smartly. "I can take care of myself." Then, after a moment, she added, "But I'm glad you came with me this time. If for no other reason than the fact that you took care of that awful snake." The corners of her lips curled up in that intriguing way, and she sort of ducked her head, Princess Diana-style, when their eyes met—almost as if she were too shy to read his gaze. Or for him to see what was in her own. "Ready?"

Oh God, was he.

"Let's go," he said, wishing he could reach across and drag her onto his horse.

She turned away and, bending low over the mustang's neck, kicked it into a great gallop.

Greenside was green. That was about all Elliott could say about the place.

It was like the scattered random villages or settlements he'd come across during the last six months: a few homes that had been cobbled together in the sturdiest buildings in the area. A cluster of maybe three dozen, maybe four, people living there. They were friendly enough, and seemed content to live their lives simply.

It reminded him of that rerun TV show his cousins had made him watch, with Laura and Mary and Pa and Ma, but without the sunbonnets. And without the prairie.

A wild river rushed by, perhaps a quarter-mile wide, and hugged one edge of the town. Beyond the river's low banks, trees offered shade, and Elliott saw small patches of garden. A few rusted-over signs and a wide patch of buckled concrete filled in with a maze of grass and small bushes indicated that fifty years ago the town had been at the junction of two highways, in the middle of what had to have been pretty much desert. But now, like Envy, the land was lush and green and overgrown except where the settlers—that's how he thought of them—had kept Mother Nature at bay.

"Why do they live here, instead of in Envy?" he asked Jade as they approached the town. He noticed what appeared to be a well-tended field of corn to his left, near the height of his horse's withers. And a low-growing patch of strawberry bushes, bright red berries glinting through the green leaves.

Jade shrugged. She'd easily managed to remain on her spirited mustang all through the day, even when they'd had to jump over a jagged crevice left by the quakes.

"They stay for various reasons," she replied. "Some of them farm or hunt and sell their extras to Envy, some of them because their grandparents had survived the Change here and never left. Some people don't like to be crowded."

Crowded? He hardly considered Envy crowded. In fact, it was a freaking ghost town as far as he was concerned.

"Plus it's safer."

Elliott looked at her. "Safer?" A little prickle lifted the hair on his arms, and it had nothing to do with the way muscular thighs held her in place on the bare back of that mustang. Although he'd taken notice of that as well.

"Away from the Strangers, sort of beneath their notice," she said. "Although that doesn't always work." Her face settled unhappily, and he knew she was probably thinking about the group of people she'd seen executed by *ganga*. He wanted to ask more about her experience with the Strangers, but now was not the time.

"Stay here for a sec," she said suddenly, and before he could reply, her horse leapt forward.

Stones clattered on the ground behind her, and . . . he waited. The thing was, he trusted her. She knew this world better than he did, and she knew what she was doing. He'd already seen evidence of that—although it was a good thing she hadn't been alone when she ran into that snake.

And it was a *really* good thing that he'd had some nasty *ganga* wounds to give the snake, right in its soft underbelly. He had Simon to thank for that unexpected weapon.

Still, the realization that somehow he not only healed

people, but took on their afflictions and then passed them on to the next person—no, apparently it was the next living thing he happened to touch—was frightening and confusing, and yet exciting and fantastic all at the same time.

Once he learned how to control this power, how to use it, he would be formidable.

That was, if he managed not to get himself killed in the meanwhile. Before he unloaded them on the snake, those *ganga* wounds had been growing ever more acute and dangerous, slowing his every movement. It was as if the injury had intensified exponentially once he took it upon himself.

If he'd "carried" Jade's fractured ulna for hours instead of minutes, would his own bone have done more than simply ache? Would it have broken? More severely? Or would something else have happened?

Elliott heard voices and looked up to see two women appear from between a couple of fairly well-tended buildings—meaning that though the windows were glassless, and the roof on one sagged (it was completely missing on the other), the brick underpinnings weren't overgrown with bushes and trees. The women were walking toward the river, carrying small baskets and a slender hoe.

"Hello," he said, moving forward in the same manner he'd done the times he'd come upon settlements in the past.

"Well, hello," said one of the women, scanning up at him with one hand shielding her face from the sun. "Where'd you come from?"

She was in her mid to late forties, and wore simple, comfortable clothing: jeans and a plain white shirt with a sort of shiny, textured wide-brimmed hat. The other woman was much younger, closer in age to Elliott himself. Her clothes fit better, showing off a nicely curved body. She wore a plain T-shirt with a sort of vest over it, also made from the same type of material as her companion's hat. Made from some sort of plastic?

Although neither appeared apprehensive or frightened by his presence, Elliott slid down from his horse and, since he had no bridle and therefore nothing to tie it with, released the mustang. Jade had assured him there was no difficulty catching another one, and if she couldn't . . . well, then, he'd have to ride with her back to Envy.

Knowing that Jade's activity as a Runner was supposed to be secret, and unsure how she would want him to react in this situation, he opted for the innocent, weary traveler persona.

"I'm Elliott," he said, giving them a warm smile. "I've been traveling all day from Envy. I don't suppose you'd have something cold to drink for a guy who's been on a horse for a couple hours?"

"I've got some iced tea," replied the older one. She had dark hair and a sweet smile and looked as if she'd be right at home baking cookies and bandaging skinned knees for a wide-eyed little boy. Did they bake cookies anymore? What did they use for skinned knees?

Elliott grinned with sincere appreciation. "I'd really appreciate that. As long as I'm not interrupting anything." He figured Jade would find him eventually—it wasn't as if he'd get lost in this skeleton of a town. Aside from that, he might have a little bit of an opportunity to check out what Lou and Jade had told him about the Strangers.

He was convinced. He just wanted . . . confirmation. Proof.

"We were just going out to pick a few beans in that field there, but I'd rather sit and chat with a handsome young man and drink tea than do that," she said, looking as if she'd like to pat him on the head. Her younger companion, who'd definitely been checking Elliott out with her big blue eyes, nodded in agreement.

Elliott accepted the glass of what turned out to be iced mint tea, which tasted clean and cool. He'd noticed that Sally, the older woman, walked with a bit of a limp and wondered how he might create the opportunity to scan her and see if there was anything he could do to alleviate her obvious pain.

While he sat, he asked general questions about the beans they grew, and the weather, and other mundane things. He felt as if he were sitting at his *abuela*'s kitchen table, chatting with her friends while they canned salsa or did perms or played cards.

He liked women of all ages. He'd often wondered, when he really got to thinking . . . usually either late at night, or when he was simply blown away by exhaustion and stress after a long stint in the ER . . . if it was because he was still looking for his mother. She'd left him and his father when Elliott was three.

She'd decided she didn't want to be a mother anymore. Simple as that. And she up and left.

Elliott, who'd nevertheless been raised with an over-abundance of motherly love from his *abuela*—his father's mother—and aunts, hadn't seen her since. And he guessed that now he never would.

Sally and her pretty niece Andrea had escorted him to a small courtyard-type place that appeared to once have been the garden in front of the town hall. The space had been well kept and looked as neat as it must have been when land-scapers did their edging and weed-whacking and seasonal planting a half-century ago. Sally lived with her family in the courthouse, on the second floor, and Andrea with her parents on the floor above.

Everyone lived on the second or third or fourth floors. It was the only way they could be safe from *gangas*.

The town and its environs struck Elliott as odd; he still wasn't used to buildings being so close to each other but with so much green. In the cities and suburbs he'd known in his previous life, the homes and structures were close together, but there was little natural growth. Here, it flourished everywhere, making him feel as if he sat in the middle of a forest, shady and cool.

He took another enthusiastic swig from the tall plastic cup and just as he was setting it down, happened to look over at an adjacent building and saw Jade through an opening in the wall.

With her arms around another man.

And there was definitely nothing brotherly about the kiss they were sharing, or where his hands were.

CHAPTER 10

"Luke," Jade said, twisting her mouth firmly away from his. This was exactly why Theo usually went to Greenside—so she could avoid Luke of the quick-draw, octopus hands. Maybe she should have had Elliott come with her. "We've got to get this stuff put away." Her knapsack had slipped to the floor when he took her by surprise, yanking her into his arms.

She supposed some women liked the strong, take-charge kind of guys who were always throwing them up against the wall to kiss them, and telling them what to do . . . but she'd outgrown that adolescent fantasy about ten years ago.

"I'd like to put something away," he replied meaningfully, with a little lift of his hips against her. *Eww. What a scrub.* "Where've you been, Jade? It's been *months*!"

It should have been longer.

"Luke! What's gotten into you?" She slipped away, taking care to keep a pleasant, regretful expression on her face and a teasing tone. She couldn't afford to get Luke pissed off, especially when she needed information—and any data he had. It was a delicate balance—remain friendly, with a hint of flirtatiousness, but keep him at arm's length. And that was why she'd asked Elliott to stay behind.

And now that he'd already told her he hadn't seen Theo

for a few weeks, she had no reason to stay once they made their data exchange. Obviously, she was wrong that Theo was trying to get her to come to Greenside for him—he just wanted her to pick up the data. So she would get it and get out of here.

She bent to pick up her knapsack, expertly dodging the swipe of Luke's large hand. "But I brought you this. Do you have anything for me?" she asked with exaggerated innocence.

He grinned a wicked grin that failed to ignite even the slightest response in her. "Of course I do." Taking her hand, he guided her out of the small room that acted as his main living space and through a short passageway to the hidden cellar.

She clambered down *ganga*-proof spiral stairs after him and at the bottom, instead of turning the light on, he turned and caught her full in his arms before she realized what was happening.

Ugh.

"Jade," he groaned into her hair. He wasn't much taller than she, and Jade was standing on the bottom step, so her mouth was a bit higher than his. His hands closed around her hips and then slid up to her breasts. *Holy crap.* His hands were fast. And strong.

A little niggle of fear threatened to sweep into panic, but she pushed it away. Never again.

"Luke," she said in a firm voice. "Let me go."

"Why?" he said, his mouth closing over her breast right through the tight, thin cotton shirt she wore.

Jade pushed ineffectually at him as she felt his tongue swishing back and forth through the fabric and her equally thin—and precious—bra, right over her nipple. *Oh, yuck.*

She resisted the automatic urge to shove him away, only

because if she pissed him off, that would be the end of their alliance. And if he got really mad, he might be loud-mouthed about Theo and the Resistance. Not that he knew that much about it, but . . . she had to be careful. Diplomatic. A lot more was at stake than just her personal space.

But he had to remove his hands—and mouth—from her. *Now.*

"Luke," she said, trying to sound breathy, "we. . . ." She let all of her weight, insubstantial as it was, lunge toward him in a sudden movement, angling her knee so that it jabbed right into his gut. "Oh, my God, I'm sorry," she said, pulling out of his grip as he gasped in pain, and she squeezed down and past him in the dark. "I slipped right off the step."

She was never coming to Greenside, or to meet with Luke, alone again.

"Jade," Luke was saying, and she felt his hand brush against her. But before he could snag her back, she turned on the light.

A smile firmly in place, she looked at him with an exasperated expression and said, "Now, Luke, you're going to put me all off-schedule. We'll have time for this later." Much later.

She moved over to the rows of computers, hard drives, and something Theo called mainframes—she guessed they were just big computers—and opened her knapsack.

"What do you have?" he asked, moving over to stand very close behind her. His finger trailed over her neck, curling around in her long hair as he looked over her shoulder.

"I need to, uh . . . upload"—she thought that was the word, but Lou talked so fast and technically sometimes she didn't always catch the correct terms—"all this data onto your machines." For backup, Lou said. So they had copies of it somewhere else in case the worst happened.

"That'll take some time," Luke said, watching her remove the assortment of flash and hard drives from her pack. "What should we do while we're waiting?" The expression in his eyes was not good.

In fact, he looked more than a little pissed. Time to soothe the savage beastie. She'd never had to resort to that before. Without letting herself think too hard about it, Jade placed her hands on his shoulders and lifted her face for a quick brush of a kiss over his lips followed by the barest of nibble.

"I wish I had more time," she murmured, trying not to gag. Then she pulled away, placing her hand on his chest to keep him from lunging forward to maul her again. "Let me get started on this while you get your stuff for me. Otherwise, I'll never get it done."

Reluctant, Luke nevertheless moved away to find the drives and disks he'd prepared for her. "Got a good delivery last week," he said from the corner, from which came the familiar sound of metal clunking and sliding against metal.

Luke collected any old computers or hard drives from various sources. He extricated the data from them and provided it to Jade, who brought it back to Lou and Theo in Envy. She "ran" the information from place to place on portable drives, and occasionally, like today, brought data that Lou wanted to make certain was protected and backed up.

This was the crux of the business relationship she had to work so hard to preserve—the exchange of information and confidentiality. The problem was, Luke was a hothead and although he had good contacts and understood almost as well as Theo how to work with computers—and he hated the Strangers, which was the key to his cooperation—he could also be impatient. The last thing she needed was for him to feel slighted by her and start running off at the mouth about her and Theo visiting and collecting data.

But now, fortunately, Luke had turned to the business at hand, leaving Jade to begin the transfer of data . . . and to wonder where Elliott was. How long had she been gone?

She checked the status of the five hard drives she'd hooked up and noted that they were in the process of transferring their secrets. It would take a while.

"I'll be right back," Jade said, rising swiftly from her chair and starting up the spiral stairs before Luke could waylay her again.

But he merely grunted, now engrossed in a different task, and she was able to make her escape to find Elliott.

She'd been to Greenside often enough to know many of the people by sight, and as far as they were concerned, she was a traveling singer who visited from Envy and brought Luke tools for his shop. Nothing suspicious about an occasional conjugal visit, if that was what they thought. And she suspected Luke wouldn't set them straight.

Since it was midafternoon, most of the town's fifty or so residents were working on their daily tasks, so Jade wasn't surprised to find few people about. But where to find Elliott?

She couldn't picture him as a patient man, waiting docilely for her to return after she dashed off like she had—and, now that she thought about it, Jade realized it was surprising that he actually hadn't followed her. Had he really listened to her when she told him to stay there?

She decided to retrace her path and hope to run into him, but she'd gone hardly a few steps when she heard voices. Jade walked toward the conversation, her skin prickling. A burst of laughter, followed by a deep rumble.

It was Elliott. As Jade approached a whitewashed build-

ing that boasted huge glassless window openings, she saw
that he was sitting beyond the building, in a courtyard with
a group of women of various ages—from grandmotherly
to a decade younger than Jade herself. Three of them were
obviously pregnant, with beautiful round bellies of varying
sizes.

Jade thought of her own flat abdomen and empty womb.
Barren bitch.

It had been a long time since Daniel's words had cut
through her memory, and she wasn't prepared for the sharp
renewal of pain they caused. He was long dead, but the voice
in her head was not.

She automatically touched the three bands on her wrist,
twisting them to line up the beads, reminding herself what
they represented. She'd come so far from that weak, inse-
cure girl—not only because of her own determination, but
also thanks in part to Flo for taking her under her wing, and
to Lou for helping her find her place. Giving her a purpose.

Giving her a chance for revenge.

Another burst of laughter, followed by a chorus of croon-
ing *awww*s drew her back to the tableau through the windows, and Jade straightened her shoulders and smoothed her
hair. As she started toward the building, she noticed the wet
spot on her shirt from Luke's overzealous mauling. Right
over her nipple.

Shit.

"Elliott," she said as she approached the large opening.
"There you are."

He looked over at her. There wasn't an element of surprise,
nor delight, at seeing Jade. None of that subtle flare of heat
she'd become used to seeing. "Jade. Are you finished?"

She counted more than five women, and recognized
some—Sally, who was as sweet as she looked, and her sister

Della, who looked more sober but was also very kind. Della's eldest daughter, Andrea, was sitting there between two of the pregnant women across from Elliott, and she seemed to only have eyes for him. In fact, from her body language, it looked as though she were ready to slide right into his lap.

Jade walked around the building and came to a low wall. On the other side sat the group of them, looking very cozy, sitting there around a table in the cheery little courtyard. "What are you all doing?" she asked, trying to sound casual, and as if it didn't bother her to see Elliott surrounded by a group of females who seemed to be hanging on his every word.

And why should it bother her anyway?

"Elliott's been predicting the sex of our babies," said one of the pregnant women. Mathilda was her name, and her belly looked ready to burst. "He says he's never been wrong."

"Is that so?" Jade looked at Elliott. When their eyes met, she read recognition of her message there . . . but, again, no warmth. "Will you be performing tonight, Jade?" asked Della hopefully.

"I'm sorry, but we need to get back on the trail before much longer. I have to be somewhere else tonight." Jade spoke quickly, then read the disappointment in the woman's eyes. "I'll come back soon, though, and stay for a show." She hoped.

"I just love it when you sing that song about the preacher man," Della said wistfully.

"I like that one too," Jade said. And because Della seemed a little sad, she sang a few bars of the beginning, about going walking with Billie Ray, the preacher's son.

It turned into the whole first verse and a couple run-throughs of the refrain, and when she finished, they all applauded. Although she hadn't wanted to sing, Jade was glad she'd done so. It seemed to give them pleasure, and she knew that the computer upload wouldn't have finished quite yet.

And then there was, of course, the added benefit of the way Elliott was looking at her. A little bit of that heat was back.

"Well, now come and have a glass of tea with us for a bit, dear," Sally said, gesturing expansively. "Elliott's been telling me how to take care of the ache in my hip too."

All of these women were fairly eating out of his hand, and Jade could see why. He looked, sounded, and acted like he really cared, yet he wasn't alienating Sally, who acted as midwife, by telling her how to do her job. He played it well. Very well.

He had a way with them—he knew how to talk to women, to treat them, to make them feel comfortable and happy. She couldn't imagine him ever raising a hand to anyone . . . although he was certainly capable of inflicting great damage. The snake he'd sliced up was a perfect example of that.

And Andrea . . . damn if she wasn't inching her way closer to him when no one was looking. Pretty soon her knees would be brushing against his. Jade was looking at the younger woman when Andrea glanced up and caught her attention. "What's that on your shirt?" she asked. There was a bit of a malicious gleam in her eyes.

"I spilled something," Jade replied coolly. Then, she smiled blandly and said, "I'm sorry everyone, but I'm going to have to take Elliott with me. We've got to get on the road if we're going to make it by dark."

Andrea must have gotten the message—whatever it was Jade was trying to tell her—because her mouth tightened just a little bit. And Jade was surprised at how relieved she felt when Elliott stood to join her.

"Ladies," he said, turning back to the group as he stepped

through the large window opening. "It's been a real pleasure meeting all of you. I'll be back in a month or so myself to see how things are going."

So much for him never seeing Andrea and her big blue eyes again.

Elliott followed Jade down the street, trying to ignore the mouth-sized wet spot over her right breast. "Are we leaving now?" he asked, catching up to Jade with an extra-long stride.

"As soon as I get my stuff." She tossed that gorgeous smile up at him.

He looked her over again, over the wet spot on her tee. He should have figured it out right away, last night when he saw her up on stage. Of course she was a man-eater. Of course a woman who looked like Jade, who performed and rode like she did—and was smart and brave to boot—had a plethora of male companionship.

Women like that attracted them in droves. And they couldn't settle on just one.

Lysney had been the same way. Beautiful, smart, confident—a skyrocketing star in the Chicago advertising industry. And she had a man in each city where she had an account.

At least Elliott had realized it before he fell too hard, for Jade or Lys.

Which was why, when he met the man who'd had his hands all over that great ass, he merely smiled at Luke instead of *smiling* at him. And he was rewarded with absolutely no vibe whatsoever.

And which was probably why Luke didn't hesitate when Elliott followed him and Jade down into another cellar complete with a NASA-like computer setup. It didn't take Elliott long to figure out what was going on—the transfer of data.

He poked around a little bit without appearing to poke— watching screens surreptitiously (simple data uploading), slyly opening a drawer when the opportunity arose (it held some flash drives and a few CDs, along with a curling-cornered picture of Jade), even looked behind the computers to see where their cords went. How was Luke generating so much power? It was one thing to run a refrigerator or television and a few lights—but at least twenty boxes, plus monitors?

The cords plugged into something that looked like a large, homemade generator boasting countless outlets that had been cobbled together. The generator was set into the ground, with all of its plugs exposed in a grid. He wanted to look beneath and find out what made it work.

So he knocked over a stack of disks, and as they spewed all over the floor, he knelt to pick them up. Out of sight under the table, he knelt next to the generator and began feeling around for the mechanism behind or beneath it. Low to the floor, he found a small metal door next to the grid of outlets. It felt warm to the touch, and its sliding bolt lock opened as if it were often moved.

The door opened with a small metallic clang, but Luke and Jade were talking on the other side of the room, and neither seemed to notice. A warm yellow glow spilled into the space, lighting the floor around him. Elliott looked down into what had to be the insides of the generator and saw a large oblong object, glowing and sparking with little blue lightninglike sparks. The object, which looked like a piece of granite with a light burning inside it, had blue and yellow veins all over it. A crystal, as large as his forearm. Generating enough power to run a classroom of computers.

Next to it were some fragments of more crystals, much smaller, as if they'd been smashed. The floor felt gritty beneath his palms, and he noticed the tiny sparkles of what looked like dust beneath the shards.

Elliott closed the door and returned to his seat with the disks in hand. Casting a glance behind him, he noted that neither of the others seemed to have noticed his nosiness.

"So you haven't heard from Theo for a couple weeks?" Jade was saying.

"Nope, but when I got this stuff, I sent him a message and said he might want to make a special trip. I'm sure not complaining that he sent you. Maybe you could come from now on," Luke replied, absently scratching what looked like a rash on the inside of his arm.

"I'd discount my prices if you made Greenside part of your regular route," he added with a leer.

Elliott resisted the urge to roll his eyes.

"That sounds like a good idea," Jade said enthusiastically, then her voice sharpened with regret. "But we're leaving now. I've got to catch up with him."

Jade didn't allow Luke's obvious reluctance at their departure to delay them, and just a bit more than an hour after arriving in Greenside, she and Elliott were on their way, back to Envy on foot.

"What happened to getting the mustangs so easily?" he asked after she'd whistled several times and there'd been no answering whinny.

"I don't know," she said, frowning. "I've never had a problem before. Maybe we'll find a herd somewhere along the way." She paused, looking toward the southwest. "Looks a little cloudy that way. Maybe there's a storm coming."

"Do you want to stay in Greenside?"

"No. I want to get back to Envy."

Elliott agreed, but he'd learned by now that Jade liked to make the decisions. And since it appeared they were of the same mind, why not let her think she was in charge.

They traveled as fast as they could, following overgrown roads. Elliott concentrated on the journey, automatically observing the environment for recognizable elements from his world—highway signs, Golden Arches, gas stations or drugstores . . . anything that seemed familiar. Those memories, those groundings of days gone by, were few and far between.

And he thought about the women he'd met in Greenside. Mathilda, with the healthy baby boy in her belly. Emily, with a little girl that would be born a month after. Sally, who had arthritis in her hip and knee, which made her move slowly and awkwardly.

And then there was Della. The moment Elliot had laid eyes on her, he'd known it would be bad news. He hadn't even needed to really scan her, but he did . . . and the moment he realized she had terminal cancer throughout her entire abdomen, he jerked his hands away as if burned.

He felt acute shame afterward, but no one seemed to notice his reaction. The shame was followed by the niggling worry that he'd touched her and somehow quickly absorbed the carcinoma. But he thought about it, wracked his memory, reliving every detail of the moment, and he knew he hadn't felt that little sizzle of power he had when he healed Jade and Simon. And, now, in retrospect, he recalled having felt a shocklike jolt when he touched the elderly man in Vineland, who'd been dying from an infection.

The problem was, he'd turned from the old man to rebandage Lenny's cut moments later . . . and look what had happened. He'd come to realize that Lenny had died from an infection—not from the rusty-metal cut, but from Elliott.

So much for "first do no harm."

Now, a deep tug of depression and grief pulled inside him. It wasn't that he wasn't used to diagnosing serious, terminal problems. Hell, he'd worked in an ER and had seen plenty of bad news.

It was that there wasn't anything that could be done to even make Della's passing easier . . . let alone cure her. Unless he wanted to die himself.

Or give the terminal illness to someone else. Accidentally.

He hiked along, grateful for the dappled shade of a small forest they'd entered. He wondered if it was safe to touch Jade again.

Meanwhile, Elliott was acutely aware that if he had absorbed anything, whatever it was was growing inside him right now . . . more quickly and venomously than it would be in anyone else.

Maybe he could find another snake. Or a horse. Or even a dog. No, not a dog. It might be someone's pet. He could touch them, passing on anything that he might be carrying. But wouldn't that be cruelty to animals?

Did it matter? When a human life was at stake, would it matter?

A thought struck him. What about a *ganga*? Could he pass it on to a *ganga*? Were they living creatures? Would it work?

That might be a solution.

First he'd have to catch one. And it would be fascinating to scan it and find out what sort of creature the *gangas* were. Of course, there was always the danger that he'd scan a *ganga* and accidentally absorb whatever it was that made them . . . well, undead, or reanimated . . . and become that way himself.

What a fucking mess. How many people would be hurt or killed before he figured out just exactly how to control this power?

After about an hour of hiking, they emerged from the forest and found themselves standing at the edge of what had been a huge parking lot. A low, sprawling building stretched in front of them. Random trees dotted the landscape of tall, meadowlike grass.

And in the distance, behind the long, low building, was a large black cloud billowing toward them, "Oh my God," Jade exclaimed from behind him.

Elliott had witnessed both tornados and cyclones, but he'd never seen anything like the roiling, evil-looking fog. It stretched as far as he could see. Yet the sky above looked like an overturned bowl of oatmeal, gray but unthreatening.

"What the hell is it?" Whatever it was, it seemed to be moving rapidly toward them.

Before he could stop her, she'd grabbed his bare arm with her fingers. They were cool and firm and he hoped like hell he wasn't "carrying" anything. "A storm. We call them blackouts. That must be why the mustangs are all gone."

"It's too wide to be a tornado, and the sky above it isn't even cloudy."

"It just rolls along the ground and destroys whatever isn't nailed down. I guess it's like a long, wide tornado. Either way, we've got to find shelter."

Elliott nodded, squinting at the rolling storm. They hadn't stopped walking, but now they had to pick up the pace. The blackout was moving quickly due east, and Envy was northeast. There was a chance the storm might miss them if they kept on their course.

"Let's keep going as far as we can," he said.

"I think we should see how far we can get. We might be able to miss it, or at least get out of the center of its path." Jade's voice was taut.

He nodded and they picked up their speed. Elliott grabbed her elbow and helped her to keep pace with his longer, faster stride, half-carrying her. They half-ran, half-jogged, passing small, rundown houses that looked as if they'd been a neighborhood of manufactured homes. Even if they wanted to find shelter now, there wasn't any safe place.

The storm seemed to pick up steam as well, and it wasn't long before Elliott felt the rush of wind chilling him through the light T-shirt he wore. He had a jacket in his pack, but he didn't stop to pull it out. The sting of biting rain began to patter over his head and shoulders. But, it wasn't rain . . . it was hail. Sharp, icy pellets the size of blueberries. Big, fat *hard* blueberries.

Glancing behind, he saw that the evil cloud now filled the horizon and rose into the sky. *Holy fucking shit.* It was like a tidal wave, rushing toward them. There was nowhere to go.

The storm bubbled and swirled, and looked like a massive purple-black steamroller careening toward them. He guessed it was moving more than ten miles an hour, and on foot, they were lucky to be doing a consistent five.

It was time to find a safe place. Something that could withstand the power of the winds that bent trees nearly double, the pounding of hail, and whatever else the storm would bring.

Leaves and debris—pieces of wood and plastic, branches and bushes—whirled, blowing into them from behind, whipping Jade's hair as the hail fell harder and faster. Elliott's nose clogged with the blast of dust, dirt, and something dank and heavy. A roaring sound surged around them, deafening and furious, as the storm rolled toward them.

Elliott scanned the horizon, looking for something promising, shading his eyes from the stinging hail and blinding dust. The little manufactured homes that had stretched in neat rows, overgrown and sagging, had given way to a wide open space that appeared to have been the intersection of two major highways.

But on the other side of the crumbling entrance and exit ramps, he saw what looked like a brick office building. Three or four stories, some glass still reflecting from the windows. "There," he shouted, pointing, but the word was lost in the maelstrom around them. Jade looked and saw where he was pointing, she nodded in agreement, the details of her face muted by the falling light.

He grabbed her hand and they ran at full speed now, clambering over the crumbling concrete wall that had separated the neighborhood from the roar of the highways, across the empty interstate, leaping over small crevices in the concrete and up and over the jagged slabs of road, and then up a small incline on the other side.

The storm blew and blustered, fast and furious around them, filling his ears and drowning out all other sounds. Then something hard and heavy slammed into the back of his head, nearly sending him to his knees.

"Elliott!" Jade shouted over the roar of the storm, holding fast to his arm, steadying him as he stumbled. Pain radiated down from his skull and for a moment, Elliott's sight blurred. But then he realized his darkening vision was partly from the storm nearly upon them.

Jade grabbed him around the waist, pulling him up against

her slender body, stumbling awkwardly at the sudden addition of the extra weight. But she kept on, her arm solid and strong around him as he blinked, trying to clear his vision and the dizziness.

Something warm and wet trickled from the back of his head, and the pounding had not eased, the world still spun, but when she tripped, he shoved an arm around Jade's waist and heaved her up against his hip, and ran. His steps wove from side to side, his knees felt as though they were going to give way at any moment, but he ran, with the sound of the freight train of a storm rushing down over him.

Hail pelted them, pounding their shoulders and backs of their legs, the back of their heads and arms, crunching beneath their feet. Debris flew about, slapping up against them, and the sounds of screeching, screaming filled his ears.

At last they gained the top of the incline. The world was dark as night, and Elliott could see hardly any details, but as they dashed toward their sanctuary, he caught sight of a large, gleaming object next to the building.

Jade saw it too, and stumbled against him, her eyes suddenly wide and white in the darkness. "*Oh no!*" her mouth said soundlessly, her shout lost in the pummeling wind. Her fingers suddenly dug into his arm, her face a mask of shock, and she tried to stop him.

But Elliott pulled her along as a massive tree branch . . . no, a whole fucking *tree*, roots and all . . . sailed past them and crashed into the brick building. Wood splintered, shooting everywhere as he scrabbled for the door, pulling on the sagging metal, and shoved her inside, where the roar and the wind became muted, and the blast shook the walls and floor.

She grabbed his arms and slammed a hand over his mouth, shoving her face up against his neck. "Strangers," she hissed into his ear. "Did you see the truck? The Strangers are here!"

And just as her furious whisper registered in his ears, dulled by the roar of the storm, he saw the black wave descend over the building in a great surge. The metal door slammed open, and he grabbed Jade, dodging away from the vortex that suddenly filled the space.

Just great. Out of the frying pan, and into the fire.

Five weeks After

Despite his injury, Theo seems the same as ever. So glad to have my twin back.

Noticed a strange thing today. Some of the bodies that were on the streets are gone. Disappeared completely.

Maybe some animals took them off, but so many are gone it seems odd. Very strange and a bit frightening.

Working with Greg Rowe and Thad Marck to divide up the tasks of scavenging, organizing, and infrastructure more effectively. Everyone is so haphazard, we need to be more organized. We four (now that Theo is back) seem to be the most able and willing to figure out the big picture. Most everyone else is still in shock.

No one goes out at night. Have heard the roar of lions and tigers, and other unidentifiable animals.

Still have power. Still no Internet.

Theo wants to find a satellite to hack into. Would never admit it, but I think he could do it faster than me.

So glad he's back.

　　　　　　　　　　　　—from the journal of Lou Waxnicki

CHAPTER 11

Jade and Elliott pressed against the wall, away from the raging storm and its weapons of hail, branches, and miscellaneous debris; whatever it could gather up and hurl in its madness poured through the open door and swirled haphazardly around the room.

Feeling around in the dark, still battling the sharp ache in his skull, Elliott found a metal door that swung wildly in the blustering storm. Praying that the Strangers weren't on the other side of it, he slipped through and pulled Jade along as the wind slammed the door closed behind them.

The pressure on the opposite side held the door closed now, and Elliott felt for Jade in the flat, unrelieved darkness. The storm's roar was even more muted, and he strained to hear and see. Groping blindly, but unwilling to move about for fear the floor was unstable or had collapsed, he felt the rough brick wall, damp and soft with mold.

"Jade," he whispered quietly, feeling it was safe to do so, for he couldn't see anything—let alone the glow of a crystal from a Stranger. If they were here, they sure as hell weren't in this room.

"Here," she said, low and to his right. The syllable was barely discernable beneath the rumbling storm. He reached out, and at last, felt a cool hand brush over his bare arm. Elliott found her, his fingers closing over her narrow wrist and the three beaded bands she wore there.

He told himself he had no choice but to pull Jade close to him so he could speak low in her ear, and gathered her into his arms. The wall behind steadied him, and though his head was still pounding, and sticky when he rested it against the masonry, Elliott had a moment of pure pleasure, just holding her as the storm crashed and battered around them.

Feeling the warmth of her skin, the damp of her clothes, the silky brush of hair over his cheek . . . not to mention all of the other attributes that had attracted him since he'd first caught sight of her barreling to the rescue on that horse . . . the soft brush of lips against the hollow of his throat, the swell of breasts pressing into his chest, the curve of her bottom. Even in the midst of the mildew and dampness, even after the wild wind tossing her hair, he smelled the fresh lemon there.

His heart, which had been racing from the adrenaline of their mad dash, began to pound in an entirely different rhythm. He closed his eyes.

"Are you all right?" Jade said in a low voice, her mouth moving deliciously against the tender skin just above his clavicle. Elliott's eyes closed again, and he concentrated on breathing easily, and not on the rush of blood surging everywhere . . . absolutely *everywhere* . . . in his body.

"I'm fine," he replied into the top of her hair, though his head still throbbed like a bitch. That was possibly the only reason he wasn't completely distracted by the woman he held in his arms. That and they were in big fucking danger if they really had found a cache of Strangers.

The problem was, what *should* be warning him away from the sweet bundle of curves in his arms was the fact that, only a few hours ago, some other guy had had his mouth on her boob. On this ruthless reminder, the wave of annoyance strengthened Elliott. He marshaled his thoughts enough to ask a relevant question. "Are you sure there are Strangers here?"

"They drive those big black trucks . . . what are they called? Hummings?"

"Humvees."

"No one else has them. Have you ever seen one?"

Not in the last six months anyway. Elliott had to shake his head, and he realized one of his hands had moved to gently lift the hair from the back of her neck. *Dammit.* But he wasn't listening to reason. He slid his fingers over her neck, gently caressing the soft indentation of her nape. It was tender and downy soft, a secret, intimate place on a woman who wore her hair long. His mouth watered. He wanted to kiss her there.

"Only Strangers, or the bounty hunters have trucks like that," she said. And he could have sworn she sagged closer against him, almost as if she were a cat purring into the stroke of his hand.

"Let's figure out where we are," he said, easing gently, reluctantly, away from her. Although they'd seen no sign of Strangers yet, if they'd come in the same way he and Jade had, it was possible they could have come through this door and followed this path. It would be best to try and get farther away from the entrance and hole up somewhere. Holding just her hand, Elliott felt along the wall, inching around, and then his foot bumped up against something. At the same time, his hand brushed a slender metal rod jutting from the wall, and then curving into . . . a stairway handrail.

Ah. That explained the severe darkness. They were in a stairwell. Definitely not a good place to stay if the Strangers had taken the stairs to another level. A bit more exploration indicated that this was the bottom floor; there were no stairs going down.

"Should we go up?" he asked softly. "It's a staircase." Elliott wished he dared pull out the matches he had in his pack, but not yet.

She nodded against him, barely missing his nose. "I don't want to be trapped in a small room like this," she whispered back.

Ditto for him.

At least any noises they made would be drowned out by the storm, which still raged like a furious bitch. Above the snarling wind, Elliott heard the dull thuds and crashes of debris slamming into the brick walls or windows. If there were Strangers here, unless they came upon them unexpectedly, they should be able to remain unnoticed.

At least, he hoped they couldn't sense the presence of humans, like the *gangas* could.

The steps felt sturdy when he stomped on the first three, and so, saying a little prayer that they would hold, he led the way up. Jade followed, her fingers still clasped in his.

At the top, he paused. Now . . . to find a way out of the enclosed stairwell.

Carefully feeling around along the wall, he oriented himself to the same position they'd been in when they came into the stairwell, two flights of stairs below. If he figured right, there should be a door . . . right . . . there.

The knob felt cool and tight beneath his fingers, and he tried to turn it. It wouldn't budge even when he tried two hands, even with the sudden surge of strength that surprised even Elliott. He pulled on it, and then pushed, but the door didn't even shudder beneath his onslaught.

Fucking great. "Up one more level," he said, feeling uneasy about getting too high up in a building that could be blown to smithereens. Or that could harbor Strangers on any level.

Yet, the brick walls seemed sturdy enough, and the steel stairs rang dully beneath his foot when he paused to stomp and test its weight. They went on, the storm howling beyond the brick walls.

The knob on the next level was loose, and he didn't even have to turn it. Carefully, he pulled and at first it didn't move . . . and then, with a grudging little sound, it came free. The wind billowed louder beyond a large window that still retained its glass, and the dark wasn't such a depthless black. Elliott could make out a few large shadows, objects that were likely old office furnishings—desks, chairs, maybe even some electronics—but nothing that glowed like a Stranger's crystal.

He hesitated, weighing the options. Stay in the small, dark, enclosed stairwell, or exit into a larger, lighter room with a window that could explode into shards, more vulnerable to the storm, and with the possibility that the Strangers would be there. . . .

"Let's go," Jade said, gently pushing him. "Too dark in here."

He nodded in agreement, though he doubted she could see, and they went into the room, closing the door behind them. Wary of the malicious bitch outside, Elliott kept Jade close as they edged along the wall, keeping clear of the window. The storm raged as strong as ever, and even as they stood there, a large branch crashed through the intact windowpane. It tumbled into the room, rolling to a halt near a large shadow in the corner.

As the storm roared and swirled around the room, the shadow moved, leaping onto two feet as if startled by the sudden wave of power. The man shifted, half turning toward them, an unmistakable glow shone in the murky darkness.

Elliott felt Jade stiffen next to him, and he shoved her away, toward the door. "Run!" he shouted. She stumbled toward the exit, but he didn't turn to watch her leave. He was looking for a weapon.

The Stranger bolted toward them and Elliott dodged, vaulting over what was, indeed, a desk. Out of the corner of his eye, he saw Jade scuttle away from the door, crawling quickly along the floor. He whipped off his pack and flung it toward her, lightening his load.

The storm swirled in the room, buffeting and whipping objects about, drowning out any sound. Elliott could see the faint glow beneath the man's shirt, as if a small light or a captured firefly burned there. Hardly noticeable even in the dark, it would have been invisible during the daylight. Blue on one side, just above where the clavicle would be. Just as Jade had described them.

Elliott ducked as something hurtled through the window at him, and shoved an old office chair at the Stranger. He pivoted, dodging some other flying object that had come from the Stranger or the storm, searching for something to use as a weapon. His eyes had become used to the low light, and he saw Jade crouched near the wall, and she seemed to be inching her way around the room. Not toward the door, but crawling toward the window.

The Stranger vaulted over a desk, and launched himself toward Elliott with a shout barely audible in the roar of the storm. Elliott spun just in time and dove toward a dark corner. Rolling to his feet, he found a long piece of wood, a beam that had fallen from somewhere long ago. It was as thick as his arm, square, and perhaps five feet long. He swiped it up, hefting it easily as the shadowy figure turned to face him again.

The wind continued to roar in the room, lifting smaller objects at them. The man leapt, Elliott swung, and felt the satisfying slam as he connected, the shock of it shooting up his arms. The man stumbled . . . but he kept coming.

Jesus Christ. Elliott raised the beam to swing again and the man ducked, diving toward his legs.

He jumped out of the way, using the beam as a sort of awkward pole vault, but the man caught his foot. Elliott fell into the wall, and by the time he got to his feet, the Stranger had turned to lunge across the room toward Jade. But Elliott brought the beam down onto the back of the man's head.

That stopped him. For about ten seconds.

Then he turned and came after Elliott, his hands wide and grasping, his teeth bared, the crystal beneath his shirt glowing brighter. He kicked out. Elliott swung, and missed, using the beam to catch himself and spin around as the man launched at him. His feet caught Elliott in the chest, slamming into him with a great force that knocked the air out of his lungs and sent him stumbling back.

Does nothing even slow this guy down?

Elliott caught sight of Jade, who was crouched right next to the window, as she flattened herself against the wall. She was gesturing at him, but it was too dark to see well, and he was a little distracted to play charades.

The man came again and Elliott dodged, slamming against the opposite wall, facing the open window. As he pushed himself away, he suddenly realized what Jade had in mind, crouched near the opening.

Brilliant.

But then something large and dark twisted through the window and he ducked, using the wooden pole to keep himself balanced. His opponent was back at him again, and this time when the Stranger attacked, hands raised, he grabbed for the beam whaling toward him and caught it with his hands in midair.

The man was strong, and he pulled, jerking the wood around, causing Elliott to stumble and splinters to drive into his fingers. He held on, yanking back just as violently, focusing on the empty, glass-edged window.

The macabre dance continued, neither of the men relinquishing the wooden beam as they circled around, pulling, pushing, occasionally kicking, jerking . . . Elliott held on as it slammed toward him suddenly, twisting so it caught him painfully in the hip instead of the gut. The pain blasted through his body, but he dug his fingers in deeper. This was the only chance.

The wind filled his ears, blasting full-force into them, and a large piece of paper or cardboard tumbled into the room, slamming into the Stranger's back. He whirled and shook it off, and at last Elliott angled so the window was behind the Stranger. He gave a loud cry and shoved as hard as he could.

The beam slammed into the man's gut, sending him buckling backward, and Elliott let go of the wood. He saw Jade surge forward behind the Stranger, who staggered back, tripping over her.

Jade raised her arms and helped him on his way out the window and into the vortex of storm.

The Stranger cried out in surprise and anger as he tumbled through the opening, and as Elliott dove over next to Jade by the window, they saw the man spin, pummeled through the air, and then off into the darkness like the house in Dorothy Gale's tornado.

Without wasting any time, Elliott grabbed Jade's hand and

they moved quickly along the perimeter of the room, back toward the door to the stairwell. Crouching low, avoiding the variety of debris spinning and blustering, they reached the door and Elliott muscled it open.

The door slammed, and they were in the darker, safer, quieter space, huddled in the corner of the stairwell.

"Brilliant," he said against her hair, breathing hard, his head pounding and something warm leaking anew from the back of his skull. "You were brilliant."

"Thank you," she said. "You were brilliantly wixy yourself."

Reluctant to release her, Elliott nevertheless did—just enough to dig into the pack she still clutched. Moments later, he had the precious lighter in his hands and flicked it on.

The little flame wavered for a moment, then settled into a small orange spike. Elliott searched for something to use as a torch, for some reason unwilling to look at Jade right now. He figured he knew what would happen if he did.

"Here," she said, as if reading his mind. She handed him a dirty piece of fabric, likely gnawed from some long-lost break-room sofa or executive chair, then found to be too big for a nest.

He took the fabric, noticing that it was a little damp in places, then wadded it into a ball and sort of tied it into itself. There was nowhere to put it in this concrete-floored and walled area, so Elliott tucked it in the corner and knelt to tip the flame to an edge. It took a few tries, along with a bit of alcohol from the bottle in his pack, before it lit—but he was glad for the delay because it gave him time to collect himself.

By the time he got it lit, Elliott had other thoughts on his mind besides the woman next to him. But before he could speak, Jade said, "I recognized him. That Stranger was the same one I saw talking to Rob Nurmikko back in Envy. He's involved with whatever that cargo is, I'm sure of it."

"He attacked us right away," he said. "As soon as he saw us."

"I noticed that too," she said. "That in itself was a little weird. Normally, a Stranger wouldn't just . . . attack."

"But what is normal for a Stranger?" asked Elliott. "I mean, how do you know they wouldn't necessarily attack a human if they came across one unexpectedly."

She looked at him, her eyes glowing incredibly green, ringed with a thin band of black and flecked with the same. "Good point. They certainly are no friends of humans, and I've certainly seen them kill without remorse. But privately. They're careful not to do anything overt that might expose their evil to the masses." She shifted, her eyes widening in horror. "My God, you're bleeding, Elliott! Are you all right?"

"I'm fine," he replied, reaching automatically to touch the wound at the back of his skull. His fingers came away sticky, but the blood wasn't bright red. Jade looked as if she didn't believe him, so Elliott changed the subject as he dug in his pack for some first aid supplies. "You know a lot about the Strangers."

She nodded, her face becoming impassive.

The roar of the storm continued to buffet the walls around them, and Elliott used another of his shirts—which left him a total of one—to clean the slice at the back of his head. "I know it's probably not your favorite thing to relive, but will you tell me how you were captured by them?"

She settled back against the wall, the meager flames burning slowly through the wad of fabric, offering a minimal amount of light. Her knees bent, her arms folded around the front of them, her hair straggling down over her shoulders and the tops of her arms. But her eyes lifted toward him, still clear.

"I was married to a man named Daniel when I was sixteen. I thought I was in love with him—maybe I was, but it didn't last long. We didn't live in Envy, we lived in another settlement, fairly large, of maybe a couple hundred people. My mother remarried and moved there when I was twelve, and so I went with her and was married four years later.

"We were married for six years, but I stopped loving Daniel long before he died," she said, bitterness creeping into her voice. "When he couldn't accept that I couldn't get pregnant. When it became clear that I wasn't able to help him contribute to society."

"Contribute to society?" Of course. "By having children. By helping to repopulate the human race."

Jade nodded, then moved on with her story. "Anyway, Daniel was a bounty hunter."

"A bounty hunter? What does that mean?"

"Bounty hunters work for the Strangers. They help manage the *gangas* and do whatever dirty work the Strangers ask. Sometimes it includes finding and abducting people, sometimes it's scavenging or stealing. They're humans like us, but allied with the Strangers for whatever reason." She looked up at him with an odd expression on her face. "As a matter of fact, there's a bounty hunter by the name of Raul Marck who's after me. He'd bring me back for a big, fat reward if he ever found me."

Elliott stared at her, surprised by the blitheness of such a statement. "And yet you run around, traveling from place to place, where he might easily find you?"

Jade shrugged. "I could hole myself up and hide away the rest of my life, or I can be very careful and work against the bounty hunters and the Strangers, using what I learned during those three years to help the Resistance. Which one makes more sense?" She brushed a lock of hair from her face and continued, obviously not waiting for his opinion.

"So Daniel was a bounty hunter," she continued. "I didn't really understand much about what he did during that time. He traveled around a lot, and I just thought he was a trader—someone who finds goods, scavenges them, and brings them back for sale or barter. Or buys things from farmers or ranchers in the smaller settlements. But the Strangers realized Daniel was cheating them, playing them against each other, and he was executed by one named Preston. They gathered us up—me, his mistresses, and children—and were going to turn us over to the *gangas*."

"Turn you over to the *gangas?* What for?"

"That's how they feed. They eat human flesh—or, rather, they prefer it. I think they'll also eat animals. But only non-blondes. The blondes are taken away to the Strangers. I'm not sure if they're the lucky ones or not."

Jade drew in a long breath, fidgeting with the bracelets on her wrist, then continued. "So it was either be fed to the *gangas* or find some way to save us. I'd noticed in the past that Preston seemed . . . interested. In me. So I took advantage of that, figuring that nothing would be worse than being torn apart by flesh-eating monsters. I soon realized there was a chance I could be wrong." She was looking at him over the tops of her knees, almost matter-of-factly. As if she didn't dare think too much about it.

Now he moved, unable to remain still. He touched her, his fingers closing gently over the top of her cool hand. "Jade."

He drew in a breath to continue, but she talked over him, as if needing to get it off her chest. "I managed to get away after two aborted attempts, and now—you have to understand, Elliott . . . now I'll do anything to destroy the

Strangers." She looked at him, looked him fully in the face. "Whatever I have to do."

Elliott swallowed, his throat so dry it constricted audibly. "You were with the Strangers for three years?" He could only imagine what happened to her there . . . at the hands of a man who would have just as soon turned her—and children—over to flesh-eating zombies. *Good God.*

Jade lifted her left wrist, showing him the trio of bands there. "Three years. One bracelet for each year, one bead for each month. I stole the beads and gems from Preston—it was a small act of defiance, to sneak them from him or his clothing and use them to mark the days until I could get away." She smoothed slender fingers over the thin braided thongs. "One is woven from a skein of rope he tied me with. This one is made of leather, from a whip. The third is from one of the laced-up gowns he liked to see me wear."

She smiled, sort of crookedly, and looked back up at him. Elliott, who'd been feeling horribly nauseated at the thought of ropes and whips, was shocked by the bolt of emotion that rushed through him when their eyes met. Something real, and strong. Tangible.

"I wasn't a very accommodating concubine," she said. "I think that's part of what kept me alive, and kept him interested. He didn't get bored." She lifted her chin and swept a long swath of hair from her face. "Preston loved my hair—it was longer than this at the time. Nearly to my waist. I shaved it off. That was one of the few ways I was able to retain any control over my own body. I bribed some of the other servants to bring me razors so I could keep it shaved the whole time I was there, and there was nothing he could do about it."

"Nothing?" Elliott felt the word catch in his throat. He had an ugly feeling that "nothing" was a lie. A man who destroyed children and employed whips likely wouldn't let an act of defiance like that go unpunished.

"Nothing that mattered. He could beat me, or rape me, or whatever, but it wouldn't make my hair grow back. I was still in control."

Or whatever?

Elliott resisted the urge to shake his head. Was she really this strong? This unemotional? He saw nothing in her eyes that seemed weak or beaten. Nothing less than determination. Her whole life had been taken from her for three years—more, really, if she was in a loveless marriage to a man who thought of her only as a brood mare and took on mistresses to impregnate. No wonder she was a control freak. "You made it through three years of what must have been hell."

"It *was* hell, no question about that," she said, a little bit of that delicious smile tipping the corner of her mouth. "But it was preferable to death. Any life is preferable to death, in my mind. Because it can always improve. Once you're dead, you're dead. End of story. You know?"

He nodded in spite of himself, in spite of the nagging realization that there had been moments since he walked out of that cave that he'd wished for death. That he'd wished not to have to go on, now that things had changed. There'd been times when he knew he could never find comfort or a place for himself, because everything he'd ever known was gone.

"The storm's stopped," Jade said suddenly, and Elliott cocked his head to listen. Sure enough, the roar beyond had ceased.

A little grateful for the chance to assimilate all that she'd told him, to get his own emotions under control, Elliott said, "Let's check things out."

Carefully, he opened the door to the room in which they'd battled the Stranger, having a much easier time of it now that the wind had died down. The room was filled with shadows—debris blown in from the storm as well as the original furnishings. He saw no sign of any glow or illumination, and opened the door wide enough to let the limited light from their fire spill into the room.

Although it had been late afternoon when the storm descended, it was obviously well past dusk now. Elliott found a rusted out waste can and scooped the burning rag into it, toting the fire into the larger room.

"I just realized I'm hungry," Jade said. "I've got some things in my pack."

"I could eat too." Elliott glanced out at the darkness, feeling a gentle breeze, still damp from the storm. "I guess we're not going to make it back to Envy tonight. Unless you want to take the chance and travel in the dark."

Her expression sobered as she looked out the window. "No, it's too dangerous." She bit her lip, obviously torn, staring into the night.

Jade dug in her bag and pulled out bottles of water and some seasoned chicken wrapped in thin bread. Elliott produced an apple and some carrots and they sat in front of the little fire, to which he added a few handfuls of debris for fuel. And they ate, quiet for a time. He hadn't realized how hungry he was until he tasted the food.

"So now that I've told you my deep, dark secrets," Jade said, breaking the comfortable silence, "are you going to tell me yours?"

Surprised out of his own meditations, concentrating on *not* thinking too much about spending the night here with Jade in this disarrayed room, Elliott looked up. "What makes you think I have any deep dark secrets?"

"A guy who was frozen in time for half a century has to have some secrets." Her lips tipped up in a little smile. She had a crumb next to the corner of her curly mouth. "Besides the fact that you wouldn't shake Lou's hand and you yelled at me not to touch you."

"Oh. That deep, dark secret." He couldn't help returning the smile. She was becoming impossible to resist.

But he needed to keep his head, at least until he figured out what kind of woman Jade really was.

Maybe a woman who'd been forced to be a whore for three years would now jealously guard her sexual freedom— or even exercise it freely, because for so long she couldn't. Maybe being involved with a variety of men was Jade's rebellion against those years—having authority over her own body again, and being unwilling to jeopardize that.

She could feel she was giving up control by committing or tying herself down to one man. He already knew she needed control.

The problem was, Elliott was and always had been a one-woman man. He'd just been searching for that one woman for too long.

And, looking at Jade over the quiet fire, her intelligent eyes focused on him, her sexy mouth in that half-smile . . . knowing what she'd been through, witnessing her bravery on the horse and knowing that her quick thinking had helped him dispatch the Stranger tonight . . . he was terribly afraid he'd found *the one*. Here, in this post-apocalyptic hell, far from houses with white picket fences and school buses and the American Dream.

He was afraid he'd found her, and that she wasn't ready for *him*.

He realized he'd been staring, and had completely lost track of the conversation.

"So my deep dark secret is, I have this . . . problem," he said, recovering quickly. He leaned back against an old metal desk, putting space between them—as if that would make him stop thinking about lunging toward her. "I am a doctor—as hard as it might be for you to believe."

"Oh, I believe it now, knowing that you're from . . . before. And you're not only a doctor, but you seem to be able to heal people. You healed me. I wouldn't call *that* a deep, *dark* secret. Can't you do any better?"

His own short chuckle caught him by surprise. Pragmatic *and* controlling. What a package. "Well, how's this? I can actually read a person's body and then, if I focus hard enough, I can heal them, simply by concentrating. But there's a catch."

"Isn't there always?" She seemed so at ease, humor lighting her eyes, the tension dissolved from her face as if once she'd spoken of the disturbing memories, she could pack them away. Just as he did. Leaning forward, she began to untie her hiking boots.

"Yeah, well this one kind of sucks." The levity slipped from his mood, and he was reminded again of how fatal this deep, dark secret could be. "The catch is, when I heal someone, I seem to take their injury—whatever it is—into my own body. If I don't get rid of it, it stays with me, and grows worse. Very quickly."

Her smile had faded, and now her expression turned grave as she paused in the middle of untying her second boot. "How do you get rid of it? Oh . . . by touching someone? Is that it?"

Elliott nodded. "Right. So I pass it on to someone else whether I want to or not. Which can be a little bit of a problem."

"Yeah. I can see that. Wow. And I thought I had problems."

He hesitated . . . but she'd been pretty open with him. And he felt the need to tell someone. "I'm afraid I accidentally killed one of the men I was in the caves with. A guy named Lenny. I'm pretty sure I passed septic infection from an old man to Lenny. I saved the old man's life, and Lenny died." He glanced out at the window as the night breeze lifted a little more strongly. "I didn't realize how it worked then. And now I've been sort of playing it by ear, and that's why I've got to be careful about touching people. In case. . . ."

"In case you're carrying something." Her eyes narrowed speculatively, and Elliott's heart shifted. She was looking at him so . . . carefully.

"Today, I scanned the ladies in Greenside. One of them has terminal cancer. It's everywhere, in most of her organs."

"You could heal her, but . . . then you'd have to give it to someone else. Or keep it yourself." Clear understanding rang in her voice. Compassion softened her eyes.

"Right. Or I might be able to pass it on to a . . . cow or something. But maybe not. I don't know for sure how it works. So how do I make a decision like that?"

She shook her head. "You do the best you can. Isn't that what you did before? Isn't that what all the doctors do— House, the hot guy from *ER*, Hawkeye Pierce?"

"In theory. Hawkeye Pierce." He laughed softly. "He was my hero. He always did everything right, and felt so compassionately about it. I grew up watching reruns of *M*A*S*H*." Elliott shook his head. Hell, she didn't have a clue what a rerun was.

Once again they lapsed into a comfortable silence, and Elliott watched as she stretched out her long, jean-clad legs in front of her, next to the fire, and crossed her ankles.

Her feet were now bare. They were slender white feet, her toenails pale and colorless in this age without makeup and nail polish. He knew a thing about nail polish, having lost many a bet with his female cousins, which invariably resulted in him either painting their nails, or, once, to his horror, painting his own. Hot pink.

He couldn't hold back another little laugh at the memory, and then became aware of how, though he grieved, the memories had become fond as well as painful. Elliott couldn't remember feeling such . . . ease since waking up in this new world.

"Are you going to share the joke?" Jade asked, sounding mildly interested.

"Sure. My mom left my dad and me when I was really young—three or four."

Her face sobered. "I'm so sorry, Elliott."

"I hardly remember her, but I got my share of maternal attention and love from my father's sisters and his mother, all of whom lived in the same neighborhood as we did. Dad and I moved in with my *abuela*, my grandmother, and I grew up with ten female cousins. I was the only boy."

"I can imagine what those girls did to you," Jade said, laughter in her voice. "Brushing your hair, dressing you up, making you their baby. I grew up in a similar sort of environment—extended families living close together. We were a mixed bunch, though there were a lot of us girls. And the poor boys. . . ." Jade's voice trailed off into a little bubble of laughter that charmed Elliott even more than her slender, naked feet. And that was saying a lot.

Hoo-boy. He was getting in deeper by the minute. Yet he couldn't keep his own smile in check, nor resist meeting her dancing eyes with his own laughing gaze. "They did. But most often, they made me be their puppy and crawl around on all fours. I ate cereal out of a dish on the floor," he added, wondering if she knew what Cheerios were.

"Poor thing," she said, the glint in her eyes belying the sentiment.

"Yeah. I was completely miserable."

"Must be why you're so good with women," she said. "All those ladies in Greenside were completely enamored with you today." Then she sobered again. "So did you heal Della?" she asked.

"Not that I'm aware of," he said honestly. "I didn't attempt it. I—well, as soon as I realized it, I stopped touching her."

Instead of looking at him as if he were a heel, Jade nodded. "That's not the type of decision that can be made in a snap like that."

"No. Definitely not."

"And it seems as if . . . well, Elliott. Your gift is pretty special. Jeopardizing your own life, and therefore your gift, could have a bigger impact. I mean, if something happened to you, there wouldn't *be* someone like you—to heal people."

That was true, he supposed. True, and a little edifying, when put that way. He could do a lot more good if he were alive than if he were dead.

"So you're safe now? You're not carrying anything?" Jade looked at him from across the fire, which had kicked up into a healthy little blaze thanks to the added debris.

"Yes."

"Good," she whispered, and, with sleek movements, moved toward him . . . and suddenly, she was looking up at him, her face close . . . so close.

His heart was slamming hard and her mouth was just . . . there. A breath away. Then she lifted her face and brushed her lips against his, so lightly it was little more than a whisper. But sweet. Oh, so sweet. He felt his body lift, tingle, come alive.

But he didn't move. Barely breathed. The ceiling seemed to drop lower, the night pressed in against him. He felt her breathing against him, gentle and easy.

And then she brushed against him again, and stopped when their mouths were aligned, lip over lip, and she pressed, slipped the tip of her tongue out and over the seam of his lips. Elliott was aware of a sudden rush of warmth, and he closed his eyes, just held there and felt the *rightness* of the moment, of the gentle, sweet kiss as his lips moved just as softly against hers. The taste. The light pressure. The tug of intimacy, drawing deep from his belly.

This is it.

After a moment, she pulled slowly away and gave a little laugh. Low and husky, the sound sent a little shiver over him. Her lips glistened and quirked at the corners, and he almost kissed her again. But instead he drew in a deep breath and remained still, stunned and fighting himself from dragging her onto the floor beneath him.

Jade was smiling when their mouths met again, but he felt the curve slip away as their lips melded together, hot and hungry and urgent. His hands came up around her shoulders, tugging her into his lap, and he felt her hand caught between them, splayed on his chest. All reason deserted him, replaced by a low-burning, deep need to delve deeper, taste more . . . to lose himself.

Elliott gave up. Those full, sexy lips covered his, all soft and warm and sinful. Want blazed through him when he tasted her, slipping his tongue into her mouth and tangling with hers, holding her head with one hand so he could delve deeper.

He closed his eyes, forgot to breathe, forgot everything but Jade and the heat of her mouth, the teasing, sultry nibble of her teeth, the softness of her lips.

He *needed* this. Her.

She sighed, turning her face away and drawing in a breath even as he couldn't stop tasting the corner of her lips, that little devious curl. Her hand slipped around his neck, her fingers touching the tender skin there.

The lemon scent from her hair was in his nose, along with the gentle smell of woman, of Jade, the faintly salty taste of her. Warm, soft flesh curving under his hands, pressing into him, even a gentle gasp when he thumbed over one of her nipples. Lifting her shirt, feeling the smooth skin, the elastic of her bra. . . .

And then, somehow, he caught himself, dragging himself back when he realized that another man's hand had been here only hours ago. And his mouth. . . .

He released her, moving away before his body overruled his head.

"Elliott?" Jade leaned awkwardly toward him balancing on one hand, her eyes heavy-lidded and bedroomy, her lips full and slick, her hair a tumbled mass around her face and shoulders.

A teen boy's wet dream, right here, right in front of him. Elliott closed his eyes, trying to reason with his raging erection, which argued, *Come on, come on, it's been fifty years.*

"Jade," he said as much to focus himself as to get her attention. And damn if he wasn't breathing like he'd run a marathon. "I'm not into this."

"Into what?" She gave a little raspy laugh of confusion. "Kissing?"

"I'm not interested in being one of your conquests."

"Conquests?"

"I don't share," he said flatly, trying to get the words out as quickly as possible, knowing it all sounded harsh and sharp. But he had to talk fast before he forgot what he needed to say. "Not with Luke, or the cowboy guy from the club last night—yes, I saw you leave with him. And not with any other man that you might booty call with on your Running missions."

She sat away, looking at him, eyes wide and startled. Then she scooted back, taking those just-kissed lips and pretty feet with her. Elliott's breathing settled and he busied himself by picking up a rusty stapler and examining it. At least, pretending to.

"So is that what you meant about my cowboy boyfriend?" she asked at last.

He nodded. He wanted to ask *Who is he?* He wanted to demand to know why she was spreading herself around like that . . . but he resisted. He suspected a woman who'd been through what she had wouldn't react well to angry male demands.

"That was Vaughn Rogan. He's the mayor of Envy," she told him. "We're old friends. Not lovers."

Elliott didn't trust himself to speak. They hadn't looked like friends.

Jade shifted and gave a soft sigh. "We tried to be lovers once, about three years ago, when I first came back to Envy. But it didn't work. I was . . . well, I was a mess, having finally escaped from Preston. And Vaughn had recently lost a woman he loved. So instead of becoming lovers, we became friends—and let everyone else think we were involved. Because it was easier for both of us."

He nodded. *Yeah, right.* She might disavow her interest in Rogan, but Elliott wasn't stupid. The Marlboro Man wannabe was definitely interested in going beyond friendship. He'd be a fool not to be even if it hadn't been blazing in his eyes for all to see.

"Thank you for telling me," Elliott said at last. And waited to see what she'd say about Luke.

She looked at him, but didn't speak. Silence hung there for a moment, blending with the dust motes that wavered in the half-light, and the only sound was the low rush of their breathing and a faint crackle in the pot of fire.

And after a long moment, she looked away. "I think I'm ready for some sleep," she said.

Elliott felt as if he'd missed something important. Had she expected him to suddenly sweep her into his arms after her confession?

"I'll keep watch," he said. He didn't think the Stranger would be able to get back, but he wasn't going to be stupid about it.

Despite the burning in his dry eyes and the continued trembling in his muscles, the ache in his head, the weariness that he'd managed to put aside for a while, Elliott knew he'd be unable to sleep.

Especially when he had to watch over Jade.

CHAPTER 12

Jade woke in a pale yellow dawn to find Elliott curled around her.

She lay there for a moment without moving, simply *feeling.* Warm, muscular arms wrapped around her from behind, her head tucked under his chin, his legs curled into hers at the backside of her knees. Even his feet angled gently beneath her heels. A blanket covered them both.

She was warm, and comfortable, and she felt . . . utterly relaxed. Free.

Free to be who she was, free to do what she wished without any expectation from the man touching her. Free to make decisions, and to have him not only listen to her opinions, but to accept them. Act on them.

Free to retreat, as she had, to the other side of the fire last night. Without feeling as if she had to follow through on what had been one hell of a kiss.

And a revelation too. Elliott had wanted her, and yet . . . he'd wanted her on his own terms.

She wasn't sure how she felt about that. And so she'd withdrawn, half expecting him to demand, or to coax, or seduce—especially after she'd explained about Vaughn. And not about Luke. Because she realized she didn't have to answer to him.

She wouldn't. He'd have to take her as she was, or not at all. She had nothing to hide or to be ashamed of.

And so he'd simply taken her explanation, thanked her for it, and that was it.

He was different. Sensitive, serious, smart . . . and holy-crap strong. Even now, the memory of those sleek muscles moving with such grace in the Tunnel, the fierce battle against the Stranger here in this very room after he'd tried to get her to run to safety . . . it made her warm and tingly inside in a basic, female way. Her mouth went dry. Her heart picked up speed. Her belly did that little flip that sent tingles through her.

That kiss had been just the tip of the iceberg, though it had been anything but cold. Hot and sleek and oh-my-God. Definitely.

But the fact that he'd wanted it too—oh, he'd definitely wanted it—and had declined . . . what kind of man did that? Especially one who'd shown off his prowess and masculinity hours earlier?

What kind of man was he, to reject her advances, and then to curl around her in the night while she was sleeping? To keep her warm, and to expect nothing else.

"Are you ready?" came his voice near her ear, surprising her. Though it was low and deep, it didn't sound as if he'd just awakened.

And then . . . *oh my*. She realized what she felt pressing into her rear, hard and rigid. A wisp of regret slipped through her, just for a moment. Then it was gone. She wanted him too. No doubt about that.

Jade twisted around in his embrace, awkward because of their position, but she managed to get halfway toward him, her face toward the water-stained ceiling instead of looking away. She saw the dark fringe of lashes over his ocean blue eyes, and how a lock of dark hair had caught just at the tips of them. God, he was breathtaking to look at, with those full lips and square chin and dark brows.

"Mmhmmm," she said. "And I'm not the only one, hmm?" She shifted her hip teasingly into his hard-on.

His face turned grim. "Sorry. I didn't mean that." He released her, and with his body no longer acting like a wedge, she rolled fully onto her back. "I meant, are you ready to get going," he said, pulling to his feet.

"Sure."

Jade wasn't certain whether to be embarrassed or elated that he'd rejected her yet again, but the look in his eyes tipped her toward the elated side. She didn't really understand why he was saying *no* when his whole body was practically vibrating with *yes*, especially since she'd told him about Vaughn. He couldn't *seriously* think she had any interest in that lunk Luke, did he? Especially after that ridiculous comment he'd made about dropping his prices if she put Greenside on her Running route. But it was all right with her if Elliott wanted some space.

At least for now. Because she had bigger things to worry about. Like where Theo was, and what kind of cargo Nurmikko was putting together.

"There's water collected outside," Elliott said as he stood. "To wash up. And I want to take a look at that humvee."

Jade frowned as she gathered up her pack. "I was thinking, as I fell asleep last night, that it was a little odd to find a Stranger alone. Usually they travel in twos or threes. And the fact that he attacked us right away . . . it made me wonder if those two facts are connected."

"Like, he was alone because he'd gone rogue or something?" Elliott asked. Her confusion must have shown on her face, for he explained, "Gone off on his own. Maybe he did and expected someone to come after him—and that was why he attacked first."

"That could be." Jade looked around the room. "He was lying there when we came in. Maybe he had something with him he was trying to protect."

The huge tree branch that had broken the window lay amid splinters and shards on the floor, and she noticed that there were other pieces of wood and glass embedded in the walls from the gale force. She shivered. How easily it could have been one of them that were skewered by the missiles.

Desks and chairs, a variety of electronics, debris from the storm, other items she couldn't identify had been strewn around the room as well. Ashes smoldered in the waste can. She walked over to where the Stranger appeared to have been sleeping, shoving the tree branch away.

"What's this?" she asked, lifting an oblong metal object that looked like it would open and close. "A stapler?"

"Yep," Elliott replied, looking up momentarily from his own explorations. "Hey. I found something." He lifted a backpack that didn't appear to be old or torn and began to rifle through it. A moment later, she heard a soft jingle and he pulled his hand out, holding a set of keys. "I'm betting these are to the humvee," he said, a smile breaking over his face. "We might be driving back to Envy."

Jade's heart leaped. She sure would like him to smile at her like that. "I haven't been in a truck for a long time," she said, remembering how unpleasant her last trip had been. That was when Raul Marck had captured her after her second escape attempt, and brought her back to Preston. For a big reward, of course.

Elliott pulled more items out of the pack, including a little book. Standing there, hips cocked to one side as he used an elbow to hold the backpack against him, he flipped through the book. The sun filtered in behind him, highlighting the dust stirred up by their investigations and tingeing the edges of his rich dark hair. Last night, she'd smoothed her hands over the wide, square shoulders and felt the swell of muscle beneath his warm skin, and watching that tall, lean figure in rugged jeans and a close-fitting red shirt made her feel all lightheaded and tingly.

Jade moistened her lips and swallowed. *Whew.* There was definitely something about Elliott Drake. Maybe she would be willing to answer to him.

No. That was ridiculous.

"What's in the book?" she asked, unable to keep from moving closer to him. His hands, large and powerful, were nevertheless elegantly shaped, with long, tanned fingers. She noticed two blackened fingernails and a few cuts on the side of his thumb.

"Lists of people, it looks like. Not an address book—it's got ages and gender listed. Hmm. Height and weight? A list of patients?" He seemed to be talking to himself, thinking aloud. "Some drawings that look like maps. And . . . hey, I've seen this before," he said, his voice taut as he stabbed one of his fingers at the book. "But I can't remember."

"Let me see," she said, moving closer, her heart suddenly clogging her throat. She was suddenly so aware of him, so eager to get close to him. And yet, her palms sprang damp and her pulse pounded.

She looked around his arm at the book, and saw the symbol there. The labyrinth with a swastika superimposed on it and a border that looked like curling waves. She knew it well. "Oh, yes. That's the symbol the Strangers use to identify themselves."

Elliott murmured, "I've seen it somewhere before." He

pressed his lips together as Jade stepped back, for self-preservation as much as to be able to look at him. "Quent will know. He's probably the one who showed it to me." He slammed the book shut and shoved it back into the pack. "We'd better get going, see if I can get the truck started."

"On to Envy."

The second morning he woke in Envy, Quent tried to find his way back to Lou's hidden computer center, and ended up in some dank, dirty, overgrown area inside the hotel. Every bloody time he touched a wall, he heard screams and saw blood and visionless eyes and other nightmarish images of crumbling walls, yawning crevices, fire, and raging destruction.

Sagging, sweat pouring down his face and terror in his brain, he closed his eyes, fighting the pull of memories that didn't belong to him. Memories he didn't want and didn't need . . . thoughts he could no longer control.

The floor rose up beneath him, and he was swept away into madness and fear and pain. . . .

"Quent!"

The sound of his name tugged at him, and then pressure on his shoulders and arm drew him from the darkness that had overtaken him. Slowly, slowly, his mind crawled back to reality, and at last he opened his eyes.

Elliott Drake looked down at him.

"Quent, what the hell are you doing here?" His face was taut with concern. "What happened?" Before he could reply, Dred's hands were moving over him, scanning to be certain he wasn't injured.

But it wasn't his body that was fucked up.

"I got lost," he said, sitting up slowly. It had never been this bad before . . . the memories had never been that strong, that overwhelming. He realized with a deep, leveling shock that he no longer recognized his environment. Hadn't his last real memory been of an overgrown part of the hotel, inside the building?

Now a blue sky blazed above him and moss-covered, mildew-blackened buildings rose in close quarters around him. He was lying on the ground, outside, and Dred and the woman . . . Jade . . . were crouched next to him.

What were they doing here? Hadn't they left Envy on some mission?

Quent reached out and connected with Dred's hand. No, it was really him, real flesh and blood. "What are you doing here?" he managed to ask.

"We just got back. We were coming into town and found you here." Dred looked as though he were ready to call the guys in the white coats, and maybe he damn well should. "How long have you been here?"

Quent shook his head. "I don't know. I was looking for Lou's room and got lost. The next thing I know, I touched something. The memories swarmed over me, the images and violence . . . I don't remember anything after that." He was sitting up fully now, and only a lingering cloudiness remained. "Is it still Wednesday? I left my room around nine thirty or so."

Elliott's face relaxed a little. "Yes. It's not quite noon on Wednesday. So you haven't been gone for too long."

Thank God.

"But you're back from . . . where did you go?"

"A place called Greenside," Jade said, speaking for the first time. "We have some things for Lou to look at, and Elliott thought you should take a look as well." She sat back on her haunches and glanced at Dred. "It's a good thing we came back in through the Tunnel, or we wouldn't have found you here, in this area of town." She glanced up and gestured to the building closest to him. "You must have come out here, which is on the unused side of the place. This is where we go in and come out when we don't want to be seen."

Dred was nodding. "Can you stand?"

"Yeah, as long as I don't fucking touch anything I ought to be just fine," he said flatly.

"Let's go in and find Lou," Jade said. "Maybe get you something to eat."

Quent nodded, standing on his own, and wondering how the hell he was going to get through the rest of his life here in this place if he couldn't touch anything unfamiliar without going into a tailspin.

He could use something to eat . . . or, better yet, something bloody strong to drink.

Elliott followed Jade back through the hotel, keeping a sharp eye on Quent. Now that he was conscious again, and took care not to do so much as brush against the wall, his friend seemed to be fully recovered. Elliott had found nothing unusual when he scanned the guy.

Apparently, like himself, Quent had contracted some sort of paranormal ability that had seemed fantastic at the outset, but was really a double-edged sword.

Elliott found it disconcerting, to say the least, that Simon, Fence, and Wyatt hadn't come away with any paranormal abilities like he and Quent had. Even the unfortunate Lenny had acquired a new skill—the ability to sense water, like a human divining rod. That had been ability that came in handy when they first emerged from the caves.

But Lenny's death had put to bed any possibility that their special skills and fifty-year "sleeps" had somehow made the six of them immortal, or immune to injury or death. Their hair and nails might not be growing, like that of mythological vampiric creatures, but the sunlight didn't bother them. Nor would they live forever.

Elliott realized Jade had led them back to the part of the hotel that teemed with activity like any other town. They walked through a walled-in area designed like the streets of a city, but which had originally been the interior lobby of the hotel. The ceiling or roof was gone, and storefronts and restaurants lined the "streets" that were now real streets with real trees and paved walkways, giving the impression of a quaint downtown area.

"Let's get something to eat," Jade said, gesturing to the same little restaurant they'd gone into the first night they were in Envy. "Then I can send word to Lou that we're back without making a big deal about it," she added softly to Elliott.

But Lou, Fence, Wyatt, and Simon were already in the restaurant, sitting in a large corner booth in the back.

"Where've you been?" Wyatt asked Quent.

"You're back," Lou said to Jade and Elliott at the same time.

As they settled in the booth with the others, Elliott still holding the pack they'd taken from the Stranger, Jade explained briefly how they'd come upon Quent.

"Everyone eats here," Lou was explaining to Fence, who must have broached the question when Elliott wasn't paying attention. "Here or at one of the other restaurants—there are five all together." He looked around the table. "I know, it's like *Cheers*, but when we first started to rebuild, it just evolved that way. Most people who live in Envy live in what were hotel rooms or suites, and have made them their homes. But no one really has the means to cook."

"So it's like a commune," Fence said. Elliott noticed he

looked rather haggard, and whoa! Was that stubble on his face? Actual stubble? And on his bald head?

Elliott dragged a hand over his own chin to check his status. Nope. Still smooth as a baby's butt. He wasn't complaining, because he'd have a full-blown Robinson Crusoe beard by now if his hair had been growing. It was just damned weird.

Lou replied, "A community, rather than a commune. The meals aren't free; people do have to pay for them. But it's easier to prepare the food with the limited electricity and supplies we have, as well as the fact that there's no reason to have a stove or fridge in every home." Then he grinned. "It suits me fine, because I've never liked to cook."

"And you never miss a meal," Jade said fondly. Elliott heard her add in an undertone, "We've got stuff. Let's make this fast and get out of here."

Lou nodded and gestured for the waitress. Elliott watched in amazement as, before his eyes, Lou turned from a sharp-eyed computer whiz into a musty-gazed, dottering old man who could barely express his request . . . which was for the woman to wrap up a couple sandwiches for the group. "You remind me of my granddaughter, you do," he said, his voice sounding aged. "She lives over there, you know. Her name is Carly. Do you know her? She comes in here all the time, you know. And I want to order four sandwiches—"

The waitress was kind, but brisk. "Of course, Mr. Wax. I'm going to get those for you right now." And she fled.

Lou turned back to Elliott, laughter in his suddenly bright eyes. "Works every time. They hate to hear me talk about my granddaughter."

"That's because you don't have a granddaughter," Jade reminded him.

"I know that, and they know that . . . but they don't realize I know that."

"So how *do* we pay for our meals while we're here?" Elliott asked. "And what do they use for currency?"

"You needn't worry about that for a while. For now, Mayor Rogan has given you carte blanche in thanks for saving the kids. If you decide to stay in Envy, arrangements will be made for what we call community service, which will assist with the costs. The rest you'll be able to pay for with income that you generate through whatever you choose to do." Lou said. "As for currency . . . what do you think? Casino chips." He grinned.

"Lou, you go on. I'll be down in a few." Jade's gaze swept everyone, but her words were for Elliott. "I've want to check on Geoff and say hi to Flo . . . she worries when I'm gone. I'll be down in a few minutes. Why don't you take this." She handed him the Stranger's pack.

Elliott wanted to say, Hurry back. But he thought that would make him sound pathetic.

What the hell. He was pathetic. He watched her as she hurried away, wondering when he'd have the chance to get her alone again.

Why had he been so foolish as to let the opportunity slip by last night?

He directed his gaze away. He knew why. Because he needed to know there was no one else. He wasn't the kind of guy to plan and execute a siege for a woman, pitting himself against a group of rivals. He'd learned that lesson back in high school when he was lobbying to take Mary Ellen Fray to the prom. He'd won that bid, paid for the limo and flowers and an expensive dinner—all so she could show off for the guy she really liked—and for whom she'd dumped Elliott two days later.

So he'd made it a policy not to waste his time unless he

knew the woman was interested enough to concentrate on him. Period.

"I want to know why there are so many pregos around here," Fence muttered in Elliott's ear as they stood to leave.

"I'd suppose that if the human race was nearly destroyed, it would make sense to try and repopulate it as quickly and efficiently as possible," Quent commented. "Looks as if it's working."

"Cool. Free love and all," Fence replied, his smile flashing wickedly. "I can help with that."

Lou must have heard them, for he stopped his fake shuffling walk, and turned to address Quent. "Actually, that was quite a bone of contention for a while, early on. There were people who wanted, literally, to set up breeding arrangements and to actually monitor them. But most of us agreed that it would be best to let nature take its course, with an emphasis on trying to find a mate and procreate."

He took a few slow steps, then turned with a smile and said, "There are, after all, no condoms or any other birth control anymore. There's no reason for it, and in fact, it would almost be considered bad taste to try and prevent a pregnancy. Our fertile women are well cared for and encouraged to have as many children as they like."

Logical and interesting. And a relief that procreation wasn't somehow managed or controlled by the governing body, for that could easily have happened in a society desperate to regenerate itself.

"Don't you worry about inbreeding?" asked Elliott.

"We do. We keep very careful records," Lou explained. "But we're only on our second generation since the Change, and so far there hasn't been a problem. And of course, now the five of you have appeared. New, fresh blood." He smiled and stroked his goatee. "Be prepared to be accosted."

"Hot damn," said Fence. "That's me. Fresh fucking blood."

"Wouldn't that be fresh blood *fucking*?" Lou said with a laugh.

Elliott snorted. He was really beginning to appreciate the elderly man's sense of humor and pragmatism. Considering what he'd lived through, and how much of a hand he must have had in the evolution of this new society, he was very practical and energetic. It could have been much different if the wrong person—or people—had survived.

Three months After

Have settled into life, such as we know it.

It's clear that no one from the outside will come to help. Whatever happened has happened everywhere. No planes, no sign of any human life besides us.

Number has grown to 765—survivors from Vegas and others that have wandered until they found us. Have made the hotel's Statue of Liberty visible. A new role for her.

Emergency and urgent task teams have now turned into day-to-day operations intent on creating a communal life. Everyone seems to have found a place of expertise: Food, Clothing, Cooks, Clean-up, Foraging, Power. (I'm working in Power and Theo and I are stocking up any electronics we can find.) He's working with Entertainment too. Need to have something to think about other than what's happened. Movies each night on a big screen. Very surreal.

Theo calls it sitting around the campfire, post-apocalyptic-style.

Some smart people have scavenged food from what's left of the grocery stores and are working to cultivate plants from seeds. Others have gone off in search of farms, trying to find anything that can be saved and grafted or otherwise propagated. Talk about thinking ahead. What a bitch it would be if someone ate the last strawberry, and we didn't have any way to grow them again.

There's talk of creating an official governing body. Makes sense as there have already been some incidents. Last night, looters came through to steal what they could—don't know where they came from, or what they think they're going to do with the money they took from the casino cash office.

Where do they think they're going to spend it? Boneheads.

Heard a strange noise last night. Sounded like someone groaning, calling for Ruth. Chose not to investigate.

All the bodies are gone, scavenged by animals. Or something.

—from the journal of Lou Waxnicki

CHAPTER 13

Sage seemed a bit less annoyed today when Elliott and the others followed Lou into the computer room. She glanced up at them briefly and noticed Elliott. "You're back. Where's Jade?"

"She'll be along in a bit," Elliott said.

Sage gave Lou a disgruntled look as if it were his fault they were interrupting her, then returned to her work.

"If looks could kill," Lou muttered with a grin. "She's really good at that."

"Don't you ever let her out into the sunshine?" Wyatt asked in his off-handed manner. He didn't have the greatest way with women. In fact, Elliott had always wondered how the sonofabitch had managed to get married.

Sage gave Wyatt a dark look from deep blue eyes, but said nothing as she presented them with her rigid back. Her fingers began to tap away again on one of the keyboards.

"Quent, you wanted to see the satellite images," Lou said. "We still have them, and others. Theo and I monitored them until the satellite burned out about forty years ago."

"I'd like to see them too," Elliott said, wondering if actual proof of the worldwide destruction would make it easier or more difficult for him to accept it. "And then I have some things to show you that Jade and I picked up from a Stranger."

"What? From a Stranger?" Lou stopped.

"We surprised him and managed to get away unscathed, and with not only his knapsack, but his vehicle as well."

"Well, that's a story I want to hear," the old man said as he sat at one of the computers in a corner. It had two big screens and a keyboard so well used that all of the letter markings had faded away, but the elderly geek didn't need them; he sat and typed rapidly, and with no indication of arthritis. "There aren't too many people who are accosted by a Stranger and live to tell about it. But let me pull these images up for you first. I know you really need to see them to believe it."

Elliott sat in a chair next to him and looked around. The room was empty of any decoration other than computer boxes and monitors. He saw no printers either, and wondered at that. On the plain white wall above Lou's computer hung a California license plate that said WIXY 97, which happened to be the year he'd graduated from pre-med. *Wixy?* Elliott couldn't help a smile. So that's where that had come from. It was the only thing hanging anywhere in the room, and it roused his curiosity.

"What's the license plate for?" he asked. "Is it from your car?"

Lou glanced up as his fingers continued to move, and he gave a little laugh. "Not *my* car. Just a plate we found. It's hanging here as a memorial. Way back when we first started to put together this network"—he gestured to encompass the room—"we knew we had to keep it secret. Underground, so to speak."

"Why would a computer network need to be kept secret?" Quent interrupted.

"Because the Strangers don't want we mortals to become

powerful again. Or to learn about them and overthrow their control. They want to keep us simple and ignorant. Aside from that, if they don't know it exists, they can't hack into it."

It sounded so paranoid, but Elliott no longer questioned it. He'd seen enough in the last two days alone for his mind, even if it had been closed, to crack wide open.

Lou continued. "We were trying to think of a password or phrase we could use to identify people who were part of the Resistance. One of our first Runners, Rick Halpert—who was killed by the Strangers about a year ago—happened to see that plate and suggested using the word 'wixy' as our password. So we tried it at first, but now it's sort of leaked out into regular conversation as a slang word—you'd try it out on someone to see if they recognized it and responded, and the next thing we knew, it had been picked up. Most passwords aren't such unique words that catch the attention of people—they're just phrases. But now you'll hear kids talk about something being 'wixy,' which means it's good or cool . . . whatever it is they're talking about. Like, that's a wixy jacket or a wixy tune. And if something's really cool or awesome, it's 'van halen.' " He gave a little chuckle.

Then he stood. "I can see that you're having trouble believing all of this, which is why we refrained from dumping it all on you before. Believe me, there's a lot to know. But I've had fifty years to figure it out, to learn and understand and believe it. You five . . . well, I can't imagine how you must be feeling."

PTSD, *anyone*?

"Here. Take a look. These are the first images we saw after Theo was able to hack into a couple satellites—almost a year after the Change. They speak for themselves."

Elliott took Lou's place at the computer, his palms suddenly sweaty, his heart pounding. Quent and the others moved to stand behind him, and together they looked at the images, which were clearly time-stamped, 14.05.2011.

It didn't take long for Elliott to see that Lou hadn't been mistaken, nor had he exaggerated. It really was the Pacific Ocean spilling over what had been California and the Baja Peninsula. And there was a large land mass, maybe the size of Colorado, about two hundred miles west of where California's coast had been.

The rest of the images left Elliott just as shaken.

"Jesus," Wyatt breathed.

"Everything I know about plate tectonics says that the legends about Mu and Atlantis and Lemuria sinking into the ocean are impossible," said Quent, his voice bleeding with disbelief. "Which would mean that continents rising *from* the depths would be equally impossible. But there it fucking is. It certainly wasn't there when I flew to Hawaii."

When Elliott turned away at last, he met Lou's gaze and saw sympathy, and a bit of hope there. How must he feel, to have more people who actually understood the gravity of what had happened? "Unfuckingbelievable," he said. "It's just . . . incomprehensible."

"Yeah. That's about what we thought," Lou replied.

"And you think that the Strangers somehow did this? How? Do you think they're aliens?"

Hell, maybe the so-called landmass was a huge space-ship that had landed on the ocean. Why not? If there were zombie-like *gangas* in this strange new world, there could be continental spaceships and aliens to go along with them.

Lou drew in a breath, hesitated, then let it out. "I have my theories about that as well."

"Lou," Sage interrupted sharply. "An email from Theo."

Elliott stood, needing to get away from the satellite

images, and wandered around the room. Nervous energy ticked through him.

"Let me see it," Lou said, his tone equally raw. He moved to her side so quickly it belied his age, and moments later, he said, "About damn time. . . ." His voice trailed off and the angry clicking of keys ensued.

Sage moved quickly to give over her chair, but still hovered behind, leaning over the elderly man with his blond ponytail and worried mouth.

"Well, at least he's okay," Lou muttered to himself, still typing furiously. "He's close to finding a way to hack into Chatter . . . says that he's not leaving until he does." He sighed, smoothed his hand over his ponytail. "Next time, don't leave us hanging for days," he added, keying in what was obviously an annoyed reprimand.

Elliott came to stand next to Sage, behind Lou, far enough away that they wouldn't feel crowded, but close enough that he could watch the five screens in a half-moon array in front of them.

Two of them held text that scrolled through, black on a white screen. A third one looked like a regular Windows-based email program, a fourth was, amazingly, Google. *Google?* No, wait . . . it was *Yahoogle*. The Waxnicki brothers had a hell of a sense of humor.

And the fifth screen. . . .

Elliott frowned and leaned closer to look at the image. "Hey, that's the symbol we found in the Stranger's book," he said, pointing to the screen and what looked like a crude drawing carved into stone. "Quent, take a look at this. Have you seen it before?"

Sage looked up, tension on her delicate face. "We've been trying to identify that symbol," she explained dismissively.

"The Strangers use it to identify themselves, and we've been looking for other uses or history that might tell us more about them."

"I know exactly what it is," Quent said, standing up straight. His face looked pale. "It's the symbol for the Cult of Atlantis."

"The Cult of Atlantis." Lou's fingers froze on the keyboard. He turned to look up behind him, and their eyes met.

Elliott could almost hear what they were thinking. He was thinking it too. No way.

Atlantis. In the Pacific Ocean.

Jade wasn't able to find Geoff, which bothered her more than it should have.

But surely he wasn't foolish enough to make another mistake like he had only three days ago. And his parents didn't seem to be concerned that they hadn't seen him since early that morning, at breakfast. School wasn't in session, and he and the other teens spent their free time doing odd jobs or learning trades, which often included discovering ways to reuse or remake scavengeable items found elsewhere and transported in to Envy.

After leaving Geoff's home, Jade thought about making a quick stop to try and find Rob Nurmikko . . . just to see if she could glean anything from him. But she decided that might be best left to someone who couldn't be recognized by a Stranger or a bounty hunter. Someone who didn't have a reward on her head.

So she went to see Flo, because she knew the older woman worried about her whenever she left Envy. It was a good thing she didn't know exactly what Jade was up to when she went on her Running missions, for then she'd worry even more.

"Vaughn was looking for you yesterday," Flo said after her greeting hug. She was shorter than Jade, but soft as a downy pillow, and she always smelled like the roses she grew in a tiny courtyard. Roses, and whatever cosmetics or beauty aid she was experimenting with on that particular day. Her short strawberry blond hair still retained its brilliant color except for an inch-wide stripe of blond coming from one side of her part—the result of a dyeing experiment gone wrong two years ago. Her current favorite style was that of the movie star Marilyn Monroe, with a deep sweep of bang over one eye and the ends flipped up all around in what she called a pageboy. Jade felt that was an improvement over the last trend Flo had attempted to imitate—something called feathering, which had been popular in the 1970s.

Despite the fact that Flo was more than a decade older than Jade, an array of freckles spattered over her round cheeks and pug nose—which was why many of her cosmetic experiments revolved around finding a way to fade freckles.

"What happened?" Jade asked, grimacing. Vaughn had had a lot of questions after her performance the other night—where she'd been, what she'd been doing, and why she hadn't rehearsed that afternoon. She'd had to evade his question by making up an excuse about taking care of Flo's granddaughter.

"I just told him you had a bad headache and had gone to rest. Thank goodness you're back already—I was wondering what to tell him if he came by again today. You'd think the mayor of Envy would be too busy to be checking up on you."

Jade smiled and shook her head. "Vaughn's very hands-on. I mean, he's more than a figurehead mayor. That's why everyone admires him so much, because he doesn't just sit around and give orders. But he's going to think I'm the sickliest thing ever. Didn't you use that headache excuse three weeks ago?"

"Now don't worry about that," Flo said, patting her hand with a small, pudgy one, beringed within an inch of its life. She wore eight rings and five bracelets on that appendage alone. "I just told him it was your time of the month, and he skedaddled before I could give him any further details. As far as he knows, when your aunt Pearl comes to visit, you get it bad."

Jade rolled her eyes, but couldn't help a smile. "I guess that'll work as long as I keep to a monthly schedule for my travels. Not that he needs such an intimate look into my life."

"Now tell me all about that gorgeous man you took off with you," Flo insisted. "I could eat him up with a spoon. Even without strawberry sauce."

"But not without whipped cream?" Jade laughed, and felt her cheeks heat under the other woman's direct gaze. "He's nice."

"Nice? Honey, that's what you say when I try a new hairstyle. Especially when you don't like it. Now tell me the truth. Did you make a nuisance of yourself by telling him how to walk, talk, and breathe?"

"No. Well, a little. He . . . well, he actually listens to me. He's not always telling me what to do." She felt her cheeks grow warmer.

Flo's brown eyes widened, and her well-plucked brows rose. "Oh-ho, so he knows how to handle the likes of you. Calm and easy does it, hmm?" She smiled, exposing three mismatched dimples on her left cheek. "Not like Vaughn Rogan, who half the time is afraid to breathe around you for fear he'll chase you off—but too afraid to let you think for yourself, for fear you'll think your way out of his life." She shook her head. "The poor mayor. God love 'im. Maybe he'll be needing some comfort for his broken heart." A decidedly pleased glint twinkled in her gaze.

Jade rolled her own eyes. "The only reason Vaughn will care is because he won't have me to hide behind anymore. Elliott asked me about him, and I explained the situation. But then. . . ." She shrugged as if she didn't care. "He backed away. And that was it."

"That was it?" Flo's eyes narrowed. "You explained about Vaughn, exactly how?"

"I told him that we were just friends. And nothing else. He did mention Luke too, though." She made a face, remembering the lunkhead's insistent kiss. "He got a little friendly."

"Elliott?"

"No, Luke. I'm not going back to Greenside alone, that's for sure. That man has one thing on his mind."

"What did you tell Elliott about Luke?"

"I didn't tell him anything. There's nothing to tell." Jade felt her mouth set firmly. "The craterhead made a move and I . . . got out of it. I saw no reason to explain myself to Elliott about something that means nothing. I don't need to defend myself to Elliott—or anyone—about *anything*. I don't need him asking me questions or trying to tell me what to do." She ended her little speech strongly, feeling her cheeks warm. "I don't even know him. And I went through that with Daniel, don't forget."

Flo merely looked at her blandly. "Uh-huh. Okay."

"It doesn't matter what Elliott thinks—I'm really not interested anyway."

But of course, Jade was lying. And Flo knew it.

Nevertheless, the older woman didn't press her, and instead produced her latest invention: lip color. "Pink as a baby's butt," she said, slipping her pinkie into a little metal pot. "It makes your lips look soft and slick, and it gives them a little color." And before Jade could protest, Flo was swiping the stuff onto her lips. "He won't be able to resist."

"Who?" Jade asked innocently, but Flo didn't bother to reply.

The lip color tasted a little chalky, but when she looked in the mirror, she could see the difference. Her lips, already naturally full with a shallow, pointed vee on the top, looked sensual and pretty, and lusciously pink.

Jade could have wiped it off, but she didn't. Just as she didn't comment on Flo's arch smile as she left, lips rosy and glistening.

Taking care that no one would notice her, Jade hurried across the thoroughfare from Flo's place and slipped into the dark recesses of the old hotel through a side door. Moments later, she opened the old door to the empty elevator shaft and climbed down the stairs hidden inside.

Just as she walked into the computer room, she heard them talking, and immediately identified Elliott's familiar rumble.

"The Cult of Atlantis?" Jade said. "What's that?" All eyes turned to her, but she felt it the moment Elliott noticed her fresh, pink lips. His chin moved in a sort of surprised little jerk, his eyes fastened on her mouth, and she swore she saw him straighten up. His own lips softened, parting as if to allow him to take in a deeper breath.

The expression on his face made her knees weak.

Don't get all jinky now, just because Flo was right about the lip color.

She walked farther into the room as Quent, the blond one, explained. "It was a society that my father belonged to. Years before the Change."

"You're certain this is the symbol?" said Sage, who'd glanced up at Jade's arrival.

She sounded a little annoyed, but Jade thought she understood why. Sage had been searching for information about the labyrinthlike symbol for five years, spending hours with bloodshot eyes, scrolling through cached computer data that Jade and Theo and the other Runners obtained, reading and cataloging any book or magazine that came to her intact—and even ones that didn't. And she'd never found anything remotely similar.

"Yes, I'm certain it's the Cult of Atlantis," Quent replied, his voice almost as tetchy. "The traditional drawing of a labyrinth is common enough, but the superimposition of the swastika near the top of it is unique. Add in the scrolls around the edges that look like waves . . . there's no question. I've seen it before."

"The swastika is an ancient Sanskrit symbol for the sun," Sage told them.

Jade hid a smile. Her friend had so much information crammed in her brain that she couldn't help but spout off with it whenever she had the chance. She knew Sage well enough to know that it was a defense mechanism—she was a social misfit and kept to herself as much as possible.

She continued her lecture. "It got a bad rap because Hitler used it to symbolize his Nazis, but he really stole it from the Hindus, and in doing so, blasphemed a religious symbol."

Quent gave Sage a measured look. "I'm fully aware of the history of the symbol, which as you likely know has also been called the hook cross, double cross, or sun wheel." He spoke precisely, his British accent more clipped and pronounced than usual.

Jade made the mistake of glancing at Elliott and felt a rush of warmth suffuse her face. He was still looking at her, although it was obvious he was trying not to. Even from across the room, she felt the heat of his blue, blue eyes.

"I thought I'd seen it somewhere before," Elliott said, and Jade felt the weight of his attention slide away from her. "Was it something you were studying?"

"My father wore a ring with that image on it, and I'd seen paperwork in his private office as well. I don't know—I must have told you about it sometime," replied Quent.

"What do you know about the Cult of Atlantis?" asked Lou.

"Not a whole lot. From what I gleaned," Quent said, "the cult was a secret society comprised of some of the world's wealthiest, most powerful people who lived . . . well, before the Change. I don't know much more about it than that—and I didn't care to learn. They had secret meetings, and didn't talk about them. I don't know if they were named after Atlantis because they believed it existed and were trying to find it, or if the name has some other significance. My father and I were estranged, and his interests meant little to me."

Lou was nodding, his face grave. Jade noticed lines of weariness around his eyes that hadn't been there before, and instead of going to sit by Elliott—as every nerve in her body urged her to do—she moved over to Lou. It would be good to get in touch with Theo and get him back here too.

"This all gives credibility to a concept that seems impossible," he said grimly. "This, combined with what we know about the Strangers—that they seem to be powered or immortalized by crystals—makes frightening sense."

Sage jumped in. "The myths and legends of Atlantis most always include elements that describe their energy as coming from crystals."

"So are you saying," Fence spoke up, "that this new con-

tinent or landmass really could be Atlantis?" There was dis-
believing laughter in his deep voice.

"It's not conclusive evidence," Lou replied. "But we do
have enough connections to theorize: the mass that appeared
after the Change, this symbol which Quent indicated repre-
sents a cult named after Atlantis, and the fact that crystals
are important to the Strangers—they wear them in their skin,
they use them for energy. It's far-fetched, but possible."

"Well, at least with your information," Sage said, "I have
a better path for my research. It could be coincidence, I
suppose."

"I'm not sure what your research sources are," Quent
said, "but I doubt you'll find much about the Cult of Atlantis. It was very clandestine; I'd never heard it mentioned or
referred to outside of my father's office—and even that was
an accident. He was livid when he realized I'd even heard
the name."

"Can you think of any other people who were involved
with it? Maybe investigating them will lead to more information," Jade suggested.

"I don't know for sure, but I would suspect people with
whom he regularly spent leisure time, or at least, didn't
have ongoing business dealings—like Bill Brass. He was a
real estate mogul. Also, a man named Remington Truth,"
replied Quent. "My father seemed to be quite in awe of
him—a shock in itself, because my father was never in awe
of anyone." Jade recognized the loathing in his voice when
he spoke of his father, and wondered what could have caused
such an estrangement. She glanced at Elliott, but he was focused on his friend. That gave her a moment to admire the
strong line of his jaw and handsome profile. Covertly.

He really had the most amazing lips.

"Remington Truth?" Lou said, looking up from the book.

"Yes. He was the head of the National Security Administration, for the second Bush administration, and left the post not long after nine-eleven," Elliott said.

Lou nodded. "Ah. Yes, I remember the name."

"Also Chas Kidley."

"The big-name actor?" Lou said. "Really?"

Quent nodded, smiling grimly. "And you thought Tom Cruise was the only actor who belonged to a special cult."

"Kidley was bigger than Cruise or Pitt," Lou said. "I'm surprised he was able to keep his involvement in the cult a secret."

"I don't know that it was a cult as much as a secret society; I mean, I don't know that there was a worship or spiritual aspect. I got the sense that it was more of a cartel—wealthy, privileged, and powerful people supporting each other behind the scenes. Perhaps not always legally. Let's see . . . there was Tatiana, the actress. The governor of Louisiana—I believe it was in the first decade of the new millennium, but I don't recall his name. Grim Halliday, the CEO of Magnew Industries. There are others, but I'll have to think to remember. These are people my father would visit often, and I'm certain they were part of the society."

"What I don't understand," said Elliott, "is how you're using the Internet when it can't exist any longer. Can it? And I saw Google—or something like it—there on your screen. How are you doing your research?"

Lou smiled and a proud gleam flared in his eyes. "That's what Theo and I have been doing for the past fifty years. We've been rebuilding as much of the Internet as we can, by using cached files on computers—PCs from homes, offices, schools, libraries, and also the caches on servers and backup servers. Google, Yahoo!, all of the ISPs like Comcast and SBC. They all had multiple caches located throughout the world, including here in the western U.S. The problem— or perhaps I should say, the challenge—is that what we have is only a snapshot of what was on the Web at any given time. The Internet that we've created is no longer the dynamic entity that you remember, but a static one, culled together from pieces that we can find."

"That means," Sage added, "that there are holes in any given place or in any given site. In fact, we run into 404 page errors all the time."

Lou laughed. "Sage, let's be honest. *You* run into the 404s. You've done most of the work and research all along, and we wouldn't have half of the information and data we have if you hadn't been working with us so steadily."

"You and Theo and Jade provide the data for me. I just churn through it."

"And never forget a thing once you've seen it," Lou said, reaching over to touch her hand, closing knobby fingers over it. "Sage has been brilliant with this because if she sees a document or Web page or something, and it's incomplete, she'll remember it when she finds another part of it later on. She's documented and indexed, and—"

"Lou," Sage said, her face bright red. Jade stifled a smile. Poor girl. Being the center of attention was definitely not her thing.

Quent appeared interested, Wyatt bored . . . but Jade noticed that Simon—the strikingly handsome guy with the dark ponytail—was looking at Sage as if he couldn't tear his eyes away. Hmmm.

"And that," Lou said as a wrap-up, "is why we've kept this whole project a secret. If the Strangers were to discover what we know, and what we're trying to find out, they'd squash us. Like bugs. Like they did fifty years ago."

Elliott looked at Jade, and then Lou. "What *are* we—you—trying to find out?"

Lou's expression sobered. "I thought you realized. They're bent on keeping us confined and ignorant. They destroyed the world. We're trying to find out how to destroy *them*."

CHAPTER 14

"I want my damned arrow back."

Quent turned slowly, as though facing a skittish cat. He'd half expected it, been waiting for it. That was why he'd left the buzz of people inside and chose to walk among what was left of the tall buildings of Vegas. Alone. For the second night in a row.

Hoping she'd find him.

Hoping she'd followed them back to Envy.

Last night, he'd walked for hours beneath the tall, deep shadows of the destroyed Strip. Tonight, after his disconcerting experience this morning, then spending too many hours in Lou Waxnicki's secret computer lab, Quent had needed fresh air.

He'd needed to clear his thoughts. And, he'd hoped. . . .

The moon glowed high and half, casting long, deep shadows among the dark juts of the few remaining structures that clustered together, mostly dark, some ragged from being half destroyed. And beyond the huddled buildings, some of which were cracked and tilting deathtraps waiting to crumble, were huge peaks of rubble from others that had already collapsed. They sat, an eerie mountain range of curling steel beams, jutting slabs of concrete, ragged metal, growing trees, vines, and grasses, making homes for any number of creatures.

"Shall I be flattered that it didn't take you long to come searching for me?" he said, looking for her in the shadows. A pack of wolves howled in the distance, the wild sound lifting prickles at the back of his neck.

"Took you long enough to leave and come outside." Her voice still sounded scratchy, as if it weren't often used.

He couldn't see her, though he examined every shadow from the direction of her voice. Then he looked up. And there she was, perched on a window ledge two floors above him.

Though it was dark, he felt the connection when their eyes met, and then after a moment, he could make out the pale hue of her shirt, so much lighter than her skin. Narrow shoulders, wings of choppy hair darker than night, the arrows spiking from the quiver on her back.

"Want to come down here?" Quent asked, realizing his heart was pounding.

Bugger it. What was it about her that drew him? There was nothing. They'd had a single conversation, he hadn't even seen her clearly—couldn't see her clearly now. And she was prickly, scruffy, and obviously a social misfit.

It was the way she had touched him. His face. He swore it still warmed there when he remembered that gentle, hesitant caress. As though doing so was foreign to her. Touching someone.

She had saved his life, which he supposed must count for at least part of his fascination. She'd done so and then disappeared. And now she seemed to have no bloody interest in him but to get her arrow back.

Quent had to admit, that wasn't something he normally experienced. Young, ridiculously rich, handsome, and an adventurer . . . he found that women were always interested in him. Too many of them.

Although . . . none of that was true any longer, was it? The realization slammed him like a cricket ball to the gut. He was no longer the heir to a vast fortune. He was no one but a blond man, in a world where blondes were abducted by monstrous creatures.

"Do you have my arrow?" Her impatience was growing.

"At least tell me your name first."

Silence for a long moment. Then, softly, quietly from the shadows . . . "Zoë."

"Zoë," he repeated. "I'm Quent."

"I know."

"And I find talking to shadows quite annoying."

"Then stop talking and give me my damn arrow."

"I don't have it with me." Purposely. "Won't you come down here?"

She made a disgusted tsking sound that clearly said, "Are you daft?"

He looked up at her, thought perhaps he could make out the lift of a chin, and the tip of a nose. "Are you afraid of me?"

This time, a derisive snort carried down to him, and Quent couldn't hold back a smile. "Then I'll come up."

And he began to climb, lodging the toe of his boot inside an old broken window, grabbing onto a vine that appeared to be sturdy. The vine gave way. Quent slid, making much more of the tumble than it actually was. And then he lay still.

Her curse carried to his ears, but then she called his name, low and urgent. He didn't reply. Then with a "fuck" and a few "damns," she clambered down, lithe and quick, landing lightly on two steady feet. When she knelt next to him, her knees brushed against his.

She laid her hand against his cheek as she had before, and he smelled the same earthy, organic scent and something else. *A little spicy. Cinnamon? How?*

Warm fingers.

He opened his eyes. Shadowed by the light behind her and the uneven edges of hair falling in her face, spiking out from around her neck, her expression was unreadable. But then their eyes met and she reeled back. He lashed out, closing around her slender wrist. It was warm, and banded with what felt like a loose leather strip.

"You faked it," she said in disgust that was clearly directed at herself. She tried to pull away, but he held tightly . . . not so much that she would be alarmed or injured, but enough that she understood he wanted her to stay.

"Sorry," he said, sitting up and releasing her hand. To his relief, she didn't move away. And now they were crouched next to each other on the ground, face-to-face, toe brushing toe. "You must really want that arrow, to come all the way down here. Next to me." He smiled, surprising himself.

"So where the fuck is it?"

Later, Quent would never be able to explain what made him do it, what made him reach for her, cupping his hand at the back of her skull and holding her there as he moved forward in what felt like slow motion. Maybe it was still that lingering warmth on his cheek, the sense that she'd needed to touch him as much as he'd wanted her to.

But he did it, rising up on his knees, steadying her warm head, feeling the tickle of her wild hair over his cheek as he found her lips with his.

Prepared to release his skittish cat the moment she made a move to twist away, he balanced on one flat palm that levered him closer. A bit of grass softened the rough ground beneath knees and hand, his fingers curled into the moist dirt.

He slid his lips up against hers, parting them enough to close over her top one with a gentle caress, then away, and then back again, to do the same to her full bottom one. And then she shocked him when, instead of pulling away, she merged into him, into the kiss, opening her mouth to close over his, tipping her head to the side and matching the sudden ferocity of his movements with her own.

Hell . . . oh, bloody hell. Just like that, he was lost.

Warm, slender, lean . . . and she tasted, smelled, sweet-spicy. Quent needed more, delved deeper, now holding her head with both hands, still gentle, but steady, near, his eyes sinking closed and the moment overwhelming. He couldn't draw in a breath. His world became heat and slick lips and tongue, and cinnamon, and warmth . . . the warmth of her up against him.

She freed herself then, and at last he could see her. Her skin was rich, the color of the cinnamon he smelled around her, and she looked like a Bollywood star with a frightful haircut. A white beam played over her face, making it exotic and mysterious with huge almond-shaped eyes, wide lips, and shadowy slashes from the uneven illumination. Elegant cheekbones and an aristocratic nose that seemed at odds with the glossy hair that went every which way, one strand catching at the corner of an eye.

"So . . ." he said when he could find his voice. "I have your arrow."

"I want it." Now her voice was even rougher than before.

"Is that all you want?"

She looked at him now, and the slant of her eyes, steady and knowing, made his bloody palms go damp. "No."

"Then I do believe I might be able to accommodate you after all."

He stood and she rose too, with spare, sleek movements,

tall and slender next to him, arrows clunking quietly. Quent brushed close to her, and then before he realized it, had his hands on her slender shoulders, her backed against the wall, his mouth devouring hers once again.

Somewhere in the back of his mind, Quent was shocked, bewildered by his ferocity. But for now, he registered only the crazy response of her lips, open and warm and sleek, the urgent wildness growing in him. The feel of her breasts, now, under his hands, the deep pleasure of a soft woman to press against, the smooth skin under his fingers. Blood rushed down, making him hard and uncomfortable, ready as hell . . . and the pressure of her grinding against him merely made Quent want to drive deep.

She pulled her face away, gasping for breath, holding his hips against hers. "Is that my arrow in your pocket . . . ?"

He laughed against her mouth, a little breathlessly, feeling her lips curve. "It's not yours . . . but you can certainly have it."

Fuck compartmentalization. Fuck stoicism. Fuck it all.

Elliott felt the tightness in his face, the tension in his shoulders, the gathering of temper deep inside him. The dull throb of weariness, the ache of gnawing grief, the fog of disbelief.

There was too much. Too damn much, and he couldn't keep it all tamped down, packed away any longer.

He had only to look at the stage here in The Pub to know part of the reason. The breaking of the last straw. The final nail in the coffin of his control.

For, up there, Jade sat on a stool under warm lights, cradling an acoustic guitar. Strumming easily, she turned an old rock song about night moves into a sexy ballad. Her voice, low and dusky, beckoned like an invitation.

Problem was, the invitation didn't seem to be for him.

Despite all that had happened last night—their conversation, their connection, that mind-blistering kiss—once they'd arrived back in Envy, she'd erected some sort of rigid wall. During the hours in Lou's computer room, Jade had remained aloof and apart from him. At the time, Elliott had accepted that as discretion, and maybe a little bit of shyness.

Plus, she'd done something to her lips that made them all lush and sexy, and it had distracted the hell out of him even though they were talking about mind-boggling, far-reaching consequences like the possibility of Atlantis, and seeing the proof that the world was indeed gone.

So he'd assumed that after they left Lou's there'd be a moment of privacy between him and Jade.

But, no. Jade had disappeared without a glance, and Elliott had learned on his own that she had to prepare for this gig tonight. And now here they were: Jade onstage, her voice, those heavy-lidded eyes, the tumble-down hair . . . feeding the imagination of every male in the room, and Elliott watching, unacknowledged, removed, and on the verge of erupting.

The balance of his control was tipping.

He slammed his beer, allowing the banter from Wyatt, Simon, and Fence (none of them knew where Quent was) around him to slip into the background and leave him with his thoughts.

Setting his empty glass on the table, he gestured for the waitress to bring another. Not surprisingly, she was the same one they'd had the other night. Trixie.

She met his eyes and gave him a long, slow smile, even as she moved efficiently to serve another table. He smiled back like he meant it, settled, slouching, in his seat, and glanced around the club, even as the low, mellow words of Jade's song wove into his consciousness.

He turned so that he didn't have to watch her onstage, giving a low, slow smile or a bit of a wave to people—well, hell, be precise; she nodded and waved to the *men* in the audience. She was a performer. She got off on the attention.

She was a control freak. She had to call the shots. She had to be stroked.

Lysney had been the same way. High-powered women who commanded interest and desire fed on it. Played the game.

Elliott didn't go for that. So he turned in his seat so that he wasn't *quite* facing the stage, but he could still watch . . . if he wanted to.

The place had been decorated by what looked like DVD or CD inserts, taken out of their cases and plastered all over the walls in a . . . what was it? His cousins used to always make them with pictures of teen heartthrobs . . . a collage. But someone with an artistic eye had seen to the arrangement, for all the images that, from a distance, appeared black or blue were on one wall, the red and orange ones were on another, and so on.

And as he looked around, as the slur of the beer settled over him, Elliott felt almost normal. Almost as if this were just another bar in Chicago, and he was hanging with the guys after a game of basketball or gone out to see a band play the blues. And the way that waitress Trixie was giving him the eye, he might not be going home alone tonight.

But the moment evaporated. He would never have normal again.

The song ended and Jade lifted the guitar and its strap up and over her head, resting it in a stand next to the microphone. She stood under the warm lights, wearing some slim-fitting trousers and a low-cut halter that tied behind her neck, lifting her breasts, showing off the deep, dark shadow between them. The material sparkled and glinted as she gave a brief bow, tossed a few kisses into the crowd, then stepped back from the stage and turned to walk off.

She'd not looked in Elliott's direction once. Not that he'd really noticed, because he'd stopped watching her. Mostly.

Trixie brought his beer, taking her time, giving him a lingering smile. As Elliott took it, he met her sloe eyes, holding her gaze for longer than necessary. A familiar step in the ritual of attraction and pursuit.

The message couldn't have been clearer, but Trixie was also a master at the game. She didn't slather, didn't come on too strong. The invitation was there, but it was one of equality, not desperation. Elliott generally liked that in a woman. Confidence. Good self-esteem.

And when she turned and hurried off to fill another order, he watched her go. Noticed the way her ass filled out her low-slung jeans. For about two seconds . . . until his attention was drawn yet again, inexorably, to the empty stage.

Someone had turned on a different sound system, and "Smells Like Teen Spirit" began to filter just above the conversations that had erupted with Jade's exit.

Several other audience members had also risen to leave, now that the show was over. Elliott couldn't help but notice that a few of them—none happened to be the cowboy wannabe, which only slightly mollified him—headed, not for the main exit of The Pub, but toward the stage, walking around and to the back of it.

Where Jade had gone.

Elliott's deep-seeded antagonism and general pissed-offness bubbled to the surface. He put his beer down, stood, and before he knew it, was striding away.

Toward the stage.

Around the back of the platform. Into the narrow hallway that led to what were presumably dressing rooms.

He knew it was irrational. He knew it was out of line, that he didn't want to play this game.

But he kept going.

He heard her dusky laugh before he saw her, which wasn't a surprise because she was surrounded in the little passageway by a small cluster of people—yes, men—all of whom were taller than she was.

Elliott hardly realized what he was doing. He felt as though he were moving underwater, but he pushed through until he found her, shouldering the others out of his way.

"Elliott?" Her green eyes flashed wide and surprised when she saw him, and later he wondered what sort of expression he must have had on his face—for hers wasn't necessarily a welcoming response.

The murkiness that pushed at him waned at bit as he focused on her. The green eyes, the lush mouth, her lifted chin. Elliott closed his fingers around her arm as he said, "I need to speak with you." He thought his voice sounded normal and calm, but he was in no state to be objective.

This isn't me. His inner voice tapped weakly at him, and Elliott, sloshing through the murky place his world had become, ignored it. "Now," he added, when she didn't leap to his command.

There was a door. He found it, hell, he didn't shove her, he knew that much, but he propelled, directed, *firmly escorted* her toward it, still calm, still in control, still damned foggy and lost . . . but focused. On her.

"Elliott," she began when they were inside whatever room it was, the door safely closed, the others on the other side. She looked up at him, her eyes wide but not frightened.

She said something else, maybe . . . but he didn't hear her. He didn't speak, he couldn't. Something rushed, filling his ears, his fingers moved to the tops of her arms, curling around her bare skin . . . he felt as if he were removed, as if he were observing himself . . . and then it all slid away as he settled into her, backing her sharply against the wall.

Warm, soft, lemon and woman, sleek and silky and sweet. The sluggishness, the tension evaporated into a blaze of heat and breathlessness.

Mine.

From the moment she saw Elliott striding down the hall, pushing his way to her, Jade's breathing fairly stopped. Her stomach slipped and slid and her palms dampened even as she pressed them against her slacks.

His blue eyes, dark and pinpointed on her, his face set, his broad, powerful shoulders parting a path between Flo and her teen-aged son Jason, coming to her.

For her.

She couldn't speak, she was simply shocked silent by his sudden appearance, the wildness edging his eyes. When he took her arm, not angrily, not painfully—but clearly willing to brook no argument—she could have been frightened or alarmed . . . but she wasn't.

She was . . . was. . . .

A door opened, closed, the crowd and Flo's fascinated expression faded away, replaced by Elliott's face, dark and shadowed, looming over her in some random room. The wall rose up behind her, chill and smooth against her bare back, and his lips moved, pressing together, as he said something soft, sharp, under his breath.

And then he bent to her and she lifted her face, her head bumping against the wall as he covered her mouth, covered any protest she might have made, drawing her up and into him, against his long, powerful body.

Oh God.

Jade closed her eyes, met his mouth, tried to keep up with the kiss as he drew deeply from her, pulled and demanded and coaxed . . . seduced and teased. What had begun as a claiming eased into a long, languorous temptation, hot and sleek and smooth. His hands moved up into her hair, sliding from shoulders bared by her halter, cupping the back of her skull, lifting the heavy weight from her damp neck.

She felt the unmistakable bulge behind the zipper of his jeans, and a blaze of heat and desire rushed over her, tingling down between her legs.

"Elliott. . . ." She twisted her face from his mouth long enough to draw in a rough breath, curling her fingers into the belt loops at his waist, pulling him closer, pressing her hips into him. He was warm, so warm, so tall and broad . . . and she realized vaguely that it didn't alarm her as he bent over her, his large, powerful body grinding her against the wall as if he needed to absorb her.

Overwhelming? No. Not at all.

She sighed, whispering his name, twisting her face away just to catch a breath. Why had she tried to ignore him? She felt so lightheaded, warm, sleek . . . alive. His hands . . . everywhere. . . .

Then, he stepped back, taking that powerful comfort away, his hands pushing her back against the wall, shoving himself away. Jade realized belatedly that they were in her dressing room, such as it was, and that the light had been left on.

"Jade," he managed to say. His voice sounded different: tight, breathless, bewildered. "I. . . ."

He stepped back, swiping a hand over his mouth, his eyes

large and deep and blue. A little shocked, even. That anguish was there again, that and something else. Heat, yes. Want, desire . . . and something fierce.

His face darkened, as though some other thought had occurred to him—an unpleasant one. "I'm not going to fight through the crowd again, Jade."

She shook her head, realizing her breathing had just begun to catch up with her racing heart. "What?"

"I don't share. I won't. I . . . want . . ." His voice trailed off as if he could make no sense of it either, but then his expression settled. His eyes sharpened, the ocean blue flattening into cold steel. "I don't know what's going on in that head of yours, but I'm not playing. You're *mine*, Jade, and—"

"Are you *crazy*?" She drew herself up. She couldn't have been more shocked at this totally out-of-the-blue pronouncement. *Mine?* "I thought you were from the twenty-first century, not the Middle Ages. I don't belong to anyone. Never again will I *belong* to anyone. You can't—"

"So do you kiss everyone like you just kissed me? Vaughn and Luke and all of your groupies?" He stepped toward her again, grimacing, almost as if he were fighting some magnetic pull. His words were furious, but they came out low, steady, unrelenting. His eyes bored into hers. "You tell them all—Luke of the fucking mega crystal, the cowboy mayor, all of them—that you're done with them."

Jade could hardly comprehend that this man, this man she hardly knew, whom she'd kissed a total of three times and had known for as many days, was hammering her with these demands. Without warning, he'd changed from the respectful, kind, sexy-as-hell Elliott, to this . . . alpha man who slammed her up against the wall.

The exact kind of man she despised.

But . . . holy crap. She'd liked it. She'd kissed him, pressed into him, moaned beneath him . . . and would have taken more.

What the hell was wrong with her?

"I," she said, drawing herself up, making her own voice calm and steely too, "do not answer to you. Or anyone. You're *insane*."

All of the heat and ferocity seemed to drain from his face. "Maybe I am," he whispered. "Maybe I am."

He drew himself up, stiffly, his gaze blank and emotionless, his face like stone. "I'm sorry if I offended you." His words were just as stiff as his persona. "But I meant what I said, Jade. You're mine. You know it. And the sooner you admit it, the better off we'll both be."

Before she could assimilate this sudden change, he spun and was gone.

And no more than a second later the door flew open again.

Jade's heart leapt, but then she saw that it was Flo. Her eyes wide, her freckles standing out in dark relief against her flushed face, the older woman burst into the room and shut the door.

"What happened?" she demanded, her voice an excited hush that Jade assumed she thought was a whisper. "Oh my saints, it was just like Rhett sweeping Scarlett up into his arms and carrying her up the stairs!" Flo clasped her hand to her pillowy breasts and pretended to swoon. "Jade, he is *mad* about you."

"Yeah, mad is the right word," Jade said, glancing at the door as if it would provide some answer to this tailspin she'd been in for the last few minutes. "He's crazy."

"What happened? What did he say? Tell me!" Flo swept over to the raggedy sofa and settled her round bottom right on the edge of its cushion, looking up expectantly.

Jade tried to explain, but even she wasn't certain what had happened. She did her best.

But apparently, Flo had all the answers. And it began with her lip color. "See, I told you it would make him notice," she said. "But it's your fault, you know."

Jade gaped at her. "My fault that he dragged me off like some Neanderthal cavewoman into a room and slammed me up against the wall?" She shivered. It seemed like every time she thought about that whole slamming-up-against-the-wall thing, her belly flipped and squished. Not in an unpleasant way either.

What the *hell* was wrong with her? She'd been manhandled enough in the past. She wasn't the kind of woman that would ever be weak enough to let that happen again. She'd grown so strong since those days.

And she'd really had no intention of having a man in her life, except for the safe and strong Vaughn Rogan. No one would mess with the mayor of Envy.

Except maybe Elliott Drake.

Tell your cowboy boyfriend you're done with him.

She couldn't help the little squiggly shiver deep in her belly, but she ignored it.

"I don't want some guy ordering me around, pretending he owns me, Flo. I've been there, done that, and bought the T-shirt," she said, quoting an old cliché that she didn't quite understand. "And that's what he wants."

"You didn't tell him about Luke. He thinks the worst, and you know what happens whenever you sing, Jade. You know how it looks." The excited glint in Flo's eyes had given way to a steely one. The one where she moved from fairy godmother to mentor. Or motherly lecturer.

"I don't answer to Elliott. I don't have to tell him about

Luke. And I'm sorry if he didn't like the way I look when I sing. I can't help it, and you know I can't see anything in the audience anyway."

"When you sing, you have every single man in the room on his knees. It's that low voice combined with the way you look. And then they all flock to see you afterward. You know that's part of the reason you let Vaughn hang around—to scare them off."

"They all flock? What . . . the three guys who play backup for me sometimes, and you and Jason and Tiger? I hardly call that flocking. Besides, the guys only come backstage to tell me if my guitar is out of tune, or whether the amp was up high enough."

Flo was shaking her head. "To a man blinded by love"— at which Jade snorted; Elliott had never said anything about *love*—"it looks like you've got a bunch of groupies hanging on you."

"Whatever." Jade shook her head, suddenly weary. "I'm tired, Flo. I'm going to go to bed before Vaughn shows up and really complicates my life."

Flo tsked, shaking her head, but Jade ignored it. Sometimes that was the only way to handle her.

Six months After

There are monsters here. They call for someone named Ruth, and they have orange eyes. Come out only at night. Saw them for the first time two weeks ago. They look just like I always pictured the blood-sucking, flesh-eating *jiang shi* monsters from China my granddad told us stories about. The *jiangs* move like they've had the crap beaten out of them. But they're huge, larger than humans, and strong and they tear people apart. We saw them. Leonard Glover went out and never came back. But we heard him scream.

Staying inside at night for damn sure.

Theo has found an intact satellite station he thinks he can hack into. Have told him he's no Torvalds, but he laughs and tells me to fuck off. He'll do it.

The crew we sent has returned from Hoover Dam. It's intact, but the power plant and generator aren't functioning well. We don't have the manpower to maintain it, so are looking for other options. Windmills. Water. Ethanol. There's a fucking ocean here, so of course we're also going to look at algae and other possibilities.

Have decided to create a governing council and elect a mayor. Rowe wants to be mayor, but Marck will fight him for it. Rowe's a better choice in my opinion—he's fair and pragmatic and reminds me a lot of Jack from *LOST*. Marck is too controlling, and he wants to enforce things like breeding plans and schedules. The man gives me a twitch.

Think I'm in love, btw. Her name is Elsie.

—from the journal of Lou Waxnicki

CHAPTER 15

Crap.

And holy hot damn.

Zoë's world had become heat and sleek muscle, warm and strong against her, around her, taking, pulling, demanding. Holy shit, the man had a set of lips on him. And he damn well knew how to use them.

She couldn't get enough of touching this man, this Quent . . . devouring his mouth, tasting the warmth and salt on his skin, the unfamiliar sensation of closeness, of strength, of comfort. She wanted to fucking crawl inside him.

And though it scared the shit out of her, she didn't give a good damn at the moment. All she wanted was skin to skin, hot and damp and hard.

And apparently, so did he.

Somehow, they'd made their way inside . . . somewhere . . . and up some stairs; she remembered little but bumping against the wall and being kissed breathless every time they went around a corner, or grabbing his shirt and yanking him to her, just to taste him again, bodies crashing against the plaster in low thuds, sagging together, knee to knee, hip to hip.

Lips, teeth, hands . . . every damn where.

At last, she heard a quiet jingle, the clink against metal,

and pulled away from his throat enough to register that he was opening a door. She tugged free of his grip, wiped her mouth, wondered briefly what the hell had gotten into her, then rejected the thought and turned to pull him through the door.

They stumbled, their feet catching and he gave a deep little laugh that sent a renewed sizzle through her, she felt something bump her from behind and realized it was the doorframe. Extricating herself, she slid one hand along the smooth wall and turned to look.

Heart pounding, mouth throbbing, fingers shaking. What the fuck? She drew in a deep breath, tried to settle.

Zoë had never been in one of these rooms, but it took only a brief glance to see that it was small, furnished with an actual bed and a table and chair, and that there was a massive window. The glass was still intact. That was pretty much all she needed to know. Other than where her arrow was . . . but that could wait.

That could damn well wait.

But . . . hell, she almost forgot. There was something else she had to take care of. She felt in her pocket. The paper was still there.

Quent closed the door and, now that they were separated by half a room's length, gave her a quick look as if to judge whether she was about to cut and run. *As if.*

His chest, covered by a shirt that she'd stretched out of shape, moved rapidly as if he'd run miles . . . maybe that was how they got up those steps so quickly. He'd half-carried her, using those wide shoulders and sleek, muscled arms. She couldn't wait to touch them.

But first . . . she had to take care of this. "Wait."

He stopped, freezing there across the room. The tension flashing between them plummeted and the expression on his face—suddenly blank and rigid—would have been comical if she wasn't cursing herself for smashing the mood. *Business before pleasure.* "I have something to show you." She dug in her pocket, pulled out the paper. "Here," she said, when he didn't move.

"What is it?" He spoke in such precise tones, with an accent she'd only heard in the movies. His voice was low, careful, emotionless.

"I found this in the van that the kids were driving. Before you came up to try and fix it. They were going somewhere, meeting someone. It looks like a map." When he didn't move, she shoved the paper at him. "And there was crystal dust all over inside."

"Crystal dust?"

"Take it," she said, rattling the paper loudly, impatient.

"That is not what I want, Zoë." The blankness left his expression.

Holy crap. Her belly tanked and her breath caught. She nearly fucking swooned.

She dropped the paper. It wafted silently to the floor.

Shit. Oh shit, she needed to touch him, feel that hair-roughened skin, warm and solid and real. Sliding her fingers under the shirt hadn't been enough . . . not nearly enough.

His dangerous blond hair, the color of fresh honey in the sunlight, rose in little licks at the back of his head, and she remembered shoving her fingers into the heavy waves. And his eyes . . . zeroing on her as if he were a feral wolf. She couldn't see their color, but the way they gleamed, and *wanted*, made her belly quiver and her breathing rise.

Come and get me.

The next thing Zoë knew, she was plastering her body over his, or maybe he'd moved first, their lips smashing together as two pairs of hands tore frantically at her shirt. She wasn't sure if he grabbed it up first, or if she did, but suddenly the tee came up and over her torso, snagging on her chin and ear because they were fused together at the mouth, desperate and fierce . . . and then he ripped it up and over and away.

And, *oh shit, crap, fuck* . . . those elegant hands found her skin instantly, covering her breasts, sliding under her bra to tip them out of the lacy cups. She pulled recklessly at him, at his clothes, her nails slipping over him, scoring, in her haste. Skin to skin, warmth to warmth. It was a craving, a need.

Then, in the flurry of tearing, pulling, slipping, they were suddenly chest to breast, melding together hot and damp. The bed was behind her, and she collapsed back onto it. He tumbled with her, one heavy thigh wedging between her legs, jolting the mattress as he caught himself over her.

She pushed her hands up onto his bare chest, feeling the muscles, taut and firm as he held himself up. He bent his head to kiss along her chin to the place just in front of her ear, at its juncture with her cheek, where even the most feathery of touch sent a blast of shivers over her body.

Oh, she was most definitely ready for this. Her body felt alive, and ready. Needy.

Zoë arched and sighed against him, sliding her hands up to feel the planes of muscle over his back and around to the smooth bulge of muscle in his arms. She had little time to explore, for his jeans were in the way, and so were her cargo pants. They clung together, torsos hot, as he grasped her hair and held her head in place, nuzzling roughly along her neck as she twisted and sighed beneath him.

Then he rolled to the side, taking her with him—a flurry of hands pulling at zippers, buttons, shucking and kicking them off, whipping them to the floor. Their bodies bare against each other, long, hair-roughened legs smoothing against hers, his mouth sucking hard enough on a nipple that she gave a little scream that made him smile while he was doing so. Hands drawing over her, her shoulders, hips, back, everywhere . . . as if he too needed to feel.

He cupped his hand between her legs, his thumb twitching around her ready clit, then slipping in and out and around. She was ready, pulsing and slick, her world centered there where he touched . . . and she reached for him, guiding him to her.

"God, no . . ." he gasped, pulling at her hand, easing back. "Wait." He sat back, chest heaving, face darkened by shadow, skin glistening. "I don't have anything. Protection."

"Wh—?" It was impossible to make her mouth form words, her brain capture coherent thoughts. Protection from what?

"Condom. I don't have a condom."

"A what?" she managed to gasp. "Whatever. We don't need that. Quent. I want you inside me."

She reached for him again, her fingers around the hot velvety skin, gave a good stroke. He groaned deep and low, the muscles in his arms trembling on either side of her. "Zoë," he said.

But she pulled him down, smashing her mouth to his. Whatever the fuck a condom was, they didn't need it to do what she wanted.

Once more she guided him to her hot, wet, ready place. "Quent. Now."

She lifted her hips and he slid inside with a deep groan, paused . . . and held.

"Move," she ordered, lifting her hips. "Dammit."

His surprised puff of humor warmed her neck, and the next thing, they were thrashing together, wild and desperate, looking for their rhythm . . . and, oh, yes, finding it.

And, oh. Sweat and salt, deep loose pleasure winding tighter, coiling, faster and harder . . . then she cried out, grabbing at him, her nails digging, her mouth free from his, as the orgasm rocked her.

His muscles bunched, she felt them, vaguely aware, as he stroked once . . . twice . . . tighter, then suddenly, shockingly . . . he pulled out, twisting away . . . then gasped a deep, pleasured groan that caused another luscious twinge in her belly.

Oh, holy hot damn indeed.

Quent walked into The Pub, looking a combination of dazed and like the cat who'd taken a bath in the proverbial cream. Elliott recognized that look right away, and settled into his seat, feeling acutely pissed off.

At least one of them hadn't made an utter fool out of himself. What the hell had possessed him to go all Neanderthal on Jade? Especially knowing her history. *Christ.*

You're insane.

That about covered it. He still felt that deep itchiness inside him, the gnawing anger and unsettled, volcanic feelings. He wanted to rage at everyone. He wanted to lock himself away and brood. But the antagonism, the murkiness, had faded into stark reality. Bleak, dark, unending, terrible.

He hated this world.

"I need a drink," Quent said, pulling up a chair next to Elliott.

"Where you been?" Fence asked Quent. "We were talking about you and suddenly you were gone."

"I went for a walk."

Fence gestured to Quent's misaligned shirt, buttoned awkwardly—a travesty for a man who'd kept himself neat and groomed even in survivalist mode. His hair was mussed and fell in his eyes. "Looks like you did more than walking, man." His infectious grin flashed bright and bold, and even in his morbid state, Elliott felt it. "So, tell . . . does it still work? It's been fifty damned years."

"Piss off." But it was clear that Quent wasn't really angry. "Zoë found me and wanted her arrow back."

"From the looks of things, she got more than her arrow back," Fence pressed, obviously living vicariously through Quent.

"She also gave me this," Quent said, pulling a wrinkled paper from his pocket. "Don't know why she thought it was important. She said she found it in the kids' van, with crystal dust all over it. Whatever that is."

Elliott reached for the paper, glad to have something else to think about. He should have just gone upstairs instead of coming back down here. He was ridiculously unfit for company.

As he glanced at the sheet, which was a precise drawing of a location—a map—Lou approached the group.

The older man sat down in a chair Fence snagged and pulled over, and Elliott noticed he was holding the small book he and Jade had found in the Stranger's pack today.

"I've been thinking," he said without preamble, as if he'd been sitting in on their conversation for the last twenty minutes. His voice was loud enough for them to hear if they leaned forward, but thanks to blasting Nickelback, anything he said would be indistinguishable to anyone else. "I have a theory about what happened to you when you were in Sedona. I suspect that you must have been in a cave that was at the juncture of many ley lines—powerful linear centers of energy—that put you into the . . . coma . . . I guess I'd call it. And that imbued you with the powers you've awakened with."

"Only Quent and Elliott have special capabilities," Wyatt commented. "Simon and Fence and I seem not to have changed at all."

"Except that we don't have to shave," Simon added blandly.

Lou smiled. "I don't know that that's something to complain about," he said, deliberately stroking his own stubbled cheek.

Elliott nodded, drawn into the conversation in spite of his foul mood. "Well, it appears that Fence is starting to sprout stubble up top, so maybe Lou's right. Maybe our bodies were . . . well, the only term I can think of is cryogenically frozen . . . for fifty years, and now that we're conscious, it's taking some time for them to learn to work properly again."

Fence began to chuckle. "That fucking figures. Why do I get the stubble while Quent gets to take his junk for a test drive?"

A rumble of laughter rippled around the table, giving Elliott another tease of normalcy. Guys laughing at a shared joke in the bar.

Elliott explained, "Once we figured out what had happened—and your theory, Lou, makes sense, and is similar to the one that we've all come to accept, although I don't think the term ley line crossed anyone's lips. Even Fence's."

"Would have if I'd thought of it, mo-fo," retorted Fence. "Now I have this image of some crazy-hot girls laying down in a long line, just waiting to be—"

"Laid, yeah, we get it," Wyatt said with a short roll of the eyes. "Anyway, once we figured out what happened, and we realized we weren't growing beards or hair or nails, we started thinking we might have gained some sort of immortality."

He had to stop speaking when Trixie sauntered over. She rested her hand on Elliott's shoulder when she leaned forward to take their orders . . . and to flirt briefly with Fence, who was still chuckling about the ley lines. Or, in his mind, lay lines.

Elliott glanced up at her and their eyes met.

And that's when it hit home that he really, truly wasn't interested in Trixie—or anyone else. Not in the way he was interested in Jade. Yeah, he could take Trixie upstairs, make sure all his parts still worked, and probably have a damn good time doing it. But that was it. And if they did, he wouldn't care if she came down and made cow eyes at Fence or any of the other guys the next night.

And that was also, unfuckingfortunately, why Andrea of the large blue eyes hadn't gotten any rise out of him in Greenside. Or his parts.

He was completely fucked. Or not. As the case might be. Jade was his.

Couldn't she see it? Feel it? Christ, the minute he touched her—even looked at her—he felt as if they were sewn together.

"Right, Dred?"

He looked up and realized that Trixie had gone, and the others were looking at him.

"Man, brother's already on that test drive," Fence said, lifting his beer mug and brushing a hand over a not-so-smooth head anymore. "Damn, I've got to get me shaved."

"When Lenny died, that pretty much put the lid on any possibility that we were immortal," Wyatt said, answering the question for Elliott. "And Dred, our resident physician, confirmed that there was nothing unusual about him or his body."

"He died from a tetanus infection," Elliott said. Which

was true. He just wasn't ready to give all the details of why yet. He hadn't told anyone about the double-edged sword of his new-found power, except for Jade. "Just like any of us would have."

Just then, a rise of voices near the bar caught their attention. "Oh no," said someone, in shock or horror. Everyone turned to look and the buzz grew louder. "My God," someone else exclaimed.

Elliott got to his feet, and the others as well. "What is it?" he asked Trixie as she approached. Her eyes were round and filled with horror.

"It's the mayor. He's hurt real bad . . ." She seemed hardly able to form the words. "He's. . . ." She shook her head. "They think he's going to die."

Elliott didn't need to hear anymore. "Where is he?"

"I'll take you," said Lou.

Elliott never got the full story, but he didn't need to scan Vaughn Rogan to know the guy was going to die.

The mayor had been found just outside the walls of Envy, a lion's corpse next to him. It had been shot by an arrow, through the skull.

Elliott looked at Lou, who'd receded into the background after their entrance into what passed for a hospital in Envy. It was more of an infirmary, but Elliott wasn't here to critique the medical facilities. He was here to do what he could.

Which was everything.

And he had little time to waste. Rogan was going fast.

"I can help him," he said, speaking to a wiry man named Ben who appeared to be as close to a physician as they came nowadays. "But I want everyone to leave."

He swept the room with his hand, encompassing the dozen

people who'd crowded into the small place. The mayor was well loved, it appeared. Well loved, respected. Important to these people.

If there was a life to be saved, at such a risk, it was this one.

At first it looked as if Ben would argue. Elliott would have—after all, they didn't know him from Adam. And Lou, who was considered the town's crackpot, wouldn't be much help when it came to vouching for him.

But perhaps Ben realized he was out of his league, and that stitches and bandages would be futile when the man— the leader of this city, the closest thing they had to a president or king—needed so much more. And aside from that, a matronly woman named Flo seemed to be on Elliott's side, and the others listened to her when she ordered them to leave, explaining that she knew he was a healer.

"I need a dog. Or a cat. Something," he ordered as he sent the man from the room. "Bring it here."

But the man was shaking his head. "I don't know—"

"Find one, dammit," Elliott ordered, suddenly feeling desperation crawling over him. "A mouse, a rat. *Something.*"

Lou was the only one who remained in the room as Elliott scanned the man, first ascertaining the extent of his injuries. *Fuck.* Punctured liver. Smashed ribs. Blood pressure in the toilet. Breath rattling ominously.

He was a bloody mess.

Elliott stared down at the man. His rival. But that didn't matter, of course.

The mayor of Envy—equivalent, in this hellacious place, to the leader of the free world.

Elliott could heal him. But then what would happen to him?

How did one determine whose life was more important? He stared down at Rogan, watching as the life literally eased from his body.

Was this the reason he was here? Was this why he'd been spared, been given this ability? To save *this* man's life? At the risk of his own?

Elliott drew in a deep breath. He thought of Jade, he watched the way the blood pumped out of the man before him. A good man, by all accounts.

And he rested his hands on him. Felt the sizzle of power as he concentrated, letting it flow into him as he moved his palms over Vaughn Rogan's battered body. Taking on his pain and injury.

When he finished, he looked at Lou. "You'll stay with him?" The older man nodded, and Elliott continued, "No one is to come in here until morning, at least, while we wait to see if this works. Lock the door if you have to." Elliott stood. "No one. Even Jade."

"You're leaving?" Lou said in surprise.

Elliott nodded. "I can do nothing else. Now we wait to see if it worked."

But the pain radiating through his body told him everything he needed to know.

CHAPTER 16

Elliott felt the blood seeping from his side, warm, sticky, onto the sheets beneath him.

The moon had begun to wane, and shone through the window not nearly as brightly as it had only three nights ago, when he watched Jade tear into an army of *gangas* on her horse.

Pain gouged him, growing slowly but steadily, dragging him into murkiness and confusion. He'd hurried, tottering back to his room after healing the mayor, careful not to brush against anyone, not to see or speak to anyone.

He'd barely made it before his knees trembled weakly, threatening collapse. He crumpled onto his bed.

The decision had been made—there'd been no other choice. But he'd hoped . . . well, that some solution would have presented itself. That someone would have brought a goddamned rat or something. That he wouldn't have to die to save Vaughn Rogan.

But there was no solution. He'd made the choice, he'd offered the sacrifice, knowing there might be no one to whom he could pass it on to.

Knowing there was nothing that could be done for him—no one could care for him, touch him, comfort him—he'd retreated to solitude. He wanted to take no chances.

No one would know until the morning, when they found Vaughn Rogan awake, completely healed. And Elliott Drake was found, drowned in his own blood.

There'd been one dark moment, one flash of thought when he wished, wryly and only half jokingly, that he could shake Luke of the mega-crystal's hand. That thought had terrified him, too . . . because it was a possibility. An evil one. One he rejected as soon as he thought it . . . but it sat there. Like an ugly toad, a horrific demon, in the back of his battered mind.

This gift . . . and he used the term in his own mind loosely . . . could be a murder weapon. One he would never contemplate . . . but one that he wielded, nevertheless.

He sank into oblivion, the moonlight wavering around him. *Anytime now.*

He wouldn't miss this world. And he felt no guilt, leaving it this way. It had been his gift to use as he saw fit. And he had.

Elliott thought he was hallucinating when a crack of light spilled into the room. He closed his eyes, opened them again, and the light was gone. Or maybe it was the light, pulling him into the afterlife. Where had it gone?

Something moved. A shadow. He was sure of it. He tried to focus, to pinpoint it, but he couldn't clear his vision. He couldn't move. His own breath caught and clogged.

It was a dream. Jade. Her long, thick hair, shining in the moonlight.

He closed his eyes, her face printed on his mind as he drifted into nothing.

Then he had the impression of a presence near him . . . my God, it wasn't a dream . . . and he gasped a warning as the silhouette came close. As she bent to him, he tried to shake his head, to speak . . . he lifted a hand, weak, word-

less, trying to warn her away . . . yet certain it was a dream
. . . but she took his hand before he could stop her, and he felt
the press of warm, slender fingers in his palm, the smooth
caress as she slid them along his arm. . . .

He gasped again, trying to comb through the pain and fog
to shout at her, to cry out. But it was too late.

"Lou forgot the Stranger's book," Quent said, noticing the
little black tome on the table as he stood. It was late, and
it didn't seem that Elliott and Lou would be returning to
The Pub. Everyone else seemed to be about finished for the
night—himself included.

He wanted to return to his room, on the off chance that
it wasn't empty, that Zoë had returned, and was waiting for
him. Now that she knew where to find him.

Bloody idiot. Of course the room would be empty, just as
it had been when he'd awakened from the glorious afterglow
of a much-needed, tear-your-clothes-off bonking. Not only
had the room been bereft of Zoë, except for the faint residual
of cinnamon, but her arrow was gone too.

The message had been clear. *See ya later, chump. Thanks
for the good times.*

And Quent hadn't really cared. It was obviously nothing
but bloody fabulous sex for either of them.

Though next time . . . he wouldn't fucking fall asleep.

Now, he reached for the Stranger's book, then hesitated,
drawing his hand back.

What secrets did the journal hold? What horrific memories would drown him if he touched it? What would he learn
if he touched it?

He was curious about these Strangers, these men who
wore crystals embedded in their skin. Were they humans?
Or aliens that simply looked like humans?

Was it possible they really were Atlanteans?

Despite everything he knew about the Strangers and their frightening actions, Quent was fascinated. Fascinated, and yet sickened. Frightened too.

If indeed these . . . beings . . . had thrust their continent up from the bottom of the Pacific Ocean—a scientific impossibility, he knew that—but what if somehow the impossible had happened?

In doing so, in reinstating their continent, they had destroyed the world, changed its entire makeup, its climate . . . and annihilated the human population. That was reason enough to despise the Strangers, to work to eradicate them without hesitation. Or mercy. Just as Lou and his brother intended to do.

And also to fear them, and their capabilities.

But . . . was it possible that they didn't know what they'd done? They didn't realize what the results were of their return to earth—either from the depths of the ocean or from somewhere outside of this planet?

Was it possible that they had innocently perpetuated the event? It wouldn't make the result any less horrific, but at least it wouldn't have been premeditated. At least it wouldn't have been so evil.

Before he could make the decision to pick up the book, Lou walked up to the table.

"How's the mayor?" asked Wyatt. "Where's Elliott?"

"I was wondering the same thing myself," Lou said. "He asked me to watch over Vaughn until the morning, but I realized I'd left the book in my haste. Didn't want anyone else to find it, and I wasn't sure if you were still here. It's getting late."

"Did Elliott work his magic?" asked Fence, finishing the last of his beer.

Lou rubbed his goatee. "He said he did what he could, and that we'd know in the morning. I left Flo there, watching over him. Anyone seen Jade? She's close to Vaughn . . . I'm sure she'd want to know about him."

"Haven't seen her since she finished singing," Wyatt replied.

"I have the book here," Quent said. "I was just about to take a look at it myself."

Using a napkin for protection, aware that the others were working on settling their bill with Trixie—which turned out to be covered under Mayor Rogan's carte blanche—Quent flipped open the book.

Drawings. Numbers . . . upon closer observation, he thought they were navigational points. Longitude and latitude. Locations, that maybe went with the drawings—maps of what looked like areas surrounding Envy, and along the new West Coast.

Rows of names, listed. Ages, genders, what looked like height and weight. They were listed in groups. He tried to read the cramped writing in the dim light of The Pub, his mind puzzling through the categories. What connected these people?

They were all about the same age. Sixteen, seventeen, eighteen . . . something creaked in his brain, shivered down his spine. All about the same ages as the blokes in the van. *The map.*

He reached for the wrinkled piece of paper Zoë had left him, his shoulders prickling like they did when he was on the trail of some fascinating antiquity. Sometimes he was right, sometimes he was wrong . . . but he felt sure he was right this time.

He yanked up the book, using the napkin to grab a corner

of it so he could compare the map to the images inside.
There had to be a connection . . . he felt it. The book opened,
the pages fanning upside down, and some folded papers fell
out, scattering on the table.

Then he remembered what Zoë had said about crystal
dust. As Lou began to scuffle up the papers, Quent explained
about the map. "She said there was crystal dust all over."

"Crystal dust?" Lou looked up from his task. Even in the
sketchy light of the votive on the table, Quent could see the
shock in his face. "In the kids' van? No fucking way."

"What's crystal dust?" asked Wyatt.

"Crystal dust, also called pixie dust or grit . . . the post-
apocalyptic version of crack," Lou explained. He removed
his glasses, setting them on top of the papers that had fallen
from the book and rubbed his eyes. "It's rare, impossible to
come by unless you're getting it from the Strangers. You say
it was in the van that Geoff had? This woman who told you
. . . who is she?"

Quent had to shrug. He wished to hell he knew more than
her first name. Even when he held her arrow and tried to
take in the images and memories, things were blurred and
swampy. "She shot these ingenious arrows at the *gangas* and
helped us chase them off. She brought the map here to me in
Envy, and told me about the crystal dust. It's a drug?"

Lou nodded and scratched his gray goatee roughly. "The
worst kind. They grind up certain kinds of crystals—this is
according to Jade, who would know—and rub it into their
skin. It sort of grinds in—they do it on their arms, for example, on the inner part of the wrist, where the skin is thin
and the blood vessels are close to the surface. The dust or
grit from the granules enter the bloodstream, and you get a
great high—you feel no pain, get very aroused, can go on for

hours. Or so they say." The description could have been said jokingly, as if it were amusing . . . but there wasn't a hint of anything but deathly seriousness in his face.

Even Fence resisted the urge to make a comment.

He picked up his glasses. "There's no grit in Envy. We don't have the types of crystals that could be ground up here. How the hell the kids ever found out about it, let alone got it, is frightening." As if needing the distraction, he began to shuffle through the papers, unfolding them. "I didn't get a chance to look closely at these earlier," he said. "These are photos."

"Hm. I don't know who this is," he said, offering one to Quent. "Must be someone important to the Strangers."

Quent eyed the picture but didn't take it. "I've seen this man before," he said. The image was of a distinguished-looking man with white hair, combed back from his fore-head. He was in his late fifties, maybe, and he wore a suit. Strong features, charisma exuding from him, he was shaking the hand of some other unexceptional companion.

Patting the rest of them into a pile, Lou picked up a smaller photo. "Oh, God. Jade. There's a picture of Jade here."

"Why would they have her picture?" Wyatt asked, reaching for it. "What happened to her hair? She shave it off?"

"Preston would do anything to get her back, and although they believe she's dead, I'd guess that they're not taking any chances." Lou's eyes had grown sober behind his glasses. "It's a damn good thing this Stranger didn't get a good look at her, and is probably dead. If word got back to Preston that she was still alive, they'd be looking for her. She wouldn't be safe here."

Pursing his lips, rubbing his forehead as if it pained him, Lou looked back down at the last photo; a large one that had been folded in quarters. "This is the triumvirate of the Strangers, the most powerful of the leaders. Preston, Fielding, and Liam. I don't know who the fourth man is—the same one who you said looked familiar in that other picture."

Quent, who could only see the vague details of the photo from where he sat, felt his breathing clog. "Let me see that."

Lou flipped up the picture and showed it to Quent. "Preston, with the bleached hair. The one in the middle is Fielding. He's a real son of a bitch. Liam. . . ."

Quent felt as though someone had punched him in the stomach, and he didn't hear anything else Lou was saying. He grabbed at the photo, heedless of his cursed ability to read its secrets, pulling it toward the small circle of light on the table so he could look at it. Dizzy. Lightheaded and nauseated. "That's. . . ." But he couldn't form the words. No fucking way. He dropped the photo onto the table, staring down at it.

"Quent?" Wyatt took his arm, looking at him in alarm. Simon and Fence were staring at him.

Quent could hardly breathe. "It's . . . Fielding. . . ." He swallowed, made himself say words, because then the others could tell him he was fucked up. Mistaken. "That man is my father."

His father was one of the Strangers.

When Elliott didn't answer her knock, Jade used Lou's passkey to open the door to his room. Her heart pounded, her palms damp. *What had he done? What had he* done?

She stepped in, and the smell of blood, of death, assaulted her. She focused on the bed, lit in a wash of morning sun and dark blood. *Oh God.*

"Elliott," she breathed, the bottom dropping out of her stomach. "No, no. . . ." She started toward the bed, heart in her throat, but then saw the trail of blood leading away.

She turned and rushed into the bathroom, stopping short when she saw the lifeless body sprawled in the tub. "My God."

Blood, everywhere, spattering the aged white tile. The light above the sink glowed. She was close enough to see her now, to recognize Trixie's face. Still and white. Blood stained her clothing, but her face was clean and peaceful. A wad of bloody towels sat on the floor, testament to the losing battle Elliott had fought.

Heart pounding, palms damp, Jade breathed slowly, trying to rid herself of the clogging scent of blood. She found the bedsheet on the floor near the toilet, twisted in a pile, and she carefully covered Trixie's face and body.

Then she left the bathroom, closing the door quietly.

And she saw him. Sitting in a chair in the darkest corner, hidden by shadows . . . as if he wished to be swallowed by them.

"Elliott," she said.

He sat like stone, hands clasped over his knees as he bent forward, his head hanging down. "Elliott," she said again, moving closer, reaching for him.

"Don't touch me." He'd lifted his face and she saw the starkness, the pain and loathing.

Jade didn't know what to say, how to react. She stilled, looking at him. Their eyes met for a moment, his black and angry in the shadows . . . then he tore them away. A suffocating silence blanketed the room, the smell of blood and death lingering, and her heart squeezed painfully. *Elliott.*

You're insane, she'd said to him earlier.

Maybe I am.

But he wasn't. An insane man would not be sitting here in agony like this. An insane man would not have made the choice he'd made.

Jade had no illusions about what had happened. This morning, she'd heard that Vaughn had been gravely injured, and that Lou had brought one of the men who'd rescued the teens to help him. As Flo blithely explained how miraculous it was that Vaughn had been cured, Jade's world had begun to splinter. *Elliott, you damned idiot.* She'd run, literally *run*, to his room.

"She touched me," he said at last, the words gravelly. He stared down at his clasped hands. "I couldn't stop her."

She took a tentative step closer.

He didn't look up, but she saw his fingers clasp and unclasp. "I tried to warn her, but I was too weak. I shouldn't have come back here." He drew in a shuddering breath. "I looked for a dog. A cat. Something."

Something to give it to.

"But it came too fast."

"Elliott," she said, his name coming out like a breath.

"I had to get away . . . I could hardly stand . . . before someone found me."

Jade moved closer. She wanted to pull him into her arms, hold that powerful, sorrowing body. "You don't need to explain. I know—"

"Don't *touch* me," he snarled.

"I need to touch you," she whispered, ignoring the command, putting her arms around his impossibly wide, iron-rigid shoulders. He stiffened, withdrawing at her touch, and she felt him gather up as if to push her away. But she tightened her hold, pulling him close to her, half leaning, half sitting against him.

"You couldn't have stopped her. She couldn't have known, Elliott." His hair slipped softly beneath her fingers, warm and wavy and thick. The brush of his lashes tickled her throat, and she felt the accompanying wetness of tears, moist in the warmth of her neck, the press of his nose against the soft part of her shoulder.

"It's all fucked up."

"You saved Vaughn's life by risking your own." It had been more than a risk, she knew. She understood now—he'd come up here to die. Where no one would find him, touch him, where he'd be safely ensconced until it was too late. But Trixie, like Jade herself, had been fascinated by him and took matters into her own hands. If she hadn't. . . .

My God, I almost lost him. "How could you have stopped her? How could you have known?"

He shook his head against her, and she realized that his arms had gone around her waist now. He was no longer pushing her away, but clinging. His strong fingers curled into her hips, his face buried against her. She felt him trembling, his deep rage, more dampness against her neck.

Her hands moved down to the broad shoulders, the wide expanse of his back, making slow, easy circles. Gentle strokes, round and round, sending her comfort into his skin.

"A fucking waste. A goddamn *waste*!" Elliott's voice lifted, rough and loud. "I knew what I was doing, goddammit. *I* made the decision. And she . . . Christ . . . she fucking blundered into it." His words were choked, tight, torn from his throat.

Jade had no answers. She could do nothing but hold him, stroking gently. There were no words. For a very long time.

He shuddered quietly against her, and she pressed a kiss to his hot temple, then down onto his cheek. It was wet and she kissed the tear gently. She drew him closer, tugging him toward her, easing him out of the chair, into her arms. "Come," she whispered, and then found his lips.

They tasted salty and soft, warm, and so tender. She kissed him, focusing with everything she had . . . lightly brushing his lips, then back to fit her mouth to them. Trying to show him she loved him without the words . . . words that didn't work right now.

His arms moved and came around her as they settled onto the floor, kissing, slowly . . . long and gently. Breaths slow and raspy, rough in the back of her throat as Jade thought about how she'd almost lost him. And what he must feel.

And why, suddenly, it wasn't important to be in control. Why it didn't matter if she answered to him about Luke . . . or anyone else.

Elliott turned his face, his breathing quiet and rough, and rested his forehead against her neck. Then, with great control, he pulled away. Hardest thing he'd ever done. He used the chair to steady himself as he started to pull to his feet.

Slow, stiff, empty. Yet . . . livid inside. Raging.

Jade looked up at him, sorrow filming her green eyes. So utterly beautiful, with the sun stealing over her shoulders and tinting her face with its glow. Beautiful, everything he'd ever wanted . . . needed. But, yet . . . not his.

What was he going to do?

With Trixie . . . with Jade . . . with this fucking curse . . . with his *life*.

He closed his eyes against it, curled his fingers over the smooth wood of the chair . . . struggled against the blistering wave of desire. Not lust. Desire . . . to hold, to have. To know.

But then she moved, reaching up toward him. He could smell the waft of lemon, he could *feel* her warmth. The blush of her nearness and her compassion. A prickling started down his back, a longing billowed inside him so strongly that his fingers shook.

"Elliott." He loved the way she said his name, long and rolling, all three syllables clear and unrushed. Like a caress.

She reached up, closing her fingers over the hand gripping the chair. She tugged them free and he let her, unable to keep the distance that he knew . . . somewhere in the recesses of his mind . . . he needed to. But she was soft and comforting and *his* . . . so very much *his* . . . only his.

He sank onto the floor, to his knees, propping his weak self up against the side of the chair as he gathered her toward him . . . into him. He was lost. Her taste, her smell, the warmth and softness of Jade filled his hands, his mouth, his senses. He could no longer hold back. This was comfort, this was simply *good* and felt perfect . . . it had been so long. So long. Not since he'd held a woman, but since he felt settled, satisfied . . . as if he could do this.

Lining his body to hers, her breasts crushed against his chest, he dipped his face, his cheek brushing the warm tickle of her hair . . . and drew in a long, embarrassingly shaky breath.

Jade. Here. Now.

"I thought she was you." The words slipped out before he could catch them. God, how did that make him sound?

Jade stilled in his arms, and he would have pushed her away, mortified and broken, but she lifted her face and turned so she could find his mouth. Her lips were sweet and soft, so soft and gentle. *Mine.*

He couldn't. Shouldn't. It was despicable. But he opened his mouth with a soft groan, took her tongue as it swept deeply, slowly . . . as if she meant to comfort him with this kiss the same way she had with her hands. His knees weakened and he settled farther back against the chair, closing his eyes. The kiss went on and on, so slow and long and deep . . . thorough and easy . . . and sad.

Elliott recognized sorrow and compassion in the way she kissed him, the thoughtful brush of lip against lip, the gentle curl of her fingers at the back of his neck. He dragged his hands through her hair, felt her hips shift against him as they moved, as he realized how easy it would be to tumble onto the floor, with this bundle of woman.

He opened his eyes. "Jade." He heard the pain in his own voice, but forced himself to continue. "No . . ." he said, but his hands wouldn't release her. He couldn't detach himself from her, keep his mouth from moving over her soft temple, his hands from drawing her up close, hard, against his hard-on.

"Yes." Her voice was steady, meant to penetrate his fog, meant to tug him along with her into the relief, the pleasure that awaited. "Elliott."

He wanted to refuse, he needed to. But his fingers had shifted lower, closing around her waist, feeling the warmth of her there in his hands, that little strip of skin that had first enticed him as she rode off on her horse. She looked up at him, desire plain in her face. Desire and certainty.

Somehow he was moving, shifting, and they sagged to the floor, soon to be a puddle of limbs and mouths and hands. His body had sprung alive, awakening from its shell of grief. It pounded and surged, the desire, the *need* taking over, destroying his will.

The swell of her breasts beneath his fingers, the curve of her hip pressing into him. The crush of her lips beneath his as he drowned out his own protestations. The rage of his own body, pounding and alive and desperate.

The floor beneath him, pulling her over on top of him, her slender legs straddling his waist . . . the rough carpet scraping his head, her hands cradling his face.

He explored, felt the weight of her breasts, the tightness of her nipples, the delicious shift of her against him as she hovered above, filling his sight, his hands, his mouth. Oh yes.

He closed his eyes, breathing deeply . . . his fingers smoothing along her torso . . . hips to waist, up her back and over delicate shoulder blades as her long hair brushed his lips and chin.

God, he *needed*. This. Jade.

She moved, her hands spanning his chest as she rose above him. Her mouth glistened, full and soft from his, her eyes shadowed and heavy-lidded. Her shirt hung loosely, gapping so that he could see a hint of shadows and curves.

She promised beauty and comfort. Pleasure. And the knowledge that he could escape the dark reality of life with this woman he had to have. The one. The one he'd been searching for.

That he should find love, here and now, in this tragic world, with a woman who couldn't return it . . . that tore at him most of all.

But he covered her mouth again anyway. He smoothed over the warmth of her skin, tugging the shirt from the waistband of her jeans, resisting the urge to move south beneath the tight denim. She rose up, sitting back on his belly and flung the shirt away. Eyes holding his, hiding nothing, she reached behind and loosened her bra, sliding it off and onto the chair.

Gloriously beautiful, breathtaking . . . refusing to think how often she'd taken the same pose . . . he reached to touch her . . . so full and warm, her body long and curvy. She arched down against him, her breasts bare, cupped in his hands, her weight pressing into the heat of his crotch, and he gave it up. Gave it away, that last bit of resistance snapping . . . and allowed himself to *take*.

Now. Oh yes.

He gave in and freed himself, pulling her down onto him, gently rolling to the side, taking her with him . . . the tight, high breast in his hand, the taut nipple beneath his thumb, the warm saltiness of her throat under his mouth, the long slide of legs spreading around his hips, pressing into the mad hard-on straining behind his zipper as her toes slid along his calves. She twisted and sighed against him, fueling the sudden rage of desire that blinded him to care, or reason.

Everything pulsed and pounded, everything focused on now, *now* . . . the silk and sleekness, her smell, her taste. He tore at the snap of her jeans, whipping them away with a loud, rough snap as she pulled on his shirt, lifting her hips against him.

Suddenly they were skin to skin . . . oh, glorious, warm, curves, sliding with him, against him. His brain shattered, shut down, when she touched his cock, down inside the heat of his jeans, closing her fingers around him as she said his name in that winsome, inviting way. Then she gave a short, quick stroke, all along the length, once, twice . . . nearly sending him off the floor.

He lost his breath, his eyes rolling back into his head as he caught himself and pulled back from the edge. "Jade," he said in a desperate little groan, stopping her hand though the rest of him battled for more.

Her answer was to yank his face down for a kiss, taking his mouth as if she were as starved as he, and she ground her hips against his even as she tore at the snap and zipper. She pressed against the screaming erection where every bit of his blood had gathered, full and raging, demanding, and the next thing he knew, he was there and free, she was there, hot and slick and ready and he didn't even have a moment to think about protection before she slipped him in . . . oh, God, oh God. . . .

He managed not to go over right then, but it was close. Jade moved, she tipped and twisted and teased, *oh, damn,* and made a soft little sound that nearly did it right then, her nails digging into his shoulders. He closed his eyes, fingers probably too tight into her arms, and fought for the rhythm . . . any rhythm . . . and then she moved against him again, hard and quick and fast, slamming up and into him, and then crying out in an unmistakable release.

That, it seemed, was what he needed to regain control. That delicious sound, low and throaty and . . . surprised.

The wildness slipped away, the desperation eased and he found himself where he needed to be: sinking into Jade, gathering her close as her eyes fluttered open, then closed as he moved with much more finesse than he'd yet shown. Long, steady, slow. . . . easy, easy . . . make it right. . . .

He even had the moment to dip and use his lips and tongue on one of her nipples, teasing and coaxing . . . something he'd neglected earlier in the frenzy. She arched and shivered beneath that new onslaught, and he sucked harder and moved faster, sliding a hand beneath her rear and the rough carpet, lifting her, holding her in the rhythm . . . oh . . . yes . . . there it was, rising, blinding him once again, coiling up hot and hard and sharp until he saw it, felt it, burst over . . . shooting into a long, low slide of heat that curled his toes, devastating him.

In the most satisfying way.

They lay, skin to skin, sticky and damp and warm, for a moment before he had the strength to open his eyes. The water-stained ceiling stared down at him, the walnut arm of the chair loomed above, and to the right of his shoulder, Jade, warm and real, next to him.

A variety of realizations slammed into him as he came back to himself, the first of which was that he'd had unprotected sex. While a body was in the next room. *Christ.*

He shuddered a long breath, easing from Jade and her

glorious self. The rough carpet scraped his arm as he shifted up and next to her. She was looking up at him, her face serious, her eyes half shadowed so that he couldn't tell if there was regret or horror at what they'd done . . . or pity.

He didn't really want to know which it was.

"I'm sorry I called you insane," she said. "You're not insane. And that was. . . ." Her eyes fluttered and she bit her lower lip. "Elliott, that was oh-my-God wonderful. That . . . just now . . . was . . . unbelievable." She looked at him bashfully, clearly unused to being so bold—at least in matters such as this—and his whole world softened into mush.

Before he could respond—which, based on the way he was feeling, would likely have resulted in a repeat of the whole event—there was a loud banging on the door. She scrambled up and away faster than he thought possible, her eyes wide and startled, breasts jouncing delightfully, and for a moment he thought he was offended. But then he thrust the thought away and stood himself, realizing once again that a body was in the bathtub, they'd just had sex—unprotected—on the floor, and he didn't know who was at the door. He dragged on his jeans and, after a glance at Jade, who was half-decent, went to open it.

It was the fucking mayor of Envy.

Seven months After

They came today. In a large black humvee.

The sound of the truck was eerie and unfamiliar after so many months of relative silence, of no cars, no highways or airplanes or trains. At first, we thought help from the outside world had finally arrived.

Then two men came out of the humvee. They looked like us, even talked like us. But I could tell right away there was something strange about them. They asked for nothing, took nothing . . . yet they didn't stay. Did little more than look around and talk with some of us for a while about how we'd survived, and how we were living. Their eyes seemed to miss nothing.

They gave what amounted to gifts to those they spoke with: beer, soda pop, chocolate, even some fresh strawberries.

And then the strangers got back in their humvee and drove off.

The *jiang shis*, or—as people are starting to refer to them because everything has to be shortened even in this world—the *jangas*, can be heard most nights. Moaning and calling for Ruth, whoever that is.

Have learned that they're not very smart, but still frightening. Don't go out at night.

Election for mayor is next week. I pray that Greg Rowe wins. If Thad Marck does, I fear what will happen. He is very rigid and controlling. Reminds me of Dimmesdale from *The Scarlet Letter*. (I hated that book.)

Theo has offered to rig the computer counting the ballots so that Rowe's a shoe-in. Am almost tempted to let him, but will resist.

It is not for me—or any one man—to make such a decision. That's why we've returned to our democratic roots, even though some of us here are not Americans.

I leave it to the Higher Power, even though many blame God for what has happened to us, calling this Judgment Day. I've pointed out that if this were the Apocalypse, we'd *all* be dead. It would be the end of the world. As it is, we're still alive.

There must be a reason for it.

Best part of the day: Elsie let me kiss her. She smiled afterward and I thought I might die.

—from the journal of Lou Waxnicki

_____

CHAPTER 17

When Elliott opened the door, Vaughn Rogan was the last person he expected to see there.

Rogan extended his hand immediately to Elliott. "I understand I have you to thank for my miraculous recovery," he said. They shook hands, and he noted that Rogan had a solid, sure grip. He looked him in the eye, was completely sincere and maybe even a little overwhelmed by the emotion of the moment. After all, he had practically been brought back from the dead. Elliott couldn't find a reason to dislike the man whatsoever, though he was looking hard.

Then he realized he was blocking the entrance, and although he bristled all over with male possessiveness, he took a step back. If there were to be fireworks, he'd take them now.

Rogan walked into the room and Elliott saw his eyes land on Jade for the first time. A quick glance told him that she was just finishing the buttons on her jeans. Her bra lay like a beacon in the middle of the room.

"Jade," Rogan said. Surprise, shock, discomfort flushed his rugged face. Then he tore his attention from her and back to Elliott, who braced himself. But the assault never happened. "I realize I'm deeply in your debt. They said I was going to die, and that you somehow . . . healed me. Completely. No scars, no weakness, no nothing." Wonder colored his voice, sincere gratitude his eyes.

Elliott felt his mouth tighten. "If you're in my debt, then I think it would be best if we didn't mention exactly what happened. It's miraculous to me as well, and I prefer to keep it a secret. Especially since. . . ." His voice trailed off. Dare he trust the man?

Jade took the decision from him by changing the subject. "Vaughn. What happened? What were you doing outside the walls at night?"

Elliott saw Rogan draw himself up, widening his impressive shoulders, as if affronted by her implication that it wasn't safe for him to go beyond the protective walls. For the moment, Elliott heartily felt for the man, especially knowing that Jade herself ventured out on a regular basis. "I saw Geoff Pinglett and some of his friends sneaking out of the city and after the other night, I wasn't about to let that happen."

"You could've sent someone else after them," she countered, sounding like a mother. Or a big sister. Definitely not like a lover.

"I'm not a goddamned figurehead mayor, Jade," Rogan said flatly. "I went after them myself because I wanted to and was fully capable of doing so."

Elliott dared not look at Jade, because he was certain her response to this obviously erroneous statement would be an arched eyebrow. His sympathy for the man grew just a little bit more.

Rogan's eyes darkened and his face settled. "Jade, you might think your own adventures out and about go unnoticed, but I can tell you that I've been fully aware of them for some time. What happened last night was not a mistake, but the result of a trap set for me, or anyone else who might have followed the kids. Including you. So consider it a warning. From me, as well as whoever nearly killed me. Don't go out beyond the walls until we find out who set up a pair of lions as a booby trap. And if it weren't for this," Rogan produced a wicked-looking metal bolt, "I wouldn't have even made it back behind the walls of the city."

Elliott recognized the arrow right away. "Is that yours?"

"No. I don't know where it came from. They found one in the skull of the lion that attacked me, and another near my hand on the ground. Wish I knew who he was, so I could thank him too."

Before the conversation could continue, another knock sounded at the door, and Elliott went to answer it. It was Lou.

"Oh, thank God," he said when Elliott answered the door. He'd never seen the man so agitated in his short acquaintance. "Do you know where Jade is?"

"Yeah, she's here," he answered, stepping out of the way to offer entrance. "What's wrong?"

"It's Theo. He's badly hurt. I need you and Jade to go after him with me. In case I need help to bring him back."

"Where is he?"

"A place called Valley Way. A few hours ride southwest from here. He can't move. We can't leave him there." Lou's glasses were streaked and his mouth set so tightly, wrinkles radiated more deeply than before.

Elliott shook his head. "Of course not. Of course I'll go."

"We'll both go," said Jade.

"Can't you go any faster?" Jade asked, her voice tight and high. Just then, the humvee bounced awkwardly into a deep rut and she slammed her head on the ceiling. "Ouch!" She rode next to Elliott in the front seat, a few wisps of her mahogany hair blustering in the wind coming through an open window. She'd pulled it back in a ponytail, but some of it still escaped.

"I could if you wanted to keep banging your head like that," Elliott told her. "It's too damn rough to go much faster." He ducked as they slammed into another small rut, then accelerated as soon as there was a smooth patch.

They had left Envy three hours ago, taking the humvee they'd acquired from the Stranger after the blackout. Lou intended to accompany them, but Jade and Sage had put their feminine feet down and refused to allow it.

In the end, Lou had no choice against their mutiny, especially when Sage pointed out that they might need him on the technical end back in Envy. Jade had also described the problem with Trixie, and Lou reluctantly agreed to stay back and help with explaining her death . . . in a delicate manner.

"What do you know about Fielding?" Elliott asked as he jerked the wheel to avoid a tire-sized rock. He still couldn't fathom the fact that Quent's father, Quentin Parris Brummell Fielding, Junior, chairman of Brummell Industries, was one of the leaders of the Strangers.

Elliott's jaw tightened. It wasn't bad enough that they had to be stuck in this godforsaken place . . . but for his friend to learn that his father surely had helped to create the mass destruction . . . He couldn't fathom how Quent was feeling. It was inconceivable.

Bracing herself with a hand pressed against the ceiling, Jade answered his question. "He's one of the leaders. I only saw him once during my time . . . with the Strangers. The most powerful ones hardly ever left their main compound. The others tended to speak of Fielding with deference and respect. Although I don't think Preston particularly liked him. You said he's Quent's *father*? From . . . before?"

"Yes. And at that time, in 2010, Quent's father . . . well, he was an extremely rich and powerful man. He had a private side too—a horrible one. He was violent and selfish and probably a little crazy." He drew in a deep breath, shaking his head. "And now he's a Stranger. He's still alive. Quent said he looks the same."

"Do you mean that this is proof that the Strangers are . . . people like us? Or, people like you and Simon and Quent? People who somehow lived through the Change without dying . . . or growing old?" She sounded breathless . . . as though someone had kicked her in the stomach. The same way Elliott was feeling.

"This means," he replied slowly, feeling his way with his words just as he was feeling his way on what was left of the road, "I *think* it means that people . . . humans like us . . . caused the Change." He closed his eyes for a minute and when he opened them, saw a tree looming. He dodged it, ignoring Jade's squeak of fear. She'd wanted him to go faster. "It wasn't aliens, it wasn't people from under the sea who destroyed the world. It was the people who belonged to the Cult of Atlantis. Fielding and the others. People like us."

People like us.

Good God. People who had actually planned to destroy the world—not in an act of war, not to expurgate their enemies, but to annihilate the whole world. Everywhere. Everyone.

Except the members of the Cult of Atlantis.

It was like the plot in a Clive Cussler novel come to pass—and this time there had been no hero to foil the plot of mass destruction.

"And," he added, "even if Fielding and his cult didn't actually *cause* the events, somehow he had to be involved with them. He's still alive, still unaged, and he's a Stranger. There's no question about that."

And that was enough for Elliott to condemn the man.

"Look," Jade said, pointing. "I think that's it."

Elliott shielded his gaze in the bright midday sun, peering at the massive, sprawling structure ahead of them. Long, with a multitude of wings, and comprised of an irregular rooftop, the building had no windows. What had once been a covered multilevel parking structure was attached, and vines and bushes grew there with abandon, making it look like the Hanging Gardens of Babylon. An empty space yawned in front of the architectural monstrosity, boasting eruptions of trees and other growth amid what had been an expanse of concrete. A parking lot.

It took him a moment, a few moments, actually, to recognize that Valley Way was a shopping mall. Then he noticed the array of letters still attached to the building:

VAL Y W Y M LL. Yep, it had once been a way for women to inflict torture on their loved ones.

He glanced at Jade, who'd never be able to experience the feminine pleasure of dragging her man from store to store.

"So, is this a settlement where people live? Like Greenside?"

Jade shook her head and shrugged. "I'm not sure. I've never been here, and Theo has only been here once that I know of. It wasn't part of his regular Running route—it's farther west than we usually go. And we never go west."

"Why?"

"Because that's where the *gangas* go. They travel west, every night when the sun starts to come up."

Elliott hadn't noticed that. Of course, he and the others had pretty much avoided the orange-eyed monsters after a few meetings. "They're like vampires and can't be in the sun?"

"They don't come out in the sun. I don't know if it's because they sleep all day so they can move around at night, or because the sun is dangerous to them. I . . . haven't asked." She flashed him an amused look from behind her blowsy hair, then her face sobered. "Elliott, before we go in . . . I want to say something."

"Go on." He wasn't sure whether to brace himself more against the rough ground, or what she was going to say. Things had moved very quickly since they'd disentangled themselves at Rogan's knock . . . and though he had a few things to say to her, he didn't like doing it while navigating this terrain. He wanted his full attention on her, and hers on him.

"About what you said last night . . . about pushing your way through the crowd. . . ." Her voice trailed off and he looked at her. She shrugged. "Elliott, there is no crowd. There's no one. Else."

"What about Luke? He had his hands all over you." Elliott couldn't quite contain the accusation in his voice, and was relieved when he had to focus on avoiding a large, rusted-out Dumpster and a deep rut at the same time.

"That's the thing," she said. "I should have told you before, when you asked about him. He was being a jerk, and nothing happened. Though he'd like something to."

"I'd be happy to have a word with him," Elliott said, realizing he sounded like a thug. Did he care? Nope.

He would have preferred to have this conversation somewhere soft and private, preferably naked, since it seemed as if it was going his way, but here they were. There'd be time later to follow up on things. He hoped.

Elliott looked over at Jade and a wave of . . . softness . . . slid over him. Like his Tía Sarita's thick quilt, covering him during a blustery winter night. Comfortable. Secure. Warm.

Was this what he needed? This woman? Was it she who

would help him find his place in this strange world, with her easy ways and pragmatism . . . and her amazing rodeo queen riding combined with her determination to save the world?

He couldn't hold back a smile at the memory of the way she swung wildly at the snake during their battle, missing him by a mile. Not funny at the time, not really funny at all . . . but proof that this woman wasn't perfect.

He couldn't live with perfect. He wanted *real*.

He wanted her.

"I can handle Luke," she said.

"What about me?" he asked, looking at her. Laying it all out there, naked as a baby.

She just smiled that curly-edged smile that made his heart funnel all the way to his toes. "I'm not sure, but I'm going to try."

"Let's find Theo," he said, his voice rough. *And then let's get the hell back to Envy so I can see just how you handle me. All night long. And then some.*

Elliott drove the humvee into the old parking structure, deciding that would be a good way to hide it from sight. He felt a definite uneasiness about this place, just as he had about that tunnel. Right before those sleek scales showed up.

"Theo's message said Mac . . . M-A-C," Jade said as they drove into the overgrown structure. "I don't know if he couldn't type the rest or if that's all he meant."

"M-A-C? McDonald's," Elliott suggested, navigating into the narrow entrance. "There's always a McDonald's in or near every mall."

A variety of cars, overgrown and rusted, were scattered throughout the structure. None of them looked as if they'd been driven in the half century since the Change. Elliott had a weird sense of déjà vu driving in, past the ticket booths, looking for a parking place. He found one big enough between a 7 series BMW and a Focus. Some bonehead had taken up one-and-a-half spaces for his Beamer fifty years ago to keep it from getting scratched. Too bad it hadn't worked.

"I'm going to leave the keys here," he said, turning off the engine. "Just in case . . . well, in case we get separated. And you need them."

"I can't drive," she protested.

"Theo can." Elliott had a really bad feeling about this place. He was going to be prepared for all eventualities. "And this is an automatic transmission." Ignoring her wide-eyed look, he continued to explain, slowly and clearly, "All you have to do is turn the key like this and move this shift into R for reverse and D for drive—to go forward. . . ." He gave her a quick lesson in accelerator versus brake, and then looked at her. "I hope you won't need to know, but just in case. It's best to be prepared."

She nodded. "You're right. But I'm not going to leave without you, Elliott."

He almost leaned forward to kiss her right then, but thought better of it. There would, God willing, be time for that later. Now he—they both—needed to be focused on finding Theo.

He tucked the keys, not under the floor mat, but into the pocket behind the driver's seat, and quietly closed the door. "Mac?" he asked. "What else did he say?"

"Not much." She pulled out a paper and read. "Hurt. Can't move. *Gangas*. At Mac."

Great. She hadn't mentioned the fact that there were *gangas* in there—although why it should be a surprise to him, he didn't know. If it wasn't *gangas*, it was Strangers. Or rabid lions. Or blackout storms.

"Why don't you stay here and let me go in and try to find

him . . . that way both of us won't get caught by the *gangas*," he suggested.

Jade shot him a glare, just as he'd expected she would: "I've been dealing with *gangas* longer than you have," she pointed out, not inaccurately. "And you know how to drive that thing. If one of us is going to stay here, it should be you."

Check and mate. *Damn.*

Moving right along. "We could try and get in on this side—there're going to be entrances all over," he said. "The problem will be finding a McDonald's. Or whatever Mac means." The problem was, Elliott hadn't paid much attention to mall stores, so he couldn't think of the name of any shop that had Mac in it. There was Abercrombie. PacSun. Had it been a typo, and Mac was really meant to be Pac?

Possible, but not likely. The keys weren't all that close together. A computer geek would be a good typist.

How the hell were they going to find him in this huge place? And avoid the *gangas*? Yeah, they were dumb, but still. . . .

One step at a time.

Jade followed him as he walked out of the parking structure and scanned the building. There was no sign of life, no sign of *living* anywhere. A jungle had begun to overtake the south side of the building, growing thick and full on those walls and beginning to spread around to the east side, where they'd approached. What had once been a glass entry near the far end of the structure had shattered long ago and it appeared that someone had attempted to board up the hole.

But whoever it was had left a door, and that was the entrance he and Jade started toward. Knife in hand, and ears sharp, he waited, then carefully eased through the door.

Silence. Stillness. Not a sign of orange eyes.

Gray shadowed the mall's interior. The only illumination came from the bit of sun that was able to filter through the dust and grime covered skylights, most of which were still intact. A musty, peaty smell told Elliott that the lack of sunlight had encouraged the growth of moss, fungus, and mildew rather than trees and bushes. The soft skitter of nails and a slithering, rustling on what had been a marble floor, had Jade shuddering behind him, but to give her credit, she didn't grab at him. Or draw back.

It took a moment for Elliott's eyes to get used to the dimness, and although he had a lighter, something warned him not to use it. He reached back and closed his fingers around her arm and drew her forward so that she could see his warning not to speak. Their eyes met and she lifted a finger to her lips, as if to shush him. He smiled. Of course. She was in charge.

The area through which they'd come was not through one of the large anchor department stores, but a main mall entrance. Thus, there were storefronts lined up on either side of the wide thoroughfare. Elliott edged up next to the nearest one, glancing at the shattered plate glass windows.

The sign was a *Wheel of Fortune* clue: PR S D NT T X DO.

If he were Quent, he'd drop in and see if there was anything left to salvage, but as it was, Elliott merely moved past. The last time he'd needed a tux was when Janelle, one of his middle cousins, got married in a Big Fat Hispanic Wedding.

A new pang swept over him. Sitting around on a Saturday night folding whatever they could find into Tía Sarita's fresh corn tortillas and drinking *cerveza*. *Christ Almighty*. He prayed they'd gone easily and quickly.

Unlike many of the other buildings he'd been in recently,

this one hadn't been completely remodeled by Mother Nature. There were remnants of her tenacity—moss, some patches of grass, even a few trees that had likely already been growing in the place. The floor was covered with dirt, and leaves had piled into corners and around kiosks, benches, and storefront corners, presumably providing comfortable accommodations for a variety of rodents.

Knife in hand, Jade close behind him, Elliott started off through the eerie mall, looking at the store signs, trying to figure out what Theo had meant by Mac.

The dank, swampy smell became stronger as they moved past The Gap—whose plastic sign was dingy, but still intact except for a crack through the P (he'd like to check in there for some shirts to replenish his stock consisting now of one), BA H & OD W RKS, and a jewelry store on the corner as the thoroughfare opened into the main part of the mall.

Elliott glanced at the broken glass cases overrun by the shadow of mildew and realized that Jade seemed not to notice. And why would she? What use would she have for a diamond—if they hadn't already been foraged—when she'd probably rather have cotton panties? Or silk ones.

That thought nearly veered him off into territories best left unexplored, but Elliott did not succumb to the temptation. Now that they'd reached the main part of the mall, he saw that a second level yawned above them. At one time, it would have been accessible by the four escalators and single glass elevator. What had been a glass or plastic railing on the upper level had cracked and now sagged in a useless wave around the opening.

So far they'd heard nothing to indicate that there was any other living creature in this building, yet he still felt uneasy.

He watched closely for any shift in the shadows, any glow of orange, and paused regularly to listen. But the only sounds were the same faint rustles and skittering, and, once, the flap of a bird's wings as it soared through the air above them.

No, that wasn't a bird. That had been a bat. Elliott glanced at Jade, but she had no reaction. They'd passed F-Y-E and POT RY B RN but nothing like Mac. If they didn't find something soon, they were going to have to start looking in each dark store.

Then he heard it. Faint but distinctive.

Ruuuuthhh. Ruu-uuuthhh.

He looked at Jade as her gaze flashed to his. *Shit*, she mouthed. *Let's get going.*

Elliott yanked them into the deepest of shadows and pressed her against the wall as he looked around for those orange eyes. If the *gangas* were upstairs, then that was a good thing; it would take time for them to make their way down those escalators. And if they were down here with him and Jade, they simply had to go back up to evade them more easily.

With a single jab of his finger, he pointed to the stairs and looked at Jade. She followed his gesture and nodded, understanding his plan.

The *ganga* moans became a bit clearer as they moved faster but stuck to the shadows more closely. Elliott felt a severe rise of frustration. How in the fucking world were they going to find Theo in this place? It was like finding a needle in a haystack. Couldn't he have given them better information? There wasn't a golden arch in sight, or even a PacSun. Nothing that even related to Mac.

And then suddenly he saw it: The Apple Store—where they sold Macs (Of course. Where else would a geek be?)—and the sounds of the *gangas* clearly emanating from a different wing of the building. But moving closer.

Elliott pulled Jade behind him as he rushed toward the

back of the store. It was dark and after he nearly tripped over one of the display cases—for the second time—he thought, *fuck it*, and pulled out the lighter.

The flame gave off a small glow, exposing the computer hardware littering the floor and the dust stirred up by his movement. Holding the beacon aloft, Elliott hurried to the back, navigating through the debris and display cases, heading to where the stockroom must have been.

Theo had been foraging for electronics. A geek was a geek was a geek.

What had been a door to the stockroom sat on sagging hinges, and moved when Elliott pushed it gingerly. The door opened a bit, but stopped at thirty degrees as if something blocked it. "Hello?" he called softly, slipping through the narrow expanse, pushing his hand behind him in a *wait* motion. "Theo, are you here?"

He heard a faint sound, breathing, and began to scan his light around the room. He wasn't worried that a *ganga* lay in wait; they hadn't that subtlety. Either it was Theo, stalling to see if he was friend or foe—or preparing to assault him—or the man was injured and couldn't move or speak.

"Lou sent us," he tried again, scanning the light as he stepped in farther. He felt Jade follow him, and the door close behind her, blocking out any little bit of light that might come from the opening of the mall . . . and the glow from his lighter for any inquisitive *gangas*.

"Here," came a voice.

Still motioning for Jade to stay back in case it was a trap, Elliott moved toward the voice, around tall metal shelf units that had tipped like rows of dominoes. White Mac boxes of all sizes littered the area, and between the shelves and the boxes, he felt like he was making his way through a maze.

Then Elliott's light fell on the unmistakable sight of a

human figure half obstructed by a huge, metal shelving unit that had crumpled on top of him. The man beneath it was about his age, with short dark hair, long sideburns, and a little stubble on his chin. The guy looked up, then squinted as Jade blasted a flashlight toward him, revealing a wristwatch with a little red light on it and a pack on the floor next to him.

"Where's Theo Waxnicki?" Elliott asked, flicking off his light. Then he knelt next to the obviously injured man. "Where are you hurt?"

"Who are you?" the man replied, his words grinding out. Then he must have looked up and seen Jade behind him, because he grunted, "Jade. What the hell are you doing here?" He was obviously distressed, but not as much as Elliott, who'd so far received answers to none of his questions.

"Who the hell are you?" he asked again.

"I'm Theo Waxnicki," said the young man.

CHAPTER 18

"Who the hell are *you*?" Theo Waxnicki asked, looking up at Elliott.

Elliott stopped gawking at the man who was definitely not the seventy-seven years old he'd expected and moved into emergency mode. "Name's Elliott Drake. Your brother sent me with Jade. He thought you must be injured. I'm a doctor. I—uh—went to Michigan." He looked at the other man steadily, and waited for the comprehension. "A real doctor. Like . . . from the past."

With only the illumination from Jade's flashlight, it was hard to see exactly what was in Theo's eyes, but it looked like an intelligent gleam settled there. "Awesome, because I can't move," he said, gesturing to his legs.

"Can you feel your toes?" he said, already moving to lift the shelving unit. "Jade, help him get out when I lift this." It was large and unwieldy, but simple to get it up and shove it to the side. He took care to be as silent as possible.

"My toes are wiggling fine. I can feel my legs—ohhh," Theo groaned. "Son of a bitch, that f—" He cut off whatever he was going to say, and Elliott understood that feeling was surging back into his limbs like a thousand acupuncture needles.

Agony for him, but a really good sign. Thank God. At

least he wasn't going to have to make a decision about healing a paraplegic.

"*Gangas* are coming. We've got to get the hell out of here," Elliott said, helping Theo to his feet.

"God, Theo, how long have you been like this?" Jade asked, deep concern in her voice, reaching to touch her friend. "I'm so glad we got your messages, or you could have been here for a lot longer."

The moaning, groaning *rruuu-uuuth*s sounded like they were getting closer.

"I'll be able to walk . . . soon," he said, sagging toward Elliott.

Mainly because he was overcome by curiosity about the man's youthful appearance, Elliott did a quick, vertical scan of Theo, noticing with interest that his body was just as young inside as it appeared from the outside. And he was, thank God, completely healthy.

There *was* an odd formation near the base of his back, in the fleshy part above the hip, but it didn't appear to be contributing to any injury. And Theo was right—he should be able to walk soon, for there was nothing seriously wrong with him. A pulled muscle, legs weakened by stasis—he wasn't certain how long he'd been trapped under the shelves—and lack of food and water were all minor things.

Elliott would have to be careful helping him so that he didn't absorb the injury himself. Taking care not to touch him directly, skin to skin, or for more than a second at a time. The one thing he'd realized about his healing power was that it took concentration and more than a brief touch to allow the healing energy to sizzle through his body to the patient. Even when he'd "healed" the old man and passed it on to Lenny, he'd been scanning and concentrating on him, not knowing what would happen. It was the getting rid of the injury, the passing it on to some other entity, that seemed to happen uncontrollably, and in a flash.

"They're getting closer," Jade said. Her eyes held worry, but not panic.

"This mall is a storage place," Theo said, his voice thready with pain as he put full weight on his legs. "For the *gangas*. A freaking warehouse for the bastards. I've been avoiding them, hiding out here for two days while trying to hack into the Strangers' Chatter. What the hell are you doing here, Jade?" He reached for his pack on the floor.

"I wasn't going to let Lou come, you craterhead."

"We can talk about the whys and hows later, dammit," Elliott said. "We've got to go."

He offered his hand to help the other man, then changed his mind and grabbed Theo's shirt-covered arm.

For a geek, Theo was fucking solid, and buff as hell, Elliott noted as he took on part of his weight. The arm that draped over Elliott's shoulder had a long, serpentine dragon tattooed on it, curling from the hand and wrist up along the forearm, and farther. Definitely the type of guy women liked. Fortunately, he didn't sense anything but sisterly love from Jade—and vice versa.

"Come on," Elliott said. He took two steps, then had a thought.

Every storefront in the mall had to have a delivery door at the rear of the backroom that usually opened directly to the outside, or at least to a rear corridor that led outside. They could slip out through that back door and be away from the *gangas*.

"The back door," Elliott said, more to himself than anyone else. "Jade, I need the flashlight."

Theo eased away from him, standing weakly under his own power, and said, "It's blocked. That's how I managed to get myself trapped for two days."

"I can move the stuff."

"No, I mean it's blocked by a huge concrete slab that must have fallen from the upper level. I already tried," explained Theo. "The only way out of this store is through the front. But there are other back doors behind other storefronts."

"They're getting closer," Jade said again, urgency in her voice. Her fingers brushed Elliott's arm in a light caress.

"How many?" Elliott asked, looking at the other man.

"Three dozen or more," Theo replied. "There are more every time I turn around. They're either fucking like bunnies and procreating right here, or more are arriving. This has to be some sort of central location for the Strangers too."

"Either way, it's going to be tight."

They left the backroom of the store, navigating around the white boxes. Elliott could fairly feel Theo's anguish at leaving possibly scavengeable electronics behind, but the other man didn't say a word. Except maybe a little groan when they passed the miraculously pristine box of a MacBook Pro, but other than that, Theo remained stoic. He seemed to be concentrating on trying to hold up his own weight, a feature that would come in handy . . . about now, because—

He heard a faint whir start up, and immediately a soft yellow glow filled the room.

"Damn," Theo said. "Someone's got the generator working again. It's not powerful enough for the lights to be on full, but this makes things a bit more interesting."

"I'll say," Elliott muttered. He didn't think *gangas* were that smart, which didn't bode well for the situation. Was someone else here, helping them?

As they hurried out of the Apple store, Elliott heard a

creaky whir, and realized almost immediately what it was. Theo did too, but Jade—who'd probably never seen a working escalator in her life—didn't.

"Fabulous. Now the *gangas* can chase us up *or* down," Theo grumbled as Elliott looked up and saw the orange eyes. They glowed from the upper level of the mall, and some of them were already beginning to lurch nervously onto the moving stairs.

It would have been humorous to watch the clumsy, staggering creatures try to navigate onto the rolling steps if Elliott hadn't noticed another group of orange eyes just across from them. On their level, moving closer. Jade bumped up next to him, and he felt her fingers close around his arm.

He counted at least ten pairs of eyes. And then another dozen or so *gangas* that were lining up to edge their way onto the escalator. "Fuck."

"More over there," Jade said, her voice steady. "We're trapped."

"There's a hallway right there, at two o'clock," muttered Theo. "That's where we have to go. Holy cats, can you smell those fuckers?"

Yeah. Elliott could definitely smell the rotting, moldy scent. "I have a bottle rocket in my pack," he said, digging for it. By the time he pulled out the small alcohol-filled bottle with a little rag tied around it, Jade was prepared with the lighter.

"Hurry the fuck up," Theo said tightly.

Jade held the lighter to the bomb's wick. The fabric was little more than gauzy cotton, and it burned as quickly as human hair.

"Go," Elliott ordered, giving Jade a little shove as he measured the distance from the gangas . . . *one . . . two . . . three*!

Elliott pitched the bottle at the group of *gangas* that were on the escalator as he dashed after Theo and Jade, who'd started off along the edge of the mall.

Boom! The little bomb exploded behind him, and he glanced back to see *gangas* scattering, tumbling, pushing. One of them tipped over the side of the escalator and crashed to the ground. Unfortunately, he got up almost immediately and started staggering toward them with half of his face burned away and an eye sagging from its socket.

Elliott scooped Theo's arm over his shoulders, relieving Jade's awkward gait, and they picked up speed. Keeping as much in shadow as possible, they passed two storefronts— BO DER and GU SS—and suddenly Elliott ducked inside the second store, pulling Theo with him. They had a few minutes before the *gangas* found them—the Guess store had display windows with backdrops that blocked the interior of the shop, giving them a place to hide until the creatures sniffed them out.

Ruu-uuthhh. Ruuuuuth. . . .

The sound of their groans echoed in the empty space, eerie and insistent. Closer. The nasty smell of rotting flesh filled the air. This was not good.

"The gate," Theo said, stopping just inside the entrance and looking up.

But Elliott had already thought of it, and found the chains that lowered the chainmail-like gate that blocked the store from the mall. The flimsy metal wouldn't last long against the *gangas*, but it would give the three of them a bit more time. It screeched horribly, but he yanked it down and they ducked farther into the store.

"I'll go to the back and see if I can find the back door. Hold them off while I get it open," said Theo, grabbing onto one of the T-shaped clothes racks.

"Go," replied Elliott, already looking around the dim place, then found what he wanted—piles of dusty clothing and the freestanding metal racks that had held them. As Theo started off as quickly as he could, Elliott tossed a lump of clothing at Jade and said, "Burn 'em."

She nodded, and began to quickly knot the sleeves of the shirts together. This turned them into little bundles of cotton that would be easier to throw.

While she did that, Elliott stood and selected one of the T-shaped clothes stands, moving it within easy reach. There were even little hooks on it for hangers, giving it a mace-like quality that would smash *ganga* brains very well.

Ruu-uuuth. Ruuuuthhhh.

The *gangas* had reached the gate. It shook and creaked, rattling ominously. It wouldn't last much longer. *Shit.*

He glanced over his shoulder, hoping for a glimpse of Theo coming back, but there was no sign of him. Then a loud crash from the front rattled the gate, making a noise sing in his ears. "They're coming, we've got to light them," Jade said.

Without waiting for his agreement, she turned and put the lighter to the edge of a sleeve, where the fabric was thinnest. The fire began to slowly eat the heavy cotton, but not nearly fast enough. *Fuck.*

"The stuff you used for the bombs," she began, her face intense, but Elliott was already digging into his pack.

He pulled out one of the bottle bombs and, opening the top, he stuck an edge of the shirt down into the alcohol until the corner became damp. This time when Jade lit the shirt, it caught quickly, blazing into the shirt's fabric. They worked together to light a second, and then a third, fourth, and fifth.

All at once, the gate crashed to the ground in a loud

clatter, and the *gangas* began to push their way in. Elliott stood and gripped the metal clothes stand like a skinny baseball bat.

Jade grabbed hold of one of the knotted sleeves, and she winged the blazing bundle out toward the advancing creatures.

It didn't go very far. At all. And it veered off to the right. "Crap," she said, reaching for another one.

"You light 'em," he said, snatching up a shirt flare. He'd tease her about throwing like a girl later. If he had a chance. Unfazed, she grabbed up the alcohol and lighter as he lobbed the flaming bundle at the closest *ganga*, even as he glanced over his shoulder.

Theo, where the hell are you?

Four years of varsity baseball—including one year of all-star MVP for pitching—served him well, and Elliott caught the lead *ganga* in the chest. He picked up another one as the leader staggered, flailing jerkily at his suddenly flaming clothing, brushing the blazing packet away from him and onto his companions. Chaos ensued among a small knot of monsters, but Elliott didn't wait. He whipped another bundle, and another.

Jade kept lighting them, giving him unnecessary directions ("Get that one!" "Over there!") and he kept winging them, perfect pitch after perfect pitch, holding them off. But they were running out of alcohol and *where the hell was Theo*?

Just then, one determined monster made it close enough, stumbling toward them. Elliott grabbed his clothes stand and whaled on him like he was a fast pitch.

The metal stand connected with the creature, and zombie brains went flying as the blow sent the lunk tumbling back into his comrades.

"Let's go," Elliott said, grabbing up the last flare and

Jade's hand, but before he could pull her off, she slipped free and shoved a large box in between them and the advancing *gangas*.

"Light it," she yelled, just as Elliott heard Theo shouting behind them.

"I found it!"

Elliott kicked the shirt flares into a pile next to the box, then lit the last bottle rocket and tossed it onto the pile.

"Run!" He grabbed Jade's hand and they dashed after Theo as the bomb exploded.

The three of them rushed as fast as they could through the small door that led to the back room. Elliott shut the door behind them, hoping that it would take the *gangas* a few extra moments to find the escape.

Now they were in the stockroom, and this one had fewer emergency lights, so it was darker than the store. But once again, Jade had been thinking, and she lit another wadded up shirt that acted as a torch.

"Save the lighter," she said.

"Service door leads to a back corridor," Theo said breathlessly as they found the back door of the stockroom. Elliott saw that he was navigating quite well on his own steam while using the clothes-stand-turned-walker. His biggest problem was getting around boxes and piles of plastic-wrapped clothing waiting to be tagged and put on shelves. Elliott wondered briefly if there were any shirts in an XL, but that was only a brief blip, for the sounds of the *gangas* were getting close.

Theo flung the door open and they went through, finding themselves in an even more poorly lit corridor. Fortunately, Jade's torch was burning slowly enough that they had plenty of light, and would for a time.

"I didn't go all the way," Theo said, "just found this hall. It should lead to the outside. What time is it anyway?"

"It's still morning, so it should be light outside. We'll be safe once we get out," Jade replied just as the splintering sound of a door collapsing reached their ears. *Damn.* One down, one to go. They had to move faster.

"I don't want to get trapped back here in this corridor," Elliott said. "If they come in from another direction, I don't want to be caught in such a small space."

They moved along the passageway, which smelled dusty and dank, but was surprisingly clear of debris. The scent of mold and mildew hung in the air, and Jade stifled a shriek when they all walked into a huge spider web. It hung across the entire expanse of the hall, and even Elliott, who used to chase Janelle and his other cousins with wolf spiders he held by one leg, didn't want to bump into the arachnid that had made that web.

Especially after the size of the snake he'd encountered in the tunnel.

"Here," Theo said, stopping. "Jade."

She quickly moved the torch toward the first and only door they'd come across on the left side of the corridor—which was the outside wall of the mall, as far as they could tell.

The door was metal and heavy—of course, for security— and still quite intact.

"If we get this fucker open and there's a goddamn slab of concrete blocking it on the other side, I'm going to be really pissed," Theo said, in the understatement of the year.

"Let's get to it," Elliott said. He looked at Theo, then at Jade. The sounds of the *gangas* were coming closer. "I have two bottle bombs left. I could use one to try and blow this up, or keep it in case we need it."

"Keep it," Theo said. "We can get this fucker open."

Elliott looked at Jade, who replied, "Keep it."

She held the torch up, steadily, as Theo and Elliott set to

opening the door. The hinges were rusted; the metal bolt lodged in place hadn't been moved for fifty years and did not want to go.

They spent several nerve-racking moments of unsuccessful work prying at the bolt with Theo's screwdriver, then the handle of Elliott's knife, to the tune of Jade's urgings, "Hurry, hurry!"—as if he weren't. Finally, Elliott took Theo's walker and began to slam it against the latch. *Clang! Clang!*

The noise echoed through the small corridor, and they heard the slam of the second door open down the passageway. It would only be a matter of moments. Elliott didn't stop swinging at the bolt, but he kicked his pack toward Theo. "Bottle bomb," he said. "Get ready."

He slammed again and felt something that time. "I think it moved!" he said.

"It did," Jade said, her voice tense for the first time. "Don't stop! Hit it harder!"

He did as Theo fumbled through the pack and pulled out the last bottle, and the metal bolt moved more and more, creaking a bit each time. "Come *on* you fucking *thing*," Elliott swore as the sounds of *ruuu-uuuthhhh* and the smell of *gangas* came closer.

"I'm going to throw it," Theo said.

"At the count of five," said Jade. "We're almost there. One . . . two . . . three. . . ."

"Four . . . *five!*" Elliott swung as hard as he could, connecting solidly with the bolt as if he'd made a homer. With the bases loaded. He felt the bolt give significantly as Theo flung the bomb.

The bottle exploded down the hall, and Elliott swung one more time. *Crash!*

The bolt slammed to the side and the door creaked ajar.

Jade pulled on it, and the door opened. A crack of light—
pure, clean, white sunlight—gaped into the darkness.

They stumbled out, blinking in the sudden brightness.

Squinting, he looked up and saw that they were not alone.

Two men were standing there, the one about Elliott's age
holding a fucking gun. Trained right at them.

The other man, with wheat-colored hair and an evil glint
in his green eyes, smiled coldly. "Well, well. Diana Kapiza,"
he said. "At long last."

Eight months After

It finally happened.

Thaddeus Marck lost it and went on another rampage. Since he lost the election for mayor, he's become more fanatical. He and some of his supporters attempted a fucking coup, tried to take over the council meeting Rowe was having. Knives, simple bottle bombs, even a gun.

Managed to subdue them, get the weapons away. More of us than them, thank God.

Voted and decided to take them out past the limits of the safe area and leave them there.

I voted for it, only because I don't think he'll change, and he'd been warned what would happen. He'll keep trying to get control. And next time someone could die. Ironic if that happened—someone dies while he's trying to get us to preserve the race.

But it was a horrible thing to do: to put them out there. Still not sure it was the right thing. Are we becoming Puritans, banishing when we disagree with others? Or was he the Puritan?

Gave them food and stuff, but left them to the *gangas*.

That's what we've taken to calling the Ruth monsters—the *gangas*. Couldn't stomach the term "zombie." It was too damn horror-movie-ish.

When I said that to Theo, he laughed. "We're fucking living an apocalyptic horror flick, don't ya know."

He's right.

As for my Elsie and me . . . we have no problem trying to repopulate the world.

—from the journal of Lou Waxnicki

CHAPTER 19

Jade's world froze.

She looked up into the startling green eyes of Raul Marck—eyes so much like hers that she'd wondered more than once if he might be her father. It was possible. Not that she cared.

He looked no different than he had the last time she'd seen him—three years ago. He had a narrow, handsome face creased by rough living and weather. Where it wasn't lined, his golden skin was smooth and shiny. She wasn't certain how long ago he'd been born—it was definitely after the Change—but his hair was silvery and his lips thin and colorless.

He was going to take her back.

No way.

She wasn't about to let this skinny, knobby-handed bounty hunter ruin her happiness. Just when she thought things were going to be all right. When she'd gotten comfortable in her own skin again, found her place, built a life . . . and had fallen in love with a man who had more empathy and courage than anyone she'd ever met, and who actually appreciated all of her. Even her need to be in control.

Elliott had moved to stand with her, his large, warm body emanating protection. He would have brushed forward to block her from the other men, but Ian Marck, who was holding a gun, made a warning sound.

"Tell your protectors not to move or I'll blow them into pieces," said Ian. He was Raul's son, and he meant what he said. His eyes, though frigid blue, not green, had the same hard expression as his father's.

"Elliott," Jade said when she felt his muscles tense. *Take it easy. We'll get out of this. It's three of us against two.* She caught a glimpse of Theo out of the corner of her eye, still leaning on the metal stand near the door. If he'd been able to move faster, he would have been next to her as well. *Okay, only two and a half of us.*

Besides, she and Elliott had bested an immortal Stranger together. They could figure out a way out of this. Jade straightened, realizing she had to keep the attention on herself. Keep it focused away from Theo and Elliott. The healer and the computer wiz—they were more important in this battle against the Strangers than she was.

"Raul," she said, looking directly at him for the first time in three years, "what an unpleasant surprise." She managed to keep her voice steady and cool. No inflection, nothing to indicate that her belly felt as though it were spinning on a nonstop carousel. And that her heart slammed hard enough to shake her fingers.

"I've been looking for you for three years. I suspected you weren't dead, and I knew if I was careful and smart, I'd find you." He smiled with delight, and she could tell he was already enjoying the reward Preston was bound to compensate him with for her return. "Incidentally, Luke Bagadasian is the one who helped confirm your whereabouts."

"Luke?" Jade couldn't hide her shock. "You tricked him?"

"Oh, no. It wasn't a trick. It was pure greed. And, I think, it might have been a bit of a bruised ego, my dear Jade. You do seem to leave a lot of broken hearts in your wake, don't you? Preston, Luke, even the mayor of Envy, or so rumor has it. But, I'm sorry to say that I've never fallen prey to that weakness."

"No. Your weakness has always been of the monetary sort. And for grit," she replied, still not believing that Luke would have betrayed her just because she wouldn't let him kiss her. "You must be the one supplying Rob Nurmikko. You and Ian," she said, tossing a measured look at the younger man.

Ian actually frightened her more than his father.

"Nurmikko's useless. He's going to eat it tomorrow, after he delivers his cargo to your friend Preston." Raul's eyes had taken on a cold gleam. "He thinks he's going to the compound, where he'll have as much dust as he can handle, but that's not the case. We'll shove him overboard at the opportune moment. All we need from him is the shipment that he's been collecting for the last few months. These things take time, you know."

If she could just keep him talking . . . it would give her or Elliott or Theo time to figure something out. But what? "Shipment of what? Furniture? Dust?"

Raul laughed. "Don't be ridiculous. I wouldn't waste my time with piddling cargo like that, Diana darling. Humans. Only the youngest, healthiest specimens, of course. Slaves. The only thing Preston and Fielding can't provide for themselves. Their weakness is my strength. My wealth."

Slaves. Jade realized all at once what the list in the Stranger's book was. An inventory—of young, healthy, teens. Perfect for replenishing their workforce. She felt Elliott's tensile reaction behind her as he obviously came to the same realization.

Oh God. Vaughn had seen Geoff and some of the others

leave Envy last night. Where were they going? They had to be meeting somewhere . . . then they could be brought into captivity and shipped off. "Nurmikko . . . he got them introduced to grit, didn't he? So he could lure them away easily."

"That was my idea. Why else would they leave the safety of Envy? How could a group of youngsters resist something so forbidden, yet so delicious? We certainly weren't going to go in and raid the place and try to steal them away. Too messy and would cause too much suspicion." Raul shifted, his eyes spanning her greedily. "Preston will be so very delighted to see you again. He's missed you."

The information clicked through her mind. If Jade went with them, she'd not only find out where the shipment was to be delivered, but she'd have the chance to help them escape.

Her palms dampened. "I hope you have more comfortable traveling accommodations than you did before," Jade said, lifting her chin and nose in a little sniff. Her heart started up again, thumping hard as ever. "The last time you transported me, I found your methods severely lacking."

Elliott's breath caught in a silent whuff, as if he'd understood her plan. She could feel the anger fairly sparking from him. She wanted to reach back and touch him, for her comfort as well as for his own. But she dared not . . . she dared not let Raul and Ian know what he meant to her. Raul gave a short bark of laughter. "As I recall, last time you weren't particularly eager to join me. But if you cooperate, there will be no need for you to ride with the *gangas*—and dressed in ropes this time."

"I'll never be eager to join you, Raul Marck," Jade said, pleased that her voice remained haughty. Despite the increased tension rolling from Elliott in waves, she didn't look at him. She could give nothing away. "But if you think to take me back to Preston, you had best be more accommodating than before. He wasn't particularly pleased with the condition in which I arrived when you delivered me last time."

Elliott made a sound, moved—and there was a loud retort, then the sharp *ping* of a bullet as it lodged into the concrete next to Jade's foot.

"I won't be so generous the next time he moves," Ian said, his blue eyes even colder than before.

Elliott. Please. Trust me. Jade shivered and her mouth went dry. She swallowed, kept her face empty, and looked at Raul. "What are we waiting for? The sooner I'm rid of the foul presence of you and your son, the better."

She actually stepped toward him, angling herself in front of Elliott.

"Ian," Raul said with a meaningful jerk of his head, and reached for Jade.

She knew what that gesture meant, and reared back into Elliott, and felt his strong arms come around her from behind like desperate bands, starting to push her behind him. Holding herself still, she kept facing the Marcks. "No, you won't shoot them," she commanded, looking at Ian. Fury burned in his eyes, but he didn't move. "They go free or I don't go with you."

Raul opened his mouth to respond, but Jade continued despite Elliott's arms crushing her waist, "It would be terrible if I got caught in the crossfire. Very unfortunate for you, after just finding me. Preston wouldn't pay as much for damaged goods. Or dead ones."

Elliott's arms tightened around her even more, but she had to get away from him. "Jade," he said angrily, his fingers closing around one of her wrists, but she refused to look at him. This was hard enough as it was. He needed to let her do what had to be done.

"Jade? Is that what you're calling yourself now?" sneered Raul.

She ignored his comment. "I think Preston would exact payment *from* the person who damaged me instead of offering it. Don't you?"

Raul's lips thinned to a thin bluish white line. "All right, then, *Jade*," he said. "Your friends won't be shot."

"I said they must go free," Jade said, trying to move away from Elliott. He was not releasing her wrist, and he was much too strong for her to break his hold. *Let go. Please let go. This is hard enough.*

At least if the two of them were set free, they would know about the slave shipment. They could find a way to stop it—and they could come after her and the slaves. They could try and get her back from Raul.

If they were shot, that hope was gone. And the hope that they could stop the cargo before tomorrow.

She had to make Elliott understand. He had to release her. But his grip was too tight, and she could feel the determination, the protectiveness in his stance and the vibration of desperation beneath his skin. Oh God, she didn't want to be the cause of more grief, more anguish in his eyes. In his life.

Especially after this morning. . . .

How could she make him understand?

"I'm going with them," she said, turning to look at Elliott. Willing him to understand. *Let me go*, she said with her eyes. *They won't hurt me. But they'll kill you.*

"I'm getting impatient," Ian said. That mercenary glint in his eyes told her he didn't care if she got caught in the crossfire.

"Elliott. I'm going with them." She pulled against his grip, hard, pleading silently. *I have to.*

At last Elliott released her, but not before she caught the expression in his eyes: blazing and intense. *No.*

"Now let them go," she said to Raul, very calmly, still angling herself between the gun and Elliott.

He laughed. "I'll let them go. Back in there. They can take their chances there."

Jade drew in her breath to argue, but Theo was already opening the door. She noticed he'd kept his face slightly averted and remained quiet, and she realized he shared her concern that he might be recognized; although as far as she knew, Raul or Ian had never had occasion to see or notice Theo. They weren't usually this far north or east. But if there were Strangers in Envy, spying or otherwise watching, it was possible.

"Come on," Theo said as he held the door open. Inside, there were no *gangas* in sight; likely they'd walked right past the door in their quest for human flesh and were, hopefully, somewhere else in the building. "No sense in getting ourselves shot over this crazy woman. If she wants to go with these guys, let her. I'll take my chances inside."

Jade dared a quick glance at Elliott and saw the way his jaw moved, his cheeks hollowed and shifting, his dark hair flat and plastered against his damp skin. His sapphire eyes nearly black, lit with wildness.

Her chest suddenly felt full and she tried to draw in a breath. It was impossible to let him go. To go *from* him.

"Get in there or I'll change my mind, Preston be damned," Raul said angrily.

Jade knew the words were an empty threat; if there was one person that Raul respected and feared, it was Preston. And with good reason.

And, oh God, she was going back to him.

No. She fingered her bracelets. *I can do this. They'll come for me. And by then, I'll know how to save the kids. I'll figure out a way.*

Elliott turned and walked briskly back into the building, without a last glance at her.

The door clanged shut.

At least he and Theo would have the chance to escape the *gangas.* They were smart and fast and strong, even though Theo was injured. They'd find their way back out. They had the truck, and they'd get back to Envy sooner. They could even drive at night if they had to.

"Don't get too excited, my dear," Raul said. "There are more than two hundred *gangas* in there. The twenty of them that we just delivered are fresh . . . and hungry. Your friends will never find their way out."

As he closed his cool, slender fingers around her upper arm, Jade saw Ian move sharply behind her.

Then . . . *pain* . . . and everything went black.

"Where is he taking her?" Elliott demanded as soon as the door clanged shut. "Where's Preston?"

"I don't know," Theo said grimly.

Elliott heard the *ruuu-uuuthhh* in the distance, closer than he wanted to hear it, but he couldn't move yet. He needed answers. He needed to know he'd done the right thing, letting her go without a fight. That he could get her back.

He stopped the next words on his tongue, for he heard a faint, familiar rumble. Touching the door, he felt the barest vibration through the metal, and then it stopped: the vibration and the rumble. "That sounded like a vehicle," he muttered.

"They drive humvees," Theo told him. "They've left."

"Let's get the hell out of here. I've got a working vehicle out there; we can follow them."

Elliott pushed against the door. Or, rather, tried to. It wouldn't budge. "Son of a bitch. They've blocked us in"—he peered through the crack—"with an old, goddamn Mercedes."

Giving the door a violent, frustrated kick, he left it open to allow for the sliver of sunlight to come in and better illuminate the place. A feeling of something like panic threatened to cloud his mind, but he didn't let it. He pushed it away. Compartmentalized. Focused.

He could worry about what was happening to Jade when he had that luxury.

Right now, they had to find another way out of here while avoiding a slew of *gangas*. And figure out how to find Preston and stop his shipment of slaves.

"They've smelled us." Theo said needlessly, for Elliott had already noticed that the *ganga* moans had become louder.

"How mobile are you?" he asked, glancing at the metal clothes stand that Theo still clutched.

"Mobile enough. Sounds like they overshot the door after we went outside, but now they're coming back."

"The way we came," Elliott said, fully aware that the groaning sounds were growing uncomfortably closer, and more quickly than he would have expected. "You first, I'll follow behind."

"You've got one bottle bomb left?" Theo said as he started off with a shaky step.

"Yep. And not much else. Any ideas which way?"

"Back out the way we came in. At least we won't be trapped in these little halls."

"Do you have *any* idea where they're taking her?" he asked again.

Theo shook his head, grimacing with discomfort. "There's been talk of a compound, but no one has seen it—even Jade, when she was with Preston. If I had to guess, I suspect it's the new landmass in the Pacific, far from the prying eyes of humans." His breathing was rough as he struggled along as quickly as he could, but he managed to get the words out. "From what Jade has said, Preston had a sort of houseboat that he lived on. Where she was with him."

"All right," Elliott said, trying not to think about what the man with the whips and ropes and laced-up gowns would do once he got his hands back on Jade. "The shipment's for Preston, right?'

"That's what it sounded like. Nurmikko's getting the kids and delivering them to him in some sort of shipment. Which implies a vehicle." Theo's words were as labored as his movements.

Elliott nodded. That gibed with what Jade had heard between the Stranger and Rob Nurmikko. The slaves had to be ready to leave by Friday. Tomorrow. "And Marck's going to take Jade to Preston . . . so they're going to the same place as the slaves. Same meeting place. That's her plan. It's got to be. She's going to try and help them."

Theo nodded. "So when we find the slaves, we find Preston."

"And Jade." *But how the hell would they find them?* Elliott glanced back. Theo wasn't moving fast enough.

"Would it really piss you off if I picked you up and carried you a bit?" The hair on the back of his neck prickled, and he knew they had to get their asses moving.

"Don't fucking carry me," Theo retorted. "Sling my arm around your shoulders."

Elliott did that and they were able to move much faster with him taking on the bulk of Theo's weight and setting the pace. "I gotta know . . . is she in imminent danger before she reaches this Preston?"

"Do you think I would have let her go if I thought she were?" Theo ground out. Elliott could feel him struggling to make his legs move to keep up with him, and knew he had to be in pain. Theo added, "Either way, he'll pay Raul Marck handsomely for her. So the good news is, Marck won't let anything happen to her till he gets to Preston."

They'd reached the entrance that had been the Guess backroom door, and Elliott hesitated. They could go in and out the same way they'd come, or they could go farther down the hall.

As if reading his mind, Theo said, "Let's keep going. At least to the next door. They're dumb enough to assume we'd go back the same way."

"Well, we did, didn't we?" Elliott grumbled. But there were lots of possible ways to get out of a mall. They just had to evade the *gangas* long enough to find another one—or get back to the entrance through which they'd originally come in. At the other end of the building. No sweat. Marck would have no clue that Elliott was familiar with this type of building.

They hurried back through the store next to Guess and out through its mall side. Orange eyes glowed in pockets to the left, on the floor above, and to the right.

"If we can make it across . . . we'll be on the other side of the mall," Theo whispered.

Elliott looked at him and nodded. Across the mall meant different service doors, and another chance for escape. "Let's go."

They were quick, and silent, and smooth, Elliott helping Theo as they boldly slipped from dark corner to dark corner as they crossed the mall.

At one point Elliott brushed no more than three feet away from, and then on past, a confused-looking *ganga* before the orange-eyed creep realized it. If he hadn't been so worried about Jade, and conscious of the fact that every moment lost she was that much farther away, he would have found it amusing. It reminded him of playing Blind Man's Bluff, for each time they passed a *ganga*, the monster would turn as the human scent touched his nose . . . but by then, they'd be long past, concealed by the darkness and shadows.

Yes, the monsters were strong and frightful. No, he didn't want to be cornered by them, or mauled by their long-nailed hands and torn apart by their feral teeth. No, he wouldn't be stupid enough to move around at night like the teens had done. But it was possible to use speed and agility to evade them if one wasn't too outnumbered, or trapped in a small space.

"What's that?" he whispered to Theo as they crouched behind a large slab of marble that had once been some decorative sculpture. He pointed to the store closest to them, about twenty feet away.

TR P T N.

"I dunno." But it didn't matter—it was the closest place and the orange eyes were closing in on them.

A trio of *gangas* had scented them, and were bearing down on them. And just then, seven or eight came stumbling down the escalator right behind them. "Let's go," Elliott said, praying there'd be a way to get to the security hall behind whatever the store was.

They ran.

But the moment they shot through and into the main part of the shop, he realized where they were. "It's a freaking tanning salon," he said. "TropiTan."

"A tanning salon," Theo said, his voice bright and enthusiastic as they brushed past a closed tanning bed, and he paused for an instant. "Oh, man, do I have an idea."

Elliott looked back at him and nodded. "I bet we're thinking the same thing."

The groans were louder and they moved quickly through the long, narrow space of the tanning shop. The generator still hummed, leaving that dirty yellow glow roughly lighting the piles of debris in the corners. Since it was a simple setup, it was easy to navigate without tripping or bumping into anything: straight down the hall lined with tanning beds and into the backroom.

Elliott could see back through the long, narrow shop out into the mall. The escalator hummed and orange eyes burned, scattered about the area, closing in on the store. There were enough *gangas* converging that Elliott knew they weren't going back out that way.

This has to work.

"Give me a hand," Theo called softly. Somehow, despite his injury, he'd managed to pull a full-sized tanning bed back into the storage room.

"How the hell are we going to get this to work? The generator's not strong enough—and what about a cord?"

"I can handle that part. I just need help standing it on end," Theo replied.

The two of them opened the clamlike steel metal bed and upended it so that it stood tall, and open.

The groans were closer now, just outside the—*Holy shit! The backroom door!* "Fuck. How the hell'd they get in the back hall too?" Elliott said. For the first time, real fear threatened to stop him. They were trapped in the tanning salon, between the service hall and the main mall.

He hoped to hell they could get the tanning bed to work, or they were going to be toast.

"I need my pack," Theo said, pulling it off his shoulder. Clanks and clunks ensued as he dug in, and Elliott was aware of the prickles on his neck growing stronger.

Listening at the backroom door, he could hear the *gangas* pass by the door, bumping it, obviously wandering and looking around for them. More had begun to stream into the tanning salon, having scented them from his quick dash across the way.

"What the hell," he said tensely. "We've got to plug this thing in *now* or we're going to be *ganga* meat."

"Bite me," Theo muttered, and then he shoved the bag back at Elliott. He was holding a metal object about the size of a large brick. "Let's go."

"Do you see an outlet or something?" Elliott demanded, then cracked open the service door that led to the narrow corridor. Was there enough energy coming from the generator to power up the tanning bed?

The *gangas* were right the fuck there and he slammed the door shut. *Christ.* They began to pound on the door. The smell of *gangas* wafted clearly to his nose, washing into the shop behind them. They were bearing down, stumbling into the store, trying to make their ungainly way down the main passageway of tanning-bed rooms.

"I've got it," Theo said, picking up the electrical cord. He moved behind the open clamshell of the tanning bed. "Ready?"

"Ready," Elliott said, maneuvering the tanning bed so it faced the door, which was shaking from the force of the *gangas'* blows.

Theo was moving next to him, and suddenly there was a

soft pop, then a buzz . . . and then the room filled with brilliant blue-white light.

How the hell . . . ?

"Fast," Theo gasped. "Hurry."

Elliott didn't know what was going on; the electrical cord seemed to be plugged into the brick Theo was holding. But his hand was inside the brick.

Whatever it was, it was working.

The blast of light had stopped the impending *gangas*, and the two men were protected by the tanning bed. When they opened the door the *gangas* stumbled back, crying out in deep, guttural voices.

"Turn it!" Theo shouted, his voice weak.

Elliott didn't need to be told; he'd already positioned it so that the ultraviolet beams caught the monsters coming in from the mall direction, and also blared toward the ones in the hall.

The creatures fell into and on top of each other, scrambling to get out of the way, groaning and tearing into each other as if in pain and desperate to get away from the light.

That answered one of the questions he and Jade had discussed: apparently light, at least this bright, was painful to the *gangas*.

Elliott managed to get the tanning bed arranged so that it blocked the doorway into the hall, trapping the *gangas* on one side of the backroom door—and those coming from the mall. That left him and Theo an expanse of service hallway down which to dash and find an exterior door that actually opened.

"Go," Theo gasped. "I'll stay here until you have the door open."

"What— never mind," Elliott said. He'd figure it out later, but the best he could tell was that Theo's hand was inside the box into which the tanning bed had been plugged. Was he giving it some sort of energy? A power surge?

He ran down the hall, prepared for any straggling *gangas*, looking for a door illuminated by the glow from the tanning bed.

At last, he found one, two storefronts away from Tropi-Tan. He began to work on the door immediately, kicking and slamming it as he'd done the other service door—but he needed the metal clothes stand that he'd used last time.

There was nothing in the hall that would help. Elliott glanced back down toward the tanning bed and its glow.

Theo was on the ground, pack over his shoulder. He wasn't moving. Shit.

Elliott had one bottle bomb left. If this didn't work, they were fucked. Digging it out of his pack, he shoved the wick into the bottle and set the whole thing on top of the door's push-bar apparatus. He lit the wick, praying, and took off back to Theo.

Ka-boom!

The explosion rocked the small passageway, sending echoes reverberating through his ears and debris flying just as Elliott reached Theo in a base-stealing dive.

He picked him up, saw that Theo's hand had slipped from inside the bricklike thing, and snatched that up too, yanking the tanning bed's plug free. The *gangas* he'd been blinding were nowhere in sight, but the sounds of their groans still rumbled through the murky darkness. They would be back as soon as they realized the light had gone.

Praying that the bomb had destroyed or at least loosened the doorknob apparatus, he dashed unsteadily back down the corridor. Theo was a solid sonofabitch, and with that pack, he was even more of a burden.

He got to the door to find it still completely closed. *Shit.*

He'd hoped it would be blown wide. He gasped for air, trying to catch his breath, and let Theo slip gently to the ground. He was a deadweight, and lay there unmoving. What the hell had the guy done to himself?

Elliott didn't have time to worry about it now. The moans were coming closer again, and he had one more chance to get this door open. He examined it in the dim light and found, with relief, that the push bar seemed to be loose.

Saying a prayer, he slammed his foot against it as hard as he could . . . and the door flew open. Sunlight splashed over him and the prone Theo, and, after a quick look to make sure there weren't any nasty surprises on the other side, Elliott wasted no time in pulling Theo out with him.

"Theo," he said, bending to his companion.

The man groaned, opened his eyes, then squinted in the bright light. "Good going," he said. "Let's go. I'll be fine in a bit."

Elliott took him at his word, and moments later he shoved Theo into the passenger seat and helped him buckle in his limp body. Then he slid into the driver's seat after retrieving the keys he'd hidden.

He started the engine and realized he had absolutely no fucking idea which direction to go.

CHAPTER 20

Elliott had started to drive west, toward the ocean, hoping that he'd either pick up the trail of the other humvee or that some other brilliant idea would strike him.

"Any ideas where we're heading?" he asked, glancing over at Theo.

Theo had pulled himself up a little and seemed to be regaining some color. "Hemps Point. Maybe." He nodded in approval, but remained slumped. "It's got to be west, by the ocean."

Elliott frowned. Why did that sound familiar?

"It's my best guess, based on what I was able to find out at Valley Way," Theo continued. His voice was getting stronger, but Elliott noticed his fingers had tightened over the handle next to him. "This was the first time I was able to hack into the system that the Strangers use to communicate with their bounty hunters like Marck. That's why I was there so long, I got in and was able to keep a good connection because Valley Way is an access point—you know, one of the anchors of the system."

"Did you know about the slave cargo?" Elliott asked grimly.

"I got that there was going to be an important shipment,

that part of it was coming from Envy, but I didn't know it was freaking *people*. I thought what Jade did—furniture or some other goods. But Hemps Point kept coming up in the Chatter, and the Friday date too, so I think it's a good guess—"

"The map!" Elliott exclaimed, cutting him off as he slammed his hand on the steering wheel. "That's it. It is Hemps Point. That's why I knew it." His mind raced as he tried to remember the details of the drawing he'd only glanced at. *Shit*.

"Map?"

He quickly explained about Geoff Pinglett and his friends, and the map that had been found in their van by the mysterious archer. "Hemps Point was on the map—that's how I know the name."

"Do you have it with you?"

"Dammit, no. It's back in Envy. Jade and I didn't see any reason to bring it with us. What?"

Theo had bent to dig in his pack. "I can take care of that," he said. "I should be able to connect through the Strangers' network back to the one in Envy. We're still close enough to Valley Way to get access, I think—and if I know Sage, she'll be at the computers anyway. We can get the information about the map from her. But you're going to have to stop so we don't go out of range."

Elliott pulled over under a tree that had sprouted next to a decrepit supermarket, and watched as the computer geek pulled out a small, paperback-sized computer and the little bricklike plug he'd used to power the tanning bed. And then another small object that looked like it had antennas.

"What are you, a walking Radio Shack?" he asked. "And a library?" He saw that a couple of books had fallen from the pack—probably scavenged from the mall. And they weren't computer manuals. "*Gone with the Wind?* Nora Roberts?"

Theo snatched them back and stuffed them into the pack. "They're not for me."

"So you gonna tell me what's up with that plug thing?" Elliott asked. Although he figured he sort of knew.

While the computer was booting up, Theo turned in his seat so that his back was to Elliott. He yanked the hem of the stained T-shirt from his jeans, exposing his lower left back.

Elliott saw another dragon tattoo curling around his hip and disappearing down behind Theo's belt . . . and then he saw the eye of the dragon. Right where, just a little while earlier, he had noticed an odd formation when he scanned Theo, in the fleshy part near the spine.

"Is that a crystal?" he said. "Embedded in your skin? Like the Strangers."

"I didn't have it embedded, it was an accident. And it's not really a crystal. It's an IC—an integrated circuit. When the earthquakes hit during the Change, I was three floors beneath the surface in a safe room working on the backup systems for one of the casinos. Things went ballistic, computers exploded and imploded, and I got knocked out . . . and, apparently, an IC embedded in my skin."

"Talk about being wired," Elliott said as Theo replaced his shirt and began to type on the small keyboard.

Theo rolled his eyes. "As if I haven't heard that one before."

"Why didn't you remove the circuit?" Elliott asked.

"Believe it or not, at first, I didn't realize what it was. I thought it was just a cut—it didn't hurt, and it's not in an area that I could easily look at. I wasn't really hurt anywhere so I never had a thorough look." He shrugged, tapped a few keys, and looked at Elliott. "There were so many more important things to be taken care of in that time. Three weeks after the world was destroyed, I wasn't worried about a fucking cut, or even a little piece of metal or glass—especially if it didn't hurt or wasn't noticeable."

"I guess you had a few other things on your mind." Elliott nodded. "But later. . . ."

"I feel a sizzle of energy in that area when I need the extra . . . I guess . . . adrenaline."

"But you don't age. Does this mean you're immortal?" Elliott asked, wondering about Fence's stubble . . . and whether he'd ever have to shave himself again.

"It took a long time, but my body has finally started to age. I've acquired some gray hairs in the last five years. Am I immortal? How would I know?" He laughed sharply. "I hope the hell not, but I'm not interested in any experimentation."

"So the plug thing? What does that do?"

Still typing, adjusting the little antennas on what was likely some sort of wireless router, Theo explained, "I can gather and pull up the energy as needed. Although, as you saw, I'm wiping the floor afterward. But this little device helps to channel it more easily into anything that plugs in. I don't need it, but it's more efficient and fast."

As he spoke, he slipped his hand into the little brick and plugged the other end into the router. Lights began to blink and as Elliott watched, Theo's face began to lengthen and pale. He obviously wasn't fully recovered from the previous exertion of energy.

"Want me to type?" Elliott asked, watching him try to do so with one hand.

"Thanks, s'all right. I'm hacking, so it's not . . . straightforward," he replied, his words a bit slurred.

This left Elliott with little to do but watch and wait and

chafe . . . knowing that as the moments passed, Jade was getting farther and farther away. And Theo, his link to Envy and the others, was getting weaker and weaker.

"I'm in," Theo said after what seemed like forever, but was probably only a few minutes. "Now, come on Sage, baby . . . be there for me." The keys clicked softly, and Elliott watched over his shoulder.

"Ah, there she is. I knew it," Theo said a second later. A smile lit his strained face, and Elliott suspected it wasn't just because he'd succeeded in the connection. So that was the way *that* wind blew. The books must be for Sage.

Hi, Theo typed, with the speed of light, not even looking at the keys or screen. *I'm fine. Elliott w me. Jade w Marck. Nd map frm Geoff P's van. ASAP. BRB fr info.*

He pulled his hand out of the little brick, eyes glazed, sweat trickling down his temple. His breath rasped loudly through the vehicle for a moment, and Elliott wished there was something he could do to help, other than sit. And wait.

Wait. Hope.

Not think about Jade.

Not remember with every agonizing detail what it had been like . . . every touch, taste, sound . . . the warm silk of her skin, the fresh lemony-Jade smell, the heavy weight of her hair. Hair that she'd shaved in defiance of Preston . . . the man who would soon have her in his possession again.

Thanks in part to Luke of the mega-fucking-crystal. A wash of red glazed his vision for a moment. He was going to kill Luke when he was done here.

There would be an innocent little trip to Greenside, where he'd scan and heal Della . . . and then he'd fucking shake Luke's hand, beat the living shit out of him, and leave the bastard to die somewhere alone. Where the *gangas* wouldn't even find him, so it would be long and slow and agonizing. . . .

Elliott flattened his lips, pulling out of the fantasy, uneasy with how quickly his thoughts had moved along that trail. Yet the desire lingered, deep and dark.

For what punishment, what law enforcement was there in this world?

He looked at Theo. "I'm going after Luke Bagadasian when we're done here. I'll bring him back to Envy, to Rogan, or whoever . . . but he's got to pay for what he did to Jade, selling her out." He'd even had a picture of her in his desk, Elliott remembered. Likely to help identify her to the Strangers.

Theo met his eyes and shook his head regretfully. "There are law enforcement and security guards that keep order in Envy," he said, seeming to choose his words carefully as much from weariness as thought, "but outside . . . well, it is a little like the Wild West. There's no far-reaching authority, no real governing body over all of the little settlements. That's one thing Rogan's trying to do—to create some sort of system of marshals and law enforcement. It's difficult, too, with the added threat of the Strangers and their hold over us." His eyes were dark and very sober. "It's a different world we live in. Very . . . gray."

Elliott looked away. Did that mean each man was a law unto himself? That if he wanted justice, he must mete it out on his own? He looked at his hands. Healing hands. Not murdering ones.

He drew in a deep breath. One thing at a time. Jade first. Always.

"So can you use your energy for things like . . . well, like if we run out of gas in this thing?" Elliott asked, changing the subject. He realized with a shock that he'd never noticed the gas gauge since they left Envy. That would just be about right if they ran out of gas halfway to Hemps Point.

Theo nodded. "In some cases, but not for an extended time."

"Good to know."

They waited another three or four minutes, then Theo stuck his hand back into the brick and turned on the router again. Moments later, he'd connected once again and Sage, efficient as she was, had the information ready so that it came through almost as if they were on a live chat.

Ur amazing. Tx. Have bks 4 u. Back soon.

Elliott almost—*almost*—felt guilty reading that over his shoulder, though the exchange wasn't really that intimate. Still. Though the words were innocuous, the expression on Theo's face said it all: he was just as desperate to return to this woman as Elliott was to find Jade.

He saw Sage's return message: *Help's coming. Tell Elliott: Simon, Wyatt, Fence. On their way to Hemps Point.*

Theo replied: *Sage U rock my wrld. Hi to L.*

And then, as if bidding a final farewell, he unplugged himself slowly from the brick, face white and tight, his mouth so flat the little bristles of his soul patch stuck straight out. "Let's get the hell going and hope we can do this."

Elliott had no reason to argue.

Sage's directions were clear and explicit, and by the time the sun had settled just above the horizon, Elliott and Theo saw the sparkle of the ocean beyond the low rise of a hill. Near the shore, which bumped out into a little point, was a large structure that at first glimpse looked like a small island with a house on it.

They'd made it without running out of gas, but the humvee was low on fuel. Elliott had a feeling he was going to need Theo's energy to get them far away from there . . . if they made it out safely.

Parking the vehicle inside an old McDonald's—which had huge drive-in holes where a play area had once been— Elliott once again secreted the keys for a quick escape.

"What's the plan?" asked Theo, digging through his pack. He pulled out the books for Sage, and a few other items that didn't appear to have any bearing on his electronics or their capabilities, and left them on the floor of the truck.

"Find Jade, find the kids, get the fuck out of there," Elliott said, already knowing it wouldn't be that easy. "If we get separated, you go for the kids. I'm not leaving without Jade."

Theo met his eyes with clear blue ones, like Lou's . . . but younger. Hard to comprehend they were twins, but for those eyes and the way their mouths moved when deep in thought. "Deal."

"Uh . . . there's one other thing you should know," Elliott said as they got out of the humvee. "I've got my own super power." He explained the situation, ending with, "So if something happens, and I touch someone to heal them . . . *don't touch me.*"

"Holy pups," Theo said. "And I thought my problem sucked."

"Not nearly as much as mine." Elliott bared his teeth in a humorless smile. "First things first . . . let's stake out the place."

He didn't think anyone would have seen the vehicle approaching, for the terrain was ripe with trees and tall grasses, and lots of buildings. A state highway must have passed through here, and settled in a small town, for there were fast-food places, stores, and gas stations galore—plenty of structures that had once held the essence of America.

As they drew closer, Elliott realized it was not an island, but some sort of floating platform. The building on it had three rows of windows and was long and low and white, with balconies that circled it at every level. It looked a little like a square cruise ship plopped on top of a low, compact aircraft carrier.

Other than the houseboat, there were no other water vehicles.

"That's got to be the boat," he whispered to Theo. "They're going to put the cargo—the kids—on there, if they haven't already, and take the whole damn thing. It's big enough."

"Nothing like traveling in style," Theo said.

Elliott noticed two other humvees parked inside a large structure with an entire wall missing, and hoped that one of the vehicles was the one Jade had been transported in. "That way," he said, pointing to the right, where a whole line of trees shaded an old road that led down to the water. There didn't appear to be any guards or watchtowers, or anything to suggest that the houseboat was protected. *Bold bastards.*

But then again, what did they have to fear? They had engineered the destruction of the whole damn world. They were immortal. They had the advantage of power and secrecy. Why would they expect anyone to know or even care about a small little houseboat fifty miles from Envy or any other human settlement?

Elliott and Theo cruised along the ridge of trees, keeping out of sight but moving quickly. By the time they got close enough to see a single person standing on the deck of the houseboat, another humvee had approached.

Dodging inside an old garage, Elliott and Theo watched as the humvee pulled up and a single man got out. Luke Bagadasian.

Elliott tensed, wanting nothing more than to spring out and throttle the man . . . but he remained still, watching. Waiting.

Just then, he felt something behind him. Reaching for his knife, he spun to find Ian Marck standing in the doorway of the garage.

"I've been expecting you," said Ian, who was, of course, pointing a gun at them. "I confess, you arrived much sooner than I'd anticipated, but it's no matter. We're all here together now, and I'm in need of your skills." He was looking at Elliott. "You're a healer."

Elliott nodded slowly, keeping his eyes on the gun. Next to him, Theo had stilled as well. Elliott's mind was working quickly. Ian Marck had been expecting them to come, and he knew he was a healer. Why hadn't he forced Elliott along when he took Jade? Because he didn't know of his skills, or because he didn't want anyone else to know? The fact that Ian had accosted them alone, without backup, supported the latter theory.

"If you want my help, I need something in return," Elliott replied. He'd declined to raise his hands, and instead met the eyes of his opponent directly.

"You must be under the wrong impression if you think you're in the position to bargain," Ian said. "You're the one looking down the barrel of the gun."

"And you're the one who is in need of a healer. Obviously, it's your last hope, or you wouldn't be so desperate," Elliott replied.

Ian's face turned even more rigid, and his eyes filled with antipathy. He looked as if he'd like nothing better than to plow a fist into Elliott's face. "I can't give you Diana."

Jade. "Is she hurt? At least tell me that, and then we'll talk."

Ian cocked the weapon. "Maybe I'll just shoot your friend here, and then you'll see how serious I am."

"You could try that. But I might get in the way, and if that happens, then I'm of no use to you." Elliott's heart pounded steadily. He felt like he had the upper hand and he meant to keep it. "Now, Jade—Diana. Is she hurt? Is she with Preston?"

"She's not hurt. As far as I know. Preston was delighted with my father's gift." Ian's mouth moved in a humorless smile, yet anxiety rolled off him like sweat on an athlete's back. Whatever he needed Elliott for, he was desperate.

"Is she here?"

"Under heavy guard. Preston's not about to let her escape again. That's why I can't help you there. Even for this."

"The slaves, then. Are they here?" Elliott asked.

"They're in the hold below." Ian's eyes narrowed as if he knew what was coming.

Elliott nodded. "All right. Here's my deal. You let my friend get onto the boat and tell him where the slaves are . . . and I'll do whatever I can for you."

"And if not?"

Elliott shrugged. "I'll walk away and you'll be forced to shoot me or let me go. Either way won't help you."

"Or you," Ian pointed out.

Elliott shrugged, concentrating on keeping an unconcerned demeanor. "If you want my help, those are my conditions. Take it or leave it."

Ian didn't seem to have to struggle for long. Whatever he was after must be of great importance. "I'll take you both there, but he's on his own getting the kids out. After that, if you don't uphold your end of the bargain, I'll put a bullet in your head."

You probably will even if I do.

"And I'll make sure Diana sees what's left of you."

Elliott blanked his mind. One thing at a time. He'd do what he could, then figure out his next step. At least if Theo got the kids out, he could always come back for Jade, now that they knew she was here.

Wyatt, Fence, and Simon would be here soon, too, God willing—a fact that Ian couldn't know. If Theo could make it out with the kids, there'd be an even better chance with the four of them coming back in for Jade. Even if Elliott was . . . indisposed.

He looked at Theo, who nodded. "It's a deal," he said. "Let's go."

Inside the houseboat, water flowed everywhere, circling the house from top to bottom, running through what Elliott had thought were balconies but instead were the levels of a giant waterfall. Water flowed up from inside the center of the structure and spilled over the top, running down and around in slender little canals.

True to his word, Ian marched them down two levels into the deepest, darkest part of the houseboat. They'd passed by the one man who stood on the deck, with Ian giving no explanation for their presence. Obviously, he answered to no one but Raul and Preston, neither of whom made an appearance.

"Behind that door," said Ian, pointing to a small padlocked door at the end of the hall. The sounds of sobbing and wailing eked through the heavy wood. Ian looked at Theo. "You're on your own. This is it from me."

Elliott grabbed Theo's wrist—the first time he'd touched him skin to skin—and Theo took his in a good-luck handshake.

"See you on the other side," Theo said.

Elliott turned and went to fulfill his part of the bargain, knowing that he had just given those teenagers their best chance of escape. That was all he could do for them, for now.

* * *

"My darling Diana."

The familiar voice, laced with kindness, cut through her. She turned slowly, heart pounding, stomach roiling. Her head still ached from the blow that had knocked her out for the trip here.

He stood in the doorway, unchanged from the last time she'd seen him, more than three years ago. Tall and slender, shiny dark hair growing from that pointed widow's peak, today pulled back into a short tail, and thin red lips curving in a gentle smile. Preston was a handsome man, with elegant, aristocratic features. In an abhorrent mimicry of a gentle lover, he carried a wine bottle and two glasses, as if in celebration.

But his eyes. Those gray eyes scored over her, hard as flint, delving into her. She felt ill, felt her head grow light and the room tilt.

"What? No greeting for me?" He'd stepped into the room and closed the door behind him. "Or do you only answer to the name Jade now?" He set the glasses on the table and began to pour the ruby colored wine.

She'd been expecting . . . dreading . . . this moment ever since their arrival here at Preston's floating residence. She'd just hoped it wouldn't happen this soon. She hadn't even had a chance to try and find out about the teenagers, although a snatched bit of conversation indicated that "the cargo" was ready and on board.

They were getting ready to launch—early.

Elliott. He had to be on his way. She knew he would move mountains to get here. But if the boat left early, he'd never find her.

She drew in a deep breath. Preston had to give the order to launch. If he was here with her, he wasn't giving orders.

He continued, his quiet voice so soft and caring. "I couldn't believe it when I got word from the Marcks that they'd found you. Although I'd never really believed you were dead, it was a most pleasant surprise to find that you were not only alive . . . but in their custody. And then when I learned they'd brought you back here. To where we'd lived in such harmony." He sipped from his wine, watching her over the rim.

Her fingers curled into the back of the leather chair in front of her as she worked to keep her face emotionless. Devoid of fear, of anything that might give him more power over her.

Elliott. He was on his way. She knew it. Just . . . hold on.

"So silent, my darling," he said, setting his goblet down and moving closer to her with great nonchalance. "What must I do to elicit some response from you?"

"You could leave. Then you'll hear me celebrating."

He smiled at that. A tender, pained smile that did not reach his eyes. "My dear Diana, you wound me. How can you say such a thing . . . after the promise you made me. In order to spare your life, and that of your friends. Remember?"

"My promise didn't include standing by and letting you beat the bunk out of me whenever you liked. Or . . . the other things."

"But . . . you did offer your services, didn't you?" He was very close to her now, and it took every bit of courage to keep from moving away from him. Her skin crawled, her hair stood on end . . . but if she moved, if she made any sign of resistance, it would only fuel him.

"You know I did. But had I known. . . ."

"Oh, you still would have done it, Diana, darling. You couldn't bear to see those children fed to the *gangas*. Or their mothers either," he said, pulling the tie from her pony-tail. He fluffed out her hair so that it fell over her shoulders,

free of its confines. His fingers were gentle, tenderly stroking one thick lock. "I'm delighted you've grown your hair
back. That's the only good thing about having lost you for
three years. And you can be certain that if anyone comes
near you with scissors or a razor, they'll die."

His hand felt so heavy on her head, over her shoulders.
She felt as though he were pushing her into the earth, shoving her down, weighting her into a puddle. Jade realized her
knees were trembling and her stomach pitched wildly . . .
and still, she could do nothing as he lifted the hair from one
shoulder and bent to kiss the side of her neck. His lips were
cool and dry.

She focused on the window in front of her, staring through
it toward the shore, the lowering sun casting long shadows
over the ground. She struggled to ignore Preston's hands on
her, fighting to stay still, to keep from spinning away and
fighting with nails and teeth and feet . . . knowing that he
was much too strong for her, that he wanted her to fight. And
trying . . . trying to figure out a way to escape.

But his hands . . . on her. So ugly, such a horrific parody
after what had transpired between her and Elliott. Grief
and despair threatened to shatter her concentration, but she
couldn't allow it. She was not the same weak woman she'd
been three years ago. Reaching automatically for the trio
of bands on her wrist, she focused on them, on the comfort
they gave her. On what she'd endured before, and how much
stronger she was now.

If she could slip past him, out of the room. . . .

"Don't even think about it, my dear," he said. "I locked
the door. I wanted us to have privacy for our little reunion."

She braced herself as his dry mouth and slender, cool
hands moved over her, concentrating on keeping her mind

clear and steady. Staring out the window, at the grassy, wooded terrain, she focused on the slender, dark shadows. Soon it would be dark and she wouldn't even be able to see them.

Preston moved closer behind her, drawing her back against him as a lover would . . . still tender, gentle. Her body rebelled as he nibbled gently on her ear and Jade stared hard into the dusk, willing herself to ignore the warm lips and damp tongue on her skin.

"Tell me about Fielding," she said. She had no idea why those words popped out, but when Preston's fingers froze, tightening on her shoulders, she knew it had been the right gamble.

"What?" he said. But there was an odd note in his voice.

"He's very powerful, isn't he?" Trusting her instincts, she stepped away from Preston. To her surprise, he allowed his fingers to slip from her.

"Why do you say that?"

She looked at him for the first time, feeling bold and superior . . . even though deep inside, she quaked with fear. He could haul off and slam his hand into the side of her face, and she'd be on the floor in a heartbeat. But . . . he seemed unsettled. "He was here before the Change. Fielding was a very powerful man even before that, wasn't he?"

Those slender lips tightened. "That means nothing now. This is what matters." He yanked aside the collar of his shirt and showed her the glowing blue crystal. She knew that it would be warm to the touch. "This makes us equal."

"I got the impression since he was here . . . well, he must have been one of the originals. He must know about . . . everything."

Suddenly hatred burned in his eyes. She'd definitely struck a nerve . . . but what? What exactly was she uncovering?

"The only one who knows about everything is Remington Truth. And until we find him, Fielding has no power over me . . . or anyone else."

Yet he was afraid of Fielding. She could see it. "Remington Truth? He sounds—"

But she'd gone too far. Preston's hand flew through the air and connected with the side of her face. The blow staggered her, and she reeled, stumbling into the leather-bound chair as he grabbed the hair he'd stroked so lovingly moments before.

For the second time that day, pain screamed through her skull and her head cracked against something hard . . . and she sank, gratefully, into oblivion.

"Who is she?" Elliott asked, looking down at the woman. Fever flushed her face and kept her eyes closed even as he touched her forehead. She breathed roughly, shallowly.

"It doesn't matter."

But Elliott hadn't waited for Ian's reply; he'd already begun to examine the young woman, careful not to let his hands linger. She appeared to be in her late twenties, with lovely, delicate features pinched by pain and illness. Pale hair, the color of wheat, lay coiled on the pillow beneath her and was plastered stickily to her temples and neck. She lay on her back, her hands stacked one on top of the other on top of the blankets, her fingers slender and frail, her nails chalky.

He could see immediately that she was very ill, and he didn't need to scan her to know how close to death she was.

"How long has she been like this?" Elliott asked now, pulling the sheets down to his patient's waist so he could more easily examine her. She wore a pastel pink nightgown with a wide, high neckline that showed only the tops of her shoulders. Just as he prepared to start the scan, he noticed the faint glow beneath her gown.

Tugging the ties to open the neckline, he pulled it away from her shoulder, careful, careful not to touch her skin directly. *Good God.* "What's this?" he asked.

Her ivory skin was fairly translucent, so thin the blue veins shone through. But in the soft part of her flesh, in the hollow below her clavicle and shoulder, the tissue had turned gray, then black and puffy. And in the center of the dark, swollen skin was the crystal he'd seen shining faintly through her gown.

The circular stone was perhaps the size of his thumbnail, and a sickly yellowish color. Embedded in the skin, this stone didn't seem to be well settled. The skin puffed horribly around it, black and shiny with a myriad of little cracks.

"What is this?" he demanded again, now raising his eyes to meet the other man's gaze. "How long has it been like this? What happened? You have to give me some information or I won't be able to do anything." He might not be able to do anything anyway.

Was she even human?

"A week ago, the stone was introduced to her body. It was a replacement for a different one that her body also rejected, but without such a violent reaction. On the other side."

Elliott pulled away the neckline from her other shoulder and saw the red puckered wound there. Anger swept over him, but he tamped it back. "How was the stone introduced?" he asked, wanting to palpate the damaged tissue around the crystal, but not daring to with his bare hands. It appeared firm and brittle. "And why?"

The woman tensed and groaned behind closed lips, shifting restlessly. He could sense the layer of infection beneath it and knew the stone would have to come out, the skin would have to be cut away. If the infection had spread. . . .

"It was a replacement, like I said," Ian replied. "There is a process by which the crystal is embedded into the skin, and for some reason, she did not accept it. The first one was not so bad—it didn't become rooted, and it fell out. And this one stayed in, but you see what's happened. They die if it becomes this bad."

Elliott resisted the urge to demand to know why they did such a thing. He didn't figure Ian would tell him anyway. "I'll need soap, towels, some small pails or bowls . . . clean cloths, forceps—something small to grab it with," he explained when Ian frowned in question, "and hot water, a very sharp knife—the smallest one you can find—and gloves, or plastic for my hands. And something for her pain. If you have anything like that. Alcohol too."

He looked at Ian. "I may not be able to save her, but I'll do what I can. It may be too late." He held the other man's gaze. "It would be much easier for me to concentrate if I knew that Jade was safe."

"You'll concentrate just fine because you know I've kept my part of our bargain," Ian said, then, with a quick glance at the woman, turned and left the room.

Elliott turned back to his patient and began to scan her. He wasn't certain what to expect, for he still wondered if she was actually human. Were the Strangers human? Fielding had been.

She must be a Stranger. But did that make Ian one as well? He'd never seen any glow through his clothing, so he suspected Ian was not crystaled. So why did he care about this woman, who was obviously a Stranger? Or at least, was trying to become one.

The obvious answer was that she was his lover. Or perhaps a sister.

But Elliott suspected it was the former that put the deep lines in Ian's face, and caused the desperation in his eyes. He knew the same lingered in his own when he thought of what would befall Jade if he didn't heal this woman . . . and find a way to save the woman he loved too.

He heard shouts in the distance. An alarm being raised, running, pounding feet. Had Theo succeeded? Had he brought the teens to safety? Or had they been discovered during the escape? He looked out the window, but the view was only an infinite expanse of ocean, black and rolling beneath a darkening sky.

A moment later, the door opened and he looked up to see Ian standing in the entrance. "They didn't make it," he said flatly.

"Is anyone hurt?"

"He's not dead, if that's what you're asking. But he's not going anywhere anytime soon either. None of them are." Ian stared at him as if to say he'd done his part, too bad it hadn't worked, but it didn't matter.

He closed his eyes for a moment. He could not be distracted now. One thing at a time.

A woman and a man walked in after Ian, carrying the items Elliott had requested. Including gloves, thank goodness. They weren't the thin-skinned latex gloves he'd been used to as a surgeon, but they were made from a slightly thicker plasticlike material that nevertheless was flexible enough to serve his purpose.

Taking a deep breath, Elliott returned to his scan. There was nothing about the woman that was unusual, as far as her internal organs were concerned. She seemed just as human as he was except for the crystal. He identified no other infection inside her, other than that which was concentrated in her shoulder.

But he did discover that she was pregnant. Approximately four months, he estimated.

He glanced at Ian, who was watching him with those cold blue eyes. Did he know about the baby? Was it his?

"She's carrying a child," he said, holding the other man's gaze.

Shock flared there, changing those flat eyes for a moment before it was quickly masked. His face remained impassive. "Then you'd best work even harder to save her."

"Tell me her name. I need to know something about her."

"Allie."

Elliott nodded and looked over at the supplies. He washed his hands and sterilized them with a generous amount of alcohol—from a bottle of vodka, which he didn't mind wasting—and the small knife as well. Then he donned the gloves and set to work.

As he turned to Allie, who appeared to be deeply unconscious, he wondered why whoever had embedded the stone into her shoulder hadn't been the one called on to remove it. He or she had to be some kind of surgeon to do such a thing, and it was obviously a common practice among the Strangers.

Then he put the questions out of his mind and bent to his task.

The knife's delicate point slipped into the flesh pillowing around the crystal, and as it punctured the tissue, Allie gasped and jerked, crying out softly in pain.

Elliott heard a low warning noise from Ian, but he ignored it and resumed his task. Allie eased back into unconsciousness and though she twitched slightly, she didn't cry out again.

A purplish green puss had begun to ooze from the incision. Its stench filled the room, heavy and appalling, and the woman who'd carried in the implements gasped and turned away. He dimly heard her retching in the corner, but he was too intent on scraping away the mess while breathing through his mouth. Only once before had he smelled anything like this, and that had been in a similar situation in Haiti, when he'd been called upon to treat another advanced infection. But at least there they'd had antibiotics and sterilized instruments.

Having released its dubious hold around the crystal, the skin seemed to deflate and the stone appeared to loosen. Gently using the knife to cut away the black, deadened skin, Elliott tried to slip its point under the crystal and grab it with the simple forceps Ian had provided. Allie jerked again and cried out, but he continued to work gently at it, dark blood now flowing from the hole around the stone.

At last he saw . . . he tasted metal in the back of his mouth as he used the forceps to lift the crystal. Unlike a bullet, the foreign object didn't simply slip out of the body. Instead, the surrounding skin and muscle seemed to be attached, to come with it as though suctioning the insides up and out.

Christ Almighty. What the hell is this?

At last it pulled free, and he saw, with a horrible fascination, that the crystal seemed to have tentacles. Slender little tentacles that had grown into the body, barely the circumference of a toothpick, some no bigger than a hair . . . and no longer than his little finger. They looked like fiber-optic cables.

He dropped the stone into a bowl, and, resisting the urge

to examine it more closely, turned back to her damaged body. Allie seemed to be breathing a bit more easily, but blood and puss still oozed from the wound in her shoulder.

Elliott cut away the rest of the dead flesh, noticing that the muscles and tendons beneath seemed to be fairly intact, despite the tentacles that had infiltrated them. He was concerned about the loss of blood, and that her skin had become even warmer since he'd started working.

All this time, Ian had watched silently, his face set. He'd made no move to touch Allie other than the moment when she first cried out.

When Elliott had done all he could, he cleaned the wound. Allie cried out again, writhing and moaning on the table as he washed it with alcohol. He hated to cause her pain, but he had nothing else. Ian moved closer to hold her steady, but his touch seemed to be more impersonal than tender.

After he finished bandaging it up, Elliott looked up at Ian. "That's all I can do for now. The infection hasn't spread to the rest of her body, so there is hope that she'll recover. But I've never seen anything like that before, so I don't know the nature of the illness. What has happened in the past?"

"Once the skin begins to darken and reject the crystal, no one has survived."

"Did they remove the stone?" Elliott asked.

"Yes. But it's always been too late. I expect this time to be different." Ian's face bore no trace of relief. "You're more than a simple doctor."

Elliott met his eyes. How Ian knew about his skills, he didn't know, but he refused to heal Allie with his bare hands. He would not attempt to take on her illness—an illness he didn't understand, and wasn't even certain he could absorb into his own body.

"You haven't laid your hands on her," Ian said. There was a definite threat in his voice, burning in his eyes.

Elliott's heart sank. *He knows.*

The gun appeared in Ian's hand and he walked over next to Elliott. "Take off the gloves and put your hands on her." The cold metal barrel touched his temple.

Elliott hesitated, despite the pressure against his head. "Pulling the trigger won't help your cause."

"It's already a lost cause—don't you think I don't know that? I have nothing to lose and you're my only hope. *Put your hands on her.*" When Elliott still didn't move, Ian stepped away and spoke through his teeth. "If that's the way you wish to do it, then."

With sharp movements, he opened the door. Three men stood there. Large men. Ian needed to give no command, for they surged in and before Elliott could react they'd swarmed around him, and forced him toward the bed, holding his arms out in front of him. Ian stripped off the gloves and Elliott began to struggle harder, knowing what was to happen next. If he moved or didn't concentrate, it might not work. If they touched his skin during the fight, it would flow into them.

But it did no good. Despite his great strength, Elliott couldn't overcome the power of the four of them. They held him by his sleeve-covered arms, and the rest of the clothing on his body protected the men as they forced his hands down onto Allie's face.

Elliott felt the sizzle of unwanted energy flow through him, warm and strong, swirling down into his limbs. It shocked and surprised him, the force of it, and his knees weakened.

When they released him, he spun immediately, trying at once to lunge at them, but one of the goons shoved a chair at him, catching him in the gut with its arm. The blow paralyzed Elliott, knocking every bit of air from his diaphragm, and, gasping for breath, he sagged to the floor.

When he looked up again, the men were gone. He was alone with Allie.

And the burn had already begun . . . just below his clavicle.

One year After

One year later.

Mayor Rowe decided to have a celebration. A new sort of Thanksgiving. It's a good idea—remind people that we've survived. And see how far we've come.

Theo was finally successful hacking into the satellite. He's been working on it for more than six months, and got in.

The images he showed me confirmed what we've believed: there's nothing much left. Of anything. But there's something odd . . . in the Pacific Ocean. Will want to look more closely at that and at the new images over the next few weeks.

It's been a month since Elsie died. I still dream that she's with me. I always will.

—from the journal of Lou Waxnicki

CHAPTER 21

Jade stared out the window into the darkness, peering through her one good eye. The pain resulting from her earlier reunion with Preston had begun to subside, except in her arm. She'd landed on it when he shoved her to the floor, and had felt it twist under her.

How was she going to get out of here? She could hear faint cries from below, and Jade knew it was the youngsters, locked in the hold. Somehow, she had to figure out a way to free herself . . . and them.

She found that watching out the window helped to take her mind off the discomfort. Perhaps she hoped she'd see Elliott and Theo riding to the rescue. A fanciful thought, but one she focused on, hoped for. The floating house had angled more perpendicular toward the shore during the last hours, and Jade now saw a different view of the shore . . . where hulking shadows lurched. Emerging from the ocean, staggering toward land.

Ruuu-uuthh. Ru-uth. . . .

Although she couldn't clearly hear their moans, she'd seen and heard them often enough. At dawn, the *gangas* trudged in a large pack toward the waves rushing onto the beach, and then, as the sun rose, they kept walking down into the water until it covered them. They emerged in the same way after

the sun had gone down, marching in a ragged army from the
depths of the sea.

But this time, as she watched them, Jade caught her
breath. She listened, and faintly heard their haunting sighs.
Ruuthh. Eddy . . . to . . . Ruuth.

She frowned, something tickling the back of her mind
. . . but the insistent pain clouded her train of thought and
she found it hard to concentrate. Yet something drove her,
something bothered at her. She knew it was important, and
she struggled to get the window open.

She listened.

Eddy . . . Tuh-ruuuth. Eddy . . . Truth?

Jade strained to listen. She'd heard them so many times
before, every night and many mornings for years and years.
Why was it so important now? Something Preston had said
. . . she filtered their conversation through her scattered
thoughts.

Ready . . . to . . . Truthhhh?

She listened, straining her ears, combing aurally through
the eerie groans to the syllables beneath.

And then she got it. Through the fog of her pain, it crys-
tallized and she understood. A glimmer of light in a murky
gray world.

A piece of the puzzle of the Strangers.

Elliott was dying.

And so was the girl.

Whatever the crystal had done to infect Allie had seeped
deep into the tissue and organs of her delicate body and
would not release it. And it had now infected him. He
touched Allie freely now, and felt life draining away. From
both of them.

Ian's gamble hadn't worked, and not only would it not save Allie, but it would soon destroy Elliott as well. There was nothing he could do for her, and only a desperate chance to save himself by getting out of this locked room.

During the last hours, Allie had grown grayer, her blue veins shining more clearly through her flesh. Despite the bandage that Elliott had dressed her wound with, blackness had crept beyond the edges and discolored her skin.

Elliott brushed his fingers over her cheeks, felt the clamminess of her skin, and, because he allowed the sensation—was looking for it—he felt the drain of life. The imposition of death. With his thumb, he made a cross over her forehead and said a silent prayer.

There was nothing else.

And so, despite his growing weakness, he turned his attention to the room—something he'd been too busy to do earlier. A generous size, well lit by a large, glazed window, the space was neat and appointed with the bed and several chairs. A table. He looked inside a small cabinet, flush with the wall, and found it empty. On the table next to the bed lay the implements provided to him by Ian—forceps, a knife too small to do much damage. But he slipped it into his pocket nevertheless. The half-used bottle of vodka, the bowl in which the crystal lay, thick black-red blood pooling beneath it. Another bowl with bloody, wadded towels.

Elliott eyed the crystal and its delicate tentacles, then scooped it up with a damp cloth and stuck it in his pocket.

The crystal . . . so important to these people. Yet so deadly.

Just then, he heard the clunking of the lock and the door opened behind him. He turned once more. The door opened and he looked up to see Ian filling the doorway. Though weak, Elliott would have launched himself immediately at the man if he hadn't seen the two men behind him. Raul Marck and Luke Bagadasian.

Elliott drew in a deep, slow breath and revised his immediate plan to attack Ian. He could kill one of them with his bare hands, but Preston was the one he really wanted.

Although Luke came in a close second.

But how much longer did he even have? He wasn't going to go out without taking one of them with him.

Trying to hide his weakness, Elliott met Ian's eyes. He saw reluctant comprehension in the other man's gaze. And anger. Deep, burning fury.

Yet . . . he didn't recognize grief. Only rage.

"I've done everything I can do," Elliott said. A strange calmness settled over him as he considered his options.

"That's not going to be enough." Ian came forward and looked down at the slight body draped in white sheeting.

Elliott ignored him and focused on Luke, who had the balls to look at him as if he were an ant. "You betrayed Jade," he said to the loathsome man. He couldn't wait much longer. It required every bit of concentration and strength to keep his knees from buckling and his breathing steady. He wasn't in pain as much as he felt like a rubber doll . . . but he knew exactly what was happening. He could feel the infection burning away his skin, into his body.

He couldn't wait for Preston.

"The reward was too good to pass up," Luke said, swaggering into the small room. *Closer now. Just a bit closer.*

Elliott felt a wave of weakness, but he braced himself against the chair. He wanted nothing to give away his position. "And you needed the money to keep yourself in a supply of crystals, so you could grind the dust," he said, remembering the gritty sparkles he'd seen in Luke's computer room. "You weren't making enough money from selling electronics."

"Not nearly enough. And I wanted to sample her before I turned her back to Preston. But the bitch was sharing her slimy gash with someone else. . . ."

The rest of Luke's taunt faded away as red rage blinded Elliott. He drew in a deep breath, calmed himself, and said, "Congratulations. I assume you were the one who sent the message that she needed to come to Greenside, pretending you were Theo. Was that so you could confirm her identity? Or set her up to be captured?" He extended his hand as if to affirm the congratulations. "But I came along with her and screwed up your plans."

Come on, you fucking bastard. Get your ego over here and shake my damned hand so I can send you to hell. Elliott no longer felt any remorse over what he intended to do.

"Yeah, that was pretty brilliant of me. Pretending to be the geek. It worked, but you left before anyone could come and collect her."

Elliott could hardly listen to the man's response . . . he was focused on his hand, still extended. *Come on, you bastard. You've got the ego. I know you want to show it off.*

Luke looked at him and Elliott allowed the anger to show on his face, taunting him. Goading him into reacting.

When Luke moved and accepted Elliott's hand in a shake, he was prepared for a fist to come flying after it. And it did.

Elliott ducked, but not before he had a firm handshake with Luke. The blow glanced off his temple and Elliott spun away. Triumphant.

Luke surged at him again and Elliott dodged once more, and the fight would have continued if the door hadn't opened again.

"What is going on here?" The tall, slender man standing

there looked as if he were about Elliott's age, perhaps a bit older. Closer to forty. His hair was jet-black, pulled back into a short tail at the base of his neck.

Luke froze and retreated to the side of the room as the new arrival walked in. He came directly to the bed, barely glancing at Elliott.

"She won't last the night," he said in a soft voice. He sounded pained, more so than Ian had. But when he lifted his eyes, Elliott felt coldness sweep over him.

Those gray orbs, the color of raw iron, didn't match his voice. They were hard and unfeeling.

"Are you pleased, now, Preston?" Ian said, confirming Elliott's suspicions.

Preston. Elliott was blinded by anger and fury, and his whole body stilled. *Dammit.* If he'd waited *two more minutes.* . . .

The weakness had already begun to leech away and Elliott knew that it was only a matter of time before Luke succumbed to the illness. It had worked. If only he'd been able to apply it to the immortal, the one he had no chance of killing.

Power surged through him, power and determination. He'd find a way to kill the man here, right now. If he touched Allie again, would he take on the illness a second time?

He realized Ian had moved. Once again, the gun was pointed at him, causing him to hesitate. "Our doctor here is a bit upset by your presence, Preston," Ian said. "He'd like nothing more than to bash your head in . . . but I'm not quite through with him yet. There's still hope for Allie, and until then, I'm not about to let him do anything foolish."

Elliott's fingers curled into his palms and he met the other man's gaze steadily.

Preston, for his part, seemed wholly unconcerned with

the interaction. Instead, he'd gently brushed his hand over Allie's cheek, trailing his fingers over her jaw. "Such a shame."

"If you hadn't insisted on crystaling her," Ian said, his voice steady . . . but cold. "Did you know she's with child?"

"I'd suspected," Preston replied.

"And you crystaled her anyway? Even after the last one was rejected?"

"Ian, my dear boy," Preston said, "you overstep yourself. And I cannot even congratulate you on bringing a *doctor*"—he said this last word with great contempt—"to our abode, for he's unable to do anything to save her. Not withstanding the fact that it's because of you that my cargo was nearly stolen."

Ian seemed to pull himself back, but revealed nothing else.

"Did you think I wouldn't find out what you'd done? You betrayed me for this little piece of nothing?" Preston jabbed his hand at the gray-faced Allie. "It's too bad you risked everything for *nothing*."

Preston turned and seemed to notice Elliott for the first time. A flare of something appeared in his gray irises. "You must be the one my darling Diana was calling for, earlier. Unfortunately, she was in distress." He smiled. A smile that one would bestow upon a babe, or a charming puppy. "Elliott, is it? What a pity." He sounded completely sincere.

Then he turned to Ian, gesturing to the bed. "She's going to die. There's nothing that can be done and we no longer need him. I see no reason to delay the inevitable. Perhaps we ought to allow Diana to watch. She'd enjoy the entertainment."

Ian inclined his head and then turned back to Elliott. The gun had not wavered. "Very well."

Preston turned back to Elliott. "I believe I'll go break the news to Diana. She'll be most inconsolable, I'm certain. Ian, I'll expect you in thirty minutes."

Elliott launched himself at Preston. The gun discharged, sending a bullet whizzing past him, and as he crashed into the dark-haired man, Elliot felt something heavy slam into him from behind. He tossed off Raul's weight, and grappled with Preston, shoving him against the wall, but the other man was stronger than he looked. They bounced against the corner, and Elliott smashed a powerful fist into Preston's face, took one in his own abdomen, and then felt strong hands yanking at him.

It took Luke, Ian, and Raul to pull him away from Preston, yet he struggled hard enough to get another well-placed kick into the man's abdomen. When Preston lifted back up, his face was ugly and the simpering was gone.

While Ian and Raul held Elliott, Preston jabbed his fists into Elliott's cheek, his jaw, nose . . . Elliott managed a whale of a kick, but Ian and Raul jerked him off balance so that he missed Preston.

By the time they allowed him to sag to the floor, he was bleeding and gasping for breath, barely able to notice that they'd released him—but fully conscious that Preston was also in pain. Not enough, but at least he hadn't gone down without a fight.

Ian stood over Elliott for a long moment after Raul, Luke, and Preston left. "That was a stupid thing to do," he said, tapping the toe of his boot sharply into Elliott's sore shoulder. "Three against one."

"Bastard." Elliott would have pulled to his feet if that gun hadn't been trained on him once again.

"This time, I won't miss," Ian told him, looking down

with flat eyes. "Stupid bastard. Now he's even more furious. And your woman will suffer for it."

"You risked everything for yours," Elliott said, swallowing blood. He swiped his hand over his mouth. It came away wet and sticky. If it were just him, he'd risk it—lunge up and swing for the gun. But with Jade at risk. . . .

"It doesn't matter any longer. As soon as I leave this room, I'm a dead man anyway," Ian said. His face had gone blank. "By his hand or someone else's."

For a moment, Elliott felt almost a kinship with the man standing before him. He'd done no more than Elliott himself had for the woman he loved.

"Will you tell me where she is? How to get to her?"

Ian looked at him for a long moment, and seemed to be ready to speak, but suddenly his lips clamped together. An instant later, Elliott understood why, for Luke and Raul had returned.

Luke had the pasty white face of a man in pain, and a glazed look that indicated he had no idea why. Elliott felt no remorse for what he'd done. He only wished he'd been able to do it twice more.

But his train of thought was interrupted as Luke lunged toward him. His arm whipped out, something hard and metal smashed into his head and everything went black.

CHAPTER 22

The door opened and Jade felt the prickle tingle her spine even before she turned.

She knew it was bad . . . she already knew it would be worse than she'd imagined. Her fingernails dug into her thighs and she forced herself to turn. To face whatever it would be.

She had to live through it.

Preston stood there, his eyes wild and furious. No longer the flat and cold, controlled gray. His hair had fallen from its queue, and hung in wicked straggles around his face, and she saw dark red marks on his face. Traces of blood near his nose.

Elliott. What have they done to you?

"So it was your friends," Preston said, his voice ugly. No longer playing gentle. "They tried to ruin everything. But they didn't succeed."

"What do you mean?" Jade was certain she knew, but confirmation would be nice. At least if she knew for certain it would be easier to handle whatever came next.

"My cargo, my specially handpicked cargo. Nearly sneaked out from under me," he said, almost to himself. "Do you know how long I've been working to get such prime specimens?"

Specimens. He was talking about *people.* Jade's belly lurched.

"That young Marck would have allowed it. All for her."

Preston looked back up and his expression sent renewed shivers down her spine. Jade stepped back, her throat dry, heart pounding. "But he knew better than to barter you, didn't he? You must be more valuable than a dozen slaves . . . to me and to them. So let's see how loudly I can make you scream. I want your lover to hear you."

When Elliott opened his eyes, it was to the sound of screams. Horrible, pained screams. Crashes, ugly thuds. Directly above him.

Jade.

He tried to move, and was rewarded by the clink of metal. His arms and legs were chained together, and anchored to the wall. A faint cast of light colored the room gray, and he realized he was in the hold of the houseboat.

A variety of manacles puddled on the floor, hanging from the walls . . . and he realized that this must be one of the holds where the slaves were kept. Where were they? Was there another storage place? Or had they somehow escaped . . . or been taken away.

But now Jade was paying the price.

Loud thumps and crashes came from above, and he could hear the grunts of exertion, followed by sharp cries of pain. Tears of frustration sprang to his eyes and he barely held back the deep roar that threatened.

"Let me go!" he shouted, bellowing at the top of his lungs, even though he knew it would make no difference. Elliott pulled on the chains, rattling and kicking and struggling with every bit of power he could muster. Even his abnormal strength would do him no good now, though he pulled and twisted, scoring his wrists and ankles with the sharp metal. *Please.* How long would he have to listen to her being beaten?

How long?

The cries and thuds continued, his desperation and hopelessness rose and Elliott wept, still battling the relentless iron.

He wept for his family and his life . . . he wept for the world, annihilated by these creatures who called themselves men, who'd lived among them . . . he wept for those who'd lived through the destruction and those who had not . . . and most of all, he wept for what he could have had with Jade.

Jade. My God. I never got to tell her . . .

A soft noise pulled him from the depths of despair and he looked up. Ian Marck stood in the doorway. Sagged.

And as Elliott watched, he sank to his knees. Even from across the room, he saw the blood staining his clothing. A dark red blossom on the center of his shirt.

"Please," Ian said. His eyes were haunted but determined. "A life . . . for . . . life." He barely managed the words.

And Elliott suddenly had hope. "I have to touch you."

It seemed like forever as Ian dragged himself toward him . . . breath by breath. He was so near death, Elliott could feel it. But . . . just a bit more.

Come on. Come *on.*

The screams above had ebbed into desperate whimpers, and Elliott couldn't allow himself to listen, to her, nor to the other distant cries of the teens, still enslaved somewhere nearby. Instead, he focused on each breath of Ian, counting between them, praying that there would be another one . . . as the man slowly worked his way to him.

Blood stained the floor, sometimes pooling there beneath

him as he waited to gain more strength and move closer. Closer. Inch by inch.

At last . . . Elliott crouched on the floor, reaching his arms as close to Ian as he could. Their hands touched, Ian's cold and deathly.

Closing his eyes, Elliott felt the sizzle of power rush through him, knowing that this would be the last time.

Ian's breathing had slowed, but now it eased into a regular rhythm. The raspiness disappeared and Elliott could almost see him come back to life.

"I don't have the keys," was the first thing he said. "I don't know—"

"I didn't think you did," Elliott replied. "Just . . . get her out of here. There's not much time. For her . . . or for me." Ian had been too far-gone, and the injury moved rapidly to take over Elliott's body. "Get her . . . safe. All of them."

Ian rose to his feet, still a bit slowly, but Elliott knew how quickly he would regain his strength.

And for the second time that day, he felt the life easing from his body.

Preston was on her, pummeling Jade with his fists, slogging her to the ground with his weight. His knee shoving between her legs, his hands pulling at her hair. She screamed when he hit her broken arm, and then felt his fingers curling into the side of her face, the dig of his nails into tender skin, the heat of his breath as he held her steady. Crashed her skull to the ground. Pulled her hair, like an enraged teenaged girl. Tore at her clothing. Smashed the wine bottle at the back of her shoulders, sending glass shattering everywhere.

She fought, bucking and kicking, trying to hold back the screams. But he was relentless and vicious and even though she knew that was his desire, she couldn't keep from crying out.

He was strong. So strong.

She lay unmoving on the floor as he pulled to his feet, breathing heavily. She heard him stagger across the room, the sound of sloshing liquid and gulping. Heavy breaths laced with fury. The back of her neck prickled, knowing the next blow would be the last. The worst.

Unless he raped her first.

Then her eyes fell on the bottle. The wine bottle . . . broken in half, smashed on the ground next to her.

Jade reached for it with her good hand, moving stealthily, and pulled it close to her. Positioning the top half of it by the neck, she closed her eyes and said a little prayer.

It was a slim chance. But her only chance. With a moan, she half rolled to her side, readying herself.

She heard him coming again, heard the unmistakable sounds of a belt buckle clinking, the swish of a zipper. And as he bent toward her, over her, grabbing at her shirt, she lunged . . . with every last bit of her strength, for her, for Elliott, for the kids . . . and as she watched, as if she were apart from it all, as she brought the jagged edge of the bottle down . . . stabbing like a knife . . . down toward Preston.

Down toward his *shoulder*. Into his flesh.

Preston screamed as the jagged glass cut into his shoulder, digging into the flesh that held his powerful crystal. His lifeline, the source of his strength. His shield.

Blood spurted everywhere, and he tried to tear away . . . but adrenaline rushed through her, fury and power and she lashed up at him and tore the bottle down into his shoulder.

He flung his other arm up, slamming it against her, trying to bat her away—but still she held on, thrashing down with the glass weapon, tearing into Preston's skin again and again, gouging the crystal out of his flesh.

Weakness seeped into Preston's face. He gasped and kicked, slowing and slowing until he was nothing but a shuddering mass.

At last, Jade staggered to her feet, breathing heavily. Blood dripped from the jagged glass, and she saw that the crystal lay on the floor in a mass of blood and flesh. Long, silvery threads tangled on the ground with it, bloody and useless. Some of them were still attached to Preston.

Just then, the door opened.

Ian Marck stood there. Jade gasped and looked around for another weapon. But he held up his hand as if to hold her back.

Shock clear on his face, Ian looked down at the other man, who was gently blowing bloody bubbles. Preston's gray eyes had gone lifeless, and his fingers had ceased to twitch. "You did that?" Ian murmured. "Unbelievable."

"Where's Elliott?" She angled the bloody wine bottle at him, ready to spring if he dared try and stop her.

That seemed to jolt Ian back to life. "He's hurt. Below. I don't. . . ."

"The kids? Where are the kids?" she demanded, brandishing the bottle as she moved toward him. She didn't want to hear what he was going to say about Elliott.

"Below. You'll need the keys. From . . . him."

Jade, beyond caring about the blood and gore, fairly dove toward Preston and found the keys clipped to his trousers. They were slick with blood, but she scooped them up and started out of the room.

Then she stopped and faced Ian. "Your father. And Luke. Where are they? And the others?"

Ian's expression hardened. "Luke's dead. And my father . . . I'll take care of him. He made his loyalty clear today, and it was not for me." He rubbed his chest as though it ached, and Jade realized his shirt was covered with blood. "The others are gone."

"Are you hurt?"

"I was," he said, his blue eyes meeting hers. Still flat, but no longer cold with loathing. "Your Elliott healed me, so I could help you."

It took only an instant for the meaning of his words to register. *Oh my God.*

"Keep your father out of my way—and you too," she said, running out the door.

Out the door, down the metal stairs, past the constantly rushing water, falling from every level . . . she reached the bottom of the stairs and didn't know which way to go. There were two rooms. Cries and shouts from the right, and she dashed that way first.

Three tries to get the right bloody key to work and at last she had the hold opened. "Theo!" she cried, seeing him slumped against the wall. The room was filled with familiar faces—the same kids she'd saved from the *gangas* less than a week ago. "Geoff Pinglett!"

Theo raised his head and squinted at her through a swollen eye. "Jade! Thank God!"

"Where's Elliott?" she asked, fumbling with the keys. There were so many of them, and they were slick with blood, and she was desperate.

"I don't know. I heard someone shouting . . . he's down here I think," he said.

Jade finally got the right keys, loosened Theo from his manacles, and said, "He's hurt. I'll be right back. It's safe now."

She ran back down the hall, heart thumping madly, to the other door. Three keys later, she got it open just as Theo dashed up behind her. Flinging the door open, she burst in and saw him, huddled on the floor.

"Elliott," she cried, starting toward him.

"Jade," he murmured, his voice thick. *"No. Don't. . . ."*

She turned to find Theo there. "Take the keys, get the kids out of here."

There was a loud noise from above and the boat vibrated. "What the hell—?"

"It sounded like an explosion," Theo said, looking up. The smell of smoke tinged the air.

"Get the hell out of here," she said. "Ian told me everyone was gone, but he must have lied. Get the others and see what's going on up there. And get away!"

Theo hesitated, then nodded and ran off with one more backward look.

That left Jade to turn back to Elliott. She moved toward him, her heart in her throat, the smell of blood deep and heavy in the room. Frightening.

"Don't . . ." he said again as she drew near, desperation coloring his voice. "Don't do it, Jade." Then he seemed to focus on her, seeing her bruised and bloody face for the first time. "My . . . God . . . Jade. I'm sorry . . . I tried. . . ." She heard him swallow . . . try to swallow. "Preston. . . ." He managed.

"He's dead," she said, almost reaching to touch him. It was automatic, she *needed* to give comfort, as well as receive it . . . but she pulled back just in time.

She saw streaks on his face, grime and sweat. His hair was plastered to his head and she nearly cried when she saw the tears in his clothing, the scrapes on his wrist from the manacles.

She wanted to brush the hair from his face, to ease the pain, wipe the blood away. Kiss him. She couldn't even do that. "Elliott. . . ."

But . . . what if she didn't touch him directly . . .? Maybe she could—

"Don't . . ." he said, as if he knew what she was thinking. "Don't chance it. Jade. *Please. Please.*"

"I want to touch you, Elliott. I can't just sit here and watch you . . . I can't even. . . ." Her voice broke. She couldn't kiss him, couldn't help him out of this room . . . she couldn't even unlock him from the damned chains. He was going to die, here, a prisoner, with her watching him. Without a last kiss or caress . . . with no comfort. She was crying in earnest now, flinging the tears away with shaking fingers.

Blood pooled around him, soaking his shirt, dripping onto the floor. She literally saw the life draining from his face even as his eyes fastened on her, focusing for a moment.

Love blazed there. Something she'd not seen before, never recognized. Not this way. This deep.

"I . . ." He began. Then coughed. The deathly rattle sounded hollow in the room.

Jade looked at him, biting her lip. *No.* There had to be something. . . .

"I . . . want . . . you . . ." he said, drawing in a damp breath.

"I want you too, Elliott," she cried, bending forward to kiss him. She didn't care.

He jerked away before she touched him, gasping with pain at the sudden movement. Fury blazed in his eyes when he turned back to look at her. *"Don't."* He pulled in a shuddering breath and said, "Don't . . . *dammit* . . . Jade." He paused, gathered himself, and continued. "I want . . . you to . . . go *back*. Rogan . . . loves you. Will take care. . . ."

"But I don't love him," she retorted. "Elliott, please. . . ."

"Let me . . . talk. Don't have much longer." He tried to smile. Failed. Pain washed over his face, his cheeks so hollow, his mouth flat and agonized. Those blue eyes, now empty and flat, closed for a moment, then opened. Slowly. "I love . . . you. So. Much. I. . . ."

Jade was shaking her head, tears coming from her eyes, dripping down her face and onto the floor. "I love you too, Elliott. I don't want anyone else . . ."

"*Listen.*" He let out a long breath. "Just once. Please."

She bit her lip, but didn't speak. Tears rolled down freely now.

"I . . . can't live . . . in this world. . . ." He made a little movement that might have been a smile, but it was more of a grimace. "It's not . . . mine."

"Yes it is. You can. With me!" she said fiercely, and by God, she didn't care anymore. She reached for him, touched him through his clothing. She felt him stiffen, in pain or fear, she didn't know, but she felt him, spreading her hands over him, felt his strong legs and hips . . . the warmth seeping through. And at last she felt a little comfort.

Jade moved her hand and felt something hard, and rounded. In his pocket. He shifted and it moved. "What is this?" she asked.

"Crys . . . tal," he breathed. His eyes had lost their focus. His lips barely moved.

But she caught the word and suddenly . . . a ray of hope. A crystal. . . .

She dug it out of his pocket and the cloth wrapping fell way, dried with blood. Slender glasslike tentacles radiated from it, and hope surged deeper. She'd just seen one. Preston's immortality crystal.

This might just work. It *might*.

"Elliott. Hold this. *Hold the crystal*," she said, moving toward his hands . . . hands that she'd had to refrain from touching, hands bloody and dirty and torn from his battles. His fingers barely moved, but she thrust the crystal into his palm, careful not to touch those lethal digits, and waited.

Prayed.

Watched.

Listened.

She knew it had worked when she heard the change in his breathing. Hardly daring to hope, she raised her face and found him looking at her. Eyes, clear. Focused.

Shining with a variety of emotions that made her suddenly feel weak . . . and comforted.

And because the moment made her feel more than a bit out of control, she seized it back, saying, "Elliott . . . I think I'm falling in love with you."

He smiled. A real smile this time. "That's a relief," he said, his words clear and strong, "because I've been in love with you for a few days now."

"A few days?" she repeated. "We've only known each other for five."

"Then I'd say it's been about four." And he kissed her.

EPILOGUE

"So you killed Preston, single-handedly," Elliott said. He looked ridiculously delicious, with mussed dark hair, well-kissed lips, and a wide, bare chest. "What a woman you are." His eyes crinkled at the corners as they focused on Jade with pride and heat, a combination that stirred her belly and made her feel as if her glow would burst forth.

Of course, that glow could have had something to do with the tangle of white sheets thrashed around them and the lump of clothes on the floor.

They'd returned to Envy late yesterday, riding in three humvees driven by Fence, Simon and Wyatt, and filled with the rescued teens. The explosion that rocked the houseboat turned out to have been a bottle rocket, lobbed by Fence, who'd arrived just as Jade was freeing Theo in the hold.

It hadn't done any real damage to the boat and by the time Theo came up to investigate, the cavalry had arrived . . . too late, as Fence complained, to do anything but shepherd the shell-shocked teens off the boat and into the waiting humvees.

"I can't believe he's really gone," she said, sliding her hand over the plains of his warm chest.

"He's really gone, Raul's gone, Ian Marck's disappeared . . . and we're really here."

"We almost weren't, Elliott." Her voice tightened and her throat closed. When she thought about how close she'd come to watching him die in front of her, chained and alone . . . "You said you couldn't live in this world." Tears stung her eyes as she remembered the stark expression on his face, the intent. "But I need you. You won't . . . you. . . ." Words failed her as fear reared inside her. Surely he wouldn't leave . . . or try to sacrifice himself again?

Elliott sat up, his expression growing serious. "Jade. . . ." He shook his head, reached to comb away the hair that had fallen into her face, his fingers strong and warm over her skin. "We woke up to find the world completely different than we'd left it," Elliott said. "We spent the last six months trying to come to terms with the fact that everything we knew and loved was gone. Had been gone, for fifty years."

He closed his eyes. Jade's heart swelled, filling her chest. What she'd been through was nothing compared to his experiences. At least she'd had some choices about her life. Sure, she'd lived through some frightening, painful moments, but at least her whole world hadn't disappeared. How *could* he ever come to accept it?

"Elliott," she said, and his eyes opened again, catching hers. For a moment, she felt like she might fall into them, literally sink right down into the rich, ocean-cool depths . . .

"I *don't* know how to live in this world. It's nothing like what I know, what I expected, planned for, nothing I could have conceived." He squeezed his eyes closed for a moment, then opened them. "But I have to learn. I need to find a place. Someplace that feels right, that . . . I guess . . . grounds me. A haven."

He planted his hand on the bed next to her, and she felt the mattress dip from his weight as he leaned closer. His eyes held hers, and she saw emptiness and sorrow there . . . and hope. Blazing hope. Something else . . . something that made her belly dip and slide.

Something infinite.

"I need you, Jade," he whispered. "Will you?"

She met his lips halfway in answer, her eyes closing as they came too close to keep hold of his gaze. Her mouth sank into his, a glorious burst of warmth cascading through her.

Her injured arm in a sling was awkward, but it didn't stop her from pushing forward, easing him back so that his head rested on the pillow. His strong arms pulled her with him, solid and gentle, curved around her back.

They faced each other, long legs shifting and twining together, his bare toes sliding up to gently caress her skin. The comforting weight of his thighs closed around one of hers and she felt the warmth of his belly and hips against her, raising little bumps all over her body.

He moved his hands down around to cup her bottom, drawing her close up against him, firmly but with tenderness, silently telling her how much he loved her. All the while, they kissed slowly, with great thoroughness, as though they would never stop. As though neither of them needed to breathe.

When at last he decided that they must breathe, he pulled gently away, his mouth pressing still against her cheek and jaw, the warmth of his breath gusting against her damp skin.

"This is much better," she murmured, pulling him up against her. She wanted that bare chest against her, the heat, the muscle and hair and strength. She wanted to taste his skin, slip her hands down over the hard, ridged belly, down farther, beyond the tangled sheets.

"Better?" he murmured against her ear, just as she managed to slip a hand down into the heat, and around her quarry. He sighed as she touched him. "Oh God. Much better."

She closed her fingers tighter around his erection, feeling the soft heaviness, the gentle pounding of his desire within her palm. "Better than last night. We were a little bloody. Dirty." She smiled against him, remembering the flurry of tearing clothes and frantic, eager bodies the moment they had a bit of privacy. "And in a big hurry. . . ." She gave a quick little stroke and smiled with delight when he breathed in sharply.

"So what's the hurry now?" he murmured, settling against her, heavy and hard in her hand, hot and smooth. His cheeks curved against her throat and his lips nibbled gently.

Then, he moved. She was on her back with the breath knocked a bit out of her before she quite realized what had happened, her hand slipping from him and sliding up his chest.

His grin was a little crooked, his eyes hot and determined as he looked down at her. "Let's see about taking our time," he said, bracing himself on one hand over her while he pulled the sheet down . . . then bent and covered her perked-up nipple with a hot, slick mouth.

Jade sighed, arched up into him, and then felt her world become sleek, languorous pleasure . . . long, slippery strokes of his tongue over the sensitive top part of her nipple, the gentle suction of his lips closing over the taut point, drawing it long and hard into his mouth. Pleasure burned through her, curling into her belly, down into her depths.

She couldn't help but smile . . . smile at the beauty of making love. So different than anything she'd known before.

His hand slipped between her legs, fingers sliding into

the slick warmth as he moved upward to nuzzle and kiss her throat.

Jade shivered, trembled, and then as he slipped and slid around, gently teasing her, she realized her whole body was gathering up . . . curling into the center of her universe, right where his hand was, his finger moving more quickly just where she needed it . . . She gasped in surprise, closed her eyes, and let the pleasure tighten up . . . tighten, unbearably sweet . . . and then roll over her in long, undulating waves, sending warmth radiating from her core to the tips of her fingers and toes. *Oh God . . . Elliott.*

"Well, now," he murmured into her ear. He sounded very pleased with himself and she smiled, her cheek bumping against his jaw.

"Your turn, Hawkeye," she said, reaching for him.

"Not quite yet." He slipped out of her range, and before she knew what he was doing, had slid all the way down, kissing her belly, until he settled between her legs. She still quivered there, her labia warm and full, and her body damp and still trembling with pleasure.

But when he bent there, his dark head rising beyond her belly, Jade lost all thought. His tongue was wicked and strong, sleek and cunning . . . and when, moments later, after her breath had gone short and rough, he lifted his face and came back up to her, she met his lips as he settled once again there . . . right *there*.

They lined up, warmth to warmth, Elliott propping himself up so as not to crush her arm. "And . . . now," he said against her mouth, "let's try this. One more time." And he slid deep inside. And settled, still.

Looking down at her with dark, glittering eyes, his mouth full and lips parted, he said her name . . . so softly and unsteadily . . . in such a way that she felt the timbre of it vibrate deep inside her.

Her heart swelled in her chest, she felt it kicking up speed as they looked at each other, waiting . . . savoring what was to come. Then his lips pressed tightly together, he drew in a breath and bent to press a tender kiss onto her mouth.

And after that, he shifted smoothly and easily, and she rose and fell to meet his rhythm, wrapping her legs around his waist. Their breaths mingled with gasps and sighs and little encouraging noises that aroused her even further. She tried to grab at him, hold on with one hand, the rhythm faster and longer and more frantic.

Just about the time she felt that familiar gathering, the peak rising, he gave a long soft sigh that tipped her over . . . and then joined her. His heartfelt moan, low and deep against her ear, sent little pleasure-shivers over her as she felt his body trembling against hers.

She gathered his head close with her one arm as he sagged against her, half lifting his damp torso away from hers.

He sighed, slipping to the side and taking her with him. "Jade."

She nestled next to him, sliding her hand through the hair on his chest, completely satisfied, wrung out, and ready to rest. At last.

When Jade began to awaken, Elliott was watching her. Miraculously, he'd slept too. He'd actually *slept*, dreamless, comforted.

She stretched like a lazy cat, purposely making her movements sinuous and slow, her bare leg brushing against his. Brushing away the cascaded hair covering part of her face, she opened her eyes.

"I love you," she said. "Will you stay with me?"

He gathered her up. "I thought I'd already made it clear that I need you. I'm not going to leave you. Even if you try and send me away." His lips quirked crookedly.

She pulled away, her heart suddenly pounding. "Elliott, we need to talk."

Wariness filled his eyes, but he didn't move. He waited, his heart bumping steadily against her hand.

"I know that you have a special gift," she said, and felt his heartbeat quicken. "I know how important it is for you to help people. I wouldn't want you to change, just like I hope you won't expect me to stop going on my Running missions."

She paused, measuring his response, but his face was blank. As if he were steeling himself against what she was about to say. "I hope now you know how important it is for us to destroy the Strangers. . . ."

"What are you trying to say?" he demanded, his eyes darkening to black. "Say it and put me out of my misery."

And then she understood. Remorse washed over her. "Elliott, I just want . . . need . . . you to be careful. With your gift. I mean . . . you almost died yesterday. Twice." She shook her head. "I don't want to have to watch you go through that again. Those choices. That pain. The risk."

At last his dark expression eased. "I see." He settled back against the pile of pillows. "I've been thinking about that too. Now that I have the crystal, it appears that I can use it to heal injuries that I might take on from others."

"But Elliott . . . what if you don't have the crystal? Or if it doesn't work? You've only tried it once."

He looked at her, face serious, eyes understanding. "I've been given this gift for a reason, but I also understand its limitations. I still have pain . . . here"—he took her hand and placed it on the center of his chest—"where I took Ian's bullet wound. And here," he moved her fingers to his shoulder, "where Allie's infection began. And in other places as well, like Simon's *ganga* scratches."

Then he curled his hand around her fingers. "It seems that each time I use the gift, even after I pass on the injury, I retain a little bit of it. That tells me that I can't do it indefinitely. That means I have to choose when and where to use it."

Jade was nodding, tears stinging her eyes. She brushed his chin with the tip of her fingers. "But you can still be a doctor, still help people, like you would before."

His eyes crinkled. "I'll just wear gloves. And, by the way, in regards to your Running missions"—she tensed, ready to argue, but he continued—"I'll just go along with you and make house calls." He leaned forward to kiss the tip of her nose. "That way you can be in charge of our travel arrangements."

She moved so that their mouths met, and that led to another long, active battle with the sheets.

Some time later, they lay, once again sated and warm, comforted and rested . . . and with a rush, Jade remembered.

She sat up suddenly, grabbing Elliott's arm. "I can't believe I forgot to tell you this."

"What now?" he asked. He looked down at her, lazily lifting an eyebrow.

"When I was with Preston, I asked him about Fielding," she said.

"What did he say?"

"He said until they find Remington Truth, no one has any great power over him. Even Fielding. He was afraid of Fielding, I think. But it sounds like he is—was—more afraid of this Remington Truth. Whatever . . . whoever . . . that is."

"Remington Truth," Elliott murmured. "Quent said he was a member of the Cult of Atlantis."

Jade continued excitedly. "But here's the important thing that I've just figured out. They're looking for him. The *gangas* . . . that's what they're looking for! That's what they're chanting, over and over: Remington *Truuuth*," Jade said excitedly. "Do you see?"

Elliott's eyes sharpened thoughtfully. "And if they're looking for Remington Truth . . . then we should do the same," he said. "Because he's obviously very important to them. And if we find him first. . . ."

"Exactly!" Jade smiled, feeling suddenly free. And light and happy. She was safe, Preston was dead, and she was with Elliott.

The only man she ever wanted. Forever.

A while later, she and Elliott joined the others and told them about her discovery.

They all turned to look at her, and for a moment, she was struck by these five men—Wyatt, Fence, Simon, Quent, and Elliott—the intensity, the energy emanating from them. She'd never felt so surrounded by power and capability.

She knew that these men were here to help. That somehow, whatever had happened to them in that cave had been because the world needed them. Now.

Fifty years ago, their world ended.
Now five men must battle the immortals
who have destroyed everything they knew ...
and save the women they love.

Turn the page for an exclusive look at

EMBRACE THE NIGHT ETERNAL

on sale February 9, 2010

Simon had found only one way into the building, and it took him right through the darkened lobby—where the *gangas* lived.

He hadn't mentioned to Sage that there were just as many canine bones as human bones littering what had once been a highly-polished black and yellow marble floor. Nor had he told her that there were about two dozen of the creatures trapped in there—obviously set to guard the place from inquisitive people like the two of them. He wondered how often someone came to provide the *gangas* with food—in the form of feral canines or unlucky humans. Or could the monsters subsist for months without food?

During the day, the gangas must stay in the building, but at night they were free to roam within the perimeter of the vehicular barrier. The wolf that had attacked Sage must have somehow escaped from the corral. Fortunately, it hadn't gone as far as the inhabited part of Envy, or something worse than a few cuts and scratches might have occurred.

Simon mulled these thoughts as he moved out of Sage's sight, forcing himself to keep his mind away from . . . other things.

If he weren't such a *chavala*, he'd have taken her back to the city and been done with it. But he'd seen the enthusiasm and determination in her eyes, and knew it wouldn't be long before she was back here.

Of course, he could have taken her back and turned her over to Theo Waxnicki, who could probably have kept an eye on her if he knew she'd try and come back. That would have been the smart thing to do.

But no. He'd let a killer body and one soul-shattering smile override that sensible solution, and now he had to find a different way to get into the building so that she could come with him.

Simon paused and listened. Silence.

With a deep breath, he stilled, focused, and drew deep down inside himself, wavered . . . and disappeared.

Now he could move quickly, walking across the empty corral toward the Beretta building. He remembered when it had been built, for Mancusi had been interested in one of the condos in what would be Vegas's premier residential property.

At least until the next hot development came along.

The *gangas* might smell him, but they couldn't see him, and Simon walked boldly through the entrance of the lobby. It had once been decorated with colorful blown glass that put the Bellagio's famed glass flower ceiling to shame, but of course, there was nothing left of that but a few swaths of dirty, broken waves. Some of the *gangas* milled about, but most of them were sleeping or lying comatose—or whatever the fuck they did. The ever-present moaning "*ruuu-uuth*" came out in the form of snores and exhales from the prone monsters.

He counted four that were up and about, and from the way they stiffened and looked in his direction, Simon knew they scented him.

Ignoring the creatures, easily evading their clumsy feet and log-like arms, he hurried through the room, wondering how long Sage would stay put.

I'm not stupid.

Fuck no. And that was a big problem.

Not that a woman like Sage would want anything to do with Simon anyway. Nor could he imagine even touching her with his corrupted hands.

He saw a door in the corner and realized it would be the stairs. And that there might be a building exit in the stairwell.

Moments later, Simon found just what he was looking for. The exit had been locked and barricaded from the inside, which was why he'd not been able to access it when he originally searched for the entrance. But it took him little effort to clear it away and open the door, thanks to the super strength he seemed to have acquired in that Sedona cave.

When he returned to Sage, fully visible again, he found her sitting in nearly the same position in which he'd left her. "Ready?"

She looked up at him, her lovely face dirt- and blood-streaked, her blue eyes accusing. "I thought you might have gone in without me."

Simon shrugged. Why should she trust him? She didn't know him, and after all, she probably sensed he was who he was. Simon Japp. Bodyguard, goon, right-hand-man to Leonide Mancusi. He might have had a chance to start over, but his sins, his choices, his corruption, still clung to him like a bad odor.

There was no sense in defending himself. "Come on."

Sage pulled to her feet, and he heard the faint groan of pain as she did so. The cut above her knee had bled into a large dark stain, and he noticed the way it stuck to her skin. That was going to hurt when she undressed—*don't think about that.* And the cuts and scrapes on her hands . . . she was lucky they weren't any worse. Maybe he should check on them before they went any further.

No. Dragon Boy will make sure she's all patched up. And then some.

They crossed the corral-like space between the vehicle barrier and the building, running the twenty yards quickly and silently to the door Simon had left open. It was unlikely that the *gangas* would see them from inside the building, and if they did, they'd never figure out where they went or how to find them. Nor could they venture into the sunlight.

Simon was confident they were safe.

"Lots of flights to go," he said once they were inside

the dim stairwell. There was only a window every three or four floors, so the light was iffy. "Twenty-three floors."

"No problem," she told him, flashing a quicker, less potent version of the smile that had fairly dropped him to his knees earlier. "I always take the stairs to my room. On the fourteenth floor."

Simon nodded. It was obvious she got her exercise despite the hours sitting at a computer table. She had a sweet ass and slender, delicate body with curves exactly where they should be.

And she was going to be climbing twenty-three flights of stairs in front of him.

"I'll go first," he said, slipping past her. "One flight at a time, then you follow."

She nodded, surprising him when he was prepared to have to argue and explain the logic of allowing his heavier weight to confirm that the old steps were stable. "Right behind you."

Simon turned and jogged up the first few flights. The steps were metal and the railings completely intact, except for peeling paint, even after fifty years. He'd gone up a different stairwell awhile earlier, and was confident that they would hold. But it was a good excuse to not have to torture himself.

Twenty minutes later, they reached the top floor of the tower where Remington Truth had a penthouse. Birds fluttered and took flight as Simon and Sage walked across what would have been the threshold to the condo's entrance. Something rustled in a pile of leaves caught up in the corner.

The apartment's expansive French doors sagged in place. On the next wall, a stream of light came through a wedge of broken window, while the rest of the plate glass shone grimy and gray. A lush patch of green grew on the floor in an elongated vee where the pure sun would shine and rain would enter, though a bit of tenacious growth attempted to spread beyond the triangular patch.

"I can't believe it's still intact," commented Sage.

Simon raised a finger to his lips and gestured for her to hold back. He didn't think anyone was here, but he wasn't about to assume anything. On feet silent over the dried leaves and branches, he moved to the doors and carefully peered into the room beyond.

The place was in shambles, as one would expect. Shadowy furnishings melded with strips and patches of sunlight, and vines and bushes sprouted everywhere. Nothing moved. No sign of life.

Easing the door open, he slipped through and crooked his finger for Sage to follow.

She raised her brows as if to ask permission to speak—why did women always have to talk?—and he nodded, shifting away so that he wouldn't brush against her shoulder.

"If he was one of the Strangers, one of the people that caused the Change, do you think he meant to live here after?" she asked, looking around the room. "I mean, it might not be an accident that his home wasn't destroyed. Do you think?"

Good point. Simon shrugged. "You might be right. But he's not here now."

"And he hasn't been here for decades. Or they wouldn't be looking for him. I mean, if you found out about this place so easily. . . ." She'd moved along the perimeter of the room, trailing her hand over leather sofas and along a long sleek table, kicking up dust and disturbing birds, mice, and God knew what else. It didn't seem to bother her, though.

Not squeamish. Smart and practical. And the most beautiful woman he'd ever seen.

Pinche.

Simon turned away and cruised along the other side of the room, then down a dark hall. Something slithered over his foot and he kicked it away, then felt something else bump into his heel as it scurried for safety. No, Remington Truth hadn't lived here for a long time.

He wasn't certain exactly what to look for anyway. Surely anything of interest would have been destroyed or found long before now.

What had been the master bedroom opened before him, complete with a waterbed long since drained and a jetted tub large enough for half a dozen people. The skylight over the tub was broken, and tall slender plants grew in the circle of light, spindly and greedy for sun. They looked like skinny bamboo plants, with their random, delicate leaves near the top.

Maybe Truth had some good luck *feng shui* bamboo
that had sprouted. Simon grimaced as he was reminded
that, along with her myriad of crystals, Florita had
grown a few stalks of curling green bamboo in a glass
vase. She'd lectured Simon on how important their position and placement was for good fortune.

That was early on, when he'd been assigned as her
bodyguard, and he'd had no choice but to listen to her
prattle on. And on. And on. But then she'd tried to get
too friendly with Simon, Mancusi found out . . . and
he'd shipped Florita and her fake tits off with her crystals and bamboo and red candles. But not long after,
in true fuck-you spirit, she'd made it huge on the big
screen.

And back in East Los, Simon had been promoted,
so to speak, because of his loyalty and prudence. And
cuffed even more tightly to Mancusi.

"Simon!"

He turned from the bamboo growth in the Jacuzzi
tub, making his way quickly toward her voice.

"I found something!"

No fucking way.

When he came into the room, which appeared to
have been an office, Sage was standing in the center
of a pool of sun. She was holding a small black item.
"Look!"

"A jump drive?"

She nodded, her aqua blue eyes shining. "It was
wedged inside that desk drawer there, and it's so small,

it would have been easy to miss. Besides, I'm sure they took any computers or files he might have had."

Simon examined the small black flash disk drive and came to the conclusion that it might just have survived fifty years exposed to the elements. The USB plug slid in and out, and the whole thing was cased in soft, protective plastic that appeared intact. "Well I'll be damned." He looked up and gave her a little smile. "It might have something interesting on it. Or it might just have a bunch of old Neil Diamond songs."

"Who?"

He smiled before he caught himself. "Look him up. Isn't that what you do?" Simon turned away before the bantering could go any further. Bantering led to camaraderie, and camaraderie led to flirtation, and flirtation could only lead to fucking trouble.

He wandered close to a massive opening in the wall, a window broken completely away, and looked out over the ruins of Las Vegas.

The ocean—the damned Pacific Ocean, here in Vegas!—sparkled blue and green to the west and north, and between this structure and the water were a variety of buildings and ruins. Brick, glass, curling steel beams, all fringed with green and other organic trim.

"Do you have to stand so close to the edge?"

He cast a look over his shoulder. "You afraid of heights?"

Sage shook her head. "No. But I don't see why you have to stand so close to the edge."

Simon shrugged, fighting a grin, and turned to look back out over—and froze. "What the . . ." he muttered, moving closer to the side of the window where he wouldn't be seen. Curling his fingers around the edge, he carefully leaned forward for a better look. Space loomed before and below him, and a little breeze skimmed his cheeks.

"What is it?" Then, she must have seen how near the edge he was, because she added, "Simon! Be careful! You're going to fall."

He swallowed a chuckle. If she only knew how close he'd come to death so many times. "Looks like a boat of some sort, on the shore. . . ." Some type of watercraft had definitely been pulled up on the rough beach. Out of sight of Envy, here on the northwest side of the deserted area. . . . That didn't bode well.

He scanned the area between the shoreline and the building, the hair on the back of his arm lifting and prickling like it did when he knew something bad was about to happen. It was like a sixth sense.

The ruined buildings and their rubble-strewn footprints hid much of the ground, but then he saw them. Three men, walking . . . pushing a large, enclosed wagon-like object . . . making their way toward the Beretta building. Much too close; in fact, they were just about to the vehicle barrier.

Pinche.

But how were they going to get that big cage through the barrier? He watched a moment longer, and then saw the ramp. The men had pulled it from a pile of debris and were putting it into place.

Damn. "They're coming," he said turning to Sage, adrenaline pumping through him and clearing his thoughts. "We've got to go *now*." Before they get over the barrier and into the corral.

"*Gangas*?" she said, following him toward the door without hesitation.

"Strangers. Or bounty hunters. But whoever they are, they're not coming from Envy. They came from the west. From the ocean." And they were either bringing something for the *gangas* . . . or more *gangas* . . . or planning to take something away.

Then he heard it . . . faint on the air. Howls.

Definitely *ganga* feeding time.

For more of Joss Ware's exciting series,
the story continues with

ABANDON THE NIGHT

on sale March 9, 2010

The elevator shaft opened, and Quent stepped into the dark, ruined hallway of what had once been a casino resort in Las Vegas. At this far side of the building, in an area that hadn't been maintained after the Change, the corridor seemed deserted and abandoned—a state the Waxnickis carefully preserved, despite their daily visits to the lab.

He could make his way along the halls back to the occupied area of the hotel, and up onto the twenty-sixth floor, where he had been given a hotel room for his own residence . . . but when it came time to make the turn that would take him in that direction, he kept straight on.

Outside, the rain poured down. Heavy, steady, but straight so that it looked like a gray and black shower curtain obstructing the night.

If Quent had hoped Wyatt was wrong, or that it might be little more than a soft drizzle, he was bloody disappointed.

Still, not because he expected anything—he wasn't

that cocked up—but because he needed to *feel*, he stepped out of the building and into the downpour.

Since the Change, the climate in Vegas had shifted from that of a dry desert to an almost tropical one. Rain was plentiful, the temperature mild or hot, and the air humid and too close at times.

Having lived in England until he was eighteen—when he moved an ocean away from Fielding and his riding crop—Quent was used to the damp. And now, as the heavy rain pounded on him, he walked, letting it soak through his stretchy silk shirt, suede jeans, and leather sandals. Good, practical clothing wasn't always easy to find, but he'd been lucky and had come across an old suitcase filled with duds from a guy about his size. And the guy had had decent taste, which helped.

The downpour weighted Quent's thick honey-colored hair and dripped from there onto his nose and cheeks. It might have mingled with some other drops—warmer, more emotional ones—but he wasn't likely to admit it.

The city known as New Vegas, N.V., or, more commonly, Envy, was the largest settlement of people in hundreds of miles—and as far as anyone could tell with the limited communication and transportation, it was the largest in the world. The irony that the formerly hedonistic city, with its superficiality and flashiness, should now be the cradle of humanity was lost on no one who'd ever visited the Strip—including Quent.

Now, with the massive shift in land mass and tectonic plates, what had been the North Strip was under water—covered by the Pacific Ocean, which, unbelievably but irrefutably, now covered California and part of Nevada and Washington. Only a cluster of high-rise casino resorts remained standing, and of those, many of them were in disrepair.

The Strip's neon lights still glowed red, blue, yellow and green, but much more feebly and in less abundance than they'd done a half century earlier. And the part of the Strip that remained visible was empty of people—a condition that would have been inconceivable back then.

Quent couldn't help himself. He looked up, trying to peer at the jagged rooftops and glassless windows above him, searching for a lanky shadow, slender and sure and sleek.

But all he got for his trouble was a face battered with sharp raindrops and another wave of anger.

At himself of course. For his foolishness. For wasting his time.

For not fucking swinging that damned five wood sixty-some years ago.

Hell. Could his one decision have made a difference? Kept the Change from happening? He might have spent the rest of his life in jail back then, but at least he'd have had a life.

Quent drew in a deep breath of clean, damp air, then exhaled. Turned his thoughts from the rage that never seemed to completely leave him.

Zoë wouldn't be out in this weather, lurking in the

shadows as she was wont to do. She wouldn't be slipping down, all warm and slender and bold, to join him in a dark corner, hot and urgent and bold.

A combination of lust and fury tightened his jaw, hitched his steps.

What the bloody hell was he doing out here in the buggering rain?

He was searching, damn fool that he was.

All he wanted to do was find Fielding and kill him. Quent's life, his purpose for being, had funneled down to nothing but that.

Everything else was just a fucking way to pass the time until then.

Even walking uselessly in the rain. Even rolling in the sheets with Zoë.

He wasn't cold, though he was as soaked as if he'd been swimming, and he kept inhaling random droplets of rain. Wet grass and bushes brushed his bare toes as he trudged away from the inhabited area of the city. The clean smell of fresh rain mingled with the underlying must of decay and mold, here in this narrow walkway. Two buildings rose, half-destroyed, jagged, and overgrown, the one on the left taller and more forbidding than on the right. If he straightened his arms to the sides, his fingertips would brush the brick. Soggy leaves and the gentle give of wet dirt softened the cracked and uneven concrete beneath his feet.

The first time he'd met Zoë, she'd saved his life, appearing from nowhere to skewer the *ganga* that had attacked him. She'd shot an arrow that lodged in the skull of the zombie-like monster, which scrambled its brains and dropped it dead.

No sooner had the creature collapsed than she demanded that Quent return her arrow.

He hadn't even been certain she was a woman or a slender young man . . . until she came close enough to touch his face.

And that first time she touched him, just a faint brush of fingertips over his cheek, as if she wasn't used to doing such a thing, it had seeped into his skin, warm and gentle. Hesitant, and yet . . . solid.

Now, Quent leaned against the ivy-covered wall, sending an additional shower of droplets scattering from the leaves. And he looked up again into the unrelieved darkness. Still fucking searching.

Rain blinded him once more, and he turned away, frustrated.

After their first meeting, she'd disappeared, slipping into the shadows, *without* her precious arrow. He'd taken it with him here to Envy, but before he turned to go, he called after her, into the dark, and invited her to come and retrieve it any time.

A few days later, she had found him in Envy, walking beneath a clear moon, and once again demanded her arrow to be returned. Despite her belligerence and god-awful haircut, Quent was compelled to kiss her.

And that had been all either of them needed. The moment felt as if something had been released, unleashed . . . snapped.

The sex that night, and the few other times they'd gotten busy since, had been hot and fast and urgent. It had left him with curled toes, breathless—and, despite its ferocity, it had left him feeling . . . comfortable. Settled.

Until she sneaked off into the night without a word. Taking her precious arrows with her.

After that first night, it had become sort of a game. From up on a rooftop, or a high window, she'd shoot an arrow where he'd be sure to find it, then disappear into the night. A day or so later, Zoë would show up unexpectedly, all self-righteous and annoyed and demanding it back, as if he'd stolen it right from her quiver . . . and then they'd get to it. On the bed. In the stairwell. Against the backside of the hotel. Wherever they managed to tear each other's clothes off. This had been going on for perhaps two weeks, but he was unable to keep her out of his mind for long.

He spun suddenly, his foot squishing into mud and then jolting against a wedge of sidewalk, nearly tripping himself. *Bloody buggering hell.*

What the fuck was he doing wandering in the rain looking for a rude, anti-social, female Robin Hood when there were plenty of other willing partners inside?

Galvanized, he started back.

But once he got inside, rain dripping audibly from

his hair and shirt and rolling off the hems of his jeans, Quent knew he had too much of a bag on to go to the Pub. Though the pints were plenty and the waitresses friendly, and Elliott's lover, Jade, often sang onstage in a definite foreplay sort of way, Quent walked past. His leather sandals squished softly.

Maybe after he changed into dry clothing—the suede jeans were already shrinking from the rain—and did something with his hair, he'd change his mind. But unlikely.

What he really should do . . . what he suddenly wanted to do . . . was to go back to the computer lab and touch that crystal again.

The idea sparked in him, and he nodded to himself. If Elliott hadn't interrupted him earlier and pulled the stone away, Quent might have been able to get more from the gem. The blur of faces might have eased from the fast-forward of a video to a slower parade, and he might have learned something. Identified someone. Seen his father.

He might be able to discover where the Strangers lived or came from. And then he could leave this fucking place and do what he had to do.

After that . . . Quent had no thought. He'd probably die in the process, for surely he couldn't simply kill a leader of the Strangers and walk away unscathed.

Inside his room, Quent moved directly to the closet and felt up behind the lip of its shelf. Force of habit, first thing he always did when he came back into his space. And when he realized he'd been checking to see if the latest of Zoë's precious arrows was still there—it was—he felt yet another blast of fury that he was still playing this game.

That he still cared to play it.

"So that's where you're hiding them now."

Quent froze. A rush of heat and anger, a sudden weakness in his knees, and the tug of a smile, conflicting and paralyzing, caught him for a moment. He collected himself, emptied his expression, and turned.

"What the hell were you doing out in the rain for so long?" Zoë said in her low, rusty voice. She looked like a Bollywood actress with a rubbish haircut—exotic features, cinnamon-skinned, and her ink black hair cropped and falling every which way around her high cheekbones and jaw. A wide mouth, pointed chin, high, plum-sized breasts and long, lanky limbs completed the package.

She leaned nonchalantly against the wall across the room, behind the door through which he'd just come. The quiver and bow she normally wore over her shoulder rested on the floor. Her entire being shouted condescension and belligerence—but for her dark, almond-shaped eyes. Even in the dim room, lit only by a small lamp in the corner, Quent felt the weight of their gaze. Hot.

His belly dropped and blood surged through his body. "Were you waiting for me?" he asked, his arrogance matching his haughty gaze. "Or was it just that you hadn't discovered my latest hiding place?"

AVON

978-0-06-172880-8

978-0-06-172783-2

978-0-06-176527-8

978-0-06-157826-7

978-0-06-185337-1

978-0-06-173477-9

Unforgettable, enthralling love stories,
sparkling with passion and adventure
from Romance's bestselling authors

YOU'RE THE ONE THAT I HAUNT   *by Terri Garey*
978-0-06-158203-5

SECRET LIFE OF A VAMPIRE   *by Kerrelyn Sparks*
978-0-06-166785-5

FORBIDDEN NIGHTS WITH A VAMPIRE   *by Kerrelyn Sparks*
978-0-06-166784-8

ONE RECKLESS SUMMER   *by Toni Blake*
978-0-06-142989-7

DESIRE UNTAMED   *by Pamela Palmer*
978-0-06-166751-0

OBSESSION UNTAMED   *by Pamela Palmer*
978-0-06-166752-7

PASSION UNTAMED   *by Pamela Palmer*
978-0-06-166753-4

OUT OF THE DARKNESS   *by Jaime Rush*
978-0-06-169036-5

SILENT NIGHT, HAUNTED NIGHT   *by Terri Garey*
978-0-06-158204-2

SOLD TO A LAIRD   *by Karen Ranney*
978-0-06-177175-0